RED SIS[…]

Mark Lawrence was born in Champaign-Urbana, Illinois, to British parents but moved to the UK at the age of one. He went back to the US after taking a PhD in mathematics at Imperial College to work on a variety of research projects including the 'Star Wars' missile defence programme. Returning to the UK, he has worked mainly on image processing and decision/reasoning theory. He says he never had any ambition to be a writer so was very surprised when a half-hearted attempt to find an agent turned into a global publishing deal overnight. His first trilogy, The Broken Empire, has been universally acclaimed as a ground-breaking work of fantasy, and both *Emperor of Thorns* and *The Liar's Key* have won the Gemmell Legend award for best fantasy novel. Mark is married, with four children, and lives in Bristol.

Follow Mark on:
/MarkLawrenceBooks
@mark__lawrence (please note: there are two underscores)

Also by Mark Lawrence

The Broken Empire
Prince of Thorns
King of Thorns
Emperor of Thorns

The Red Queen's War
Prince of Fools
The Liar's Key
The Wheel of Osheim

RED SISTER

MARK LAWRENCE

Book One of the Ancestor

HARPER
Voyager

Harper*Voyager*
An imprint of HarperCollins*Publishers* Ltd
1 London Bridge Street
London SE1 9GF

www.harpercollins.co.uk

This paperback edition 2018
3

First published in Great Britain by
Harper*Voyager* 2017

A catalogue record for this book is available from the British Library

ISBN: 978-0-00-815232-1

Set in Plantin Light 10.5/12 pt by
Palimpsest Book Production Limited, Falkirk, Stirlingshire

Printed and bound in the UK by CPI Group (UK) Ltd, Croydon CR0 4YY

FSC
www.fsc.org
MIX
Paper from
responsible sources
FSC® C007454

This book is produced from independently certified FSC™
paper to ensure responsible forest management.

For more information visit: www.harpercollins.co.uk/green

To Celyn, who needs no words for eloquence.

Author's Note

Rather than place this background information in an appendix at the back where you might not notice it until you've finished the book (I've done that before) I'm putting it here at the front. However, it is best to skip it and return only if you find you need it. All the information here is given to you in the text and unfolds naturally with the story.

The people of Abeth descend from four 'tribes'. These tribes were:

Gerant – distinguished by their great size
Hunska – distinguished by their speed. A dark-haired, dark-eyed people
Marjal – distinguished by their ability to tap into the lesser magics
Quantal – distinguished by their ability to walk the Path and work greater magics

The great families of empire adopt the suffix *-sis* when the head of the family is named a lord by the emperor. The emperor's own family are the Lansis. Other families of note include the Tacsis, Jotsis, Memsis, Galamsis, Leensis, Gersis, Rolsis, and Chemsis.

In the Convent of Sweet Mercy novices move through four

classes on their way to taking holy orders. A novice must graduate from each class. The classes are named after the four orders of nun:

Red Class – typical novice age 9-12
Grey Class – typical novice age 13-14
Mystic Class – typical novice age 15-16
Holy Class – typical novice age 17-19

On taking holy orders novices become nuns. They follow one of the following paths:

Bride of the Ancestor (Holy Sister) – a nun concerned with honouring the Ancestor and maintaining the faith. The most common calling
Martial Sister (Red Sister) – a nun skilled in armed and unarmed combat, usually showing hunska blood
Sister of Discretion (Grey Sister) – a nun skilled in espionage, stealth, and poisons. Often showing marjal blood and a talent for shadow-work
Mystic Sister (Holy Witch) – a nun able to walk the Path and manipulate threads. Always showing quantal blood

Dramatis Personae

Nuns (in order of superiority)

Glass: Abbess of Sweet Mercy Convent, also known as Shella Yammal
Rose: Sister Superior, Holy Sister, runs the sanatorium
Wheel: Sister Superior, Mistress Spirit, Holy Sister, teaches Spirit classes
Apple: Mistress Shade, Grey Sister, also known as the Poisoner, teaches Shade classes
Pan: Mistress Path, Holy Witch, teaches Path classes
Rule: Mistress Academia, Holy Sister, teaches Academia classes
Tallow: Mistress Blade, Red Sister, teaches Blade classes
Chrysanthemum: Holy Sister, mostly known as Sister Mop
Flint: Red Sister, Grey Class mistress
Kettle: Grey Sister

Oak: Holy Sister, Red Class mistress
Rock: Red Sister

Novices

Alata: junior novice
Arabella Jotsis: junior novice, quantal and hunska blood
Clera Ghomal: junior novice, Nona's friend, hunska blood
Croy: junior novice
Darla: junior novice, gerant blood
Ghena: junior novice, hunska blood
Hessa: junior novice, Nona's friend from Giljohn's cage, quantal blood
Jula: junior novice, Nona's friend, studious
Kariss: junior novice
Katcha: junior novice
Ketti: junior novice, hunska blood
Leeni: junior novice
Mally: junior novice, Grey Class head-girl
Ruli: Nona's friend, marjal blood
Sarma: junior novice
Sharlot: junior novice
Sheelar: junior novice
Suleri: senior novice

Others

Emperor Crucical: his palace is in the city of Verity
Sherzal: the emperor's sister. Her palace is close to the Scithrowl border
Velera: the emperor's sister. Her palace is on the coast
High Priest Jacob: head of the Church of the Ancestor
Archon Nevis: high-ranking priest
Archon Anasta: high-ranking priestess
Archon Philo: high-ranking priest
Archon Kratton: high-ranking priest
Thuran Tacsis: lord, head of the Tacsis family
Raymel Tacsis: heir to Thuran Tacsis, Caltess ring-fighter, gerant blood
Lano Tacsis: Thuran Tacsis's second son, hunska blood

Academic Rexxus Degon: senior Academy man
Markus: child from Giljohn's cage, marjal blood
Saida: child from Giljohn's cage, gerant blood
Willum: child from Giljohn's cage, marjal blood
Chara: child from Giljohn's cage, marjal blood
Partnis Reeve: owner of the Caltess fight-hall
Gretcha: Caltess ring-fighter, gerant blood
Maya: Caltess apprentice, gerant blood
Regol: Caltess trainee, hunska blood
Denam: Caltess trainee, gerant blood
Tarkax: known as 'the Ice-Spear', renowned warrior from the ice-tribes
Yisht: warrior from the ice tribes, serves Sherzal
Zole: girl from the ice tribes, Sherzal's ward
Irvone Galamsis: high court judge
Sister Owl: legendary Red Sister (dead)
Sister Cloud: legendary Red Sister (dead)
Safira: former senior novice, works for Sherzal
Malkin: Abbess Glass's cat
Argus: prison guard at Harriton
Dava: prison guard at Harriton
John Fallon: prison guard at Harriton
Herber: graveman
Jame Lender: prisoner executed at Harriton

Red Class

Prologue

It is important, when killing a nun, to ensure that you bring an army of sufficient size. For Sister Thorn of the Sweet Mercy Convent Lano Tacsis brought two hundred men.

From the front of the convent you can see both the northern ice and the southern, but the finer view is out across the plateau and over the narrow lands. On a clear day the coast may be glimpsed, the Sea of Marn a suggestion in blue.

At some point in an achingly long history a people, now lost to knowledge, had built one thousand and twenty-four pillars out on the plateau: Corinthian giants thicker than a thousand-year oak, taller than a long-pine. A forest of stone without order or pattern, covering the level ground from flank to flank so that no spot upon it lay more than twenty yards from a pillar. Sister Thorn waited amid this forest, alone and seeking her centre.

Lano's men began to spread out between the columns. Thorn could neither see nor hear her foe approach, but she knew their disposition. She had watched earlier as they snaked up the west trail from Styx Valley, three and four abreast: Pelarthi mercenaries from the ice-margins, furs of the white bear and the snow-wolf over their leathers, some with scraps of chainmail about them, ancient and dark or bright as new, depending on their luck. Many carried spears, some swords; one man in five carried a short-bow of recurved horn. Tall men in the main, fair-haired, their beards short or plaited, the women with lines of blue paint across their cheeks and foreheads like the rays of a cold sun.

Here's a moment.

All the world and more has rushed eternity's length to reach this beat of your heart, screaming down the years. And if you let it, the universe, without drawing breath, will press itself through this fractured second and race to the next, on into a new eternity. Everything that is, the echoes of everything that ever was, the roots of all that will ever be, must pass through this moment that you own. Your only task is to give it pause – to make it notice.

Thorn stood without motion, for only when you are truly still can you be the centre. She stood without sound, for only silent can you listen. She stood without fear, for only the fearless can understand their peril.

Hers the stillness of the forest, rooted restlessness, oak-slow, pine-quick, a seething patience. Hers the stillness of ice walls that face the sea, clear and deep, blue secrets held cold against the truth of the world, a patience of aeons stacked against a sudden fall. Hers the stillness of a sorrow-born babe unmoving in its crib. And of the mother, frozen in her discovery, fleeting and forever.

Thorn held a silence that had grown old before first she saw the world's light. A quietude passed down generations, the peace that bids us watch the dawn, an unspoken alliance with wave and flame that lets both take all speech from tongues and sets us standing before the water's surge and swell, or waiting to bear witness to fire's consuming dance of joy. Hers the silence of rejection, of a child's hurt: mute, unknowing, a scar upon the years to come. Hers the unvoiced everything of first love, tongue-tied, ineloquent, the refusal to sully so sharp and golden a feeling with anything as blunt as words.

Thorn waited. Fearless as flowers, bright, fragile, open to the sky. Brave as only those who've already lost can be.

Voices reached her, the Pelarthi calling out to each other as they lost sight of their numbers in the broken spaces of the plateau. Cries rang across the level ground, echoing from the pillars, flashes of torchlight, a multitude of footfalls, growing closer. Thorn rolled her shoulders beneath black skin armour.

She tightened the fingers of each hand around the sharp weight of a throwing star, her breathing calm, heart racing.

'In this place the dead watch me,' she breathed. A shout broke out close at hand, figures glimpsed between two pillars, flitting across the gap. Many figures. 'I am a weapon in service to the Ark. Those who come against me will know despair.' Her voice rose along with the tension that always presaged a fight, a buzzing tingle across her cheekbones, a tightness in her throat, a sense of being both deep within her own body, and above and around it at the same time.

The first of the Pelarthi jogged into view, and seeing her, stumbled to a halt. A young man, beardless though hard-eyed beneath the iron of his helm. More crowded in behind him, spilling out into the killing ground.

The Red Sister tilted her head to acknowledge them.

Then it began.

1

No child truly believes they will be hanged. Even on the gallows platform with the rope scratching at their wrists and the shadow of the noose upon their face they know that someone will step forward, a mother, a father returned from some long absence, a king dispensing justice … someone. Few children have lived long enough to understand the world into which they were born. Perhaps few adults have either, but they at least have learned some bitter lessons.

Saida climbed the scaffold steps as she had climbed the wooden rungs to the Caltess attic so many times. They all slept there together, the youngest workers, bedding down among the sacks and dust and spiders. They would all climb those rungs tonight and whisper about her in the darkness. Tomorrow night the whispers would be spent and a new boy or girl would fill the empty space she left beneath the eaves.

'I didn't do anything.' Saida said it without hope, her tears dry now. The wind sliced cold from the west, a Corridor wind, and the sun burned red, filling half the sky yet offering little heat. Her last day?

The guard prodded her on, indifferent rather than unkind. She looked back at him, tall, old, flesh tight as if the wind had worn it down to the bone. Another step, the noose dangling, dark against the sun. The prison yard lay near-deserted, a handful watching from the black shadows where the outer wall offered shelter, old women, grey hair trailing. Saida wondered what drew them. Perhaps being so old they worried about dying and wanted to see how it was done.

'I didn't do it. It was Nona. She even said so.' She had spoken the words so many times that meaning had leached away leaving them just pale noise. But it was true. All of it. Even Nona said so.

The hangman offered Saida the thinnest of smiles and bent to check the rope confining her wrists. It itched and it was too tight, her arm hurt where Raymel had cracked it, but Saida said nothing, only scanned the yard, the doors to the cell blocks, the outer buildings, even the great gates to the world outside. Someone would come.

A door clanged open from the Pivot, a squat tower where the warden was said to live in luxury to rival any lord's. A guardsman emerged, squinting against the sun. Just a guardsman: the hope, that had leapt so easily in Saida's breast, crashed once more.

Stepping from behind the guardsman a smaller, wider figure. Saida looked again, hoping again. A woman in the long habit of a nun came walking into the yard. Only the staff in her hand, its end curled and golden, marked her office.

The hangman glanced across, his narrow smile replaced by a broad frown. 'The abbess…'

'I ain't seen her down here before.' The old guardsman tightened his fingers on Saida's shoulder.

Saida opened her mouth but found it too dry for her thoughts. The abbess had come for her. Come to take her to the Ancestor's convent. Come to give her a new name and a new place. Saida wasn't even surprised. She had never truly thought she would be hanged.

2

The stench of a prison is an honest one. The guards' euphemisms, the public smile of the chief warden, even the building's façade, may lie and lie again, but the stink is the unvarnished truth: sewage and rot, infection and despair. Even so, Harriton prison smelled sweeter than many. A hanging prison like Harriton doesn't give its inmates the chance to rot. A brief stay, a long drop on a short rope, and they could feed the worms at their leisure in a convict ditch-grave up at the paupers' cemetery in Winscon.

The smell bothered Argus when he first joined the guard. They say that after a while your mind steps around any smell without noticing. It's true, but it's also true of pretty much every other bad thing in life. After ten years Argus's mind stepped around the business of stretching people's necks just as easily as it had acclimatized to Harriton's stink.

'When you leaving?' Dava's obsession with everyone else's schedule used to annoy Argus, but now he just answered without thought or memory. 'Seventh bell.'

'Seventh!' The little woman rattled out her usual outrage at the inequities of the work rota. They ambled towards the main holding block, the private scaffold at their back. Behind them Jame Lender dangled out of sight beneath the trapdoor, still twitching. Jame was the graveman's problem now. Old Man Herber would be along soon enough with his cart and donkey for the day's take. The short distance to Winscon Hill might prove a long trip for Old Herber, his five passengers, and the donkey, near as geriatric as its master. The fact that Jame had no meat on him to speak of would lighten the load. That, and the fact two of the other four were small girls.

Herber would wind his way through the Cutter Streets and up to the Academy first, selling off whatever body parts might have a value today. What he added to the grave-ditch up on the Hill would likely be much diminished – a collection of wet ruins if the day's business had been good.

'...sixth bell yesterday, fifth the day before.' Dava paused the rant that had sustained her for years, an enduring sense of injustice that gave her the backbone to handle condemned men twice her size.

'Who's that?' A tall figure was knocking at the door to the new arrivals' block with a heavy cane.

'Fellow from the Caltess? You know.' Dava snapped her fingers before her face as if trying to surprise the answer out. 'Runs fighters.'

'Partnis Reeve!' Argus called the name as he remembered it and the big man turned. 'Been a while.'

Partnis visited the day-gaol often enough to get his fighters out of trouble. You don't run a stable of angry and violent men without them breaking a few faces off the payroll from time to time, but generally they didn't end up at Harriton. Professional fighters usually keep a calm enough head to stop short of killing during their bar fights. It's the amateurs who lose their minds and keep stamping on a fallen opponent until there's nothing left but mush.

'My friend!' Partnis turned with arms wide, a broad smile, and no attempt at Argus's name. 'I'm here for my girl.'

'Your girl?' Argus frowned. 'Didn't know you were a family man.'

'Indentured. A worker.' Partnis waved the matter aside. 'Open the door, will you, good fellow. She's down to drop today and I'm late enough as it is.' He frowned, as if remembering some sequence of irritating delays.

Argus lifted the key from his pocket, a heavy piece of ironwork. 'Probably missed her already, Partnis. Sun's a-setting.

Old Herber and his cart will be creaking down the alleys, ready for his take.'

'Both of them creaking, eh? Herber and his cart,' Dava put in. Always quick with a joke, never funny.

'I sent a runner,' Partnis said, 'with instructions that the Caltess girls shouldn't be dropped before—'

'Instructions?' Argus paused, key in the lock.

'Suggestions, then. Suggestions wrapped around a silver coin.'

'Ah.' Argus turned the key and led him inside. He took his visitor by the quickest route, through the guard station, along the short corridor where the day's arrivals watched from the narrow windows in their cell doors, and out into the courtyard where the public scaffold sat below the warden's window.

The main gates had already opened, ready to admit the graveman's cart. A small figure waited close to the scaffold steps, a single guardsman beside her, John Fallon by the look of it.

'Just in time!' Argus said.

'Good.' Partnis started forward, then faltered. 'Isn't that…' he trailed off, lips curling into a snarl of frustration.

Following the tall man's gaze, Argus spotted the source of his distress. The Abbess of Sweet Mercy came striding through the small crowd of onlookers before the warden's steps. At this distance she could be anyone's mother, a shortish, plumpish figure swathed in black cloth, but her crozier announced her.

'Dear heavens, that awful old witch has come to steal from me yet again.' Partnis both lengthened and quickened his stride, forcing Argus into an undignified jog to keep pace. Dava, on the man's other side, had to run.

Despite Partnis's haste, he beat the abbess to the girl by only a fraction. 'Where's the other one?' He looked around as if the guardsman might be hiding another prisoner behind him.

'Other what?' John Fallon's gaze flickered past Partnis to the advancing nun, her habit swirling as she marched.

'Girl! There were two. I gave orders to— I sent a request that they be held back.'

'Over with the dropped.' Fallon tilted his head towards a

mound beside the main gates, several feet high. Stones pinned a stained, grey sheet across the heap. The graveman's cart came into view as they watched.

'Damnation!' The word burst from Partnis loud enough to turn heads all across the yard. He raised both hands, fingers spread, then trembling with effort, lowered them to his sides. 'I wanted them both.'

'Have to argue with the graveman over the big one,' Fallon observed. 'This'un.' He reached for the girl at his side. 'You'll have to argue with me over. Then those two.' He nodded at Dava and Argus. 'Then the warden.'

'There'll be no arguing.' The abbess stepped between Fallon and Partnis, dwarfed by both, her crozier reaching up to break their eye contact. 'I shall be taking the child.'

'No you won't!' Partnis looked down at her, brow furrowed. 'All due respect to the Ancestor and all that, but she's mine, bought and paid for.' He glanced back at the gates where Herber had now halted his cart beside the covered mound. 'Besides … how do you know she's the one you want?'

The abbess snorted and favoured Partnis with a motherly smile. 'Of course she is. You can tell by looking at her, Partnis Reeve. This child has the fire in her eyes.' She frowned. 'I saw the other. Scared. Lost. She should never have been here.'

'Saida's back in the cells…' the girl said. 'They told me I would go first.'

Argus peered at the child. A small thing in shapeless linen – not street rags, covered in rusty stains, but a serf's wear none the less. She might be nine. Argus had lost the knack for telling. His older two were long grown, and little Sali would always be five. This girl was a fierce creature, a scowl on her thin, dirty face. Eyes black below a short shock of ebony hair.

'Might have been the other,' Partnis said. 'She was the big one.' He lacked conviction. A fight-master knows the fire when he sees it.

'Where's Saida?' the girl asked.

The abbess's eyes widened a fraction. It almost looked like hurt. Gone, quicker than the shadow of a bird's wing. Argus decided he imagined it. The Abbess of Sweet Mercy was called many things, few of them to her face, and 'soft' wasn't one of them.

'Where's my friend?' the girl repeated.

'Is that why you stayed?' the abbess asked. She pulled a hoare-apple from her habit, so dark a red it could almost be black, a bitter and woody thing. A mule might eat one – few men would.

'Stayed?' Dava asked, though the question hadn't been pointed her way. 'She stayed 'cos this is a bloody prison and she's tied and under guard!'

'Did you stay to help your friend?'

The girl didn't answer, only glared up at the woman as if at any moment she might leap upon her.

'Catch.' The abbess tossed the apple towards the girl.

Quick as quick a small hand intercepted it. Apple smacking into palm. Behind the girl a length of rope dropped to the ground.

'Catch.' The abbess had another apple in hand and threw it, hard.

The girl caught it in her other hand.

'Catch.'

Quite where the abbess had hidden her fruit supply Argus couldn't tell, but he stopped caring a heartbeat later, staring at the third apple, trapped between two hands, each full of the previous two.

'Catch.' The abbess tossed yet another hoare-apple, but the girl dropped her three and let the fourth sail over her shoulder.

'Where's Saida?'

'You come with me, Nona Grey,' the abbess said, her expression kindly. 'We will discuss Saida at the convent.'

'I'm keeping her.' Partnis stepped towards the girl. 'A treasured daughter! Besides, she damn near killed Raymel Tacsis. The family will never let her go free. But if I can show she has value they might let me put her into a few fights first.'

'Raymel's dead. I killed him. I—'

'Treasured? I'm surprised *you* let her go, Mr Reeve,' the abbess cut across the girl's protests.

'I wouldn't have if I'd been there!' Partnis clenched his hand as if trying to recapture the opportunity. 'I was halfway across the city when I heard. Got back to find the place in chaos … blood everywhere … Tacsis men waiting… If the city guard hadn't hauled her up here she'd be in Thuran's private dungeon by now. He's not a man to lose a son and sit idle.'

'Which is why you will give her to me.' The abbess's smile reminded Argus of his mother's. The one she'd use when she was right and they both knew it. 'Your pockets aren't deep enough to get young Nona out of here should the Tacsis boy die, and if you did obtain her release neither you nor your establishment are sufficiently robust to withstand Thuran Tacsis's demands for retribution.'

The girl tried to interrupt. 'How do you know my name? I didn't—'

'Whereas I have been friends with Warden James longer than you have been alive, Mr Reeve.' The abbess cut across the girl again. 'And no sane man would mount an attack on a convent of the faith.'

'You shouldn't take her for a Red Sister.' Partnis had that sullen tone men get when they know they've lost. 'It's not right. She's got no Ancestor faith … and she's all but a murderer. Vicious, it was, the way they tell it…'

'Faith I can give her. What she's got already is what the Red Sisters need.' The abbess reached out a plump hand towards the girl. 'Come, Nona.'

Nona glanced up at John Fallon, at Partnis Reeve, at the hangman and the noose swaying beside him. 'Saida is my friend. If you've hurt her I'll kill you all.'

In silence she walked forward, placing her feet so as not to step on the fallen apples, and took the abbess's hand.

Argus and the others watched them leave. At the gates, they paused, black against the red sun. The child released the abbess's hand and took three paces towards the covered mound. Old Herber and his mule stood, watching, as bound by the moment as the rest of them. Nona stopped, staring at the mound. She looked towards the men at the gallows – a long, slow look – then returned to the abbess. Seconds later the pair had vanished around the corner.

'Marking us for death she was,' Dava said.

Still joking. Still not funny.

3

A juggler once came to Nona's village, a place so small it had neither a name nor a market square. The juggler came dressed in mud and faded motley, a lean look about him. He came alone, a young man, dark eyes, quick hands. In a sackcloth bag he carried balls of coloured leather, batons with white and black ribbons, and crudely made knives.

'Come, watch, the great Amondo will delight and amaze.' It sounded like a phrase he didn't own. He introduced himself to the handful of villagers not labouring in field or hut and yet brave enough to face a Corridor wind laced with icy rain. Laying his hat between them, broad-brimmed and yawning for appreciation, he reached for four striped batons and set them dancing in the air.

Amondo stayed three days, though his audience dried up after the first hour of the first evening. The sad fact is that there's only so much entertainment to be had from one man juggling, however impressive he might be.

Nona stayed by him though, watching every move, each deft tuck and curl and switch. She stayed even after the light failed and the last of the children drifted away. Silent and staring she watched as the juggler started to pack his props into their bag.

'You're a quiet one.' Amondo threw her a wizened apple that sat in his hat along with several better examples, two bread rolls, a piece of Kennal's hard goat's cheese, and somewhere amongst them a copper halfpenny clipped back to a quarter.

Nona held the apple close to her ear, listening to the sound of her fingers against its wrinkles. 'The children don't like me.'

'No?'

'No.'

Amondo waited, juggling invisible balls with his hands.

'They say I'm evil.'

Amondo dropped an invisible ball. He left the others to fall and raised a brow.

'Mother says they say it because my hair is so black and my skin is so pale. She says I get my skin from her and my hair from my da.' The other children had the tan skin and sandy hair of their parents, but Nona's mother had come from the ice fringes and her father's clan hunted up on the glaciers, strangers both of them. 'Mother says they just don't like *different*.'

'Those are ugly ideas for children to have in their heads.' The juggler picked up his bag.

Nona stood, watching the apple in her hand but not seeing it. The memory held her. Her mother, in the dimness of their hut, noticing the blood on her hands for the first time. *What's that? Did they hurt you?* Nona had hung her head and shook it. *Billem Smithson tried to hurt me. This was inside him.*

'Best get along home to your ma and pa.' Amondo turned slowly, scanning the huts, the trees, the barns.

'My da's dead. The ice took him.'

'Well then.' A smile, only half-sad. 'I'd best take you home.' He pushed back the length of his hair and offered his hand. 'We're friends, aren't we?'

Nona's mother let Amondo sleep in their barn, though it wasn't really more than a shed for the sheep to hide in when the snows came. She said people would talk but that she didn't care. Nona didn't understand why anyone would care about talk. It was just noise.

On the night Amondo left, Nona went to see him in the barn. He had spread the contents of his bag before him on the dirt floor, where the red light of the moon spilled in through the doorway.

'Show me how to juggle,' she said.

He looked up from his knives and grinned, dark hair swept down across his face, dark eyes behind. 'It's difficult. How old are you?'

Nona shrugged. 'Little.' They didn't count years in the village. You were a baby, then little, then big, then old, then dead.

'Little is quite small.' He pursed his lips. 'I've two years and twenty. I guess I'm supposed to be big.' He smiled but with more worry in it than joy, as if the world made no more sense and offered no more comfort to bigs than littles. 'Let's have a go.'

Amondo picked up three of the leather balls. The moonlight made it difficult to see their colours but with focus approaching it was bright enough to throw and catch. He yawned and rolled his shoulders. A quick flurry of hands and the three balls were dancing in their interlaced arcs. 'There.' He caught them. 'You try.'

Nona took the balls from the juggler's hands. Few of the other children had managed with two. Three balls was a dismissal. Amondo watched her turning them in her hands, understanding their weight and feel.

She had studied the juggler since his arrival. Now she visualized the pattern the balls had made in the air, the rhythm of his hands. She tossed the first ball up on the necessary curve and slowed the world around her. Then the second ball, lazily departing her hand. A moment later all three were dancing to her tune.

'Impressive!' Amondo got to his feet. 'Who taught you?'

Nona frowned and almost missed her catch. 'You did.'

'Don't lie to me, girl.' He threw her a fourth ball, brown leather with a blue band.

Nona caught it, tossed it, struggled to adjust her pattern and within a heartbeat she had all four in motion, arcing above her in long and lazy loops.

The anger on Amondo's face took her by surprise. She had thought he would be pleased – that it would make him like her. He had said they were friends but she had never had a friend and he said it so lightly... She had thought that sharing this might make him say the words again and seal the matter into the world. Friend. She fumbled a ball to the floor on purpose then made a clumsy swing at the next.

'A circus man taught me,' she lied. The balls rolled away from her into the dark corners where the rats live. 'I practise. Every day! With … stones … smooth ones from the stream.'

Amondo closed off his anger, putting a brittle smile on his face. 'Nobody likes to be made a fool of, Nona. Even fools don't like it.'

'How many can you juggle?' she asked. Men like to talk about themselves and their achievements. Nona knew that much about men even if she was little.

'Goodnight, Nona.'

And, dismissed, Nona had hurried back to the two-room hut she shared with her mother, with the light of the moon's focus blazing all about her, warmer than the noon-day sun.

'Faster, girl!' The abbess jerked Nona's arm, pulling her out of her memories. The hoare-apples had put Amondo back into her mind. The woman glanced over her shoulder. A moment later she did it again. 'Quickly!'

'Why?' Nona asked, quickening her pace.

'Because Warden James will have his men out after us soon enough. Me they'll scold – you they'll hang. So pick those feet up!'

'You said you'd been friends with the warden since before Partnis Reeve was a baby!'

'So you *were* listening.' The abbess steered them up a narrow alley, so steep it required a step or two every few yards and the roofs of the tall houses stepped one above the next to keep pace. The smell of leather hit Nona, reminding her of the coloured balls Amondo had handed her, as strong a smell as the stink of cows, rich, deep, polished, brown.

'You said you and the warden were friends,' Nona said again.

'I've met him a few times,' the abbess replied. 'Nasty little man, bald and squinty, uglier on the inside.' She stepped around the wares of a cobbler, laid out before his steps. Every other house seemed to be a cobbler's shop, with an old man or young woman in the window, hammering away at boot heels or trimming leather.

'You lied!'

'To call something a lie, child, is an unhelpful characterization.' The abbess drew a deep breath, labouring up the slope. 'Words are steps along a path: the important thing is to get where you're going. You can play by all manner of rules, *step-on-a-crack-break-your-back*, but you'll get there quicker if you pick the most certain route.'

'But—'

'Lies are complex things. Best not to bother thinking in terms of truth or lie – let necessity be your mother … and invent!'

'You're not a nun!' Nona wrenched her hand away. 'And you let them kill Saida!'

'If I had saved her then I would have had to leave *you*.'

Shouts rang out somewhere down the steepness of the alley.

'Quickly.' The alley gave onto a broad thoroughfare by a narrow flight of stairs and the abbess turned onto it, not pausing now to glance back.

'They know where we're going.' Nona had done a lot of running and hiding in her short life and she knew enough to know it didn't matter how fast you went if they knew where to find you.

'They know when we get there they can't follow.'

People choked the street but the abbess wove a path through the thickest of the crowd. Nona followed, so close that the tails of the nun's habit flapped about her. Crowds unnerved her. There hadn't been as many people in her village, nor in her whole world, as pressed into this street. And the variety of them, some adults hardly taller than she was, others overtopping even the hulking giants who fought at the Caltess. Some dark, their skin black as ink, some white-blond and so pale as to show each vein in blue, and every shade between.

Through the alleys rising to join the street Nona saw a sea of roofs, tiled in terracotta, stubbled with innumerable chimneys, smoke drifting. She had never imagined a place so big, so many people crammed so tight. Since the night the child-taker had driven Nona and his other purchases into Verity she had seen almost nothing of the city, just the combat hall, the compound where the fighters lived, and the training yards. The cart-ride to Harriton had offered only glimpses as she and Saida sat hugging each other.

'Through here.' The abbess set a hand on Nona's shoulder and aimed her at the steps to what looked like a pillared temple, great doors standing open, each studded with a hundred circles of bronze.

The steps were high enough to put an ache in Nona's legs. At the top a cavernous hall waited, lit by high windows, every square foot of it packed with stalls and people hunting bargains. The sound of their trading, echoing and multiplied by the marble vaults above, spoke through the entrance with one many-tongued voice. For several minutes it was nothing but noise and colour and pushing. Nona concentrated on filling the void left as the abbess stepped forward before some other body could occupy the space. At last they stumbled into a cool corridor and out into a quieter street behind the market hall.

'Who are you?' Nona asked. She had followed the woman far enough. 'And,' realizing something, 'where's your stick?'

The abbess turned, one hand knotted in the string of purple beads around her neck. 'My name is Glass. That's Abbess Glass to you. And I gave my crozier to a rather surprised young man shortly after we emerged from Shoe Street. I hope the warden's guards followed it rather than us.'

'Glass isn't a proper name. It's a thing. I've seen some in Partnis Reeve's office.' Something hard and near invisible that kept the Corridor winds from the fight-master's den.

Abbess Glass turned away and resumed her marching. 'Each sister takes a new name when she is deemed fit to marry the Ancestor. It's always the name of an object or thing, to set us apart from the worldly.'

'Oh.' Most in Nona's village had prayed to the nameless

gods of rain and sun as they did all across the Grey, setting corn dollies in the fields to encourage a good harvest. But her mother and a few of the younger women went to the new church over in White Lake, where a fierce young man talked about the god who would save them, the Hope, rushing towards us even now. The roof of the Hope church stood ever open so they could see the god advancing. To Nona he looked like all the other stars, only white where almost every other is red, and brighter too. She had asked if all the other stars were gods as well, but all that earned her was a slap. Preacher Mickel said the star was Hope, and also the One God, and that before the northern ice and the southern ice joined hands he would come to save the faithful.

In the cities, though, they mainly prayed to the Ancestor.

'There. See it?'

Nona followed the line of the abbess's finger. On a high plateau, beyond the city wall, the slanting sunlight caught on a domed building, perhaps five miles off.

'Yes.'

'That's where we're headed.' And the abbess led away along the street, stepping around a horse pile too fresh for the garden-boys to have got to yet.

'You didn't hear about *me* all the way up there?' Nona asked. It didn't seem possible.

Abbess Glass laughed, a warm and infectious noise. 'Ha! No. I had other business in town. One of the faithful told me your story and I made a diversion on my way back to the convent.'

'Then how did you know my name? My real name, not the one Partnis gave me.'

'Could you have caught the fourth apple?' The abbess responded with a question.

'How many apples can you catch, old woman?'

'As many as I need to.' Abbess Glass looked back at her. 'Hurry up, now.'

Nona knew that she didn't know much, but she knew when someone was trying to take her measure and she didn't like things being taken from her. The abbess would have kept on with her apples until she found Nona's limit – and held that knowledge like a knife in its sheath. Nona hurried up and said nothing. The streets grew emptier as they approached the city wall and the shadows started to stretch.

Alleyways yawned left and right, dark mouths ready to swallow Nona whole. However warm the abbess's laughter, Nona didn't trust her. She had watched Saida die. Running away was still very much an option. Living with a collection of old nuns on a windswept hill outside the city might be better than hanging, but not by much.

'Master Reeve said that Raymel wasn't dead. That's not true.'

The abbess pulled her coif off in a smooth motion, revealing short grey hair and exposing her neck to the wind. She quickly threw a shawl of sequined wool about her shoulders.

'Where did— You *stole* that!' Nona glanced around to see if any of the passers-by would share her outrage but they were few and far between, heads bowed, bound to their own purposes. 'A thief and a liar!'

'I value my integrity.' The abbess smiled. 'Which is why it has a price.'

'A thief and a liar.' Nona decided that she would run.

'And you, child, appear to be complaining because the man you were to hang for murdering is not in fact dead.' Abbess Glass tied the shawl and tugged it into place. 'Perhaps you can explain what happened at the Caltess and I can explain what Partnis Reeve almost certainly meant about Raymel Tacsis.'

'I killed him.' The abbess wanted a story but Nona kept her words close. She had come to talking so late her mother had thought her dumb, and even now she preferred to listen.

'How? Why? Paint me a picture.' Abbess Glass made a sharp turn, pulling Nona through a passage so narrow that a few more pounds about her middle would see the nun scraping both sides.

'They brought us to the Caltess in a cage.' Nona remembered the journey. There had been three children on the wagon when Giljohn, the child-taker, stopped at her village and the people gave her over. Grey Stephen had passed her up to him.

It seemed that everyone she knew watched as Giljohn put her in the wooden cage with the others. The village children, both littles and bigs, looked on mute, the old women muttered, Mari Streams, her mother's friend, had sobbed; Martha Baker had shouted cruel words. When the wagon jolted off along its way stones and clods of mud had followed. 'I didn't like it.'

The wagon had rattled on for days, then weeks. In two months they had covered nearly a thousand miles, most of it on small and winding lanes, back and forth across the same ground. They rattled up and down the Corridor, weaving a drunkard's trail north and south, so close to the ice that sometimes Nona could see the walls rising blue above the trees. The wind proved the only constant, crossing the land without friendship, a stranger's fingers trailing the grass, a cold intrusion.

Day after day Giljohn steered his wagon from town to town, village to hamlet to lonely hovel. The children given up were gaunt, some little more than bones and rags, their parents lacking the will or coin to feed them. Giljohn delivered two meals a day, barley soup with onions in the morning, hot and salted, with hard black bread to dip. In the evening, mashed swede with butter. His passengers looked better by the day.

'I've seen more meat on a butcher's apron.' That's what Giljohn told Saida's parents when they brought her out of their hut into the rain.

The father, a ratty little man, stooped and gone to grey, pinched Saida's arm. 'Big girl for her age. Strong. Got a lick o' gerant in her.'

The mother, whey-faced, stick-thin, weeping, reached to touch Saida's long hair but let her hand fall away before contact was made.

'Four pennies, and my horse can graze in your field tonight.' Giljohn always dickered. He seemed to do it for the love of the game, his purse being the fattest Nona had ever seen, crammed with pennies, crowns, even a gleaming sovereign that brought a new colour into Nona's life. In the village only Grey Stephen ever had coins. And James Baker that time he sold all his bread to a merchant's party that had lost the track to Gentry. But none of them had ever had gold. Not even silver.

'Ten and you get on your way before the hour's old,' the father countered.

Within the aforementioned hour Saida had joined them in the cage, her pale hair veiling a down-turned face. The cart moved off without delay, heavier one girl and lighter five pennies. Nona watched through the bars, the father counting the coins over and again as if they might multiply in his hand, his wife clutching at herself. The mother's wailing followed them as far as the cross-roads.

'How old are you?' Markus, a solid dark-haired boy who seemed very proud of his ten years, asked the question. He'd asked Nona the same when she joined them. She'd said nine because he seemed to need a number.

'Eight.' Saida sniffed and wiped her nose with a muddy hand.

'Eight? Hope's blood! I thought you were thirteen!' Markus seemed in equal measure both pleased to keep his place as oldest, and outraged by Saida's size.

'Gerant in her,' offered Chara, a dark girl with hair so short her scalp shone through.

Nona didn't know what gerant was, except that if you had it you'd be big.

Saida shuffled closer to Nona. As a farm-girl she knew not to sit above the wheels if you didn't want your teeth rattled out.

'Don't sit by her,' Markus said. 'Cursed, that one is.'

'She came with blood on her,' Chara said. The others nodded.

Markus delivered the final and most damning verdict. 'No charge.'

Nona couldn't argue. Even Hessa with her withered leg had cost Giljohn a clipped penny. She shrugged and brought her knees up to her chest.

Saida pushed aside her hair, sniffed mightily, and threw a thick arm about Nona drawing her close. Alarmed, Nona had pushed back but there was no resisting the bigger girl's strength. They held like that as the wagon jolted beneath them, Saida weeping, and when the girl finally released her Nona found her own eyes full of tears, though she couldn't say why. Perhaps the piece of her that should know the answer was broken.

Nona knew she should say something but couldn't find the right words. Maybe she'd left them in the village, on her mother's floor. Instead of silence she chose to say the thing that she had said only once before – the thing that had put her in the cage.

'You're my friend.'

The big girl sniffed, wiped her nose again, looked up, and split her dirty face with a white grin.

Giljohn fed them well and answered questions, at least the first time they were asked – which meant 'are we there yet?' and 'how much further?' merited no more reply than the clatter of wheels.

The cage served two purposes, both of which he explained once, turning his grizzled face back to the children to do so and letting the mule, Four-Foot, choose his own direction.

'Children are like cats, only less useful and less furry. The cage keeps you in one place or I'd forever be rounding you up. Also…' he raised a finger to the pale line of scar tissue that divided his left eyebrow, eye-socket, and cheekbone, 'I am a man of short temper and long regret. Irk me and I will lash out with this, or this.' He held out first the cane with which he encouraged Four-Foot, and then the callused width of his palm. 'I shall then regret both the sins against the Ancestor and against my purse.' He grinned, showing yellow teeth and dark gaps. 'The cage saves you from my intemperance. At least until you irk me to a level where my ire lasts the trip around to the door.'

The cage could hold twelve children. More if they were small. Giljohn continued his meander westward along the Corridor, whistling in fair weather, hunched and cursing in foul.

'I'll stop when my purse is empty or my wagon's full.' He said it each time a new acquisition joined them, and it set Nona to wishing Giljohn would find some golden child whose parents loved her and who would cost him every coin in his possession. Then at last they might get to the city.

Sometimes they saw it in the distance, the smoke of Verity. Closer still and a faint suggestion of towers might resolve from the haze above the city. Once they came so close that Nona saw the sunlight crimson on the battlements of the fortress that the emperors had built around the Ark. Beneath it, the whole sprawling city bound about with thick walls and sheltering from the wind in the lee of a high plateau. But Giljohn turned and the city dwindled once more to a distant smudge of smoke.

Nona whispered her hope to Saida on a cold day when the sun burned scarlet over half the sky and the wind ran its fingers through the wooden bars, finding strange and hollow notes.

'Giljohn doesn't want pretty,' Saida snorted. 'He's looking for breeds.'

Nona only blinked.

'Breeds. You know. Anyone who shows the blood.' She looked down at Nona, still wide-eyed with incomprehension. 'The four tribes?'

Nona had heard of them, the four tribes of men who came to the world out of darkness and mixed their lines to bear children who might withstand the harshness of the lands they claimed. 'Ma took me to the Hope church. They didn't like talk of the Ancestor.'

Saida held her hands up. 'Well there were four tribes.' She counted them off on her fingers. 'Gerant. If you have too much gerant blood you get big like they were.' She patted her broad chest. 'Hunska. They're less common.' She touched Nona's hair. 'Hunska-dark, hunska-fast.' As if reciting a rhyme. 'The others are even rarer. Marjool … and … and…'

'Quantal,' Markus said from the corner. He snorted and puffed up as if he were an elder. 'And it's marjal, not marjool.'

Saida scowled at him, and turning back she lowered her voice to a whisper. 'They can do magic.'

Nona touched her hair where Saida's hand had rested. The village littles thought black hair made her evil. 'Why does Giljohn want children like that?'

'To sell.' Saida shrugged. 'He knows the signs to look for. If he's right he can sell us for more than he paid. Ma said I'll find work if I keep getting big. She said in the city they feed you meat and pay you coins.' She sighed. 'I still don't want to go.'

Giljohn took the lanes that led nowhere, the roads so rutted and overgrown that often it needed all the children pushing and Four-Foot straining all four legs to make headway. Giljohn would let Markus lead the mule then – Markus had a way with the beast. The children liked Four-Foot, he smelled worse than an old blanket and had a fondness for nipping legs, but he drew them tirelessly and his only competition for their affection was Giljohn. Several of them fought to bring him hoare-apples and sweet grass at the day's end. But, of all of them Four-Foot only loved Giljohn who whipped him, and Markus who rubbed him between the eyes and spoke the right kind of nonsense when doing it.

The rains came for days at a time making life in the cage miserable, though Giljohn did throw a hide over the top and windward side. The mud was the worst of it, cold and sour stuff that took hold of the wheels so that they all had to shove. Nona hated the mud: lacking Saida's height she often found herself thigh-deep in the cold and sucking mire, having to be rescued by Giljohn as the wagon slurped onto firmer ground. Each time he would knot his fist in the back of her hempen smock and heft her out bodily.

Nona set to scraping the goo off as soon as he set her down on the tailgate.

'What's a bit of mud to a farm-girl?' Giljohn wanted to know.

Nona only scowled and kept on scraping. She hated being dirty, always had. Her mother said she ate her food like a highborn lady, holding each morsel with precision so as not to smear herself.

'She's not a farm-girl.' Saida spoke up for her. 'Nona's ma wove baskets.'

Giljohn returned to the driver's seat. 'She's not anything

now, and neither are the rest of you until I sell you. Just mouths to feed.'

Roads that led nowhere took them to people who had nothing. Giljohn never asked to buy a child. He'd pull up alongside any farm that grew more weeds and rocks than crop, places where calling the harvest 'failed' would be over generous, implying that it had made some sort of effort to succeed. In such places the tenant farmer might pause his plough or lay down his scythe to approach the wagon at his boundary wall.

A man driving a wagonload of children in a cage doesn't have to state his business. A farmer whose flesh lies sunken around his bones, and whose eyes are the colour of hunger, doesn't have to explain himself if he walks up to such a man. Hunger lies beneath all of our ugliest transactions.

Sometimes a farmer would make that long, slow crossing of his field, from right to wrong, and stand, lean in his overalls, chewing on a corn stalk, eyes a-glitter in the shadows of his face. On such occasions it wouldn't take more than a few minutes before a string of dirty children were lined up beside him, graduated in height from those narrowing their eyes against the suspicion of what they'd been summoned for, down to those still clutching in one hand the stick they'd been playing with and in the other the rags about their middle, their eyes wide and without guile.

Giljohn picked out any child with possible gerant traits on a swift first pass. When they knew their ages it was easier, but even without anything more than a rough guess at a child's years he would find clues to help him. Often he looked at the backs of their necks, or took their wrists and bent them back – just until they winced. Those children he would set aside. On a second pass he would examine the eyes, pulling at the corners and peering at the whites. Nona remembered those hands. She had felt like a pear picked from the market stall, squeezed, sniffed over, replaced. The village had asked nothing for her, yet still Giljohn had carried out his checks. A space in his cage and meals from his pot had to be earned.

With the hunska possibles the child-taker would rub the youngster's hair between finger and thumb as if checking for coarseness. If still curious, he would test their swiftness by dropping a stone so that it fell behind a cloth he held out, and make a game of trying to catch it as it came back into view a couple of feet lower. Almost none of the children taken as hunska were truly fast: Giljohn said they'd grow into it, or training would bring their speed into the open.

Nona guessed they might make ten stops before finding someone prepared to swap their sons and daughters for a scattering of copper. She guessed that after walking the lines of children set out for him Giljohn would actually offer coins fewer than one time in a dozen, and that when he did it was generally for an over-large child. And even of these few hardly any, he said, would grow into full gerant heritage.

After Giljohn had picked out these and any dark and over-quick children, he would always return to the line for the third and slowest of his inspections. Here, although he watched with the hawk's intensity, Giljohn kept his hands to himself. He asked questions instead.

'Did you dream last night?' he might ask.

'Tell me … what colours do you see in the focus moon?'

And when they told him the moon is always red. When they said, that you can't look at the focus moon, it will blind you, he replied, 'But if you could, if it wasn't, what colours would it be?'

'What makes a blue sound?' He often used that one.

'What does pain taste of?'

'Can you see the trees grow?'

'What secrets do stones keep?'

And so on – sometimes growing excited, sometimes affecting boredom, yawning into his hand. All of it a game. Rarely won. And at the end of it, always the same, Giljohn crouched to be on their level. 'Watch my finger,' he would tell them. And he would move it through the air in a descending line, so close his nail almost clipped their nose. The line wavered, jerked, pulsed, beat, never the same twice but always familiar. What he was looking for in their eyes Nona didn't know. He seldom seemed to find it though.

Two places in the wagon went to children selected in this

final round, and each of those cost more than any of the others. Never too much though. Asked for gold he would walk away.

'Friend, I've been at this as long as you've tilled these rows, and in all that time how many that I've sold on have passed beneath the Academy arch?' he would ask. 'Four. Only four full-bloods … and still they call me the mage-finder.'

In the long hours between one part of nowhere and the next the children, jolting in the cage, would watch the world pass by, much of it dreary moor, patchy fields, or dour forest where screw-pine and frost-oak fought for the sun, leaving little for the road. Mostly they were silent, for children's chatter dies off soon enough if not fed, but Hessa proved a wonder. She would set her withered leg before her with both hands, then lean back against the wooden bars and tell story after story, her eyes closed above cheekbones so large they made something alien of her. In all her pinched face, framed by tight curls of straw-coloured hair, only her mouth moved. The stories she told stole the hours and pulled the children on journeys far longer than Four-Foot could ever manage. She had tales of the Scithrowl in the east and their battle-queen Adoma, and of her bargains with the horror that dwells beneath the black ice. She told of Durnishmen who sail across the Sea of Marn to the empire's western shore in their sick-wood barges. Of the great waves sent up when the southern ice walls calve, and how they sweep the width of the Corridor to wash up against the frozen cliffs of the north, which collapse in turn and send back waves of their own. Hessa spoke of the emperor and his sisters, and of their bickering that had laid waste many a great family with the ill fortune to find itself between them. She told of heroes past and present, of olden day generals who held the border lands, of Admiral Scheer who lost a thousand ships, of Noi-Guin scaling castle walls to sink the knife, of Red Sisters in their battle-skins, of the Soft Men and their poisons…

Sometimes on those long roads Hessa spoke to Nona, huddled close in a corner of the cage, her voice low, and Nona couldn't tell if it were a story or strange truths she told.

'You see it too, don't you, Nona?' Hessa bent in close, so close her breath tickled Nona's ear. 'The Path, the line? The one that wants us to follow it.'

'I don't—'

'I can walk in that place. Here they took my crutch and I have to crawl or be carried … but there … I can walk for as long as I can keep the Path beneath me.' Nona felt the smile. Hessa moved back and laughed – rare for her, very rare. She told a story for everyone then, Persus and the Hidden Path, a tale from the oldest days, and even Giljohn leaned back to listen.

And one day, wonder of wonders, the twelfth child squeezed into the cage, and Giljohn declared his wagon full, his business complete. Turning west, he let Four-Foot lead the way to Verity, soon finding a wide and stone-clad road where four hooves could eat up the miles double quick.

They arrived in the dark and in the rain. Nona saw nothing more of the city than a multitude of lights, first a constellation hovering above the black threat of the great walls, and once through the yawn of the gates, a succession of islands where a lantern's illumination pooled to offer a doorway here, a row of columns there, figures hidden in their cloaks, emerging from the blind night to be glimpsed and lost once more.

Broad streets and narrow, cut like canyons through the neck-craning height of Verity's houses, brought the wagon in time to a tall timber door. A legend set in iron letters above the door declared a name, but recognizing that the shapes were letters took Nona to the borders of her education.

'The Caltess, boys and girls.' Giljohn pushed back his hood. 'Time to meet Partnis Reeve.'

Giljohn pulled up in the courtyard that waited behind the high walls and ordered them out. Saida and Nona clambered down, stiff and sore. Before them a many-windowed hall rose to three times the height of any building that Nona had seen until she reached the city. The yard was largely deserted, lit by the flames guttering in a brazier set at the centre. Peculiar equipment lay abandoned in corners, including pieces of leather-bound wood the size and shape of men, set on round-bottomed bases. A few young men sat on benches beneath the lanterns, all of them polishing pieces of leatherwork, save one who was mending a net as if he were a fisherman.

Partnis Reeve kept the children lined up for more than an hour before he emerged from his hall. Long enough for dawn to infiltrate the yard and surprise Nona with the knowledge that a whole night had passed in travel.

Saida fidgeted and pulled her shawl about her. Nona watched as the sun edged the ridge of the hall's black-tiled roof with crimson. Beyond the walls the city woke, creaking and groaning like an old man leaving his bed, though it had hardly slept.

Partnis came down the steps, always taking the next with the same leg. A heavy-featured man, tall and well fed, with iron-grey hair, dark eyes promising no kindness, wrapped against the cold in a thick velvet robe.

'Partnis!' Giljohn held his arms wide and Partnis Reeve copied the gesture, though neither man stepped forward into the promised embrace. 'Celia well? And little Merra?'

'Celia is … Celia.' Partnis lowered his arms with a wry grin. 'And Merra is living in Darrins Town, married to a cloth merchant's boy.'

'How did we get so old?' Giljohn returned his arms to his sides. 'Yesterday we were young.'

'Yesterday was a long time ago.' Partnis turned his attention to the merchandise. 'Too small.' He walked past Nona without further comment. 'Too timid.' He passed Saida. 'Too fat. Too young. Too ill. Too lazy. Too clumsy. Too much trouble.' He turned at the end of the line and looked at Giljohn. They were of a height, though Partnis looked soft where Giljohn looked hard. 'I'll give you two crowns for the lot.'

'I spent two crowns feeding them!' Giljohn spat on the grit floor.

The haggling took another hour and both men seemed to enjoy it. Giljohn enumerated the reasons why the children would become valuable fighters in Partnis's contests, pointing out gerant or hunska traits.

'This girl here is eight!' Giljohn set a hand to Saida's

shoulder, making her flinch. 'Eight years old! Tall as a tree. She's a gerant prime for sure. A full-blood even!'

'Even a full-blood's only got labour value if there's no fight in 'em.' Partnis barked a wordless shout into Saida's face. She stumbled back with a shriek of fear, raising both hands to her eyes. 'Worthless.'

'She's *eight*, Partnis!'

'So her father said. She looks fifteen to me.'

Giljohn grabbed Saida's arm and pulled her forward. 'Feel her wrists!' He pushed her head forward and ran a finger over the vertebrae knobbling the back of her neck. 'Look here!' He straightened her by her hair. 'Fathers lie, but bones don't. This one's a prime at the least. Ain't seen a gerant to beat her this trip. Could be full-blood.'

Partnis took Saida's wrist and squeezed until she whimpered. 'She's got a touch, I grant you.'

'Touch? She's no damn touch.'

'Half-blood if you're lucky.'

And so it went on, Partnis allowing some of the children might be a touch or even half-bloods, Giljohn insisting they were all primes or even full-bloods.

Nona and a boy named Tooram he claimed showed clear evidence of hunska bloodlines. He slapped Tooram, then tried again and the boy interposed his arm before the blow could land. When he tried it on Nona she let him slap her, the hard length of his hand impacting the side of her head, leaving her ear buzzing and her cheek one hot outrage of pain. He did it again, with a scowl, and she scowled back, making no effort to avoid the blow which took her off her feet and replaced the grey sky with bright and flashing lights.

'...idiot.'

Nona found herself on her feet, her shoulder in Giljohn's iron grip, blood filling her mouth. She remembered the force of the slap, how her teeth had seemed to rattle.

'You saw how fast she turned towards me.'

It was true – Nona's lips felt four times their size and white spears of pain lanced up her nose. She had faced into the blow at the last moment.

'I must have missed that part,' Partnis said.

Nona swallowed the blood. She let the pain run through her – the cost she paid for taking money from Giljohn's pocket. Some of the children, sold by their own fathers, almost saw the child-taker as their replacement. Stern, certainly, but he fed them, kept them safe. Nona took a contrary view. Her father had died on the ice and what memories she kept of him warmed her in the cold, tasted sweet when the world ran sour. He would have known how to treat a man like Giljohn.

The gerants had no such choice to make, their size argued their case without need for demonstration. Though in Saida's place Nona thought she might have agreed with Partnis when he accused her of being fifteen.

Partnis took them in exchange for ten crowns and two.

'Be good.' Giljohn, a father to them all for three long months, had no other words for them, climbing up behind Four-Foot without ceremony.

'Goodbye.' Saida was the only one to speak.

Giljohn glanced her way, stick half-raised for the off. 'Goodbye,' he said.

'She meant the mule.' Tooram didn't turn his head, but he spoke loud enough for the words to reach.

A grin slanted across Giljohn's face and, shaking his head, he flicked at Four-Foot's haunches, encouraging him through the doors that Partnis's man had set open once more.

Nona watched the wagon rattle off, Hessa, Markus, Willum and Chara staring back at her through the bars. She would miss Hessa and her stories. She wondered who Giljohn would sell her to and how a girl unable to walk would make her way in the world. She might miss Markus too, perhaps. The miles had worn away his sharp edges, the wheels had gone round and round … somehow turning him into someone she liked. In the next moment they were all gone.

'And now you're mine,' Partnis said. He summoned the young man mending the net, lean but well-muscled under his woollen vest, hair dark, skin pale, but not so dark or so pale as Nona. 'This is Jaymes. He'll take you to Maya who is your mother now. The slapping kind.' Partnis offered them a heavy smile. 'I don't expect to notice any of you until you're this high.' He held his hand to his chest. 'And if I do, it will probably be bad news for you. Do what you're told and you'll be fine. You're Caltess now. Bought and paid for.'

Maya stood more than a foot taller than Partnis, arms thick as a man's thighs, her face red and blotched as if a constant rage held her in its jaws. To compensate for her complexion the Ancestor had given her thick blonde hair that she braided into heavy ropes. She stood on the attic ladder after shepherding the new arrivals up it, only her head and shoulders emerging into the gloom.

'No lanterns up here. Ever. No candles. No lamps. Break that rule and I break you.' She made the motion with heavy-knuckled hands. 'When you're not working you're up here. Meals are in the kitchen. You'll hear the bell when it's time. Miss it and you won't eat.'

Nona and the others crouched close to the trapdoor, watching the giant. The musty air reminded Nona of James Baker's grain store at the village. Around them the shadows rustled. Cats most likely, rats and spiders of a certainty, but also other children watching the new arrivals.

Maya raised her voice. 'Don't pick on the new meat. There's time enough for that down below.' She stared at a patch of darkness seemingly no darker than any other. 'I see any lumps and bumps on Partnis's new purchases, Denam, Regol, and I'll knock your heads together so hard you swap brains. Hear me?' A pause. 'Hear me?' Loud enough to shake the roof.

'I hear you.' A snarl.

'Heard.' Chuckled in the distance.

The others emerged as soon as Maya withdrew. Two long-limbed boys dropped from the rafters into the midst of the newcomers. Nona hadn't seen them lurking there. Others scampered in from the shadows, or strolled, or crept, each according to their nature. None of them as small or as young as Nona, but most of them not many years older. From the direction in which Maya had stared came a huge boy, a scowl beneath a thick shock of red hair, muscles heaped and shifting below his shapeless linen shift. Moments later a lad near as tall but willow-thin joined him, black hair sweeping down across his eyes, a crooked smile hung between the corners of his mouth.

A throng gathered, many more than Nona had anticipated. Huddled and watchful, waiting to be entertained.

The red-haired giant opened his mouth to threaten them. 'You—'

'Oh hush, Denam.' The dark-haired boy stepped in front of him. 'You're newbies. I'm Regol. This is Denam, soon-to-be apprentice, and the toughest, fiercest warrior the Caltess attic has ever seen. Look at him wrong and he'll chew you up then spit out the pieces.' Regol glanced back at Denam. 'That's the gist, ain't it?' He returned his gaze to the newbies. 'Now we've got the chest-thumping out of the way and saved Maya the bother of spanking Denam you can find yourself a place to sleep.' He waved a hand airily at the gloom. 'Don't tread on any toes.'

Regol turned as if to go then paused. 'Sooner rather than later someone will try to convince you that the reason so many of us up here are titchies like yourselves is that Partnis eats children, or there's some test so deadly that almost nobody survives it, or sometimes Maya forgets to look before she sits down. The truth is that you've been bought early and cheap. Most of you will be disappointments. You won't grow into something Partnis can use. He'll sell you on.' Regol raised a hand as Denam started to speak. 'And not to a salt mine or to be used as the filling in a pie – just to any place that has a need you can meet.' He lowered his hand. 'Any questions?'

A cracking sound filled the immediate silence and it took Nona a moment to realize it was Denam's knuckles as he formed fists. The giant's scowl deepened. 'I really hate you, Regol.'

'Not a question. Anyone else?'

Silence.

Regol walked back into the darkness, stepping rafter to rafter with the unconscious grace of a cat.

⋆ ⋆ ⋆

Life in the Caltess proved to be a big improvement on an open cage rattling along the back-lanes of empire. Truth be told, it was an improvement on life in Nona's village. Here she might be the smallest but she wasn't the odd one out. The isolation of the village bred generations so similar in looks you might pick any handful at random to make a convincing family. Nona alone hadn't fit the mould. A goat in the sheep herd. The family Partnis's purse had furnished him with mixed every size and shape, every colour and shade, and in the attic's gloom they were much of a muchness even so.

In addition to the four dozen children Partnis kept immediately beneath his roof, he housed a dozen apprentices, and seven fighters in their own set of rooms around the great hall. The apprentices shared a barracks house out in the rear of the compound.

Nona found a spot wedged between grain sacks larger than herself. Saida had more difficulty finding a space to squeeze into and was turned away by older residents time and again, even those she dwarfed. But in the end she settled on the boards close to Nona's sack-pile, further back where the roof sloped so low that she had to roll into place.

That first night the hall opened its doors and the world flowed in to see men bleed. Denam and Regol got to watch from the highest rungs of the ladder in the furthest corner of the great hall, behind counters where the apprentices sold ale and wine to the crowd. The eldest of the remaining children crowded around the trapdoor. Everyone else had to find some chink among the rafters through which the events below might be glimpsed.

Nona's spot afforded her a narrow view of the second ring. She wondered that they called it a ring when in fact the ropes strung between the four posts enclosed a square perhaps eight yards on a side, the whole thing a raised platform so that the fighter's feet were level with the average man's brow. She could see the tops of many heads, hundreds packed tight. The hubbub of their voices filled the attic. As the crowd built so did the noise, each of them having to shout just to be heard by their neighbour.

Saida lay close by, her eye to a crack. At her side an older boy, Marten, peered through a knot hole to which he laid ownership.

'It's all-comers tonight,' Marten said, without looking up. 'Ranking bouts on the seven-day, all comers on the second, exhibitions on the fourth. Blade matches are the last day of the month.'

'My da said men fight in pits in the city...' Saida said timidly, waiting to be told she was wrong.

'In the Marn ports some do,' Marten said. 'Partnis says it's a foolishness. If you've got willing fighters and a paying crowd you put them up on a platform, not down in a hole, where only the first row can see them.'

Nona lay, watching the throng below her while fights progressed unseen at the hall's far end. Her view offered only the tops of heads, but she judged reactions by the pulse and flow of the crowd. Their roaring sounded at times like the howl of a single great beast, so loud it resonated in her chest, throbbing in her own voice when she yelled her challenge back at them.

At last a figure climbed into the ring beneath them. All around her Nona could feel other children scrambling for a view. Someone tried to lift her from her spot but she caught the hands that grabbed her and dug her nails in. The unknown someone dropped her with a howl and she put her eye back to the crack.

'Raymel!' The voices around her echoed the cries of the mob.

In the ring he looked a heavily-built man with thick blond hair, naked save for the white cloth bound around his groin, his skin gleaming with oil, the muscles of his stomach in sharp relief, showing each band divided from the next. Nona had glimpsed him wandering the hall earlier in the day and knew that he was enormous, taller even than Maya, and moving with none of her awkward blunder. Raymel prowled, a killer's confidence in each motion. The man was a gerant prime. In the attic's dimness Nona had learned the code that Partnis and Giljohn had used when selling her. The range ran from touch through half-blood and prime to full-blood. A touch could be thought of as quarter-blood and a prime as three-quarters. For gerants, primes often made the best fighters, full-bloods though rarer still and larger were too slow – though perhaps they just said that at the Caltess as they had none to show.

'You'll see something now!' A girl's voice, excited, at Nona's left.

Marten had explained that any hopeful wishing to win a fight purse, or even to join the Caltess, could present themselves on all-comers' night and for a crown they might pit themselves against Partnis's stable.

'Raymel will kill them,' Saida said, awestruck.

'He won't.' Even shouting above the roar Marten managed to sound scornful. 'He's paid to win. He'll put on a show. Killing's not good for business.'

'Except when it is.' Another voice close at hand.

'Raymel does what he wants.' The girl to Nona's left. 'He might kill someone.' She sounded almost hungry for it.

A challenger entered the ring: a bald man, fat and powerful, the hair on his back so thick and black as to hide his skin. He had arms like slabs of meat – perhaps a smith given to swinging a hammer every day. Nona couldn't see his face.

'Doesn't Partnis tell Raymel—'

'No one tells Raymel.' The girl cut Saida off. 'He's the only highborn to step into a ring in fifty years. Regol said so. You don't tell the highborn what to do. The money's nothing to him.'

Nona had heard the same tone of worship in the Hope church where her mother and Mari Streams called on the new god and sang the hymns Preacher Mickel taught them.

The bell sounded and Raymel closed with the blacksmith.

Nona saw a slice of the ring, from one fighter's corner to the other's. When they stepped to the side she lost them. Raymel moved with an unhurried precision, stopping the blacksmith's advance with punches to the head, moving back to let him recover, luring him forward into the next. It didn't seem a contest, unless you considered the blacksmith to be competing to see how many times he could stop the giant's fist with his face.

The baying of the crowd rose with each impact, with each spray of blood and spittle. By the time Raymel stopped punching the smith long enough for the man to fall over, his opponent had yet to land a blow.

'Why would anyone do that?' Saida asked, lifting from her peephole, shuddering. 'Why would they fight him?'

'Lot of money in that fight purse,' Marten said. 'It gets fatter every time someone tries and fails.'

Nona kept watching as Raymel strode back and forth across the ring. She said nothing but she knew there was more to it than money. Every hard line the fighter owned was a challenge, written across him. The masses' roar fanned the fire, but it was Raymel that lit it. *Come and try me.*

Two more tried before the night was over, but the fighter in the other ring, Gretcha, had more takers. Perhaps she was more of a performer, letting her opponents take a shot, putting them down with more style and less brutality. Raymel treated his foes with disdain, dropping them to the boards bloody and humiliated.

The work Maya set was neither long, nor arduous, being split between more children than was necessary. In the great hall Nona polished, swept and scrubbed. In the kitchens she peeled, carried, washed, sliced and stoked. In the privies she slopped, bailed, wiped and retched. Maintenance of the fight equipment, the sparring rings, the training weapons and the like all fell to the apprentices. The fighters cared for their own weapons, as would anyone who trusted their life to a sharp edge or sturdy mail.

Sometimes groups of the older children were hired outside the Caltess to pick fruit, and dig ditches, but mostly, as Regol had said, their main task was to grow and to show the promise for which they had been purchased. Maya confided that none of them would be sold on for at least a year, probably two or three.

'Sometimes the promise won't show properly until a girl bleeds. I wasn't half my height at thirteen. Ain't no point Partnis putting you in training until he knows what you'll be.

Training costs. And it's wasted on most. Nobody ain't never going to make ring-fighter without the old blood showing in them. And even when he's sure you've got the gift for it Partnis likes to wait – says best training's done when you're mostly grown into your size and speed, so you don't have to be adjusting all the time.'

Twice a day Maya had the whole attic out in the yard for an hour, first clearing the fighters' weights back into their chests in the storeroom, then running endless laps, regardless of rain or wind. Nona looked forward to these daily escapes from the closed-in boredom of the attic and the routine of indoor chores. She worked with Saida and Tooram, who had been the last of Giljohn's acquisitions, to lift the smaller dumb-bells abandoned in the yard and return them to the equipment room. In truth, she and Tooram were probably more hindrance than help to Saida. Denam would pass them as they struggled up the steps, one of the heavier dumbbells in each hand, just the sweat plastering the red flame of his hair to his forehead to let them know the effort he was hiding.

They stopped to let him pass, then Saida led them on. 'Heave!'

Nona didn't mind that she wasn't helping much, or that her arms ached, her back hurt and her eyes stung with sweat. She liked to feel part of something. Saida was her friend and whilst she might not need Nona's help with the weights, she appreciated it.

In their friendship Nona found something absent in the faith of the village, or her mother's Hope, absent in Nana Even's moral instruction, or in the bonds of family she had seen break. Something she considered holy and worthy of sacrifice. Making friends came hard to Nona – she didn't see how it worked, only that sometimes it happened. She had had just one friend, only briefly, and lost him, she wouldn't lose another.

'Tell me how you ended up at Harriton, child. Looking up at a noose.' Abbess Glass's voice punctured Nona's remembering and she discovered herself walking along a stony road that divided broad, windswept fields given over to horses and sheep.

Left and right the occasional farmstead dotted the terrain, the low-gabled roofs of a villa lay ahead, and beyond that the steep escarpment below the plateau.

'What?' Nona shook her head. She had almost no recollection of leaving the city. Glancing back, she saw it lay a mile or more behind her, and that two nuns now flanked the abbess.

'You were going to tell me what happened with Raymel Tacsis,' the abbess said.

Nona looked again at the nuns, both taller than Abbess Glass, one very lean, the other with more curves to her, their habits fluttering about them. She half-remembered them joining the abbess at some small gate through the city wall. One had perhaps as many years as the abbess, her face pinched and weathered, eyes cold, lips thin. The other was younger, green-eyed, returning Nona's distracted inspection with a full smile that made her look away.

Nona fixed her eyes on the horizon. The convent was no longer visible, set back from the edge of the escarpment. 'Saida was told to clean the floors in Raymel's rooms. I heard her screaming.' It hadn't sounded like a person. In the village when Grey Jarry slaughtered pigs … it sounded like that. Not until one of the boys crowded around the trapdoor had said 'Raymel's rooms' had some cold hand taken hold inside Nona's chest and drawn her forward.

'I came down the ladder. Fast.' It had been slower than falling, but not much slower. She had run into the foyer. Saida had left a bucket and mop to hold the door open, a great slab of oak with scrolling brass hinges.

'There were pieces of pottery all over the floor. And he was hurting her.' Saida had knocked something from its niche – she was always clumsy. Raymel had her arm in his fist, his hand swallowing it from wrist to elbow, and he'd lifted her from the ground. He just stood there turning his hand from one side to the other while Saida struggled and wriggled, trying to reduce the awful strain on elbow and shoulder, shrieking all the while.

'I told him to put her down but he didn't hear me.' Nona had run to try to support her friend's weight, but Saida weighed twice what she did. Raymel noticed her then and, laughing, shook Saida so that Nona flew free. Something cracked in Saida's arm when he did it – loud enough to register over her screams.

'So I stopped him. I cut his throat.'

The younger nun snorted behind her. 'They say he's nine foot tall.'

'I climbed.' Raymel wasn't nine foot but he was over eight. He had gone down on one knee, still holding Saida off the ground by her broken arm, taunting Nona with an ugly grin on his handsome face.

Nona had sprinted forward. There was time for the surprise to register in Raymel's eyes, but not for him to move. She had leapt onto his knee to gain the necessary height then slashed her hand across his throat.

'How did you cut him?' The older nun, from behind.

'I...' Nona pictured Raymel, golden hair curling across an unfurrowed brow, the smile opening into something else, blood sheeting crimson from the slices she'd set deep in the meat of his neck. 'I pulled the dagger from his hip as I climbed.'

'That,' said the younger nun, 'sounds unlikely.'

Abbess Glass replied before Nona could deliver her sharp reply. 'Nevertheless, if you look more closely, Sister Apple, you will see that the girl's tunic was once white rather than brown – a brown which, if the guards at Harriton are to be believed, is a combination of drying blood and prison grime. Moreover she and her friend were both to be hanged for the murder of Raymel Tacsis.'

'Then why isn't he dead?' Nona asked. She wanted Raymel to be dead.

'Because his father is very rich, Nona.' The abbess led them from the road onto a narrower track aimed towards the towering walls of the escarpment. 'Not just a little bit rich but rich enough to buy a different mansion to sleep in every night from now until age claims him.'

'Money doesn't matter when you're bleeding.' Nona frowned. Rich or poor, people looked the same on the inside.

'Thuran Tacsis is rich enough that he owns Academy men.'

The abbess hitched up her habit to help her climb the slope. 'I miss my crozier already. An old lady without her stick to lean on is a sad thing indeed.'

Nona said nothing, not understanding the abbess's words.

'Academy men... Wizards, Nona! Mages. Sorcerers. Witches and warlocks. Children with marjal blood. Educated and raised at the emperor's expense and bound to the Ark and to his service, but free to earn a living outside the palace until such time as he requires their skills.'

'They can raise a man from the dead?' Suddenly she thought of her father, unable to remember anything of him but thick black hair and strong, safe arms.

'No, but they can stop a live one becoming dead. There's a boundary, a place where we cross over to join the Ancestor. Some among us can visit that boundary and hold a person there while their body heals from wounds that would otherwise make an end of them.'

'So rich people never die?' Nona wondered at it, buying off death with gold coins.

The abbess shook her head. 'No warlock stays by the boundary for long.' Her breath came shorter now as the way grew steeper. 'Thuran has a dozen warlocks working in shifts to hold his son from crossing. And many of the things that kill us the body can't repair, no matter how much time it is given. Cut flesh though, and lost blood ... a healthy body can mend one and replace the other. The real risk is when they bring a person back to their body – there are ... beings ... that will try to follow in their wake and find a home in their minds. The longer the person is kept on the boundary, the harder it is to keep out such passengers.'

Nona thought of Raymel Tacsis lying in his father's halls surrounded by Academy men sweating to keep him from death. Saida was dead – Nona had seen her feet poking beneath the sheet in the prison yard, their wrappings still stained with Raymel's blood. She had no pity for him.

'I hope he comes back full of devils and they eat his heart.'

4

'You could send the child on her way here, abbess.'

They stood at the point where the track began its steep ascent up the tumbled cliffs of the plateau, cutting back and forth across the gradient in a dozen hairpin turns. The older nun turned to Nona and pointed across the woods and fields to the west. 'Morltown is five miles that way. A girl could make herself useful there, find fieldwork.'

Sister Apple stood shoulder to shoulder with Sister Tallow. 'The high priest will be on this in a heartbeat. The Tacsis won't even have to ask.'

'Pick your fights and pick your ground, abbess,' Sister Tallow said. 'Jacob would love to get his feet back under the convent table. This would be the perfect excuse.'

'And you did just steal her from prison…' Apple frowned, glancing back towards the distant city.

'Mistress Blade tells me not to fight.' A smile, then the abbess turned to begin the climb. 'And Apple tells me not to steal…' Nona started to follow her. 'You're nuns. Show a little faith.'

A last edge of the sun clung to the horizon as Abbess Glass led the way towards a peculiar forest of stone pillars, their shadows reaching across hundreds of yards of rock towards the travellers' approach. Nona followed, flanked by the two nuns, neither of them winded by the long climb that had set the abbess wheezing. The old one, Sister Tallow, looked as if she could climb all day. The younger, Sister Apple, at least had the decency to appear flushed. Nona, toughened by endless laps at the Caltess, felt the climb in her legs, and the dampness of her shift where sweat stuck it to her back, but made no complaint.

The plateau, really one huge slab of rock, narrowed to a neck of land before widening into a promontory. The pillars stood across the neck, from cliff to cliff, dozens deep, scores across. Abbess Glass led the way through – finding her path seemingly at random. All about them the columns, taller than trees, stretched towards the darkening sky. The place held an odd silence, the wind finding nothing to sing its tune, only stirring the dust and grit among the towers of carved stone. Nona liked it.

The pillars bounded Sweet Mercy Convent one side, and on the other the edges of two cliffs marched towards a sharp convergence. The main dome rose black against the crimson sky, a dozen and more outbuildings visible to either side. Nona followed the nuns towards its arched entrance, the weight of the day on her shoulders now, fatigue wrapping her in its dull grip, making both her anger and her sorrow grow more distant, shaping them into things that might be set apart for a night of dreams.

'You live in there?' As they drew closer Nona began to realize how large the dome was. The whole of the Caltess would fit inside several times over, stacked on top of itself.

'That's the Dome of the Ancestor, Nona. The Ancestor lives there, nobody else.'

'Is he terribly big?' Nona asked. Behind her Sister Apple stifled a laugh.

'The Ancestor occupies any space built in their honour. In Verity the Ancestor is present in ten thousand household shrines, some into which even you would find it hard to squeeze, others larger than most houses. Here on the plateau the church was able to give the Ancestor a grander home – a gift of Emperor Persus, third of his name.'

Nona followed on in silence, her lips buttoned against the thought that the Ancestor seemed very greedy to be taking

Somewhere a few cells back a woman coughed in her sleep, breaking the silence and the strangeness. Freed from both paralysis and compulsion, Nona raised a hand to shield her candle's flame and advanced into the narrow room that Sister Apple had led her to.

Even her cell at the Harriton had boasted a window, high and barred perhaps, but offering the condemned the sky. Nona's new cell had a slit wide enough to reach her arm through, shuttered with a pine board. She made a circle. A sleeping pallet, a pillow, a chair, a desk. A pot to piss in. Last and strangest, a length of metal running along the outer wall at ground level. It emerged from the cell to the left and vanished through the wall to the right. Round as a branch and just a little too thick to close her hand around.

Nona sniffed. Dust, and the stale air of an unused room. She went to the pallet. Heat rising from the metal stick burned on her cheeks. The whole cell held the warmth of it. Nona pulled the pallet away from the hot metal, mistrusting it. She set the candle down, pulled the blanket over her, and laid her head on the pillow. One last look at the room and she blew out the flame. She stared at the darkness, her mind too full for sleep, certain that she would lie awake the whole night.

A moment later the clanging of an iron bell opened Nona's eyes. The door swung open, banging against the wall. Nona levered herself up from the pallet and blinked towards the entrance, the darkness now a gloomy half-light. A groan escaped her, every limb stiff and aching though she only recalled straining her legs on the climb.

'Up! Up! No slug-a-beds here! Up!' A small, angular woman with a voice that sounded as if it were being forced violently through a narrow hole. She strode into the cell, reaching over Nona to throw back the shutter. 'Let the light in! No hiding place for sin!'

Through fingers held up to defend against the daylight Nona found herself staring into a humourless face pinched tight around prominent cheekbones, eyes wide, watery and accusing. The woman's head, which had seemed a most alarming shape in the gloom, sported a rising white headdress, rather like a funnel, and quite different to those the other nuns had worn the previous evening.

'Up, girl! Up!'

'Ah, I see you've met Sister Wheel.' Sister Apple stepped through the open doorway holding a long habit, the outer garment grey felt, the inner white linen.

'Sleeping after the morning bell, she was!' The old woman raised her hands, seemingly unsure whether to strike Nona or to use them to better depict the enormity of her crime.

'She's new, Wheel, not even a novice yet.' Sister Apple smiled and looked pointedly at the doorway.

'A barefooted heathen is what she is!'

Sister Apple spread her fingers towards the exit, still smiling. 'It was commendable of you to notice the cell had an occupant.'

The older nun scowled and ran her hands over her forehead, tucking a stray strand of colourless hair back into her headdress. 'There's nothing that goes on in these cells I don't notice, sister.' She narrowed her watery eyes at Sister Apple then sniffed hard and stalked back into the corridor. 'The child stinks,' she offered over her shoulder. 'It needs washing.'

'I brought you some clothes.' Sister Apple lifted the habit. 'But I forgot how dirty you are. Sister Wheel is correct…' She folded her arms over her stomach. 'Come with me.'

Nona followed Sister Apple out of the room, weaving around various nuns emerging from their cells or speaking in low tones in the corridor. A couple raised an eyebrow at her approach but none addressed her. At one point an angular nun brought Sister Apple to a halt by laying a hand upon her shoulder. She towered above the others, her height seemingly gained by stretching a regular woman far beyond her design, leaving her dangerously thin.

'Mistress Blade reports armed men beyond the pillars. An emissary came before first light.'

'Thank you, Flint,' Sister Apple nodded.

Sister Flint tilted her head, her face so dark that in the gloom Nona could see only black eyes, glittering as they made a study of her. The nun took her hand from the smaller woman's shoulder, releasing her to her task.

Sister Apple led the way out into the brittle light of morning. By daylight Nona could see that the convent comprised so many buildings that back in the Grey it would qualify as a village. She suspected it had more stone-built buildings than Flaystown, though she had only glimpsed that metropolis from Giljohn's cage on the day he drove her from her home.

'Sister Flint said men are coming. Are they here for me?' Nona asked. She wondered what help a score of nuns would be if Thuran Tacsis had sent his warriors for her. She should have lost herself in the city when she had a chance.

'Perhaps.' Sister Apple glanced back at the great Dome of the Ancestor and frowned. 'Perhaps not. In any case, it would be best if you joined our order sooner rather than later – and you can't do that dirty, now can you?' She led on at a brisk pace.

'Scriptorium, refectory, bake-house, kitchens.' Sister Apple reeled off names as they passed various buildings. Few of them meant much to Nona but bake-house she knew and the aroma of fresh bread when they passed the door filled her mouth with drool. 'The Necessary.' The nun pointed to a small building, flat-roofed and seemingly clinging to the edge of the cliff a hundred yards off.

'Necessary?' Nona asked.

'You'll go there when you need it.' Sister Apple shook her head and smiled. 'The smell will let you know it's the right place.'

They passed a long range of buildings with many small square windows, all shuttered on the windward side. 'Stores and dormitories.'

Nona found herself observed, a dozen pairs of eyes at various of the windows. Some of the girls called out, perhaps to each other. She caught snatches, carried by the wind.

'…chosen … never!'

'…that can't be her…'

'…peasant…'

'...she's not the…'

'*Chosen?*'

The voices followed them, words lost in the distance but

the tone still hanging in the air. Nona knew it well enough, sharp and unkind.

'Bathhouse.' Sister Apple pointed to a squat building built of unadorned black stone, steam escaping from a row of narrow windows, only to be stripped away by the wind. The Corridor wind scoured the plateau, and crossing the gap between the dormitories and the bathhouse Nona found herself exposed to its teeth. She'd spent a lifetime learning to ignore it – just another hard edge of a hard life – but one warm night had left her soft and shivering.

They reached the shelter of the bathhouse walls. The nun unlocked the heavy door and ushered Nona in. Hot wet air wrapped her immediately, the steam reducing her vision to a few yards. Wooden benches lined the foyer and a tall arch gave onto what might be a rectangular pool, its surface offered only in glimpses.

Metal shafts ran beneath the benches in profusion. 'One of those was in my room!' Nona pointed.

'Pipes, child. They're hollow – mineral oil runs through them. Very hot.' Sister Apple nodded at the arch. 'Let's get the prison filth off you.'

Nona started uncertainly towards the pool, wondering how deep it was, and how hot. The streams around the village never reached much past your knees and quickly stole the feeling from everything below that point.

'You're not going in wearing clothes.' Sister Apple's voice held a mixture of amusement and exasperation.

Nona turned to stare defiantly up at the nun, her lips pressed together in a puckered scowl. Sister Apple stood with her arms folded. One silent second followed the next and at last Nona started to tug off her Caltess smock, stiff with Raymel Tacsis's dried blood. She made a slow and awkward job of it: in the village even the littlest of the littles rarely ran around naked; the ice stood too close for that. Only around the harvest fires or in the all-too-brief kiss of the focus moon had Nona ever been as warm as there in the convent bathhouse.

'Hurry along. I doubt you're hiding anything unusual under

there,' Sister Apple said, pulling back her headdress as the heat got to her too. She had long hair, red and curling in the wet air.

Nona stepped out of her smock, arms folded about herself, with only the steam for modesty. She made a dart for the pool.

'Wait!' Sister Apple raised a hand. 'You can't go in filthy. You'll turn the water black.' She took a leather bucket from one of the many pegs lining the walls above the benches. 'Stand over there.' She pointed to an alcove between the benches on the left.

Nona did as directed, her whole body clenched. The alcove was wide enough for two or three people. The floor, tiled and perforated by finger-width holes, felt strange beneath her feet.

'What—' An explosion of hot water stole the rest of the question. Nona wiped her eyes clear in time to see the misty outline of the nun at the poolside having refilled the bucket.

'There's a brush on the floor. Use it.' Another wave of hot water broke across Nona's chest.

Nona reached, dripping, for the brush. She'd never felt anything quite as wonderful as a bucketful of hot water. Not even fresh bread and butter came close. Not even eggs, or the bacon she had smelled cooking at the Caltess. If scrubbing herself with a bristly brush was the price she had to pay to get into a whole pool of it, she would scrub.

Two buckets later Sister Apple declared her clean enough for the pool. Nona ran to the edge and lowered herself in, toes questing for the bottom. 'How deep is it?' The rising steam blinded her, the heat delicious.

'This end is shallow. On you … to your shoulders?'

The water reached her neck before Nona's feet found a smooth floor and she released her death-grip on the side. She stood, arms floating at her sides, sure that she had never been truly warm before.

Time skipped a beat. It skipped an untold number of beats. Nona hung in the blind heat of the pool. A sharp clap brought her attention back to the world.

'Out you get. You're clean … well, cleaner.' Sister Apple

stood at the water's edge. In concession to the heat she had hung the outer cloak of her habit up on the pegs. She clapped again. 'Out! We've both got things to do.' She pointed to the corner of the pool. 'There are steps there.'

Nona went to the steps, too limp to want to struggle back over the edge. At the top she found the nun holding out a large rectangle of thick cloth towards her. It didn't seem to have any armholes or ties. 'How do I…'

Sister Apple snorted. 'It's a towel.' She thrust the thing into Nona's hands. 'Dry yourself with it.'

Nona wrapped herself in the towel, finding it thick and luxurious. If it had arms she would have worn it.

'Dry your hair too.'

When Nona finished rubbing at her hair she was alarmed to see Sister Apple had sprung a second head, this one young and impish with short black hair, chin resting on the sister's shoulder, cheek next to hers.

'What is it?' the new head asked.

'It's a Nona,' Sister Apple replied.

'A what?'

'A ring-fighter from the Caltess.'

The new head frowned. Two slim hands slid into view holding the tops of Sister Apple's arms. 'It looks rather small and skinny for that. Someone should feed it. It looks more like a farm-girl.' The second nun slipped away from Sister Apple. 'Are you a farm-girl, Nona?'

Nona clutched her towel to her and found she was biting her lip too hard to explain that her mother wove baskets. She shook her head.

'I don't much care for farm-girls,' the new nun sniffed, her smile removing any sting.

'This is Sister Kettle,' Sister Apple explained, shooing the other woman away. 'And,' raising her voice as Sister Kettle vanished into the steams, 'she loves country girls.' She returned to the benched area. 'Come on. Get dressed.'

Nona followed her and reached for the habit. Sister Apple brushed her hand away with a tut. 'Smallclothes first.' She held out a confusing piece of white linen. Nona took it, frowning. Sister Apple watched her a moment then shook her head. 'Farm-girls…'

It took a couple of minutes and significant amounts of advice before Nona finally stepped out of the bathhouse in the full attire of a novice of the Sweet Mercy Convent of the Ancestor. The wind was shockingly cold on her face but the rest of her seemed surprisingly well protected. She stood in her double-sleeved robe, tied at the middle with a woollen belt, two underskirts rustling beneath, her feet feeling most strange in leather shoes drawn tight around them with laces. The only difference between her habit and Sister Apple's appeared to be the lack of a headdress, the nun having restored the garments she'd shed inside.

'The novices will be at breakfast in the refectory.' Sister Apple turned her head sharply and waved to someone across the wide yard. 'Suleri!'

The figure stopped, turned, and hurried towards them, a tall girl with long dark hair. 'Yes, sister?'

'This is Nona: she's to join Red Class for lessons. Take her to their meal table.' Sister Apple seemed suddenly more stern, someone to be reckoned with.

'Yes, sister!' The older girl, perhaps fifteen, glanced down at Nona, 'Come on.' And she walked away at a brisk pace, forcing Nona to run to keep up.

They crossed a courtyard and turned a corner into a passageway, the bake-house on one side, the kitchens on the other. Suleri stopped and rounded on Nona, blocking her path.

'You're not her!' She seemed both furious and unconvinced. 'The Chosen One wouldn't be a skinny little hunska.'

5

When hunger has been your lifelong companion the smell of food is a physical thing, an assault, a seduction, a deep-sunk hook that will reel you in. Nona forgot about Suleri's anger. The convent's wonders slipped from her mind. The flood of warmth on passing through the tall oak doors, the rapid, high-pitch babble of many voices that became almost a roar … none of it mattered. The aroma of fresh bread held her, the captivating scent of bacon sizzling, buttery eggs, scrambled and sprinkled with black pepper.

'This way!' Suleri's voice carried the edge added when someone has had to repeat themselves.

She led Nona through a crowd of older novices chatting animatedly by the entrance. Nona's head barely rose above belt-height on many of them.

Four long tables ran across the width of the hall, each surrounded by high-backed chairs and with large bowls set along the centre. A dozen or more girls sat around each table save the nearest one where only a couple of novices had yet taken their place, both looking like grown women to Nona.

'Is that her?' A voice from behind.

The conversation around the doorway died to nothing and, glancing back, Nona found the novices staring down at her.

'Red Class at the back, Grey Class next, Mystic...' Suleri slapped the table immediately before them. 'And Holy!' She waved Nona away. 'Go!'

Nona advanced into the room under the scrutiny of the girls by the doors, arms straight at her sides, hands in fists. Despite the crowd she had never felt more alone. She bit her bottom lip hard enough to taste blood. Easing her jaw, she pressed her lips together in a thin, defiant line.

The conversation failed at each table as she passed; by the time she reached the fourth the girls there were turning their chairs to watch.

Nona stopped at the last table. The girls there ranged across a few years in age, though none looked quite as small or young as her. The hunger that had wrapped her stomach in its iron fist slipped away under the stares of half a hundred novices. She looked for a chair but all of them were occupied.

'She's not the one.' Suleri's voice cut across the room. 'She's the dirty peasant we saw earlier. Look at her!' Ignoring her own command, the novice turned her attention to the plate before her, heaping it with bacon and bread.

Nona's treacherous stomach chose that moment to rumble more loudly than she had thought possible. The laughter that followed made her cheeks blaze and she stood, furious, staring at the floor, willing it to crack and burn. Instead, it was the laughter that cracked and fell into silence.

Tall men in the furs of the red bear, and armoured beneath in bronze scales, came through the doors, novices scattering from their path. The warriors carried themselves imperiously, as though they might just walk over any too slow to get out of their way. Each wore a helm coiffed with chainmail and visored to mimic the sternest of faces without hint of mercy.

Tacsis men! Come with their own rope to set right the mistake at Harriton, or perhaps to administer crueller justice of their own. Nona snatched the knife from the nearest girl's plate and holding it before her, level with her eyes, she started to back towards the service door in the rear wall.

The men ignored her. They stepped to either side, clearing the main entrance, and raised their visors to reveal faces that admitted no more compassion than had been engraved upon the metal. The abbess came through the open doors behind them, one hand gripping her crozier, its golden curl rising above her head, the other resting on the shoulder of a blonde girl perhaps a year older than Nona.

'Novices, this is Arabella Jotsis. She will be joining our order.'

'As was foretold!' Sister Wheel stepped out from behind the abbess, Sister Tallow to the other side. 'As was foretold!' She cast about rapidly, her watery stare challenging anyone to disagree.

Abbess Glass frowned. 'We can be sure she is Arabella and that she is Jotsis. Anything else is open to interpretation.' She struck the heel of her staff to the floor, the sharp retort cutting off the novices' mutterings. 'We can also be sure that Arabella will study hard and be treated no differently from any other novice.'

Sister Wheel seemed on the point of saying something but at a glance from the abbess closed her mouth with a snap.

'Additionally, we may be certain that Novice Nona understands that it is impolite to point a knife at guests,' the abbess added, tilting her head in Nona's direction.

Nona set the blade back on the table with a guilty hand as laughter rose about her.

'Gentlemen.' Abbess Glass looked left then right. 'Your duty is dispatched. Arabella is now the charge of the convent and her care rests in my hands.'

The four men inclined their heads and turned, marching out of the building without a word to either the abbess or the girl they had delivered.

Arabella herself didn't appear to notice their departure. She looked, to Nona, like a different kind of creature, set apart from the dull and dirty humans who scurried about the world. Her hair seemed to glow golden in the light that reached through the still-open doors. Her travelling clothes were a wonder of brushed suede and fur-edged leather, with a magnificent dark red cape across her shoulders secured by a gold chain. Where others might be described by their collection of flaws Arabella Jotsis's only identifying feature seemed to be that she was without blemish. Perhaps the Ancestor looked like this, but people didn't.

'Your table is at the end, Arabella. I'm sure Red Class will welcome you into their ranks. Nona too.' The abbess nodded towards the end of the room and took her guiding hand from the girl's shoulder.

'Best behaviour!' Sister Tallow added, running a hard stare across the room. And with that, Abbess Glass led the nuns from the refectory.

Arabella Jotsis surveyed her new classmates with a sort of serene confidence and stepped forward as if not only had she lived here all her life, but also as if she owned the place and paid the wages of everyone around her. As she drew near the table an older girl from table three hurried up behind her with a spare chair.

The girl whose knife Nona had snatched stood up the moment the doors closed behind the departing nuns. Tall, slim and pale, her hair a black and wild tangle of curls, she seemed less impressed with the golden newcomer than the rest of the novices. 'You'll find that the Ancestor doesn't order any special treatment for royalty here, Arabella. Minor or otherwise. Your father's title might let him crush honest men down in Verity, but up here fights are one on one and it's skill that counts, not rank.'

Arabella hardly deigned to glance at the girl. 'Your father put himself in prison, Clera Ghomal. He made a poor merchant.' She sat, like a princess, in the offered chair. 'And a worse thief.' Her accent was new to Nona, rich and precise, words clipped, the emphasis on odd syllables.

Clera balled her hands into fists. 'Be careful what you say—'

'Oh please. You come from a family of money-grubbers who have lost their money … which makes them just … grubbers. Let it lie. From what I understand we will all have plenty of opportunity for hitting each other later. So do be quiet and let me eat.' Arabella took a roll of crusty bread and broke it onto her plate.

'Thank you for making it so clear.' Clera sneered. 'How terrible for you to have to endure the company of people who don't own their bodyweight in jewellery. How can you stand to mix with us?' She reached out and took Nona's hand. 'I suppose you hate Nona here most of all. Imagine, a peasant girl dining at the same table as a daughter of the Jotsis!'

Arabella spread butter onto the halves of her roll. 'I'm not in the least interested in you or your skinny hunska peasant, Ghomal. Now do sit down, you both look ridiculous.'

Clera dropped Nona's hand and took a step towards Arabella. 'I—'

'Clera!' Suleri's voice cut across her from the far end of the room. 'Sit down. Shut up. Save it for Sister Tallow's class or you'll find yourself working in the laundry for a month.'

Clera sat down, mouth set in a vicious line. A heartbeat later she grinned, leaned back and pulled across a chair just vacated by a novice leaving the next table. 'Nona. Take a seat. You look hungry.'

6

On his wagon Giljohn had fed Nona far better than her mother had ever been able to. At the Caltess the food had been better still and Nona's bones had begun to sink from sight like a city child's. The refectory at Sweet Mercy Convent put the Caltess meals to shame. Nona ate meat in whole pieces for the first time she could remember, not just a shred here or there but thick slices of bacon still hot from the pan. She wrapped them in crusty bread and chewed with dedication, scattering crumbs everywhere, while Clera chatted easily at her side.

The merchant's daughter made no further mention of Arabella, not even glancing down the table in her direction. Instead she rattled on cheerfully about what could be expected from the day, requiring little from Nona in return save the occasional grunt or 'yes' in the brief gaps when her mouth wasn't full.

'Ghena's the youngest in the class, she's still nine. Me and Ruli are eleven. We'll probably move into Grey soon – that's Class Two. Class One is Red. Sister Oak is our mistress but we don't see a lot of her.' Clera paused to watch Nona eat. 'You really *were* hungry!'

'Mgmmmm.'

'Our first class is Academia with Sister Rule – that's everything from numbers and reading to history and geometry. Right now we're doing geography.'

A full mouth saved Nona from having to admit that she didn't know what geometry or geography were.

'We have Blade this afternoon – we're doing unarmed, but later we learn knives and stars, the older ones learn swords, and tactics and strategy too. In Red Class everyone studies everything. Later on the Holy Sisters do more Academia and Spirit classes. Martial Sisters do mostly Blade. Sisters of Discretion concentrate on Shade. Mystic Sisters spend their time learning Path. Everyone calls the Martial Sisters the Red Sisters, and the Mystic Sisters are Holy Witches – but don't let a nun hear you call them witches!'

Nona kept eating, letting the confusion of names wash over her. It would sink in given time. She finished the bacon, struggled through the scrambled egg, but the bread bowl defeated her, sitting before her with three crusty rolls still nestled at the bottom. She had never stopped eating while food remained before her: to do so seemed desperately wrong.

'Come on!' Clera put a hand on her shoulder. 'We'll be really late.'

Looking up, Nona saw that they were the last two at the table. She glanced behind her and saw that only three other novices remained in the hall.

Clera hurried towards the main doors. 'Come on!'

Nona followed, hands folded over her aching belly, so full it hurt to walk, let alone run. Clera led the way back past the dormitory building and across a quadrangle, cloisters to one side, a rectangular pool and fountain in the middle. Above the range forming the western end the sails of a windmill could just be seen passing through the top of their cycle. Clera hurried Nona out through a corridor penetrating the north range.

'That's the Academia.' She pointed ahead to an ornate tower close to the cliffs on the plateau's north side. Together they half walked, half ran to the archway at its base. A rapid ascent by the stone steps of a spiral staircase brought them to an oak door, the steps continuing up. Clera stopped at the door and pushed on through to the room beyond.

'There's no one here.' Nona felt stupid the moment the

words left her, a peasant girl stating the obvious. The classroom lay in shadow. A large, elderly cat watched from its grey curl in the far corner: Malkin, the abbess's beast. Four rows of empty desks faced a polished table in front of a chalk-marked board. A confusion of maps and charts decorated the wall behind that, so many that pieced together they might show the whole world.

'Damnation!' Clera ran to one of the windows and threw open the shutters. Diamonds of glass, leaded together into a continuous sheet, ensured that only the light came in while the cold stayed out. She pressed her face to the panes, turning one way then the other. 'She's taken them out somewhere – can't see them…'

Nona advanced towards the desk. It held all manner of fascinating objects, not least three leather-bound books and a large ledger beside a quill and inkpot. The objects that drew her though were a dog's skull, a clear crystal nearly a foot long and too wide to close her hand about, and a glistening white ball in a brass stand. This last held her attention until she found herself beside it, knees bumping against the desk.

'What is it?' Nona set a finger to the enamelled whiteness of the ball, finding it rough beneath her touch, tiny ridges catching the light. It was a little larger than her head and perfectly round. A stand held it top and bottom so that it could rotate. And around its middle, like a belt, a very thin strand of colour no thicker than a piece of string.

'Don't touch! Mistress Academia would have a fit!' Clera elbowed Nona out of the way and immediately ignored her own instruction by setting the thing spinning on its pivots. 'It's the world, silly.'

'The world?' That made no sense at all.

'Abeth.' Clera huffed her breath out as if Nona's stupidity had hit her in the stomach. 'A model of it.'

Nona blinked. Her world had been the village, the forests, the fields, and in the distance the northern ice forming one wall of the Corridor. She hadn't ever considered that it might have a shape and if she had she would not have guessed at a ball, white or otherwise.

'It's a globe.' Clera reached out to stop it spinning. 'We live … here.' She put her finger on the line around the middle.

'We do?' Nona leaned in to look more closely.

'Want to see something special?' Clera grinned. Without waiting for an answer she set one hand to the top of the globe and the other to the bottom then, with a little effort, rotated each in opposite directions. Smoothly and without noise the lower part of the white surface began to retreat. Nona saw that it was not one piece as she had imagined but comprised many bladed parts that shuffled beneath each other like the feathers of a folding wing. In consequence the cord-thin strip of colour girdling the globe widened, first to a finger's width, then wider and wider still until Nona's whole hand couldn't cover it. The pattern of jewel-enamelled blues and greens and browns fascinated her eye.

'What—'

'That's the world fifty thousand years ago, long before the tribes even came.' Clera rotated the halves back slowly and the ice advanced. 'All the people that lived across all these lands, pushed back.' She returned the ice sheets to their original position. 'Pushed into this tiny corridor as the sun got old and weak.'

'How could they fit?' Nona imagined them running before the ice.

Clera shrugged. 'Mistress Blade says people need room. You can squash them in only so far, then the bleeding starts, and when it's done … there's just about enough room again.'

'It's good to see that some of your lessons stick, Novice Clera.'

Both girls turned to see the doorway behind them now almost entirely full of Sister Rule, the convent's Mistress Academia, a woman of considerable height and still more considerable girth, all wrapped in the dark grey of a nun's habit. Sister Rule pushed on into the classroom, the rest of Red Class filing in behind her, diverging towards their allotted desks. Arabella already had three girls pressed around her and they took seats beside each other, all of them smirking behind their hands.

'Explain yourselves, novices.' The nun fixed them with dark and beady eyes.

'We were...' Clera searched for an explanation ... and could find nothing better than the truth, which she settled on with a sigh of defeat. 'Nona was *very* hungry!'

A scatter of laughter went up at that, cut off sharply as Sister Rule's yardstick cracked across a desktop. She reached the table, looming over both girls. 'Well, Nona does appear to need some feeding up. Do not be late to my class again, Nona. Today you missed a quick observation of the layered structure of this plateau where the Glasswater sinkhole exposes it. Next time you could miss considerably more than that – dinner included.'

Clera slipped away to her desk near the door. Nona stayed by the table. She looked up at Sister Rule's face, which was at once both fleshy and severe, then let her eyes slip to the globe again.

'You can take either of those two desks at the back, Nona.' Mistress Academia laid her yardstick against her table and let out a sigh. 'I do hope you're not going to slow us down too much, child. The abbess casts her nets very wide sometimes...'

Nona dropped her gaze to the floor and took a step in the direction the nun had waved at. A mixture of anger and defiance boiled behind her eyes but stronger than that, more than that, was the desire to know. Besides, she was too full to be properly angry.

'I ... don't know what geography is.'

Sister Rule's yardstick killed the laughter before it started. 'Good. You're clever enough to ask questions. That's better than many I've had through these doors.' She took her seat behind the desk, straightened her habit, then looked up. 'Geography is like history. History is the story of mankind since we first started to record it. The story and the understanding of that story. Geography is the history of the world beneath our feet. The mountains and the ice, rivers, oceans, land, all of it recorded in the very rocks themselves for those with the wit to read what's set there. Consider this slab of rock our convent rests upon, for example. The history of this plateau is written in the limestone layers that can be seen in the sinkhole two hundred yards west of this tower.' She sent Nona on towards her desk with a gentle poke of her stick. 'Our history is wide and we are narrow, so perhaps its lessons no longer fit. Cut your cloth to your measure, some say. But the history of the land has lessons more important than those of kings and dynasties. The history of the ice is written there. The tale of our dying sun, etched into rock and glacier. These are the lessons we all live by. And when the moon fails we will die by them too.'

7

Nona resolved to make it to Blade on time. Over lunch in the refectory Clera explained the meaning of the various bells that sounded throughout the day.

'There are three bells. That's the iron bell, Ferra, which just rang. It's got a hollow sound and dies off quickly. That's for the sisters, to tell them about prayers mainly. It hangs in the little belfry up on the Dome of the Ancestor. The one that looks like a nipple.'

'Clera!' Jula scolded. She had taken the chair on Nona's other side and now turned to join the conversation. 'Bray is the brass bell that hangs in the Academia, at the top of the tower. It sounds the hours, and that's what you have to listen to for class and meals.'

'And lights out and getting up.' Clera cut back in. 'Bray has a deep voice that hangs.' She made her own deep and sonorous, a singer's voice, Nona thought. 'Afternoon class is sixth bell, lunch is fifth, dinner is seventh.'

'Blade this afternoon.' Jula rolled her eyes. 'I hate Blade.'

'Holies always do.' Clera smirked.

Nona considered Jula for a moment. The girl had a studious look about her, slender despite more than a year eating at the convent table. She had mousey hair, cut at neck length. Nothing about her suggested that hunska or gerant blood might show in years to come. Almost nobody showed up quantal or marjal, however good the signs, so Jula would almost certainly be a Holy Sister. Nona knew very little about the Church of the Ancestor but the idea of a life spent in prayer and contemplation held no appeal at all. If the life in question didn't also include being well fed and having a warm safe place to live then Nona might have felt sorry for the girl.

'After Blade you'll think you've met the hardest mistress,' Clera said. 'But Mistress Shade makes her seem gentle. Everyone calls her the Poisoner or Mistress Poison because she always has us grinding up stuff for one poison or another. She's supposed to teach us stealth, disguise, and climbing and traps … but it's always poison. Anyway, don't *ever* call her Mistress Poison.' Clera shuddered.

Jula nodded, looking grim. She picked up her fork and got it halfway to her mouth before remembering the bells. 'Bitel is the third bell. The steel bell.' She returned the fork to her plate, perhaps still thinking of poisons. 'That's almost always bad news, and you won't confuse it for the others – it's sharp and very loud. The abbess will ring Bitel if there's a fire, or an intruder, or something like that. Hope you never hear it. But if you do and if nobody tells you different, go to the abbess's front door and wait.'

'I heard…' The girl across the table spoke up, loud enough for everyone to hear. 'I heard the abbess herself brought you up from Verity.' The rest of the class had been focused on Arabella who had been telling them some story about the emperor's court. Nona had only caught the odd word and had imagined it a fairy tale of the sort told about princesses around the hearth in her village … but then she had remembered Clera calling Arabella royalty and it struck her that the fairy story might actually be true.

'I heard Abbess Glass brought you up the Seren Way in the middle of the night.' The speaker was the one Clera had called Ghena and had said was the youngest in the class, a girl with a tightly curled cap of short, black hair. In the village Grey Stephen had a staff that had been his father's and *his* father's: where so many hands had polished the dark wood for so long it was the colour of Ghena's skin. 'I heard you're a peasant. Where are you from? How did your people even pay the confirmation fee?'

'I—' Nona found she had the whole table's attention. Even Arabella broke off her tale to stare.

'You hear too much, Ghena.' Clera cupped both hands behind her ears and laughed. 'You were at the window all night looking to see "the Chosen One" arrive.' She tilted her head just a fraction in Arabella's direction. 'Did you see the abbess going by with dust on her skirts and know she'd come up by Seren Way?'

Ghena scowled and looked away.

After lunch, and before Bray spoke for the sixth time that day to let them know they must hurry to class, there was time to wander or to sit. Arabella left the refectory with most of the class at her heels.

'They'll take her to the novice cloisters,' Clera said.

'It's where most of us spend time after lunch,' Jula explained. 'It's not like the nuns' cloisters – it's full of chat – too loud to think.' She looked disapproving where Clera looked wistful.

'We'll take you to the sinkhole,' Clera said. 'You missed it today—'

'I'm not swimming!' Ruli interrupted, the last of those who'd stayed.

'Me neither.' Jula crossed her arms and pretended to shiver.

'We'll just sit and throw stones,' Clera declared. 'And my new friend Nona can tell us why her parents gave her up.'

The Glasswater sinkhole awed Nona. It looked as if some giant had poked a finger into the plateau when it was soft and new, leaving a perfectly round depression whose vertical stone walls dropped forty feet to the surface of dark and unrippled waters. She wondered what lay beneath the surface – hiding in unknowable depths.

The pool was about forty foot across. On the far side an iron ladder, bolted to the stone, led down into it. Nona could see the layers that Sister Rule had mentioned, showing in the sinkhole's walls, as if the whole plateau were made of one thin slice laid atop the next.

The four novices sat on the edge, legs dangling out over the drop. Nona's shoes were the finest pair she had ever owned, the only ones made of leather. She was terrified she'd lose them and clenched her toes inside, even though they were laced on tight. For a while none of them spoke. Clera played a copper penny across the backs of her fingers with practised ease. Nona enjoyed the silence. She didn't want to tell her story, not yet … not ever. She didn't want to lie either.

'Everyone tells,' Clera said, as if reading her mind.

'Mother died trying to give me a little brother,' Jula spoke into the awkward gap. 'Father got very sad after that. He's a scribe, not a practical man, he said. He thought the nuns would look after me better than he could.'

'My dad ships convent wine across the Sea of Marn but he wasn't paying the duty.' Ruli grinned. 'My uncles are all smugglers too. The ones they haven't hanged. The abbess came to the trial and said she'd take me in. Dad had to agree, and it saved his neck.'

They both looked at Nona, waiting.

Clera raised her eyebrows, inviting Nona to speak. When they could rise no further, she herself spoke. 'On the first day you tell why your parents didn't want you any more. It's supposed to stop it hurting. Sharing does that. Later you hear everyone else's stories and you know you're not the only one. If you'd ever been to prison you'd know that's the first thing people do there – they tell what they did.'

Nona didn't like to say that she *had* been to prison and that she hadn't needed to tell because the guards had shouted it out as they led her to her cell. *Murderer.* It was on her lips to ask what a merchant's daughter knew about such places – but as she opened her mouth to speak she remembered the cruel things Arabella had said about Clera's father. *He put himself in prison.* And instead she began to answer the question that she had been trying to avoid. Nona's story should have begun, 'A juggler once came to my village. He was my first friend.' She didn't start there though. She started with a question of her own.

'Did you ever have a dream that they were coming for you, in the night?' she said, staring at her feet and the black water far below them.

'Who?' asked Clera.

'Yes.' Ruli lifted her head, shedding long pale hair to either side to reveal her long pale face.

'They?' Jula frowned.

'*They*. Them. Bad people who want to hurt you,' Nona said, and she told the girls a story. And though at first her words stumbled and she spoke as a peasant girl from the wild Grey lands of the west, out where the emperor's name is rarely spoken and his enemies are closer than his palaces, she found her tongue and painted in the girls' minds a picture that took hold of them all and wrapped them in a life they had never tasted or imagined.

'I dreamed I was asleep in my mother's house in the village where I had always lived. We weren't like them, Mother and me. The villages along the Blue River are like clans, each one a family, one blood, the same looks, held by the same thinking. My father brought us there, me in my mother's belly, but he left and we didn't.

'I dreamed of the focus moon, burning its way down the Corridor, and the boys and girls rising from their beds to play in the heat of it. The children joined hands around my mother's hut, singing that old song:

She's falling down, she's falling down,
The moon, the moon,
She's falling down, she's falling down,
Soon, soon,
The ice will come, the ice will close,
No moon, no moon,
We'll all fall down, we'll all fall down,
Soon, too soon.

'In the focus the boys and girls look so red they could be covered in blood. They're coming. The bad ones. I know they're coming. I see their path in my mind, a line that runs through everything, zig-zagging, curving left, right, coiling, trying to throw them off, but they're following it – and it leads to me.

'Outside the hut the children fall down. All at once. Without a scream.

'I wake. All at once. Without a scream. It's dark, the focus has passed and the fields lie restless beneath the wind. I sit up and the darkness moves around me like black water, deep enough to drown. For the longest time I sit there, shivering, my blanket wrapped tight around me, eyes on the door that I can't see. I'm waiting for it to open.'

Dogs barking. A distant scream. Then a crash close at hand. The door-bar breaks at the first kick and a warrior fills the doorway, a lantern in one hand, sword in the other. He's tall as any man in the village and muscle cords the length of him.

'Take her!' He steps in and others follow. The lantern finds dull glints among the iron plates on his leather shirt. He moves towards the workshop door, the other room where Mother sleeps on the reeds piled for her weaving.

Strong hands seize me, iron-hard and pinching. The men have braided beards. A woman slips a loop of rope around my wrists and draws it tight. Her face is marked with vertical bars of paint. Wooden charms hang in her tangle of dreadlocks. A Pelarthi. Raiders from the ice-margins.

Mother breaks from the workshop as the first raider reaches it. She's very fast. Her reed-knife makes a bright sound as the blade skitters across the iron plates over his stomach. He swings his heavy sword but she's not there. Her hand is at the neck of the woman holding me – the knife buried in the woman's throat. My mother hauls me towards the main door. We nearly get there, but the man in leather and iron turns and swings again. The point of his sword finds the back of her neck. She falls. I fall beneath her. And the night goes dark again, and quiet.

'The raiders sold you?' Jula asked, horrified.

Nona had fallen silent, staring down at the water far below. 'No. My village did.' Nona looked up and saw the three girls staring at her as if she was something altogether new to them. 'The raiders took me, but they didn't get far. When dawn broke they camped in the Rellam Forest. The village hunters don't go there. They say there are spirits in those woods, and not kind ones.

'The Pelarthi broke into small groups. There weren't more than twenty to start with. Five stayed with me: four men and the sister of the woman my mother stabbed. I found I had blood on me.' Nona looked at her hands, turning them over as if the story might be written there. 'While the Pelarthi were settling to sleep the forest fell silent. They didn't seem to notice but I felt it watching us, the whole place – the trees, the ground, the darkness – all of it watching. A warrior came out from the shadow where the trees grew thick. He had bramble in his beard and a shock of wild hair. He didn't speak, just raised his sword and came on barefoot. None of the Pelarthi even looked up – just me, lying on my side with my hands tied behind my back. I thought he might be one of them, only he looked too … wild, as though he hadn't ever lived anywhere but right there in the Rellam. And his sword was polished wood, black, or very deep brown.

'First the wildman slew the warrior who had killed Mother. He just swung his sword overhead and brought it down on the Pelarthi's neck. The man's head came right off. The others jumped up then and they weren't slow, but he moved among them as though it were a dance – didn't say a word, didn't make a sound … none of them met his blade with theirs … and every time he changed direction there was a wound behind him spraying blood, and someone falling.

'The woman fell over me, stumbling away from a swing of the wildman's sword. By the time I'd struggled out from underneath her it was all over. The Pelarthi lay dead and the man had gone. Just me and the corpses and the forest moving all around us.

'A party of hunters that had tracked the raiders out from the village found me an hour after sunrise, covered in blood and with bodies all around me … in the haunted wood. They brought me back but the old women were already washing

Mother for the pyre and Mari Streams had run off to White Lake to get Preacher Mickel to stop them. Preacher Mickel says when the Hope arrives then all the dead will step from their graves and be made whole … so they must be buried and not given to the fire, because even the Hope can't make live men and women from smoke and ash.

'It didn't take long for the whispering to start. *…came out of the Rellam covered in blood – not a scratch on her… …who killed the Pelarthi?… …bodies… …blood… …spirits…*

'I don't know who said *witch* first, but the first to hiss it at me was the smith's wife, Matha. She'd hated me since her little Billem tried to beat me with a stick and I hurt him back. It didn't take long before they were all saying it, as if the Pelarthi hadn't even come, as if the bodies in the forest hadn't belonged to men who killed my mother and dragged me off. I think they were angry that of all those stolen by the Pelarthi I was the only one they got back. The one they hadn't wanted in the first place.

'The smith and Grettle Eavis wanted to tie me in a bag and drown me in the Blue River. They said that's the way to kill a witch so she doesn't come back – wrap her in iron chain, put her in a bag and drown her. Grey Stephen said no – he's the one who gets to say how things will be in the village on account of he fought the Pelarthi way back when there was an empress, and he killed some too. Grey Stephen said no and that the tinker had seen a child-taker on the road and if the village wouldn't have me the "taker would".

'I—' The voice of a bell spoke over her, deep and throbbing in the sinkhole's void. 'Bray! That's for the lesson!' Nona leapt to her feet, unconcerned that she stood on the very brink of a high fall.

The other girls were slower to get up, pushing themselves back from the sinkhole's lip.

'That's horrible,' Jula said, brushing the grit from the seat of her habit.

'It's incredible!' Ruli said. 'Weren't you terrified when—'

'Is it true?' Clera frowned, weighing Nona with a speculative gaze.

'We have to get to Blade.' Nona was already hurrying towards the Academia tower. 'I can't be late twice!' She hesitated and looked back. 'Where's the lesson?'

Clera laughed at that. 'Come on. She's right – Sister Tallow will have us running up and down the Seren Way, you know what she's like!'

A moment later the three novices were walking briskly towards a building at the far edge of the plateau, with Nona jogging to catch up.

'That's the Blade Hall.' Clera pointed to a tall building with high arched windows. Walls of huge limestone blocks supported a peaked roof with stone gargoyles roaring beneath the eaves. To the south a row of carved buttresses reinforced the wall that faced out over the plateau's edge. 'And that's the Heart Hall.' Clera nodded to the building on their left as they passed its many-pillared portico.

'The Persus Hall.' Jula finished tying her hair back with a black cord. 'After Emperor Persus, third of his name, whose line ended when the current—'

'Everyone calls it the Heart Hall because it was built for the shipheart.' Clera led up the steps of Blade Hall, almost running but not quite.

'What's the ship—'

But Clera had already pushed open the heavy door and slipped inside. Ruli followed.

'I still don't understand who paid your confirmation fee.' Jula came up behind Nona.

Nona didn't understand either. She worried that perhaps it had been overlooked and this evening or maybe tomorrow a sister would come with ledger and quill and a demand for ten gold sovereigns. Talking about it with the others seemed like tempting fate.

'Nona!' Sister Tallow called her name the moment Nona stuck her head around the door. 'Come here beside me.'

Nona, saved from answering Jula, hurried across. The old woman shot her a narrow look then returned her gaze to the rest of Red Class, the last few of them lining up in a second rank. Arabella, now in a habit, stood at Mistress Blade's other side, golden and perfect, her hair looking as if a trio of handmaids had spent an hour combing and pinning it.

The hall extended about half the length of the building, ending in galleried seating around a short tunnel that led to the remaining chambers. The ceiling vaulted above them high enough for an oak tree to grow to maturity at the centre. Apart from a collection of a dozen or so man-height leather-wrapped wooden posts on stands in a far corner the hall lay echoingly empty, the floor an inch of sand over flagstones.

'I need partners for these two.' Sister Tallow had enough steel in her voice that even simple observations became life or death ultimatums. She cast a dark eye across the girls lined before her. 'Novice Ghena, you will be with Nona. Novice Jula, with Arabella.'

Ghena fixed her gaze on Nona and allowed herself a thin smile. Jula looked surprised.

'Time to change.' Sister Tallow clapped her hands. 'Anyone dawdling gets their head shaved.' She directed her attention to Ghena who, now that Nona considered it, looked as if she might have suffered just such a fate only a few weeks ago. 'Make sure the new girls get habits that fit.' Another clap of the hands. 'Go!' And the dozen novices were off, running towards the tunnel beneath the tiered seating, sand spraying out beneath their heels.

Ghena moved swiftly and Nona had to sprint to catch up. The gloom of the tunnel stole Nona's sight after the brightness of the hall. As she slowed to let her eyes adjust Ghena pulled away while others came pounding up behind. At the end of the passage most of the girls bundled to the left, but Jula led Arabella to the right, and Nona followed.

Ghena was waiting for them in a long and narrow storeroom. She pulled back the shutters and light from the window at the far end revealed both walls lined with shelves. Further back all manner of goods were stacked: earthenware jars, rolled mats, heavy leather balls, staves, sticks, canes, even the hilts of what might be daggers or swords. Closer at hand shelves boasted piles of neatly folded tunics and shoes of thick black cloth.

'The smallest are by the door. Make sure you get one that fits well,' Jula said. 'Too tight and if someone wants to get a hold they'll have to grab a handful of you as well. Too loose and you'll be tripping up or have it pulled off.'

Nona and Arabella pulled out fighting tunics, each top paired with ankle-length trousers, holding them against themselves under the critical eye of their partner.

'Too small, even for you,' Ghena barked. Jula had already led Arabella off to the changing room, the new girl seemingly more anxious to keep her golden curls than worry overmuch about the fit of her tunic.

'It looks about right…' Nona hadn't ever chosen clothes before, but it *did* look about right.

'When someone grabs you.' Ghena lunged forward and seized a fistful of the tunic. 'Do you want them to have a handful of this or a handful of your skin?'

'I don't want them to grab me,' Nona said. 'A loose tunic makes it easier.'

Ghena snarled and ripped the tunic top from Nona's hands. 'You're partnered with me, farm-girl. Every mistake you make makes me look bad. Mistress Blade will test you and if you fail *I* get punished. And if that happens I'll take it out on you.'

Nona snatched the top back. 'Winning is never a mistake.' She met Ghena's dark and furious eyes, feeling her own snarl begin to twist her face, remembering how she had screamed out her fury as she ran towards Raymel Tacsis. A second later the heat blew from her, as if a cold wind had rattled through the room. She saw the hangman's sheet again, Saida just a shape beneath it. Anger hadn't saved her. Winning hadn't saved her. Nona took the tunic two places along from the one she'd tried last and held it up against her. 'Good enough?'

'Good enough.'

They reached the changing room to find the first novice already leaving. 'You two will make a lovely couple with your shiny heads.' Ketti ran her hands over her brow as she passed them, grinning, her own thick cascade of black hair tied back tightly with a white cord.

'…pigs and cows.' Arabella broke off, aiming a bright smile at the door as Nona and Ghena entered. All the novices laughed, a couple trying to hide it behind their hands.

Nona set her teeth, and finding a space on the long bench began to struggle out of her unfamiliar clothing, throwing it up on the pegs above as the other girls had. The room smelled of old sweat, of bodies packed close – you could smell it out in the main hall, faint but pervasive. It reminded her of the village.

'Hurry up!' Clera offered the advice apologetically as she left, ready in her fighting habit, belt tight about her waist, hair scraped back with not so much as a single curl escaping.

'Come on! Come on!' Jula stood at the door frantically looking down the corridor. 'Arabella!'

Arabella ran for the door and both of them sprinted away. Nona and Ghena were last to leave the changing room.

'Come on!' Ghena started running.

Nona made to give chase but at the doorway she spotted one of the dark linen belts, abandoned on the floor. Without thinking, she scooped it up and took it with her to return to its owner, tucking it down the front of her tunic to keep her hands free. Moments later she was sprinting down the tunnel towards the bright hall beyond. Dazzled by the sunshine as she emerged Nona couldn't see who ran past her in the opposite direction.

'Cutting things fine, novice.' Sister Tallow turned to watch Nona's breathless arrival hard on the heels of Ghena's.

Nona bowed her head and went to join Ghena at the end of the second row. She looked about … one person missing. She opened her mouth to comment but Ghena deployed a swift, sharp elbow to her ribs.

A moment of silence passed. Another. A whole minute where eleven novices watched the sandy floor beneath their feet and tension rose around them.

'And here she comes.' Sister Tallow dropped the words with the same weight the judge had spoken Nona's death sentence.

Arabella came running from the tunnel, clutching her fight

tunic closed across her chest. 'I couldn't find it! It wasn't anywhere!' She pulled up breathless and close to tears.

'An inventive child would have taken a replacement from the stores and claimed it as hers. An attentive child would not have lost her belt within moments of receiving it in the first place.' Sister Tallow returned her gaze to the class. 'At convent the rules apply to king and commoner alike. Once the class is finished Novice Jula will shave Novice Arabella's head and then Arabella will perform the same duty for her.'

Nona realized her mistake. She hesitated, then reached beneath her own tunic to draw out Arabella's belt. 'Sister—'

'Ah!' Mistress Blade proved to have quick eyes. 'I see that Nona has demonstrated an enduring and valuable truth. We may fight here in this hall and think that because our battles are unconstrained by rules that we truly understand what it is to make war.' Sister Tallow strode the length of the first line. 'Do not be deceived. No real fight is bound by four walls. No real fight ends at a particular doorway or when we wash off the sweat and the blood. Fights end with defeat. And death is the only defeat a warrior understands. While we draw breath we are at war with our enemies and they with us.' The nun turned at the end of the line and approached Nona, taking the belt from her hand. 'In future, Nona, save such demonstrations of the secret war for Mistress Shade's class where they will be better appreciated. Though try not to irk her. Our sister of the shadow is far less … kind … than I am.' She tossed the belt to Arabella. 'Laps! Sharlot, lead off.'

The tallest girl in Red Class, a willowy redhead, took off running, the rest falling in behind her.

Nona was used to laps from the Caltess and she fell into an easy rhythm. She could sense Arabella behind her, last in the running order, and doubtless staring daggers at the back of her neck. At each corner Clera glanced back, offering a grin. After the first few circuits of the hall Nona let her mind empty of everything except the pattern of her feet hitting the sandy floor. She let go of the story she had told at the sinkhole, let the worry over her confirmation fee slip away, let Arabella Jotsis and her revenge fade, even thoughts of Raymel Tacsis and *his* revenge becoming lost beneath the placing of one foot before the other. Only the line remained, bright and burning, as it had been in her dream.

'I will repeat myself for the new girls,' Sister Tallow said when she had them in two rows once more, sweating and labouring over their breath. 'It's a message many of you could do with hearing again. Perhaps you'll take more meaning from it after so many lessons in this hall.

'We are not built for war. We are not fast – most every animal can outrun or evade us, be it hound, cat, rat, or sparrow. We are not strong – a mule, a hoola, a bear, all of them are pound for pound three, maybe five times as strong as man. And you are not men.

'What we are is clever and precise. These are our tools. Wit and precision. I am teaching you to fight without weapons for two reasons. First, because there are times when you will be without a weapon. Second, because in training for such conflict you will learn about pain without getting broken, and you will learn about rage without killing.' She held up her hands. 'These are poor weapons. When we fight we fight to win. This—' From nowhere six inches of gleaming steel appeared in her hand. 'This is a better weapon. However, I can punch you with my fist and you will learn a lesson. The knife's lesson is short and terminal.'

Sister Tallow flexed her wrist and the blade vanished into her sleeve. 'The stories tell us that battles are about right and wrong. That winning requires heart and passion. That the Ancestor will reach out to those who believe and lend strength to their arm. The truth is that the Ancestor will gather your essence to the whole when you die. I'm sure you're told more about that in Spirit, but in Blade just know that until you die the Ancestor will only watch.

'Fighting is about control. Control of your fear, your pain, and your anger. Control of your weapon. Control of your opponent. Fighting is about mechanics, levers, breaking points, and speed. Your body is a mechanism. It is time to learn how it works, how far you can push it or allow it to be pushed, not before it hurts, but before it breaks. Unarmed combat requires the application of force to disable the opponent's machine before they disable yours.

'In Blade we value quickness. Sufficient speed makes every other aspect of combat irrelevant. If your opponent is a statue it doesn't matter how strong or skilled they might be – find their throat or an eye and make an end of them. Speed is the way of the sisterhood.

'You will have heard the old stories of Red Sisters, of Sister Cloud and the Western King, or Sister Owl maybe, when she tamed the Black Castle. The wordsmiths in Verity will spin such tales out for you for a quarter penny and tell you about the fist storm, about a dozen of the king's close-guard left lying in Cloud's wake.' Sister Tallow spat into the sand. 'Stories are just words. Words have no place in a fight. The truth is that almost every time two people raise their empty hands against each other they will both end up on the floor long before one of them dies or is otherwise broken.

'On the ground strength tells, and very often you will not be the strongest. I will teach you about joints. How they will and won't move. In which direction they tear most easily. In which place the force you apply will find the longest levers to stress those joints. How to twist yourself out of similar holds. How to bite and gouge. How to win where winning is an option.

'More importantly you will learn about pain, fear, rage, and control. You will learn how to balance the first three to achieve the fourth. And you will carry those lessons into Grey Class where I will put weapons in your hands and teach you what it is to be a Red Sister. In Grey Class I will teach you how to make the fuckers bleed.

'Arabella, Nona, Jula, Ghena, to the front.'

Nona followed the others to the spot Sister Tallow indicated.

'You two over there—' Sister Tallow waved Arabella and Jula off to the side. 'Both of our new arrivals come with reports of great potential. Let's see how far potential gets them. Jula and Arabella first. Don't hurt her, Jula.' She stepped back and clapped once more. 'Fight.'

Jula snapped into a fighting stance, body turned sideways to Arabella, fists raised at chest height, one a few inches behind the other, legs wide and braced. Arabella ignored her, looking instead at Sister Tallow. 'Fight, Mistress Blade? How should—'

'Fight!' Sister Tallow spread her hands. 'Kick her, punch her, bite her if you must. Put her down.'

'But...'

Sister Tallow nodded to Jula. She exploded forward into a flying kick that hit Arabella on the shoulder and sent her sprawling to the floor.

'The leg is stronger than the arm. The foot less delicate than the hand. Though to strike with them sacrifices balance.' Sister Tallow motioned upward with fingers. 'Get up, girl.'

The attack surprised Nona. Jula looked so bookish ... she found herself smiling at the contrast, then noticed Arabella scowling at her from the ground.

Arabella rubbed her shoulder and got slowly to her feet.

'Fight!' Another clap.

Jula repeated the kick. Arabella stepped to the side, her speed remarkable. Jula kicked again, missed again. The two girls squared up, fists raised. Arabella threw the first punch, a swing, blindingly fast. Somehow Jula stepped into it and caught the blonde girl's wrist, twisting her own body under Arabella's to throw her over her shoulder. Arabella landed heavily on her back and, along with all the air in her lungs, spat out a word that Nona wouldn't have thought ever got used in the emperor's court.

Nona looked up at Sister Tallow for her reaction to the display and found her, together with the whole class, staring at Arabella, wide-eyed. The nun's surprise was mixed with some emotion that Nona couldn't identify but it was strong enough to make the lines of old scars stand out against her paling skin.

Jula said it first, even as she stood there in her victory. 'She moves like a hunska.'

As a child in the ignorance of her village Nona had barely

known about the four tribes of men or how their blood might show, but her months with Giljohn and then at the Caltess had taught her how deep one simple truth ran. Hunska-born were dark of eye and hair. She knew then why Arabella might be so special that the Church of the Ancestor would have negotiated to take her from a noble house. She knew it even before the first of the novices whispered 'mixed'. Two-bloods were rare as a sheet-thaw. There hadn't been a three-blood in the three centuries since Aran the Founder who carved out the realm from the chaos of wildmen and petty kingdoms. At least that's what they said at the Caltess. If Arabella Jotsis showed the signs of the gerant line too she would be stepping into history. If she showed up quantal or marjal she could be stepping into legend.

'Enough.' Another of those claps that hurt the ears. 'Nona, our ring-fighter from the Caltess…' The novices laughed at the joke. 'It's your turn. Ghena? Are you ready?'

Nona turned to face Ghena and found her already in the fighting stance, eyes narrow with concentration, no smile, no snarl. The girl was perhaps an inch taller than her, making them the two smallest in the class. Her dark limbs were nearly as lean as Nona's, every part of them muscle and bone.

The common sense behind the blade-stance was obvious: it presented a smaller area for attack while keeping a wide, stable base. Nona stood as she always stood though. She would learn and use the blade methods but it felt foolish to ape the stance immediately and face her first fight in a position she wasn't used to.

'Ready?' Ghena asked. She hadn't taken the advantage of surprise like Jula had, but looking at her Nona knew pride lay behind the restraint, not kindness. Ghena wanted to own her victory whole.

Nona gave a slight nod and Ghena snapped a punch at her, a straight jab, not Arabella's clumsy swing announced by her whole body before she even started. This came sudden and direct. Nona blocked the fist with both hands, palms crossed before her face. The smack of flesh on flesh echoed in the space of the hall and the impact hurt far more than Nona had imagined.

She lowered her hands to see a look of surprise on Ghena's face.

'You're fast.' Ghena tilted her neck left, then right, stretching.

Without warning the novice launched a flurry of punches, advancing a step with each, a furious attack with no quarter granted. Nona let the world slow around her, the split seconds crystallizing into that clarity she had always been able to call upon. She stepped back, swaying out of the path of one punch, knocking the next aside so it passed within a hair's breadth of her cheek. Ghena was quick. Very quick. Hunska-fast. Nona pushed aside another punch, another, sidestepped a third. Ghena's mask cracked and her fury showed. Anger made her blows more wild but only seemed to increase her speed. Nona found herself having to work harder, saving herself only by the narrowest of margins. She gritted her teeth and dug deeper into the moment until her brain buzzed inside her skull like a trapped bee and even Ghena's whip-crack blows became lazy things that she could step around.

Nona saw, even in the fractions their fight occupied, awareness start to enter Ghena's eyes, a widening, a dilation of pupils. She knew the look – she had seen it before in the eyes of her first friend when he had tossed her a fourth ball and she added it to her juggling thinking to please him… She let Ghena's fist catch her on the left shoulder, and spun with the impact, allowing it to carry her to the floor. A great spray of sand marked her arrival and she stayed there, panting.

A long moment passed and Nona let the world run at its own pace again, feeling the sand grains between her lips, the ache in her shoulder, the sting still in her palms. At last Mistress Blade's clap broke the silence. Nona sat up, climbed slowly to her feet, and went to rejoin the line. The novices nodded their approval. Clera and Ruli looked impressed, Arabella sour. Of all of them only Ghena's gaze held a measure of confusion, and in Sister Tallow's there was a quiet speculation.

8

Nona liked the dormitories better than the nun's cell of the night before. The building had three storeys, Red and Grey classes dividing the ground floor between them in two long, low rooms, Mystic and Holy each having their own floor, with study rooms for the Holies at the top. The beds were larger and more comfortable too, being raised on legs, each with a mattress of folded blankets over boards. Nona lay on hers while the class moved about her, chatting and getting ready for sleep. In the bed to Nona's left Ghena had already crawled beneath her covers and lay dead to the world.

Nona stretched, yawning. The exercises in Blade, one punch and one throw repeated over and over, never quite to Sister Tallow's satisfaction, had left her sore and sweat-soaked. The bathhouse afterwards took away the ache and stink of exercise and left in its place a warm and bone-deep weariness. If Clera hadn't reached down a hand to help her out of the pool Nona suspected that she might still be there, floating helpless amid the steam.

Ruli came to sit at the end of Nona's bed, her long hair pushed up into a nightcap bulging comically atop her head. 'I'm surprised you can keep your eyes open after that.' She nodded towards Ghena's bed.

'Did I do all right?' Nona asked.

'You were great! You're fast, Nona! Ghena doesn't have a lot of technique because she's only been here three months, but she's really, really quick, a prime for sure. Only Clera's quicker than Ghena and some say—'

'They say I'm the fastest the convent has seen in years.' Clera sat on the next bed along and favoured Nona with a dangerous smile. 'Hunska full-blood.'

'Are there other convents?' Nona remained flat on her back, the blanket pulled to her neck, gaze returning to the dance of shadows on the ceiling.

'Six.' Ruli began to count them off on her fingers. 'Silent Patience, Chaste Devotion, Gerran's Crag—'

'Sweet Mercy is the only one to teach Blade, Path, or Shade. The rest just train Holy Sisters.'

'Just?' Jula from a nearby bed, still sounding sour about her lost hair.

'Holy Sisters are as important to the Ancestor as any other sister,' Ruli chipped in with a conciliatory tone. 'The abbess is a Holy Sister and she's in charge of us all.'

Nona let them talk and watched the shadows play. She didn't want to see Arabella, strangely alien now with her pink scalp and patchy blonde stubble. She didn't want to catch the girl's eye and start another round of accusations. Jula had taken her shaving with poor grace but her reaction was as nothing compared to Arabella's outburst. Nona had wondered for a moment if Sister Tallow would have to hold her down…

Abbess Glass had said Nona was free to leave at any time, but when Arabella had demanded to go home in the tone of someone used to being obeyed, Sister Tallow had said no.

'I'm not letting a novice hack at me with a razor because some wild-land peasant stole my belt!' And with that Arabella had started to stride towards the main doors.

What followed had been ugly to watch, but no matter how Arabella raged or how dire her threats the nun had shown no hint of backing down, and eventually a tearful Arabella Jotsis sat in the chair provided while Jula removed her golden hair with a long razor and a trembling hand.

By the time it was Arabella's turn to shave Jula's head she did so with a steady grip on the blade, her eyes red-rimmed and full of cold accusation aimed in Nona's direction.

Nona opened her eyes with a start. Sleep had nearly taken her. She rolled her head to the left. Clera sat on the edge of the bed in her long white nightgown, the copper penny she so often played with in her hand. The other girls were settling into their beds. 'We're friends then?' she asked without preamble, watching Nona's eyes.

'"Friend" can be a dangerous word,' Nona said.

Clera laughed. 'Friend? Really?'

'It is if you mean it.' Nona didn't smile. She thought of Amondo and of Saida. 'Friend' was a bond. Much of what people did, how they acted, confused Nona. But 'friend' she understood. A friend you would die for. Or kill for.

'Well I mean it.' Clera let her own smile slip.

'Then we are.'

It seemed enough for Clera. She rose from Nona's bed and went to her own, flipping the penny once and humming some tune, low and sweet.

Nona let exhaustion close her eyes. The dormitories were heated by the same pipes that ran in the bathhouse and cells. She hadn't imagined that commoners ever wholly escaped the cold, perhaps the emperor before his ever-blazing fires, but not girls like her, not like this. One of the high windows was even a quarter open to stop it being too muggy, as if heat were something that could be given to the wind rather than something precious to be hoarded.

In the village mothers cut their children's hair to a fuzz whenever the weather turned. When the ice-wind surrendered to the Corridor wind and the cold grew less bitter the knives came out. They did it to reduce lice, fleas, and nits to a manageable level, but Nona had always felt it marked the start of something new: new growth, new possibilities. Her last thoughts before dreams stole her were that if a shaved head were the worst thing to have happened to Arabella Jotsis so far then she had lived a charmed life. Also, Nona thought, annoyingly the loss of that golden mane had done nothing to mar the girl's beauty. If anything she looked somehow more perfect.

* * *

Folded in the soft hubbub of voices and with the warmth of her bed drawing her down into sleep Nona let the contest with Ghena play across the back of her eyelids. The whole thing had lasted only moments, moments in which Ghena had thrown a dozen or more punches, a well-practised dance on her part, instinct and reflex on Nona's. Memory of one fight slipped into memory of another, returning Nona to the sawdust and sweat of the Caltess, watching the apprentices spar. Partnis Reeve's fight-masters taught discipline but left room for aggression.

A week or two after Nona's arrival Raymel Tacsis had strolled into the great hall where the apprentices were training. Nona, Saida and two other attic children engaged in sweeping the floor paused their labours and leaned on their brooms to watch the fighter. Up close his size was intimidating. Nona realized that her head wouldn't even reach the man's hip and that with the strength of one arm he would be able to toss her, Saida, and the other two sweepers across the room, not separately but together.

'I've a better lesson for these puppies.' Raymel climbed over the ropes into the ring where two gerant apprentices had been wrestling, both of them enormous but lacking more than a foot on the older man. He stood huge, blond, and glorious between them, somehow wearing his wealth though all that covered him was a loincloth and a sheen of oil.

The fight-master stepped forward, an objection on his lips, but Raymel boomed across him, 'And the rest of you.' He beckoned another three apprentices from across the hall. Two hunskas holding nets and a gerant girl with a ponderous brow that looked as if it would break the fist of anyone foolish enough to punch her in the head.

As the girl clambered in behind the two swifter apprentices Raymel drove an elbow into the throat of the gerant behind him. 'Don't ever wait to attack.' The apprentice fell, clutching his neck. The rest stood, too stunned or nervous to act. Raymel slapped the girl, his huge hand covering half her face and sending her back into the ropes, spitting blood. His grin was an ugly thing, corrupting the good looks he'd been born with.

Beside Nona, Saida covered her eyes, turning to reach for her broom.

'Aren't you going to watch?' Nona couldn't look away. The hunska apprentices had launched themselves at Raymel, two blurs of fists and feet.

'I hate it.' Saida resumed her sweeping. 'It makes my stomach feel bad, seeing people hurt.'

'But…' Nona winced as Raymel trapped one hunska against the ropes and snatched him up by the leg. 'Partnis bought you to fight. You're going to have to.'

She sensed rather than saw Saida's broad shoulders shrug. 'I'd rather mend people than break them. Is that a thing in the city? Mending people?'

'I don't know.' Nona watched Raymel swing the hunska apprentice against the ring post. Part of her wanted to be unleashed within the roped enclosure. Another part wanted Saida's hope to be true, wanted there to be people who put as much passion into healing as Raymel did into hurting.

'Raymel!' the fight-master barked. 'Ease up.'

Raymel continued to choke the apprentice in his hands, still seemingly impervious to the attacks of the last hunska remaining on her feet.

Nona found herself turning away too, the undirected anger that built in her whenever she saw a fight now dissipating. 'You won't have to fight, Saida. They'll see you're no good at it and give you a different job. Regol said the old man who comes to the horses can sew up wounds like a seamstress. Perhaps he'll need an apprentice soon. He is *very* old.'

Saida managed a shy smile. 'I'd like to help. I don't want Partnis to give me away. I would miss you.'

'I'd miss you too.' Nona found her chest aching at the thought. 'So I won't let it happen!' She said it with such fierce confidence that Saida's smile had widened into something that made her blunt face suddenly beautiful.

The dream turned darker, colder, shadows invading the Caltess hall. They were alone now, Saida and Nona, a sense of profound unease stalking between them.

'Don't hurt me!' Saida was suddenly backing away from Nona, terrified.

'Saida! I won't let anyone—'

'Don't hurt me!' Saida pointed at Nona, cowering.

Nona tried to reassure her but found instead that she towered over Saida, holding her friend's arm in a massive fist. The grey hall around her became the walls of Raymel's apartment, Saida dangling above the thick luxury of a bearskin rug.

Nona tried to let Saida go. 'It's not me. I'm not like him. I'm not!'

'No, please! I didn't mean to.'

Anger flared somewhere deep in Nona's chest. She was trying to help the silly girl. Why was she scared? Did she think Nona had anything in common with a creature like Raymel Tacsis? 'I'm not going to hurt you.' She found to her horror though that she was shaking Saida, the fist on her friend's arm emphasizing her points as she spoke.

'Let go!'

'I am letting go…' But the fist gripped tighter, twisted, and Saida's screaming began.

Nona drew a sharp breath and opened her eyes. The colours of her nightmare vanished leaving only black. It took a moment to realize where she was. The soft sounds of sleeping surrounded her on each side. At the back of her mind the dream carried on as if it neither wanted her attention nor required her permission to proceed. She had been following something, a line that ran its narrow path with danger to either side, on one flank a dark and consuming hunger, on the other a blindness, fierce as staring at the sun. And somehow she had been following someone else at the same time, black-clad, swift, certain, moving through a starless night, plotting a sure path between high buildings. The figure had found what it sought, looked up, reached out to find cold stone walls, and had started to climb.

Nona strained her ears, hunting beneath the novices' gentle snores and sighs, the soft turning of a body in sleep, the whisper of the wind … a scrape, a sudden movement … hard to judge at what distance in the unbroken night. Without warning, surprising herself, Nona jolted upright, as swift a motion as she had ever made, the blanket pulled from her. Perhaps some new sound had sat her up, perhaps nothing, just one of those twitches that comes out of nowhere and jerks your body as if by a string. Somewhere else in the dark a muffled impact, the sound of air leaving lungs fast and without orders...

'Wuh-what?' At the end of the row Ketti, the eldest of them, unhooded the lantern that sat beside her bed for anyone needing to make the trip to the Necessary in the dead of night.

Just below the rolled blanket where Nona's head had lain a small black object stood proud of the bed. She blinked, trying to focus – the hilt of something? Close by, Clera rose groggily from her own bed. 'Can't be morning already?' Her voice thick with sleep. A figure stood between them, revealed in the light of the unhooded lantern – Arabella Jotsis, her face a mask.

Nona took hold of the hilt – leather-bound, the pommel a ball of iron the size of an eye – and tugged. It took most of her strength to free the point from the boards, and when she saw the gleaming blade start to slide out from the slot it had put in her blankets she quickly covered it. Only Arabella noticed, her eyes moving from Nona's hand on the hilt to Nona's face as their eyes met.

'Get back in bed! It's the middle of the night.' Ketti closed the lantern's cowl until just a glow remained.

Arabella hurried towards Ketti and moments later left the room holding the lantern.

'Shut the window. It's cold in here.' Clera from her bed, the words all running together. Nobody replied.

Nona lay back, pulling the blankets over her. It *had* grown cooler – the wind must have caught the window and pulled it wide – even so, if Clera called this cold then she had never known what it was to face the ice-wind, hungry and with only wattle walls for shelter.

She drew out the knife from under the covers. The blade reached for about two widths of her hand, narrow as two fingers, all of it cold steel. Nona could only think that Arabella must have stolen it from the stores at the training hall. The real question though, was had she meant to stab Nona to death or just to leave her a pointed warning? At the core of her something red and primal snarled at the blade's challenge, demanding blood, demanding the weapon be returned with a hard lesson. Nona fought the impulse to go after Arabella. She could catch her before she reached the Necessary hunkering on the edge of the cliff. How would that encounter end? Nona with a sharp knife in her hand and blunt accusations in her mouth? Anger had its place, it was a weapon not to be neglected, but so did patience, and Nona decided that control lay in deciding which to use and when.

She stayed in her bed. It was cold outside and dangerous in all manner of ways. The knife must have been meant to scare her. Even someone as high-born as Arabella Jotsis couldn't expect to murder people in their sleep in a crowded dormitory and get away with it… Unless she really did think a village girl was no more than a cow or pig compared to someone who had been invited to the emperor's palace?

At some point, with one thought chasing the next in endless circles, Nona fell asleep and though she tossed and turned she didn't wake until Bray spoke the waking hour and all across the dormitory grey shapes started to move beneath their covers, grumbling at the day.

'Path and Spirit today,' Clera groaned. 'Worst of the lot.'

'Breakfast first!' Ruli with a grin, pulling off her nightcap and shaking down her hair.

'Spirit is what we're all here for.' Jula gave a sniff, patting her head and finding her hair hadn't returned overnight.

'I'm here because I was sent here,' Clera said. 'When I'm a Red Sister if anyone asks me to repeat the catechism I'll stab them in the eye.'

'If you paid closer attention in Spirit, you would know that stabbing people in the eye is frowned upon.' Jula straightened her habit and started to make her bed. 'Anyway, it's Path first.'

'Yawn!' Clera tugged her habit over her underskirts. 'I hope Pan lets us pathless go play again.'

Nona slid from her covers and started to dress. She reached beneath her pillow, to touch the knife one more time to reassure herself it hadn't been a dream. Still there, warm from her body now, a hard, sharp, and undeniable truth. She wanted to take it with her, strapped to her body, the blade wrapped in a strip of linen, but she lacked both time and privacy. She would have to leave the weapon in her bed and hope that Arabella had no chance to reclaim it.

Nona found herself one of the last out of the dormitory, hurrying with Clera to the refectory for breakfast. The pair of them clattered down the front steps, finding an unusually still day, a cloudless sky, and a rare warmth on offer.

By the dormitory wall a plump, red-faced sister attacked an area of the flagstones with a stiff brush, pausing to slosh down more water from her bucket. She glanced up at the girls. 'Hurry!' And returned to her task, scrubbing furiously at a dark stain. 'Away with you.'

Clera stuck her tongue out at the woman's back and ran off towards the refectory, giggling. 'That's Sister Mop. She thinks novices only have two aims in life: to get stuff dirty and to get in her way.'

'She called herself Mop?' Nona running behind.

'No, but everyone else calls her that. She chose some flower name, Crysanthe-something, but nobody can pronounce it or remember it.'

A hundred yards on they passed Sister Tallow, coming from the abbess's house. She looked away towards the eastern sky as they ran by but not before Nona saw the abrasion across the left side of her face and the bruise darkening around it.

Nona waited until they were out of earshot around the corner of the refectory. 'What happened?'

'Don't know. Can't imagine anyone getting the best of old Blade,' Clera panted. 'Maybe the abbess slapped her!' She laughed, then more serious, 'Did you see she had her arm hidden inside her habit?'

Nona hadn't and once through the doors the sight of food bowls, full and steaming, pushed any questions from her mind.

Breakfast was a hasty affair but Nona still made a valiant attempt at leaving nothing edible behind by the time she left the table.

'Come on!' Clera turned and beckoned as Nona jogged to keep up, one arm over her over-full stomach. Fortunately the Path cloisters came into view soon enough, past the beehives lined in the lee of the abbess's house. Four arms of the building reached towards the compass points from a round central tower. Each arm was a framework of ornately-worked stone, open to the elements, with delicate corner pillars and trellised masonry reaching between them to complete the structure. The central tower stood dark against the sky, defying the years with the arrogance of stone, seeming in one moment foreboding and in the next beautiful. Four doors gave onto the ground floor, one for each arm of the surrounding structure.

Ahead of Nona and Clera a novice laboured towards the tower in limping steps, a crutch under her left armpit.

'Someone must have got kicked a bit hard in Blade yesterday!' Nona slowed her pace as they caught the girl up. No one had been limping in the dormitory, and yet there was something familiar about the novice.

'Ha!' Clera shouted, 'That's just Stumpy!' She raced past, jostling the girl enough to make her stagger.

Nona came to a halt, almost level with the novice, reaching to catch her, then pulling back her hands as she saw it wasn't needed. The girl was hardly taller than her, hair the colour of straw set about her head in a hundred tight curls. 'Nona,' she said, without turning.

Nona knew the voice. 'Hessa?'

Hessa pivoted on her crutch. The length of the habit hid her withered leg, but only the tip of her shoe touched the ground on that side. 'We've come a long way from Giljohn's cage.'

Nona had her arms about her before she had time to blink. 'They killed Saida.'

'I'm sorry for it.' Hessa lifted a hand uncertainly to pat Nona between the shoulders.

'How are you here? Why haven't I seen you?' Nona released her and stepped back.

'I've been in the sanatorium. Sister Rose wanted to keep me in until I got rid of this cough.' Hessa thumped a fist against her narrow chest. 'I've been here for weeks. Giljohn tried to sell me at the Academy but I failed their tests. They said I was the wrong sort, quantal maybe, but definitely not marjal. He tried to sell me to three different mages. Their houses are so big, Nona! I thought we were going into the emperor's palace—'

'NooooOOOooona!' Clera hollering from the north door. 'We'll be late!'

'Coming!'

'We'd better hurry.' Hessa shifted her weight and set her crutch forward.

A bony hand closed on both their shoulders. 'The heathens have found each other, I see!' Sister Wheel pushed between them. 'The peasant and the cripple, plotting together. We'll soon clear out those muddy little minds. Scrub away heresy and falsehood so the Ancestor may find you worthy. Even simple clay can be moulded and fired into something of worth.'

Nona opened her mouth to say something sharp. 'I—'

'Yes, Sister Wheel! I'm looking forward to our Spirit class.' Hessa smiled up at the nun so sweetly that Nona almost believed she meant it. 'But we'd best go now or Mistress Path will be cross with us.'

Sister Wheel made a sound of disgust and released both of them, wiping her hands on her habit. 'Quickly then!'

Hessa showed a fair turn of pace with her crutch, her withered leg swinging beneath her skirts. Nona matched her speed, glancing back at Sister Wheel, now making for the dome. 'I don't like that old woman!'

'Hah, Wheel's all right once you know her ways.' Stump, swing, stump, swing. 'Just wait till you meet the Poisoner. Now she *is* scary!'

Nona entered the Tower of the Path with Hessa, using the east door. Novices were supposed to be drawn to a particular door but none of them called to her. All four doors led into the same room – an echoingly empty one with a stone spiral stair at the centre, and around the walls the strangest pictures Nona had seen, though in truth until she entered the ring-fighters' rooms at the Caltess she had never seen paintings. While Hessa laboured up the stairs Nona took a moment to glance around at the two dozen or so portraits, nuns all of them, but with their hair uncovered and the most peculiar flights of fancy added. One lacked half a face, with tatters extending across the gap out over a night-black background. Another in place of one eye had a red star, its rays reaching in all directions. Another still had no mouth and in her hair flowers of a kind Nona had never seen, the deep blue of evening sky.

'Nona!'

She sped up the stairs after Hessa. The stairway seemed long enough to reach the tower top but offered no doors into any rooms along the way before emerging into the middle of a classroom. At least Nona assumed it to be a classroom – it looked more like a church. Apart from the chairs on which Red Class sat, and a large iron-bound chest at the front, the room was completely bare. Even so, it had a beauty to it. Four tall and narrow windows broke the light into many colours. Scores of stained-glass panels made each window into a glowing, abstract picture that threw reds, and greens, and blues, across the walls and floor. For a moment all Nona could do was gape at the alien wonder of the place.

The nun standing before the chest was the oldest Nona had seen. Quite possibly the oldest woman she had ever seen. Nana Even's older sister, Ora, had died a year back. Nona's mother claimed the woman had seen eighty years come and go. Yet lying there on the pyre in the square before Grey Stephen's stone-built home old Ora had looked young compared to Mistress Path.

'Take a seat, Hessa.' The ancient nun had a surprisingly young voice. 'You too, novice…?'

'Nona.' Nona took a chair, little more than a stool really, the back a single narrow plank.

'Knower?' Mistress Path came a step closer, leaning in.

'Nona!' Clera all but shouted it.

'Ah, Nona.' The nun clapped her hand to Nona's shoulder. 'Like the merchant-queen?'

Nona wasn't alone in offering this last question a blank look, though she caught Clera nodding.

'No matter – no matter.' Mistress Path moved off, shaking her head. 'It was long ago and her sons are all gone to dust.'

'We're all gathered now?' Mistress Path looked around the room, her eyes so pale as to be without colour, the whites creamy with age. 'Two new girls, yes?'

'Yes, Mistress Path.' A loud chorus.

'I'll do my introductions then. I am Sister Pan. Within these walls, Mistress Path is my name.' She paced towards the front of the class and, with an exaggerated sigh, settled herself upon the great chest. Nona noticed that the woman's right hand, that she had thought lost in the sleeve of her habit, was more lost than that, the arm ending at the wrist in an ugly mess of scar tissue.

Sister Pan lowered her head and tapped her fingers on the lid of the chest. She was quiet for so long that Nona wondered if she had dropped into a doze, but a moment later she looked up, eyes bright. 'In these lessons we study the Path. For most of you this will be a journey to serenity, to states of mind that can help you with patience or with concentration. Or perhaps they may help quiet your fears, or put sorrow aside for a while until you have time for her visit. For those few of you who might have it in your blood to see the Path clearly rather just sense it as an idea these lessons are the first steps to discovering hidden worlds, the boundary between them, and the power that may be won by those who dare to venture in such places.'

Clera leaned across to Nona, speaking in a low voice. 'If any of us do go there we'll be doing it alone. They say the old girl hasn't put a toe on the Path for thirty years.'

Nona pressed her lips together, gesturing with her eyes towards Mistress Path.

'She's deaf as a post, silly.' Clera grinned and raised her tone a fraction. 'Those that can, do – those that can't, teach. At least in Path. The doers are too valuable to waste on us.'

Sister Pan paused and frowned at Clera, who dutifully faced front and centre. 'Now, we have … Arabella.' The nun focused on the Jotsis girl, whose shaved head was spattered with coloured light. 'A bold stare she has. Hmmm. But what can she see?' Sister Pan approached and leaned in close. 'Don't look away, dear. Keep your eyes on mine. In this place the world sings for us. Can you hear it?' She took Arabella's wrist in the gnarled claw of her hand. The nun's skin was the black of a dusty slate, darker than her habit: Arabella's fingers looked white as bone in that grip. 'A three-part song. Life.' She lifted their joined hands. 'That which has never lived.' She moved her stump into a pool of deep red light and followed the shaft of it up towards the window. 'And death.' A quick glance back towards the chest. 'The notes of the song…' Sister Pan intoned three notes, pure but somehow sad, the start of a melody that Nona wanted to hear more of. The nun released Arabella's wrist and started to pace before the seated novices. 'There's a boundary between what lives and what does not. It runs through all things, and around them. It's a path that is hard to follow but each step taken is a holy one. When you walk the Path you approach the divine. The Path flows from the Ancestor and the Ancestor waits at the end of it. At the end of all things.

'We are mortal though. We are flawed. Poor vessels for divinity. Each step is harder than the last, the Path twists and turns, it is narrow and in motion, the power that it gives is … difficult to contain. Sooner rather than later everyone slips from the Path no matter what their heart desires, no matter how pure their faith.

'Our knowledge of the Path is the gift of the fourth tribe – the last to beach their ships on Abeth. Among the stars the quantal built their lives around the Path, generation upon generation, until it lived in their veins. That blood was mixed to meet the challenges of a new world – but in some few it shows, even now after so many years have passed.

'Have you seen the Path, child?' Sister Pan, at Arabella's shoulder once again, took the girl's chin, angling her eyes back to her own.

'I... Sometimes I see a bright line, like a crack running through my dreams...'

'Have you touched it?' Sister Pan asked.

'A-almost. One time. I reached out for it...' Arabella looked away, towards one of the glowing windows. 'It felt as though I were running ... my heart ... and my head filled with angles. All sharp and wrong...'

'And then what happened?' Sister Pan released the girl's chin.

'I fell out of bed and woke up with a headache.'

Laughter rippled, half amused, half nervous.

'And what about...' Sister Pan blinked and looked around until she found Nona, sitting on the far side of the class. '... our other new girl?'

'She's hunska, Mistress Path!' Clera called out, slapping Nona on the shoulder. 'One of us reds!'

'Hmmm...' Sister Pan turned her gaze back to Arabella and started to ask more questions.

'She'll leave you alone now,' Clera said in an undertone. 'Only cares about the mystics.'

'The what?' Nona whispered.

'Mystics. If Empress Arabella isn't lying then she'll be the second quantal in the class, the other being your friend hop-along. Only our bald friend is also hunska-fast which makes her oh-so-special, which is why all the nuns are wetting themselves over her – the Chosen One.' Clera raised her hands in mock worship. 'At the end of our studies, if we're judged fit, we take holy orders and join the convent as nuns. Girls who follow the Path take their orders as Mystic Sisters – everyone calls them Holy Witches. I told you before. You and I, we'll focus on Blade and take our orders as Martial Sisters, which everyone calls Red Sisters. Most who come here end up as Holy Sisters ... and everyone calls them Holy Sisters ... or if they're being fancy, Brides of the Ancestor. That sounds creepy to me... And some take Shade in the last year. Those are Sisters of Discretion. Grey Sisters. There are lots of other names people use for those, none of them nice. But—'

'Novice Clera!' Deaf or not, Sister Pan had good enough eyesight to spot two novices with heads so bowed in conversation, they nearly touched.

'I was telling Nona about the blade-Path, Mistress! Can I show her? Please!'

Sister Pan lifted her eyes to the heavens and signed her faith, laying her index finger over her heart, pointing upward. 'The child has only been here a few moments!' She drew a deep breath. 'Today we will be meditating. Continuing to develop the serenity that helps to bring us to the Path. And, Nona, whilst it is true that for many of you girls no amount of quiet contemplation will bring the complexity and beauty of the Path into focus within your mind's eye there are many other benefits, both spiritual *and* physical, to achieving the mental states we seek to unlock in this class. In a girl's first year I endeavour to teach her, through meditation, mantras and the control of breathing, the three-fold mind. The necessary states of clarity, patience, and serenity. When you have the basics of the trio my seal will be on your scroll for advancement to Grey Class.'

Sister Pan left Arabella's side and hobbled towards Nona and Clera. 'Whilst it is essential that a Mystic Sister be the mistress of these techniques, all three are of benefit to any novice. The Holy Sister will find her communion with the Ancestor deepened by reaching clarity. The Sister of Discretion will carry out her duties with greater efficiency if she attains patience. And, ironically, the Martial Sister will be all the more deadly if before combat she has reached the peace of serenity. However, as this is Nona's first day and I have a number of tests to go over with Arabella any novice who wishes to practise their blade-path may do so.'

The scraping of half a dozen chairs immediately followed this pronouncement as girls leapt to their feet all around the room and started to head for the stairwell at the centre.

'Clera!' Sister Pan called after them, her voice resonating down the stairs with surprising volume. 'You can ask for the key to Blade Hall at the sanatorium!'

* * *

The six girls burst laughing from the base of the Tower of the Path and ran off towards the plateau's narrowing point. The four hunska girls outdistanced Ruli and Kariss, but their natural speed counted for less in a race than it did in a fight: hunska blood gave whip-crack reflexes and a startling twitch that could move a hand from one place to another seemingly without the tedium of having to occupy any of the spaces in between, but it couldn't, for example, move a full body-weight faster than a horse over four hundred yards.

The sanatorium sat at the compound's outermost edge, built from limestone blocks hewn from the plateau itself, hunkered down against the wind, with a long and pillared gallery on the lee side. Clera ran on into the office while the other novices came to a halt by the door. 'Why did we have to come here?' Ketti frowned, hunched over to make herself a height with the other girls.

'I saw Sister Tallow limping this morning,' Ghena said. 'She must be hurt.'

'How?' Ruli asked.

Ghena shrugged. 'I don't know.'

Nona tried to imagine Sister Tallow slipping and coming to grief on a flight of stairs. She couldn't do it. She had yet to see Mistress Blade fight but everything about the way the woman moved said she would not be taken unawares by the inanimate. Which left…

'Maybe someone sent assassins after Arabella,' Ketti said.

'Assassins? Why?' Nona had only heard of assassins in the old stories. The Noi-Guin, trained in secret, deployed to end wars, or start them, or to cut away any life that might constitute an offence to someone with enough money to pay fees that even old nobility found staggering.

Ghena grunted at Nona's obvious stupidity. Ketti raised both eyebrows and did something with her lips that signalled supreme surprise at the depths of Nona's ignorance. 'She's the Chosen One. The Ancestor's gift. You think there aren't people fighting over who owns her? Or, if it's clear that the person who owns her isn't going to be them, you think they're not ready to kill her just to stop someone else gaining the benefit?'

'I heard Sherzal tried to take her from the Jotsis estate,' Ruli said.

Even in the village the names of Emperor Crucical's two sisters were known. Sherzal was said to be the worst of them, a plotter that the emperor had had to banish almost to the Scithrowl border before he felt safe behind his walls.

Clera interrupted Nona's questions by hurrying out of the office, a grin on her face, a large iron key swinging from her hand. Behind her the bulky form of Sister Rose waddled to the door, her cone-like headdress just like Sister Wheel's. 'Careful on the line, novices. I mean it, Ketti! Make sure the new girls don't end up on my doorstep this afternoon…'

Clera led the race back to Blade Hall and hurried them on across the training floor, along the corridor beneath the stands and straight on to the door at the end.

'Shouldn't we change?' Ruli, turning left towards the changing room.

'We need balance sticks…' Kariss, panting as she caught them up and turning right towards the stores.

'Pah. Sticks are for babies, and hunska balance better in their common habits.' Clera flapped her sleeves like wings. She pushed on through into a corridor too dark to yield any detail.

Nona, Ketti, and Ghena followed, Nona at the rear, stumbling blind up a tight wooden stairway. Somewhere far above a door opened and light reached down towards her. She kept climbing.

'Careful up here,' Ketti warned. 'There's not much space on the platform.'

Nona edged out through the door behind the older girl, her initial questions immediately replaced by new ones. They stood on a platform just below the ceiling of a huge room lit by many small square windows in the furthest wall. Apart from great nets strung between posts in each corner and suspended a couple of yards above a sand-covered floor the room was almost completely empty. A great pendulum hung on the wall to the left, thirty yards long, nearly the height of the room, a heavy brass bob on the end of a long thin iron rod. Above it a round dial, as wide across as Nona could stretch her arms and marked around the edge with evenly spaced graduations. Running in a convoluted path from the platform where the girls stood to a door at ground level on the opposite side was a pipe of the sort that carried the hot oil through the nuns' cells and bathhouse. It rose, fell, twisted, turned, and at one point made a corkscrew with three turns.

'What is it?' Nona found herself the only one still standing. The others sat on the edge of the platform, removing their shoes, their valuables in linen bags against the back wall. Ketti had hers off already, legs dangling over the drop.

'The line,' Clera said. 'Blade-path.' She pulled a small earthenware tub from her habit and started to dab the dark substance in it onto the soles of her feet. 'This is—'

'Pine resin.' Nona could smell it.

'I use tar,' Ketti said. 'Better grip.'

'Pine resin's cheaper.' Clera applied it with a miser's care.

'The blade-path?' Nona asked.

'It's the closest a hunska can get to the Path. Closest anyone who's not a quantal can get. They say it helps the body teach the mind – but really it's just to give us humble mortals something to do, and so we appreciate how hard it is for the poor witches sitting back there in Path with legs crossed and eyes closed.'

'You walk down it,' Ghena said in a rare helpful moment. 'The pendulum counts how long you take.' She pointed to a lever in the wall behind her. 'That starts it and there's one down there by the door that stops it.'

'I'll show you,' Clera said.

But Ketti had already shuffled to the start, careful not to make the platform sticky, and stood just before the start of the narrow pipe. 'Too slow!' And she stepped out with infinite care, arms spread.

To Nona's horror she saw that the cables reaching down from the roof to eye-rings on the pipe weren't there to help steady the structure – they were its only support and the moment Ketti settled her weight on it the whole edifice began to sway, even rotating about joints at half a dozen spots along its length.

Ghena pulled the lever on the wall to release the great pendulum. It swung, swift and silent, taking perhaps ten beats of Nona's heart to reach the limit of its range and start to return. During that first swing the wheel above turned through five of the small divisions on its rim.

Finding her balance, Ketti began to advance, being careful not to let the slope of the pipe accelerate her. She moved with a certain grace, her long thin body making a dozen subtle shifts each moment, swaying in counterpoint to the path beneath her, each new step changing the rhythm.

Coming to the first rise, Ketti slowed still further, and waited for the whole structure to adjust to her weight that now levered it in a new direction. The drop beneath the platform seemed huge to Nona. More than enough to kill. Tall as a tree. How much would it hurt to hit those nets at such speed? Would they hold?

'Ah!' Ketti found herself in trouble, arms wheeling at full extent.

The three girls on the platform watched, transfixed. A moment later Ketti had control again and advanced twenty feet along a steeply descending curve.

'Now it gets difficult,' Clera said.

Ketti stepped towards the rise where the pipe began its spiral of three complete turns, so tall that she could fit within them. With agonizing slowness she began the transfer from the inner to the outer surface, relying on the traction from her tarred feet to anchor her to the cold metal. Against Nona's expectation she reached the top of the first spiral.

Nona turned to see the dial, now almost through a complete circuit. 'How long will it take h—' A wail of rage and despair cut her off. Far below them Ketti hit the net and bounced, screaming in frustration.

'She does better than that normally,' Ghena said.

'Your go, Nona!' Clera gestured towards the start point.

Nona glanced at the resin pot in Clera's hand but Clera looked away, leaning over to tease Ketti, who was now scrambling for the edge of the net by the door. Ghena pulled the lever, which trapped the pendulum at the end of its swing and set the dial to its original position. Turning back, she nodded to the dark patch on the platform just where the pipe started. 'Stamp about there. You'll get your soles sticky enough. Mistress Blade has the path cleaned every day – we think she must have a deal with the resin sellers. But she doesn't tell us to clean the platform … so we don't!'

Nona slipped her shoes off. The tar and resin felt tacky under her toes. She tried to concentrate on the sensation rather than all the empty space between her and the ground. Clera's hoarding of her resin pot hurt a little but Nona knew that need and generosity have their own cycles. In hungry times the village was wont to share food – but when the hunger built to a certain point everybody, even the kindest of them, closed in on themselves, sharing only with their closest family. Perhaps there even came a point when famine could stop mother feeding child. Nona understood better than most that even the most sacred bonds could be broken under enough stress. Clera wasn't hungry – but she was once rich and now was not. Perhaps to someone raised in luxury that was like starvation…

Nona tried to push thoughts of her mother aside and seal her anger away. Gritting her teeth, she stepped forward. The pipe shifted beneath her foot the moment she pressed down. Far below the net trembled.

'The convent keeps records of the best times,' Clera said. 'The best time in each class in each year, the best time in the whole year, the best time ever.' The lever made a deep clunk as Ghena set the pendulum going again.

'I don't— How can—' Nona found her other foot glued to the platform by more than a sticky patch of floor. No part of her wanted to commit herself to the path. She had never been a great climber of trees, fearing the helplessness of the fall almost as much as the pain of reunion with the ground.

'Go on!' Clera urged.

The sound of footsteps on the stairs behind her pushed Nona out over the drop. Shame can exert as much pressure as anger. She put her arms out and slowed the turning of the world just a fraction. Balance relies on an understanding of the motion of things: of swing, of momentum, of the constraints that gravity's laws place on all matter, be it flesh or stone. Slow the world too much and you lose that intuition, you break your connection to the interlinked web of moving pieces, and while you may fall by degrees, taking an age to realize you've passed the point of no return, you will still fall.

The slope of the path pulled at Nona, her feet on the point of slipping at every moment. The pipe swayed treacherously. She came to the curve, her shallow breaths drawn in time to the motion of her body as she struggled to stay upright. Her arms ached already as if she were hanging by them not merely balancing. Somehow she made it around the first long and descending curve!

The steep rise of the corkscrew seemed an impossible barrier, lifting above her head in the space of a few strides. Nona took it in tiny steps, hearing nothing but the rasp of her breath and the pounding of her heart. To her surprise she found herself at the top of the spiral's first turn, staring down at the impossibly steep descent to the bottom of the next turn. She knew her feet would slip there with the path running away from her.

'Go on!' Shouted from the platform, almost angry.

Nona held for a moment, with the drop to every side screaming for her to fall, the tension in her legs unbearable. Then she jumped.

Her lead foot caught the top of the next loop of the spiral and, swinging her trailing leg, thrusting up with both arms, she carried on to the top of the third and final loop. Where, with arms pinwheeling, she caught herself with one foot. She had in two leaps carried herself to a point a little over a quarter of the way along the blade-path.

Nona brought her other foot onto the pipe and, with the exaggerated care of a drunkard, turned to the side. In that movement she saw the other novices crowded onto the platform staring at her, mouths open. It was a look she knew: the same shock had registered on Amondo's face when she had learned too quickly to do his tricks. It was the start of a look that ended in hurt and anger.

Nona's heel slipped from the iron pipe. She let out a yelp and fell backwards. By the time she hit the net she was screaming.

She bounced twice and rolled over, wheezing as she tried to draw the air back into her lungs. An awkward scramble brought her to the edge of the net and strong hands helped her down. She found herself looking up into the impish eyes of Sister Kettle who had last appeared behind Sister Apple in the steams of the bathhouse.

'Well that was … unorthodox.' Sister Kettle smiled. 'Not strictly what I would call *following* the path, but an impressive piece of acrobatics even so!'

'H-how long—' Nona heaved in a breath.

'Did you take?' Sister Kettle looked up at the platform. 'Ghena? How long before she fell?'

'One and twenty!'

'One cycle and twenty,' Sister Kettle repeated. 'That's eighty counts. Do you know what your class record is for completion, Nona?'

'No.'

'Guess.'

Nona tried to imagine it. 'Three hundred counts?'

'Ketti?' Sister Kettle asked.

'Nobody currently in Red has completed the blade-path. Suleri was the last to finish it while still in Red. Her count was two hundred and ninety.' Ketti was standing by the door. Her eyes flitted to the path above them. 'I've almost made it to the end though. Almost.'

'Suleri can do it faster now,' Sister Kettle said, turning for the door. 'She's the fastest novice still at the convent. Her record is one hundred and eighteen.'

'What's the fastest it was ever done?' Nona asked.

Sister Kettle paused, the door half open. 'Our records say that a little over two hundred years ago a certain Sister Owl – yes, the one in the stories, the Black Fort and all that – the ledgers record her setting a time in Holy Class of twenty-six counts. It does seem hard to credit though. Perhaps the timing mechanism has been adjusted over the years…'

'Twenty-six!' Nona blinked. It didn't sound even vaguely possible.

'Something to aim for.' Sister Kettle went through the door with a slight limp, leaving Nona and Ketti to stare at each other. Way above them Ruli started out on the path.

'Why was Sister Kettle here?' Nona asked, to break the silence more than anything.

'To watch the new girl, of course,' Ketti said. 'She'll be reporting back to Sister Tallow. That's what she does. Watches and reports. She'd be Mistress Shade if we didn't already have the Poisoner! I expect—' She paused as Ruli plummeted down into the net with a shriek of frustration. 'I expect she'd have come anyway to size up the competition. Kettle holds the convent record for the blade-path – the record for anyone still living here – sixty-nine counts.'

Nona tried the path half a dozen more times, moving less quickly and falling, not to stay part of the group but because gravity seemed to have got its hooks into her. Quite how she had got so far before she couldn't say, for now the path swayed beneath her like a foreign sea, its ways alien to her feet. Even so she got further along than Ruli, Ghena and poor Kariss, who barely made the first yard and never the third.

The sixth impact with the net left her ears ringing.

'Bray!' Clera shouted. 'Oh hells!' She dropped off the platform, habit swirling about her head, long legs out before her.

Nona hung on tight to the ropes. The only rule they'd told her was not to try the path while someone is still in the net, as you could bounce them out.

Clera scrambled for the edge. 'We'll be late for Spirit!'

Nona glanced up at the platform. Empty. She and Clera had been so deep in their competition they hadn't seen the others leave.

'Come on!' Clera tossed Nona her shoes and dropped to the floor. 'Mistress Spirit is the worst!'

'I thought you said the Poisoner was the worst!'

'They're all the worst when you're late!' And Clera was running.

9

Racing around the Dome of the Ancestor Nona started to think that the place had no door, her breath came ragged and Clera's longer legs were opening a lead. The pain of a stitch stabbed beneath her lungs and she slowed, grabbing her side. Fortunately a few more paces brought sight of the great doors that she had seen on her first night. The line of Red Class was already filing in through the narrow gap where a hand held the leftmost door ajar. Clera and Nona joined the end of the line, sweaty and breathless, just as Ketti and Ruli slipped through ahead of them. Ketti had to duck below the hand which turned out to be attached to Sister Wheel. Nona scowled, having yet to forgive the nun for turfing her from her bed with such holy zeal on her first morning at the convent.

'Quickly! Quietly!' Sister Wheel ushered them on.

At first the dim light yielded only an impression of great columns and a polished floor, with some brighter space beyond. Nona followed Clera's back, blinking to help her eyes adjust. They were in a grand foyer that itself was bigger than all but the richest houses in Verity. Sister Wheel led them along the wall to the left towards a small door at the side of the foyer, as if allowing novices to venture any further in would sully so holy a place. From the view of the interior, glimpsed between sleek columns of black marble, Nona understood the space to be both singular and vast, lit by scores of long and narrow windows radiating from the dome's apex, with a statue gleaming at the centre, tiny in such a space but far bigger than a man.

The pull that Nona had felt that first night in the nuns' cells was here too. Not so strong as it had been when she stood just yards from the black door that entered the rear of the dome … but there even so. The huge and echoing space, the sunlight shafting in through many windows, the golden statue, they were grand things, impressive, perhaps even holy, but they were not the source. Something filled that dome, almost to bursting, but its centre lay deeper…

'Nona!' Clera at the open side door, beckoning. 'Stop dawdling!'

Nona hurried on into a small classroom dimly lit by three of the high porthole windows that formed a ring perforating the wall of the great dome.

'Late to class but never late to dinner!' Sister Wheel's fingernails-on-slate voice reached a surprising volume as she pointed Nona and Clera out in the doorway.

This seemed a harsh judgement to Nona, who had attended just one convent dinner so far.

The sister stood at the far end of the classroom in one of the circles of light cast by the windows, the white funnel of her headdress all aglow and the wisps of grey hair that escaped it seeming to float about her face. 'Come along! The road to damnation is paved with tardy steps!'

Nona hurried to an empty desk near the door, head down, puzzling over how a road might be paved with steps. Clera took the next desk along, flashing a grin towards her. Fishing in her habit, she pulled out a tightly rolled scroll of parchment, a slate, a piece of chalk, a small and stoppered pot, and a quill. This latter gave the impression that the bird from which it was taken had died of some wasting disease, falling from its perch into a dirty puddle before being run over by several carts and finally thoroughly chewed by a hungry cat.

The novices at the other desks already had their scrolls unrolled before them, some dipping their quills into inkpots. Arabella's quill caught the light, becoming something ethereal. A perfect swan's feather, pristine and glistening.

'We will continue with the eighteenth part of the catechism. Later I will be examining you on the names of the saints, the dates of their name-days, and the services and traditions particular to each— New girl! Get your parchment and quill out! Or do you not consider my remarks worthy of record?'

'No…' Laughter on all sides, Arabella's a musical peal. 'I mean yes, Sister Wheel.'

'Sister Wheel? There's no Sister Wheel in *this* class, girl. You will address me as Mistress Spirit. Now get your scroll out!'

'But— I don't…' Nona patted her habit as if the items she required might somehow have been stowed in one of the interior pockets without her knowledge.

'Quickly!' Sister Wheel slapped an iron hand on Jula's desk in the front row and began to advance on Nona, weaving her path between the desks, the girls head-down as she passed.

Nona felt a familiar anger starting to boil deep down where her thinking never ventured. Even if she had been given such things as quill and parchment she had never held either in her life and could no more make the required marks with one upon the other than she could fly.

'Well?' Sister Wheel, now looming above Nona, her pale and watery eyes meeting Nona's stare.

Nona stood up, sharply.

'Novice Nona's entry to the convent was … non-standard.' Abbess Glass had entered without being noticed and now settled a hand on Nona's shoulder, returning her to her seat. 'This precluded the usual correspondence regarding the supplies an entrant is expected to bring with them, Mistress Spirit.' The abbess laid a grey-plumed quill and fat scroll of parchment on the desk. 'Nona will, however, be a listening pupil rather than a writing one until such time as Sister Kettle pronounces her sufficiently advanced in her extra-curricular studies. She will—'

Sister Wheel's pale face reddened. 'I know *exactly* what kinds of extra-curricular activity Sister Kettle gets up to, and with whom, and I—'

'Sister Kettle will improve Nona's reading and writing to

the standard required in Red Class.' The abbess fixed Sister Wheel with a stare. 'The matter is now closed.'

Sister Wheel scowled and stumped off towards the head of the class.

Abbess Glass rolled out the top portion of Nona's scroll and produced an inkpot to hold it in place. She dipped the quill and in what seemed one flowing motion left a beautiful confusion of lines upon the parchment, black and glistening, coiling like a vine. 'Your name,' she said. She dipped again, and beneath it placed three very different lines, interlocked squiggles, careless where the name had been precise. The abbess produced a blotter and patted the design. 'And there is you.'

Nona stared at the pattern, furrowing her brow.

'And since I am here,' the abbess continued, 'I shall address the novices.' She followed Sister Wheel, smiling at the girls to either side. 'Some here may not yet have heard my welcome to the faith – certainly Arabella and Nona will not have – and it will do no harm to refresh those that have.'

Nona reached out a finger to trace the lines of her name, and as she did so the larger pattern beneath her name suddenly made sense … her face, caught in three black squiggles. A face that had last stared at her from a mirror on Raymel Tacsis's wall. She blinked and stifled a laugh, wondering how she could ever not have seen what the lines meant. Perhaps writing would reveal its meaning to her in the same manner one day.

Abbess Glass reached the front and shooed Sister Wheel aside to take centre stage. 'Sister Wheel teaches the important details of our veneration of the Ancestor. The mechanics of the thing, if you like. The *hows* and the *whens*. She does it well and we thank her for it. It falls to me though to remind us all of the *whys*.

'Nona, for example, was a follower of the Hope before she came to us, and whilst the Hope is a sanctioned heresy that falls within the framework of the Ancestor we— Yes, Nona?'

Nona had raised her hand like the bigs did when they wanted to ask a question in Nana Even's seven-day class in the village. Few of them ever did actually ask because the answer was generally: *because I say so*. 'My mother went to the Hope church in White Lake but I never said the words. One star is white and the others red … why should I kneel to it?' That's what her father had said. 'In my village they pray to the gods who are many and have no names.' The novices tittered as if this were funnier than their dome and golden statue.

Abbess Glass pursed her lips. 'Such practices are unusual in Verity, Nona. In the wild lands to the east and across the border into Scithrowl there are remnants of many faiths and the emperor is tolerant of them, at a distance, but the Ancestor—'

'My father hunted on the ice and even in the tunnels that go beneath.' Nona remembered almost nothing of her father save the stories he told. None of those tales had stuck with her quite so strongly as the ones that told of the tunnels. River-carved, they ran beneath the ice, drained when the waters found some better path or froze at source. In those stories her father and his clan had hunted beasts from every tale she'd ever heard. But the best of his stories told of the Missing, those who were not men and who lived on Abeth before the four tribes descended from the stars. No man had ever set eyes upon the Missing but their servants remained, a remnant now, haunting the dark places beneath the ice where sites holy to the Missing lay exposed once more. Such ruins could be found here and there where the tunnels ventured across the cities that the Missing had carved deep into the very rock itself. 'My father said that the Ancestor might watch over us in the Corridor but in the dark places of this world it's the gods that the Missing left behind who matter.'

There was no laughter at this, only the silence of held breath, waiting for the hammer to fall.

Abbess Glass pursed her lips as if she had tasted something particularly sour. She studied Nona a moment, raising one hand towards Sister Wheel as the nun seemed about to get her first word out around her outrage. The abbess relaxed her face into a smile.

'The emperor has forbidden worship of false idols, Nona. Much of our own history – ten thousand years and more of it – lies buried beneath the ice. A record of triumphs, follies, and a slow defeat beneath a dying sun. There are enough heresies and heathen gods of our own devising without pursuing the mysteries of creatures less like you and me than a dog is like a fish.'

The same anger that had boiled out of some red place within Nona when Raymel hurt Saida began to bubble through her again. She stood up so fast that her chair would have fallen but for Clera's quick hands. 'My father—' The words, hard and angular, stuck in her throat. She bit down on them – anger had lost Nona her place in the village, then the Caltess…

'I am here to address the *why*.' Abbess Glass continued smoothly as if a small girl weren't standing in defiance before her, fists balled at her sides. 'We venerate the Ancestor because in doing so we connect with what is holy in the human spirit, what is holy in us—'

'You're not holy!' Nona couldn't stop the words. Warm beds and good food were too great a treasure to be sacrificed, but with them came knives in the dark and laughter behind hands and this woman calling herself holy. 'You watched Saida die! You watched her strangle and choke!'

'Sister Wheel!' The abbess raised her voice to a shout, drowning whatever the nun had to say. 'Bring me a wire-cane from the Blade stores.'

A sharp intake of breath sounded all around the room. Sister Wheel's face split with an uncustomary grin. 'Yes, Abbess Glass, yes indeed. A good choice. A fine choice for a beating.' And she hurried from the room, her speed surprising.

The abbess waited for the door to close. She pulled up one of the chairs from an unused desk and sat on it, presenting a slightly comical image, portly abbess perched on child's seat. 'I'm not holy? What *is* holy? Nona? Anyone?' Silence. Nona would have answered but found that she didn't know. 'I believe in the Ancestor – in the spirit of the Ancestor.'

'Believe? Like Sister Wheel believes?' Nona couldn't keep the venom from her words – when she looked at Wheel it seemed that something had been left out in the making of the woman. Nona felt the same way about herself most of the time – as if some part had been omitted in her construction, so wholly absent that she couldn't even say what it was, only that a void lay where it should be. 'I hate Sister Wheel.' It's harder to forgive someone else your own sins than those uniquely theirs. Much harder.

'You don't know Sister Wheel, Nona. You've only just met her.'

Nona scowled. 'I know plenty. I've seen plenty. More than you can see from up here in your nice warm convent, paid for by all the people working down there in the city and out in the Corridor growing your food from the mud. What good is holy if it can't feed and clothe itself? This is a place to turn children into old women, praying for the sins of the world and never seeing them.' Some of the words were her father's but she owned all the anger. 'What good is holy if it watches my friend die – not because she did something wrong but because her blood wasn't good enough?'

Around her the novices' faces had frozen into a range of expressions, from horror and shock on Jula and Ruli, to amazement on Clera, and on Arabella a smile that could mean anything. Nona wanted to take back what she said – even now she wanted to apologize and beg to stay … but she couldn't get the words past her locked jaw.

'You're right, Nona.' The abbess nodded to herself, her attention resting for the moment on her only ring, set with a large amethyst.

Nona blinked, she'd been tensing for the blow, or the condemnation.

'If we spent our whole lives here we would have little to offer the world and know little enough of the world to have context for our prayer…' Seeing Nona's frown she spoke more simply. 'We wouldn't understand what we're praying for. Without knowing the chaos and confusion that washes all around this plateau, our Rock of Faith, we could not appreciate the serenity we seek.' Abbess Glass paused and fixed Nona with dark eyes. It seemed important to her that Nona understand … that Nona believe. 'I wasn't always a nun. I had a son and I breathed for him. When we buried him my sorrow consumed me. Was my grief holy? Was it unique? All our hurts and follies are repeated time and again. Generation after generation live the same mistakes. But we're not like the fire, or the river, or the wind – we're not a single tune, its variations played out forever, a game of numbers until the world dies. There's a story written in us. Your parents – your father and his ice tunnels, your mother and her Church of Hope, both of them, whether they loved you or left you, are in you bone-deep, remembered in your blood. The hunska has risen to the surface in you, the quickness of some relative dead these past ten thousand years – you think your mother and father are less present?'

Nona found her teeth clenched too tight for reply. Anger over her mother seethed through her and her hands twitched for violence.

'There's a story written in us, added to with each conception – it remembers and it changes us – we move to something from something.' Abbess Glass held her two hands before her side by side, palms out, thumbs folded in, very close together so that the narrowest of gaps stood between the index finger of both. 'Life.' She raised one hand a fraction. 'Death.' She raised the other to match it. 'We spend all our years on the short journey across this gap. But look – the gap is narrow if you cross it, but follow it and it's long. As long as you like. You and I journey across the gap, but as a people we *follow* it. The Ancestor stands at both ends. The Ancestor watches us from before the flight – before the shiphearts first beat their rhythm. That is the Ancestor of singular form, the origin, the alpha. Along our journey we have become many and varied. The Ancestor watches us from the start *and* from the end, from beyond the death of stars, in the cold dark of beyond. That is the Ancestor of singular mind, the destination, the omega.

'The Ancestor is meaning in chaos, memory in time, and *that* is holy. The ritual that Sister Wheel teaches is part of that memory – our connection to it, and it is important, whatever you think about the person who delivers the message. But what I really care about is the knowing behind it. We are many parts of the one. We are the steps, the Ancestor is the journey.' She stood and reached for Nona's hand. 'Come on, we'd better go.'

Surprise loosened Nona's tongue. 'Why? Where?' She stepped back, suspicious.

'By now Sister Wheel will have found the Blade Hall locked, gone in search of Sister Tallow, found her in the sanatorium and recovered the key. Do you want to be here when she gets back with that wire-cane?' She reached the door and opened it, pulling Nona after her. 'Behave yourselves, girls. Mistress Spirit will be looking to use that cane and won't require much excuse.'

'Sister Wheel will calm down soon enough.' The abbess crossed the foyer to open the main doors. 'At least as calm as she gets. Though I won't pretend that she's not the sort to hold a grudge. She carries her passion for the faith in both hands, does Sister Wheel, and any disrespect to me, real or assumed, is to her an attack on that faith, Nona. Stay on her good side and pay attention: you need to know what she teaches.'

They approached the abbess's house, where her cat, Malkin, lay sleeping on the steps. Abbess Glass paused. 'You can always speak your mind to me, Nona, but it will go easier on you with Sister Wheel and others if you're seen to be punished for disrespect for the office I represent. Today you will spend an hour in contemplation at the sinkhole instead of joining your class for the evening meal.'

'Yes, abbess.' Nona had eaten a week's worth of food in two days: she could miss dinner and hardly notice it. She had known hunger before. True hunger.

A figure came running towards them across the ground between the dome and the forest of pillars. The abbess stared at the approaching nun. 'You need to learn what Mistress Spirit teaches. Once it is given over you can make it your own. You can order and prioritize the tenets of the faith to your own liking, as do we all. But first you need to know what they are…' She trailed off distractedly as the runner drew close, sleeves and skirts flapping, and came to a halt before them.

'Sister Flint?' Abbess Glass tilted her head.

The etiolated nun inclined her head, seemingly untroubled by her long sprint. 'Visitors approach, abbess. A judge of the high circuit and nine men-at-arms.'

'Curious.' The abbess pursed her lips. 'Not by the Seren Way, nor the Vinery Stair, or we would have had warning. Is Sister Oak still patrolling the Cart Way?'

Sister Flint nodded.

'Then our visitors have either flown here on the backs of eagles or taken a very long walk in order to come upon us unannounced…'

'Eagles?' Nona asked.

'A joke, dear.' The abbess frowned and looked up at Sister Flint. 'When will they arrive?'

'A few minutes.'

'Hmmm.' Abbess Glass lowered herself, with a little difficulty, to sit upon the steps of her official residence. 'Fetch my crozier, Nona, will you? Just behind the front door. It's open.'

Nona hurried up the steps and pushed through the panelled door into a dim hallway tiled in black and white. Her footsteps echoed in the vaulted space above her as she entered. A rack of five identical croziers stood against the wall a little way in, hefty staves bound with iron hoops, the top coiling like a shepherd's crook, the flat spiral covered in plates of very thinly beaten gold, each one embossed with scenes from the book of the Ancestor. She took the first, surprised at its weight, and hurried back to the abbess.

'Thank you.' Abbess Glass took the crozier and patted the step beside her. 'Sit.'

Nona sat, and Malkin stalked away. Sister Flint waited at the bottom of the steps, the wind wrapping her habit tight about her painful thinness.

Before too long they saw the visitors making their way through the pillars, ill at ease among the forest of stone. 'Did you know, Nona, that the stone from which those pillars are made can't be found anywhere in the Corridor? It's all beneath the ice now. Lost to us.'

Nona started to reply then let the words fall. Abbess Glass knew she knew nothing.

The approaching men wore long red cloaks and breastplates of burnished steel, their helms gleaming and ornate. They flanked a grey-haired man in a thick black robe riding an enormous horse, one built for endurance rather than speed. A second man, also in a black robe, but a thinner one, tossed by the wind, followed, leading a mule with laden saddlebags.

By now half a dozen nuns watched from the doorway of the Ancestor's dome, Sister Wheel among them, having paused on her return to Spirit class with wire-cane in hand.

The nine guardsmen arrayed themselves before Abbess Glass's steps and the old man dismounted from his giant horse. He held himself with a degree of confidence and dignity that would put Grey Stephen to shame. Nona wondered if he were a lord or some close relation to the emperor. A thick circlet of twisted gold strands held a white mane from his patrician's face. He regarded the abbess from beneath neatly trimmed eyebrows, channelling a slight air of distaste down either side of a prominent and angular nose.

'Those are quite the grandest city guardsmen I've ever seen,' Abbess Glass murmured. 'I smell money here, and lots of it.'

The younger man came forward clutching a heavy book bound in black leather. Nona had watched him tugging it from the mule's saddlebag.

'Judge Irvone Galamsis offers the Abbess of Sweet Mercy Convent his greetings and felicitations on this the birthday of Emperor Hedral Antsis, fourth of his name.'

Abbess Glass bent towards Nona, her voice low and carrying a smile. 'Almost every day is the birthday of some emperor or other if you dig deep enough.' With a grunt she got to her feet, using her crozier to lever herself up. 'Irvone, a delight to see you again. Will you be staying to dinner? The novices would be so excited! A judge visiting us, and not just some common sort but one third of the highest jury in the land!'

'I've come for the girl, abbess. I don't plan to stay long.'

'Girl? We have lots of those here, Irvone. I'm charged to look after them, body and soul.'

'The convicted murderer that you helped abscond from Harriton prison two days ago.'

'Convicted?' The abbess rubbed her chin. 'There was a trial? Or was a rope merely purchased for her?'

Judge Irvone snapped his fingers and the young man hefted up his book, opening it to a page marked with a silk ribbon. He read from it, his voice precisely measured. 'In the ruling of Judge Maker, esteemed of the high court: Within the sound of the palace bells a stateless person may be convicted by any prison official of more than three years' service on the evidence of five or more eyewitnesses of good standing. YoM 3417.'

The golden head of the abbess's staff made slow revolutions. 'Such a new cover for such an old book, judge. Year of the Moon 3417? Your law predates this convent. It predates most of Verity! And I doubt if it has been used in the time these buildings have stood here.'

'Even so, Warden James passed sentence upon the girl when she arrived at Harriton.' The judge looked towards the convent. 'If you would be so good as to have the child brought out – that would be preferable to a search of the premises.'

Nona realized with a start that none of the men knew that she was the one they were looking for.

'Of course.' The abbess nodded. 'Of course, I would be glad to help. But it seems to me that even in these modern times, and even with a law so old … would one not require someone to have been murdered in order to hang another person for murder? Or has poor Raymel gone to his accounting with the Ancestor?'

The judge waved a bored hand at his assistant who turned to another page marked with a length of silk. 'YoM 3702, Judge Arc Leensis rules that in cases of attempted murder the perpetrator may hang for murder if the original conviction were based upon the reasonable belief that the victim would die.'

'Thuran Tacsis must have paid out a considerable weight of gold to have your clerks scouring the law books with such diligence, Irvone.'

'What man would not want justice for his son?' The judge inclined his head, apparently solemn and thoughtful. Nona wondered if he had ever met Raymel Tacsis. 'Lord Tacsis is prepared to overlook your interference with the due execution of the law, Abbess Glass, and out of respect for the church I do not propose to press the case on behalf of the city. However, you would be well advised to place the murderer known as Nona Reeve into my custody without delay.'

Nona ground her teeth tight against the urge to spit. Partnis

Reeve had given her nothing she wanted to keep, his name least of all.

'I would never disobey the high court, Irvone.' Abbess Glass stopped turning her crozier. The judge snorted. Abbess Glass waited a moment then continued. 'But—'

'Ha!' The judge shook his head.

'But Nona is now a novice at the convent and as such any and all misdemeanours, past and present, fall under the jurisdiction of church law. As do mine. I'm sorry that you've had a wasted trip. You really should stay for dinner, the girls would be delighted—'

The big black book of laws hit the ground with a resounding thump. 'That's her, isn't it?' The young assistant advanced towards the steps, finger pointing at Nona. 'That's the little bitch who did it!'

'Lano…' The judge shook his head, more in resignation than anger. 'I told you you should not have come.'

Nona stared at him, seeing the man for the first time and finding something familiar in the narrow cast of his features, perhaps the pale fury in his eyes or the slant of his lips.

'He would have killed Saida!' The anger of that moment in the Caltess returned to Nona in an instant, as if it had never left. 'He deser—'

Lano Tacsis moved faster than anyone Nona had ever seen, a blur of dark robes, twisting past Sister Flint even as she reached for him with reflexes to shame a cave viper. Nona barely had time to throw up her hands in front of the fingers reaching to seize her by the throat. A moment later Lano was being hauled backward, a scream of anger choked off by Sister Flint's slim arm fastened about his neck.

'What?' Abbess Glass, locked into the moment of the attack, now found her voice, only realizing there had been an assault as the perpetrator was pulled away. 'Nona! Are you hurt?'

Nona stared up at the abbess's concern. 'No.'

'Your hands!'

Nona raised them, both dripping crimson. There was no pain.

'The bitch cut me! That little gutterling actually *cut* me!'

Lano, thrown back into the arms of the closest guardsmen, clutched one hand with the other, blood pulsing between his fingers. 'Arrest her!'

Other nuns now stood between the judge's men and the abbess, Sisters Kettle and Apple flanking Sister Flint along with two Nona didn't know.

'Lano Tacsis?' Abbess Glass took a step forward. 'Does your father know that you're here, young man?'

Lano snarled and took a step forward, but slowly enough to allow the guardsmen to hold him back.

'I see your time at the Tetragode has been well spent. Your disguise and turn of speed were both admirable.' The abbess looked to Judge Irvone, sighed, and returned her gaze to the young man before her. 'It seems that both of Thuran Tacsis's sons have yet to learn that beating little girls is not a pastime that can be pursued entirely without consequence… I do have a number of older girls here who would be happy to teach you that lesson if you care to make a challenge within the Blade Hall?'

'You don't scare me, Shella Yammal!' Lano spat the words, white-faced in fury, hectic patches of red around his eyes. 'Yes, I know your line and your family, old woman. My father could buy this rock from under your miserable collection of old hags and rejects.'

'What Lano means,' Judge Irvone raised his voice, a deep and impressive instrument full of gravitas and authority, 'is that we will return to Verity and pursue this matter through the appropriate channels.' He motioned to a guard to retrieve the dropped legal tome then used another man for support as he mounted his horse.

'High Priest Jacob dines at my father's table, you miserable sack of blubber!' Lano roared. The judge waved for the men holding him to start back towards the pillars. 'I'll sink you for this!' Lano let them drag him as he shouted. 'I'll have that girl roasted! I'll serve her to my brother on a dinner plate! The high priest will have you beaten from this place, old woman. You'll beg on the streets before I'm done!'

Now about twenty yards off, heels dragging, Lano Tacsis

shook off the men holding him and stalked to the front of their party to remonstrate with the judge. The nuns watched in silence. The harsh edges of Lano's outrage stretched back across the plateau even as the men reached the pillars.

'Well.' Abbess Glass sat down heavily on the steps once more. She didn't seem inclined to say more. Sister Apple turned towards her but the abbess waved her away. 'You heard the man – we can expect a visit from the high priest soon enough. A good time to clean the place up a bit and make sure everything is in order. I'll leave you in charge of that, Apple dear.'

Sister Apple pursed her lips, glanced at Nona's hands, then nodded and led the others away. Sister Wheel lingered, but a gesture with the crozier sent her hurrying after the others.

'So,' the abbess said, patting the step beside her. 'You have a knife?'

Nona nodded and took her place on the cold stone.

'Understandable, I suppose.' Abbess Glass kept her eyes on the distant pillars. 'But I must ask you to return it to the Blade stores.'

'Yes, abbess.' Nona looked down at her hands, conflicted. The abbess had done more to protect her than her own mother had: she might lose everything just for some peasant girl she barely knew. Nona hadn't told a lie, but even so it felt wrong to deceive her. 'I will.'

'Are you sure none of that blood is yours?' the abbess asked.

Nona flexed her hands, the fingers already sticking to each other. 'I'm sure.'

'Run along then. Put that knife back and we won't speak of it again. It's my duty and the duty of all your sisters here to protect you. You don't need a blade.'

'Yes, abbess.' Nona got quickly to her feet. 'I will.' She wanted to thank the abbess, but nothing she thought to say sounded right. And whatever had happened Abbess Glass had still watched Saida hang.

Nona ran off, the Corridor wind trying to steer her. She would put the knife into Blade Hall's stores straight away … but first she would run to the dormitories and retrieve it from her bed.

10

Nona came late to the dormitory, having slipped into the bathhouse on her way back from contemplation at the sink-hole to avoid Sister Wheel, only to have the woman hold an endless conversation right outside the door with some unknown party. Nona thought she heard her name mentioned but maddeningly the thickness of the door, the splashing of two or more older novices in the pool, and the soft but constant gurgling of the pipes kept the actual words just beyond hearing. At one point Wheel raised her voice enough for Nona to catch, 'Assassin!' and a moment later, 'Blood!' but after that only muttering.

Eventually Sister Wheel ran out of opinions, or at least time to deliver them in, and left, allowing Nona to escape. She stepped out from the steams and instantly discovered the misery of mixing a warm damp habit with a cold and invasive wind.

Rain started to splatter about her as she passed the laundry. Despite her haste to reach the dormitories Nona paused at the laundry side door. A nun held it open a hand's-width, having stopped to finish her conversation with someone further inside.

'...Ancestor! We don't want him here again.'

'...'

'You weren't even here back then to see it, girl. Abbess Shard hadn't the guts to keep him out. He'd have the novices over to Heart Hall for "special testing". And not just the older ones.'

'...'

'Just an archon. And if he was like that as an archon what do you think he's like as high priest? No wonder he hates Glass! They say—' The door shut again as the conversation drew the sister back into the laundry.

Nona waited a minute, then another, then moved on, as wet with the rain as if she'd swum from the bathhouse. On opening the door to the Red sleeping hall she found the class chatting in various groups around the beds, a few of the girls starting to undress but nobody in any particular hurry. Arabella's voice carried through the mix, though she was hidden by the three or four novices around her. '—could say those things to Sister Wheel!'

'And we got shaved just because she took your belt, Ara!'

Nona saw that Jula was one of those in Arabella's circle. It stung to see her there, but what she'd said was true. And the attention of a noble, an almost princess, must be very flattering to a scribe's daughter. Head down, Nona walked to her bed.

'Heard the law came looking for you.' Clera, lying on top of her blankets, put down her class scroll at Nona's approach. 'I hate those judges.' She set her penny spinning on the writing slate beside her, spattering the lamplight.

Nona offered up a weak smile and turned to her bed. Clera patted her own. 'You look half-drowned. Use this.' She tossed over a rough grey towel. 'What did you do, Nona? Did they come to arrest you for cheeking the abbess? Or for being a tunnel-worshipper?' She grinned, pushing aside her hair, and patted again. 'Come, tell Clera everything.'

Nona pulled her wet habit off, wiped her face, rubbed at her hair, then despite her mood sat where Clera indicated.

Clera leaned in close. 'A judge? A damned judge rode all the way up here to get you? What the hell did you do, Nona?' She took hold of Nona's arm. 'And how are you still here? I don't want them to take you away!'

Nona sighed. Sooner or later the whole convent would know about Raymel Tacsis. She was surprised the story wasn't circulating among the novices already. Sooner or later. She would rather it was later though…'You're my friend?' she asked.

'I am.' The grip on her arm strengthened.

'I lied.' Nona looked up. Ruli was sat on the next bed now, nightcap in place, one pale strand of hair escaping. 'I wasn't taken from the village by raiders…'

Clera and Ruli shuffled closer, saying nothing, and Nona started her story anew.

'A juggler once came to my village. He was my first friend—' Nona backtracked. 'In my whole life I'd had one friend. It's a hard thing to live in as a stranger in a small village. There's nowhere to hide, nowhere you're not known. I used to think there was something wrong with me to make the other children turn me away. Something more than being dark… I've never understood people – not truly – not how to be at ease with them and make them be at ease with me. Sometimes I feel as though I'm playing a part, like those mummers who travel the roads, only I don't know the words properly, or how I'm supposed to act.

'I had one friend. I don't know if he was a proper friend, but he said he was, and nobody had told me that before, so it was something special.'

'The juggler? How old was he?' Clera asked, leaning in with Ruli. Jula sat nearby now, watching, her expression unreadable.

'Twenty-two,' Nona said, remembering Amondo's face, light and shadow in the brilliance of the focus moon.

'Twenty-two!' Clera gasped and exchanged glances with Ruli. 'That's a grown man.'

'What was he called?' Jula from the next bed.

'Amondo. He only stayed three days. He said he had to keep travelling to find new people who would pay to see his show. But on the morning that she found him gone my mother was very angry. I hadn't seen her like that before, at least not so bad, throwing around her baskets and cursing him. Then she saw me standing in the corner, trying to be out of the way, and she said it was my fault, all of it was my fault, and that I'd driven Amondo away and that she hated me.'

'Did he *touch* you?' Clera demanded.

'Yes.' Nona frowned. It seemed like a stupid question.

Ruli drew in a sharp breath.

'I mean … in a *bad* way?' Clera said.

'He didn't hit me…' Nona's frown deepened. 'He showed me how to juggle.' She pursed her lips and shrugged. 'And when he left I went after him. I told myself I was going to get him to come back so my mother wouldn't be so angry with me. She was cross most of the time, as though something was wrong with everything. I don't remember her laughing. Ever. But I thought if Amondo came back that might change and we could be happy. I told myself I was going to get him to come back – but really part of me hoped he would ask me to come with him, and another part of me knew I would say yes.

'My father told me stories and they were different from the ones Grey Stephen would tell the village on fire-nights. They were different because I *knew* he had been to the places he was describing, and they made me want to go too. Da's stories made me feel that the world went on so much further than I could see, and that the Corridor was a road that could take me anywhere. I could reach the Marn Sea and sail on a fishing boat, or dig emeralds from the ground in Tecras, or hunt whiters on the ice, or explore the tunnels and discover the Missing. Anything.

'Old Mother Sible saw Amondo leave along the Rellam trail. She told him the forest was a haunted place but he just laughed and said everywhere had its ghosts.'

Nona fell into her own story as she had before, not hearing the words as she spoke them, only seeing events play out before the eye of her mind.

Mother Sible called after me to stop. 'You won't catch him 'fore he gets to the woods.'

I kept running, foot-wrappings soaked and muddy, flapping as I dodged the wheel ruts.

'You won't catch him…' The old woman's voice lost itself in the distance.

I'd been as far as the Rellam Forest before. I'd gathered sticks in the margins, hunted for hedgehogs among the dry leaves, peered into the dark spaces between the boles of the trees, looking for the faerie lights that folk in the village spoke about. Seen nothing, found nothing, except for sticks, and back at the hut they'd burned the same as any others. I'd been to the Rellam Forest before – but not as the sun was falling. And I'd never ventured in.

Still, Amondo and I both stood on the same road. We both stood beneath the same clouds, hung with sun-bright edges and rain-dark hearts – rain comes from a dark heart. I would catch up with him before it fell.

Amondo had more than an hour's head start on me and Mother Sible proved right in her prediction. I found myself panting, sore-footed and sweaty, the trail now just a band of beaten green, winding its way into the first trees as if it too had heard the woods' reputation and was trying to delay entering.

Everywhere has its ghosts, Amondo had said, but in most places those ghosts are at least hidden in the corners, or tucked away at right angles to the world, waiting their moment. In the Rellam Forest you could see the ghosts, patterned on the gloom beneath the canopy, the distortion of their faces frozen into the bark of ancient trunks. And you could hear them too, screaming into the silence, not quite breaking it but making it tremble.

I was scared. More scared than I'd ever been of the bigs who chased me, or of Black Will's hound that took Jenna's fingers the year before. What made me follow that trail with the sun falling, and the cold wind speaking through the branches, was a larger fear, one that had been with me ever since I had words to put around it: the fear that I wouldn't ever leave that village, that I would stay and grow old and bent and be put in the ground there, wasting all the years of my life as an outsider, inside.

I got a few miles along the trail before the gloom thickened past the point that I could find my way. Hungry and cold, I crouched with my back to an old tree and waited. A light rain started to fall, the sort that's half ice and hits the leaves with a splat, gathering in wet clumps before it drops to ground.

When you're moving in a dark and haunted forest the urge is for every step to be taken more quickly than the last. There's a pressure between your shoulder blades. Each creak and groan is a hunter stalking you, each flutter of wind its breath, close against your neck. You want to break and run, in any direction, just so long as it's fast.

When you're still the urge is to be stiller. The knowledge that eyes are turned your way quietens the air inside your lungs. You make yourself small. You hold every muscle tight. And you listen. Above all you listen to the woods as they close about you.

I stayed there, cramped and shivering and terrified, until the moon's focus found me. The light filtered down, slow at first, making the impenetrable gloom penetrable once more, recreating the forest around me, resolving monstrosities into chance alignment of unconnected branches. Within minutes I could see the trail. I started to run. For all that time walking the path I had wanted to break and run, but that way lies madness: you don't run from terror, not if you ever want to stop again. Now though, with the red light shafting down all around me to dapple the ground in bright patches, I ran.

Soon the focus reached its height, boiling through the clouds. The leaves began to steam, the icy rain now a warm fog. I ran, and I ran, and I ran, and I saw him.

'Amondo!' Just a darker blur in the fog but I cried out and raced towards him.

The man who turned and caught my arm was taller than Amondo, tall as any man in the village, all hard muscle, dirt, and the stink of old sweat. A beard tangled to the base of his neck.

'Take her!' He passed me to another behind him and drew his sword. Even in the fog the focus moon found dull glints among the iron plates on his leather shirt. 'How many more of you?' he asked.

There were four or five of the men. They all had the same

iron-plated leathers, the same dark and heavy capes, red under the grime, rich cloth, the colours of some army perhaps. Some had helms, the guards around their eyes lending a strange owlish cast to their faces. Strong hands seized me, hard and pinching.

'Amondo, she said?' The tall man turned slowly in the steaming mist, sword before him. 'I told you that weasel would be around here somewhere.' He made something thin and high-pitched of his voice. 'Amondo! Amondo! Help me, Amondo!'

One of the men holding me chuckled into his hand.

'Make her sing,' the tall man hissed. 'That'll bring him if he's close.'

One of them twisted my arm behind me. I ground my teeth together and grunted. He tugged it harder and the pain lanced through me. It's easy enough to make a body hurt past the point of any resolve. Within a few more seconds I was screaming and screaming was all I knew about. I don't know how long it took. It seemed like half a lifetime. It stopped suddenly. The man doing the twisting let go and sat down, clutching his neck. The focus had nearly passed, the mists glowed crimson with the last of the light.

'What are you playing at?' The man holding my other arm.

Blood, dark as wine, leaked between the fingers his friend had clasped around his throat.

'He's here!' My captor drew his sword, still holding me. 'He's—' The handle of a knife appeared under his chin, blade hidden in his neck.

'Get among the trees!' The tall man barked the order and followed it in the same moment.

The man holding me released my arm and wrenched the knife from his neck, as if that might save him. He stood for three or four heartbeats, blood spraying from the wound, warm, the salt of it on my lips, then sank to his knees, using his sword as support. He didn't look angry, or scared, just disbelieving, eyes staring into the mist.

'Run, Nona!' Amondo's shout.

I saw a dark shape moving among the trees, cries, curses, the light dying moment by moment. A scream. A wet thunk.

Low branches snapping. My legs wouldn't take me anywhere. I had nowhere to go.

Darkness. No noise but the creak and moan of the Rellam once more, as if it had just bitten its tongue, waiting for the light to move on. I held my breath, and somewhere in the distance, just audible above the night sounds, the broken stumble of someone limping away, or dragging themselves through the undergrowth.

I stayed there, small and silent in the restless dark, waiting for the ghosts of the dead to leave their flesh and find me like they did in all the stories. But in the end the dawn made its way among the trees and with it James Baker and Willum Streams. They weren't searching for me, they were thinking to catch up with Amondo – Baker's hoard of coin went missing the day the juggler left. They were lucky only to find me, all bloody and surrounded by corpses.

Nona drew a deep breath and looked up. 'The rest is as I told you before. They called me a witch, and a thief, and gave me to the child-taker.'

'Only your mother wasn't dead,' said Clera, almost a whisper.

'No.'

'She let them do it,' said Ruli, without surprise as if perhaps her mother had done the same, albeit wrapped in different circumstances.

'She said I'd helped Amondo steal from the Bakers.' Nona bowed her head.

'And that's why the judge came…' Clera said. 'Because of the dead men. And the missing money. Were they soldiers? Or some local lord's men?'

'I don't know.' Nona got off the bed and went to her own, weighed down with memories and the lies she had told.

'How did Amondo throw his daggers?' Jula, still on the other bed, frowning. 'You said the mist was—'

'I'm going to sleep now.' Nona fell headlong onto her bed, and lay silent and unmoving until the lanterns were extinguished and the sounds of sleeping rose around her.

11

The focus woke Nona. Every crack in the shutters wrote itself red upon the dormitory walls, snaking over the novices in their beds, describing each in as few lines as Abbess Glass had used to capture Nona's face. She watched the lines move with the moon's passage, flowing over the sleeping forms about her. The building creaked and groaned as the heat penetrated. Somewhere, far away, the great walls that stepped up to the White would be weeping, shedding rotten ice, losing the slow gains they had made during the day. That battle ebbed and flowed of course. For a century the Grey and all its towns and villages had been swallowed by an advance before the focus finally wore the ice back. Even now the topsoil lay thin, poor stuff that only the desperate would farm and the wild hunt upon. The glaciers had pushed the good black earth of millennia thirty miles into the Corridor and made the Hernon territories the garden lands of empire.

Nona lay back and thought of her village, the people scraping their living from the shallow ground. Even after just a few months it was hard to imagine it – hard to imagine that their world rolled on without her.

'Nona.'

Nona sat up. Looked around.

'Nona.'

Nothing. Nobody.

'Nona.'

For a moment the moon's light, caught in bright lines upon the floor, seemed to align into a single thread, leading from the room. Nona slipped from her bed, barefoot on the cold stone. She wrapped a blanket around herself and followed, with the hall whispering all about her and her sisters sleeping.

'You came!' Hessa sat on the steps of the scriptorium across the square from the dormitory block, wrapped like Nona in a thin convent blanket. The heat from the focus moon made the puddles steam and set Nona sweating beneath her cover.

Nona looked up. The line she had been following was gone. She wasn't sure now that there had ever been one. 'Why are you up?'

'I don't sleep well.' Hessa patted her bad leg. 'Not since the cage.' She frowned. 'Not since ever.'

Nona sat beside her on the steps. 'It's a strange place, this convent.'

'Yes.'

'I don't trust them.'

Hessa shrugged. 'I like most of the nuns.'

'I don't trust the Ancestor either,' Nona said. 'But I'm not running away. Not yet, anyhow.'

'The faith is one thing, the church and its people are another.' Hessa shifted her leg and leaned back to bathe in the moonlight. 'You can believe in the Ancestor, or not. But the church is just people, some good, some bad.'

They sat in silence for a long minute, then another, the focus reaching its peak and starting to slide.

'I had a bad dream,' Hessa said.

Nona looked around at her.

'About Markus.'

'Markus?' Nona hadn't thought of the boy since she cut down Raymel Tacsis. 'Where did Giljohn sell him? Did he have to throw Four-Foot into the bargain?' She smiled, remembering Markus's bond with the child-taker's mule.

'I had a bad dream,' Hessa repeated herself, staring over the rooftops, a tremble in her voice, 'but the real thing was worse.' She turned to Nona. 'I can show you, I think. Sister

Pan said I had a gift for stories, for the path they take. And memory is its own story with its own path…'

'Show me.'

Hessa reached out her hand, cupped and ready, her eyes on Nona's. And Nona, having nothing else to give, placed her own there. Hessa turned Nona's hand palm up. 'I've only tried this with Sister Pan. You might get a sort of fuzzy idea, or nothing. Nothing is probably better…' She set her index finger so that the edge of her nail bit against the base of Nona's palm. 'I might have to do this several times.' She started to trace a line across Nona's palm, scoring hard enough to make her want to fold her hand up.

'What—' Hessa's story swallowed Nona's voice first, then took the rest of her.

The Academy purchased Willum and Chara. Like the Caltess it kept a reserve of young potential, but while Partnis Reeve stored his children among the sacks and boxes in his attic the Academy had a school for the purpose, a sprawling range of buildings that looked to Hessa more like a fairy castle than a place to teach ragged peasants plucked from Giljohn's cage.

Four-Foot's hooves clattered on the cobbles as he brought them in under a great sandstone arch, every inch of it carved with sigils, some that seemed to fold the world around them, and others that made her smile, laughter bubbling up from places Hessa had forgotten even before the journey. A strange energy suffused the air, tingling on Hessa's skin, pricking along her cheeks, singing in the marrow of her bones.

'You're as close now to the emperor's palace as you're ever likely to get.' Giljohn seemed nervous – worry looked as out of place on him as kindness or sentimentality might. 'Closer than most ever get. The Academy Hall lies behind this school, and it practically backs against the Ark.' He brought Four-Foot to a halt before a complex of buildings, under the watchful eyes of stewards in spotless black uniforms. 'Get out.' Giljohn ushered them from the cage. 'Quick about it!' He aimed a half-hearted swipe at Markus. 'And try to look valuable, damn you!'

They had been examined, all four of them, Markus and Hessa too, in a hall as grand as any church. Each of them in turn, inspected across the width of a polished ebony table. Hessa sat in the uncomfortable chair that Giljohn had carried her to, on a cloth that the Academic's assistant had laid atop smooth wood. The assistant had wrinkled his nose as he retreated.

In this place Hessa supposed even Giljohn looked like a beggar. He stood ill at ease among the gleaming marble columns, watching as Markus took his turn at the table.

The Academic sat in a high-backed chair, itself a work of turned pillars and ornate turrets, her fingers steepled before her, thin arms emerging from sleeves of lustrous purple fabric embroidered with the same sigil repeated time and again. Her neck seemed too long and thin to support her head, and all across one side of it a stain spread, a dull scarlet thickening of skin, like a hand reaching up to choke her.

She spoke to each of them at length, looking down from her elevation with coldly curious eyes. Hessa came away confused and drained, as if each answer had taken something from her.

When it came to the sale Giljohn had none of the banter that he'd shared with Partnis. Rather he spoke more like a stall-keep at a peasant market faced with some high lady wandering through for a moment's diversion. He stated his price and the Academic either paid or enquired after the next child. For Chara and Willum she handed over twelve crowns apiece, more for each of them than Partnis had given for all eight that he took.

'The dark boy, he's likely to show some marjal blood, but his aura is too wild for Academy work. He'll end up a hedge-mage or turn native. If that happens, better he end up a forestling than take to the tunnels, mark me.' The Academic turned away, down the long gallery of pillars, and Giljohn pushed her purchases after her, his hands to their shoulders. 'And the girl?'

'Nothing. Perhaps she sees the Path … perhaps some-one taught her what to say so that she might get fed. Take her to the sisters, or Caiphus, if he'll see you. Or one of the rogues. I don't really care – the Path is not Academy business.'

After the Academy Giljohn drove his cart along the smaller streets, muttering to himself. The tenements had a sour smell and tall chimneys behind the houses pumped out a dark, almost green, smoke that even the wind didn't seem to want.

'Damned if I'm taking you to the witch, girl!' Giljohn raised his voice without warning, turning in his seat. 'I don't like the way she looks at me. 'Sides, it's a steep haul to the convent and the mule ain't up to it.'

Hessa shrank back into the far corner of the cage, raising her hands. Witch, mage, Academic, it made no difference to her – they all sounded terrifying.

'I'll take the boy to church first. The priest knows his business. Not a judger, that one.' Giljohn shook the reins and Four-Foot picked up the pace. The sky lay sullen overhead, the air heavy with the kind of heat that makes a body sweat.

They passed through the dour streets of the eastside and came by rising and tree-lined avenues to a more opulent quarter where, over a sea of tiled roofs, the spires of some great cathedral challenged the sky. Hessa felt as uncomfortable passing by the good-folk of Verity as she had beneath the Academic's scrutiny.

'They don't look like they're real people…' Markus whispered beside her.

Hessa nodded. All of them, whether old or young, whatever their shade or blood, seemed a different breed, glowingly clean, full-fleshed, their clothes both strange and costly. Hessa had seen the major of Morltown once, back in the Grey, as he passed by on his horse. Here even he would look shabby, his colours dull.

Giljohn drew up beneath a large tree and jumped out into the road. 'Covering you up. Stay hid.' He pulled out the hides he hung when the rains came and pushed them through the bars. Hessa and Markus hunched down beneath them.

They rattled along in stifling darkness for a while with only the change from cobbles to paved road and back again to mark their passage.

'I didn't like that woman,' Markus said.

'The Academic? She was … strange.'

'My great-nan was a hedge-witch. She said that the marjal who work with the land don't twist like the rest. That's why they hate us.'

'Twist?' Hessa lifted the edge of the hide for enough light to see Markus's face.

'Twist.' He put a hand to his neck where the woman had borne a livid mark. 'The marjal tribe learned the deepest secrets of their world, tasted its blood, knew it down to the bedrock and beyond – it let them work it with their minds, draw on its strength, understand its beasts and draw its fire. But this isn't that world, it belongs to someone else. You take too much here and Abeth takes back. This place still belongs to the Missing.'

Giljohn drew up again. 'Wait here.'

An age later, or perhaps a couple of minutes, Giljohn returned and drove the cart around a corner into some echoing space. He halted and pulled the hides clear, leaving Hessa blind in the daylight.

First she saw that they were in a high-walled garden on the gravel between house and grounds. Next that the house was as grand as any she had yet seen, the windows beneath huge sandstone lintels boasting sheets of glass bigger than her head, held within a criss-crossing of wooden frames.

'Priest'll be out in a minute,' Giljohn said. 'Show him what he's looking for, boy. He's not a man you want to disappoint.'

Hessa shuffled along to sit on the tailgate while Markus clambered out and went to stand beside Giljohn up by Four-Foot. The garden walls seemed to hold back what little wind the day had to offer, the air hanging close and wet around them.

'He's a priest?' Markus asked.

'Of the Ancestor, so mind your heathen mouth.'

'I'm not a heathen—'

The main door to the house opened, a tall and exquisitely dressed man stepping through. He took in the cart and three travellers with a disapproving eye, as if mere proximity might sully the dark blue of his velvets. A moment later the priest walked out, a broad-chested guardsman behind him. Hessa stared, lips parted. The servant had been more richly dressed than anyone she had ever seen, but the priest wore a robe of dark material that seemed to glisten even as it ate the light, so thick and so folded that stretched out it might cover the cage that for months had been her home. Gold chains gleamed on both his wrists, an amethyst the size of a hen's egg hung from the rope of woven gold about his neck, and in his right hand he held a sick-wood staff, the end stamped with the alpha and omega of the Ancestor, each letter inlaid in silver.

'Giljohn. I hope your arrival was unremarked. What do you have for me?' The priest spoke with casual authority, making no effort to hide his distaste.

'The boy, your worship. Marjal true-blood. Thought of you straight away. He's the sort you send to that monastery on the coast. More than a touch in him, make a fine Mystic Brother this one would.' On the road Giljohn had ruled them with an iron hand and dealt with the farmers of the Grey as if he were a lord dispensing favours. But here, with the stone house rising before him and formal gardens to his back, he seemed a peasant himself, servile and ill at ease.

'I've had seven boys off you, Giljohn. Abbot Tae reports that only two showed any touch of marjal, and one of those was half-wild.' He descended the steps, staring at Markus. 'The wild ones have to be broken early if they're to be kept. Break them properly and their minds *can* be retrained to more useful ends. But it's a lot of effort.'

'Strong signs with this one, your worship, strong signs. Half-blood at the least! Clever too. Could take to sigil-work double quick.' Giljohn nodded.

The priest, though short beside his guard and Giljohn, loomed over Markus. He looked an old man, his hair grey, face craggy, but his eyes were sharp, slicing across Hessa, discarding her. His arm when he reached for the boy was snake-fast. 'Sigil worker?' His hand fastened about Markus's wrist. 'Or wild boy?' A sharp jerk brought Markus staggering forward with a cry.

Fast as the priest was Four-Foot moved faster, leaning in to bite the fingers clutching Markus's wrist. The priest released him with an oath, and Four-Foot set to braying loud enough to bring maids to the upper windows to stare.

Giljohn, all apologies, stepped in to check the hand the priest held cradled to his mouth but the guardsman sent him reeling back with a straight arm to the chest.

'Never seen that mule bite anyone before, your worship, Ancestor's truth!' Giljohn looped an arm about Markus's neck and pulled him back behind him. 'It's the marjal in the boy – like you said, your worship. Wild. But emfy can work on people too, if it's trained right. That kind of influence can be gold in your pocket.'

'It's empathy, you idiot, not emfy.' The priest lowered his hands, one clutching the other, red-fingered. He had blood on his mouth too, and an ugly look beneath it. 'And there are a hundred touched whispering to beasts for each prime that can turn a man's mind. And ten primes for each full-blood that can own it… But I will take the boy. And the mule.'

'Ah. Well the lad's twenty crowns, your worship. Like a son to me … he is. But Four-Foot, he's not for sale. Been with the old fellow twelve years now.'

'You'll take ten for the boy and a crown for the mule. You'll get a young one for pennies at the Brown Fair. My gardener and his son will help you push your cart there.' The guardsman stepped in close behind the priest's shoulder.

Giljohn swallowed, still holding Markus behind his back. 'Ten. Ten I can take, from a man of the cloth. A sign of my devotion to the Ancestor. But Four-Foot—'

'You'll sell me that mule, Giljohn, or you'll never sell anything in this city again. A word in Captain Herstin's ear and the guard won't even let you past the city gates. So, enough with this foolishness. A crown for a vicious mule that's a season from being rendered for glue and hound meat.' The priest waved to his servant. 'Pay the man.'

'Don't do it!' Markus broke free of Giljohn and ran to Four-Foot, taking the mule's head over his shoulder. 'He wants to hurt him.'

The adults paid no attention. The servant produced a worn leather pouch from within his velvets and brought forth the first crown to count into Giljohn's palm. The child-taker held out his hand reluctantly, face twitching with warring emotions.

'Don't!' Markus shouted, eyes wild. 'It was my fault, not Four-Foot's!'

The servant laid the crown on Giljohn's creased and dirty palm: a silver coin, polished with use, traces of tarnish in the grooves picking out the emperor's features. He counted out the rest, each chinking against the next. At ten Giljohn closed his hand.

'See... Four-Foot is family—'

'The animal bit me.' The priest held his hand up, sticky trickles of blood reaching down as far as his wrist. 'Accept your coin, child-taker. Or are you so wealthy that you'll sacrifice your livelihood over an elderly mule?'

The servant pushed the last coin into Giljohn's half-open hand. The rain that had threatened for so long began to fall.

'Tie the beast up over there. Use a heavy rope.' The priest gestured to the pillars holding the roof above his rear door.

Giljohn took Four-Foot's halter in his hand, ignoring Markus's cries. 'Sorry, lad,' he muttered as he took the mule. Four-Foot let himself be led, but whinnied his distress, rolling a dark, liquid eye at Hessa. She clutched herself tight, not wanting to see but unable to look away.

Giljohn left Four-Foot tied to the nearest pillar with the thick tow-rope used to get the cart, and sometimes other travellers, out of deep mud. He returned to the cart looking a poorer man despite the additional silver in his pocket.

The gardener and his boy came to roll the cart back out through the gates, but the priest didn't seem inclined to wait. 'You know, Giljohn, how to break someone? Of course you do – the Scithrowl had you a while did they not?'

Giljohn said nothing, just bent his back to the task of pushing, but before his shoulder set against the cart's edge his hand reached up to touch the empty socket of his left eye.

The rain thrummed down around them, dripping from Hessa's nose, running down the bars of the cage.

'You break a man, or a boy, most easily by breaking something that they love. Better still if it loves them too.' The priest's voice didn't turn them but the crack of wood against flesh and the startled bray did. He had his staff raised again as Hessa looked around, both hands at the end, swinging it over his shoulder.

'No!' Markus darted forward but the guardsman caught him by an arm.

The priest swung again with all his strength, bringing his staff down across Four-Foot's back. The mule, already straining, threw himself against the rope, braying his surprise and pain. The priest struck again, and again, and Four-Foot strained against the rope, eyes wild and staring. Markus was screaming, struggling to be free, but over the cracks of each blow and Four-Foot's loud distress Hessa couldn't understand the words.

'You don't—' Giljohn stood and raised his voice and his hand before letting both fall. Rainwater trickled from the socket of his eye in place of the tears that should have been there. 'You don't… Pulling's all he knows… He thinks you want…' Giljohn shook his head, lowering his face to hide his emotion.

'Stop him,' Hessa begged, but Giljohn, the thickset gardener, and his lean son, all looked away, each of them broken in some manner that Hessa, even with her useless leg, was not.

The staff made its own rain of blows, thick and heavy, the tempo regular, not frenzied. The priest, breathing hard, marked each blow with a word. 'You. Bit. Me. You. Filthy. Animal.'

Four-Foot, the fur across his back and sides dark with blood, threw his weight against the rope, anchored to the immovable pillar, not braying now but heaving desperate breaths through a muzzle thick with crimson-specked foam.

Giljohn and the gardener pushed the cart. The boy unbarred the gates. All of them needing to be away from there.

Hessa, in the cage and paralysed with grief, found she couldn't draw breath, couldn't move. Her chest hurt. Her face contorted into a grimace so fierce it hurt. The priest's cruelty had reached inside and twisted something vital, drawn it to breaking point, reducing her to snot and tears. Through half-blind eyes she watched Four-Foot strain, hard enough to burst his heart, uncomprehending beneath the blows, knowing only what his simple life had taught him: to pull.

With his own animal cry Markus got his teeth into the guardsman's knuckle. Rain-soaked, he was hard to hold onto. He twisted free while the man whipped his hand away, cursing. Markus ran, not for the priest but for Four-Foot, throwing his arms about the mule's neck, pressing his face to an ear. The priest's next blow hit Markus's hip, not with the same fury as those for Four-Foot, but loud and hard and agonizing. Even so, Markus hung in place.

Hessa didn't see it, she didn't hear it, it registered on none of her senses – but inside, in the core of her, she knew the moment that Markus found the edge of his power. Whether it was a word whispered into Four-Foot's ear, or something that bled between them from hand to hide, Hessa couldn't tell. What she saw was Four-Foot raise his head, unflinching as the next swing of the staff cracked more ribs. The mule snorted, the kind of snort he would give for a fresh meadow of long grass or a delicious bank of celembine, and pulled again…

The pillar shifted. The thick mass of stone, fifteen feet high and wider than a man, jolted forward. Amid the spilling rain terracotta tiles came flowing from the roof above, a waterfall in red. The priest went down beneath them. A heartbeat later the rope snapped and Four-Foot collapsed gently, his legs folding beneath him. Markus followed him down. The mule took one more shuddering breath. And died.

The scene narrowed. Narrowed again. The priest's gates closed behind the cart.

'No! No!' Hessa shouted but the hands kept hold as she struggled. 'No!' She opened her eyes. Hessa was leaning over her, the moonlight bright behind her. '*Hessa?*' And Nona knew herself again. 'I thought … I was you.' She reached up and they held each other as they had back in Giljohn's cage, weeping together as if tears might somehow wash away the pain.

12

'Tell us then.' Clera put down her fork and stared pointedly at Jula.

'What?' Jula crammed in another mouthful of bread. 'Wuff?'

'You know,' Ruli said.

'*Her* story.' Clera tilted her head ever so slightly towards the far end of the Red table. The four of them were huddled at one end, Arabella held court at the other, her group the larger.

'Ara says—'

'Ara? Who's Ara?' Clera's face hardened.

'Arabella,' Jula replied. 'Everybody calls her Ara. You know that.'

'Her *friends* do.'

Jula shrugged. 'She's okay. It's not her fault she was born so rich. Anyway, do you want to hear her story or don't you?'

Clera tapped at her plate. 'Go on.'

'Well…' Jula looked around, savouring the attention. 'Well… the priests have been going on about the Argatha for years, right? But over the last few months they've really been building up excitement, sending assessors out to the provinces, even to the wild towns along the border.'

'Argatha?' Nona hunched in, waiting to be told how stupid she was.

'It's an old prophecy,' Ruli said quickly. 'A Holy Witch called Sister Argatha made it, back when the first emperor took the Ark from the Sarmarians. It says that the Ark will open when the four tribes demand it with one voice.'

'Couldn't you just get a gerant, a hunska, a marjal and a quantal to do it?' asked Nona.

'Right! That's what I said.' Jula nodded. 'But they tried that ages ago and it didn't work. So ever since then the priests have been saying "one voice" means one person exhibiting all the bloods.'

'Everyone knows it's just theatre to take people's minds off the war that's coming,' Clera said. 'Every time there's a crisis, and the emperor wants to shut up dissent, all of a sudden there's a big hue and cry over searching for the Chosen One. That's what my father says…' She trailed off, staring at the table.

'So … the abbess thinks Arabella's going to show up as both the mage-bloods?' Nona asked.

'Pan seems pretty sure she's quantal, and more than a touch,' Jula said. 'A touch doesn't count. You could have a touch of all four and nobody would get excited. Sister Kettle's a hunska prime with a touch of marjal, and nobody's calling her the Argatha's Chosen One.'

'She is?' Nona asked. 'How do you know?'

'Kettle can shadow-weave. It's the easiest marjal trick and even touches can do it near the shipheart.'

'Does the abbess think Arabella will show up gerant too?' Nona frowned. Arabella was far from the tallest in the class. 'Unless she's six and nobody told me then she's not gerant.'

'She's close on eleven,' Jula said. 'But sometimes gerant doesn't show till you're grown and just don't stop growing… *Anyway*.' She pushed her hands together as if trying to steer the conversation back on track. 'Anyway, Ara's family saw how quick she was and because she didn't look hunska that got them worried. So her father took her to the Academy.'

'Stupid thing to do,' said Clera. 'Once the Academy knows, everybody knows. Too many fingers in that pie.'

'Your father say that too?' Ketti slid her chair noisily over to join them, wiping her mouth.

Clera turned on her, eyes fierce, and Ketti raised her hands.

'My father collects taxes. He says if the emperor wasn't standing behind him he'd be called a thief every day.'

'Anyway!' Jula raised her voice, then lowered it, glancing down the table at Arabella's group, deep in their own conversation. Only Hessa and Ghena sat alone at the middle of the table now, opposite each other, focused on their plates. 'The emperor called her whole family to court. So Malcan Jotsis, Arabella's uncle who's head of the family, gathers everyone at his estate out in Ledo and then leads them all to the palace, but on the way they're intercepted by Sherzal's house-troops, like a hundred of them … all the way from the Scithrowl border. And this was just days after the testing at the Academy!'

'What did they do?' Ruli asked.

'Nothing,' Ketti said, earning a scowl from Jula as she stole the story. 'Because the Jotsis had already sent Ara on in secret with four trusted men to meet with the abbess so she could join the convent.'

'Which,' said Jula, pushing both hands back across her bristly scalp, 'puts her out of the emperor's control and even his sisters aren't mad enough to try to steal a novice. And however much High Priest Jacob is pressed he can hardly give her up what with all the noise the priesthood have been making about the Argatha.'

'Exactly.' Clera stood up, brushing crumbs from her habit. 'None of them really expected to find a candidate, so they didn't have a plan for what to do if one turned up.'

Academia that morning saw Clera and Nona first through the door. Sister Rule waited behind her desk, massive even when seated, her headdress bulging as much as her habit as if it too had a lot to confine. The abbess's cat, Malkin, lay on the desk in an arthritic coil.

'Good morning, Mistress Academia,' they both chorused, taking seats at the front of the class.

Sister Rule watched them with dark eyes and said nothing. Behind them other novices began to file in. Nona's gaze was drawn again to the globe on the mistress's table, Abeth wrapped in ice with its thread-thin girdle of green. Nona had always considered the Corridor to be vast – endless really. It was hard to imagine how much space there had been before the ice advanced.

'Why…' So many questions twisted half-formed across her tongue that Nona didn't know what she would say before the words came. 'Why isn't the moon round too?'

Sister Rule's voice overrode the smirks from behind her. 'That, Nona, is an excellent question. Though you should say, why is the moon not also a sphere?'

'Sphere.' Nona rolled the word in her mouth.

'Why do you think the moon should be a sphere?' Sister Rule asked.

'Well…' Nona didn't really know – it just seemed right. 'Well… the world is. And in the sky Badon is round sometimes and a crescent other times … if you really squint at it. And at the Hope church they say that Badon is a whole world like ours, not a star like the Hope and that Badon isn't coming to save us like the Hope is because Badon is ice and more ice and locked to our sun just like we are…' Nona took a breath. 'So … I just thought that everything really, really big seems to be round…' She looked up at Sister Rule – who it had to be said was really big and, whilst not spherical, beginning to head that way.

Sister Rule only had to reach for her yardstick to silence the titters.

'You know that, with the blessing of the Ancestor, our forebears put the moon in the sky in the distant long ago, Nona?'

Nona nodded, she wasn't wholly ignorant, though she didn't know the name for the shape of the moon.

Sister Rule reached into her drawer and picked out something. She raised her hand and held it towards the class. 'The moon.' A silver circle-square in her palm. She turned it sideways and Nona saw with surprise that it was a dish, paper-thin. 'Watch!' Sister Rule held the 'moon' behind Abeth's globe, positioning it where the morning sun slanted down from the windows, filling it full of light. She tapped the globe and Nona saw a bright red spot, moving as Sister Rule moved her hand

and the 'moon' held in it. 'All the light it gathers is thrown down onto this one spot. The focus. Put your hand there, child.'

Nona stood and did as she was told. 'It's warm! Hot!'

'And that's how the moon keeps the Corridor open. The sunlight from a large area focused by a vast mirror into a small area. There's no reason for it to be circular.' Sister Rule put the mirror away. 'We stand between two huge walls of ice, Nona, and winter has been coming for fifty thousand years.' She held her hands as if they were the two walls and pressed them together with disturbing finality. 'Today though, we're talking about rocks!'

The girls groaned at that and got out their slates. Nona did her best to pay attention, but rocks proved less interesting than they sounded, and they hadn't sounded that interesting to being with. Time and again she found herself thinking of the moon that some distant ancestor of hers had set to hang above the world, and about how one thin and breakable mirror seemed to be all that stood between everyone she might ever know and the ice advancing from north and south.

After lunch Clera led Nona to the novices' cloisters, flipping her penny as she went.

'Why are you always playing with that?' Nona asked. It seemed that Clera, who thought herself poor now her family's fortune lay ruined, considered the penny a trivial sum, no more than a toy, but Nona had seen a child purchased from her parents for a single penny and to see one tossed about so lightly always gave her a sense of disquiet.

'My father gave it to me. Told me to learn how to turn one into many.' Clera shrugged. 'The Corridor is divided into a hundred lands, maybe a thousand, but you know what doesn't care about those borders or who rules there? Two things.' She counted them off on her fingers. 'The Corridor wind, and money. Traders move through it like blood in a body. No queen or emperor is stupid enough to try to stop them. That's why the rich spice their food with black-salt from the mines in Cremot. Nobody from Cremot has ever set foot in the empire, but the money flows and the trade flows.' Clera flicked her penny up and caught it. 'Money is at the centre of everything we do: it has the loudest voice.' She sounded as though she were quoting her father.

'But … you're training to be a nun. Nuns don't have money.' Nona wasn't even sure if Clera was allowed to own the penny. She certainly kept it hidden in classes.

'When I'm trained I'll leave.' She put the coin into a pocket. 'The kind of education we get here is highly sought after…'

'But—' Nona was going to ask who paid her confirmation fee – it must be a hefty sum to pay for board and keep along with an education that gave such valuable qualifications – but she bit down on the question, not wanting to find it pointing back at her. Instead she nodded. 'I'm going to do the same thing.' She thought of the priest who took Markus and beat Four-Foot to death. 'I don't want to be a nun.'

The novices' cloisters proved to be a galleried walkway around the internal courtyard of the building that served both as laundry and repair for nuns and novices alike. Fifty or so novices of all ages either walked slow circuits, chatting as they went, or sat on the long stone benches looking out through the arches onto the gravelled yard at the middle. At the middle of the yard a single huge tree, the centre oak, spread its branches, though quite what anchored it to the rock Nona couldn't guess.

'The nuns' cloisters are much grander,' Clera said. 'The sisters come out in the dead of night and lie in the centre waiting for the focus.'

'No they don't,' Nona said.

'Naked!' Clera nodded her head.

'Clera!' Ruli made a face.

'Well they didn't do it when I was sleeping in the cells,' Nona said.

'You were sleeping,' Clera said.

Nona tried to imagine Sister Wheel, Sister Rule, and the matronly Sister Sand moonbathing. 'I think you're the one who's dreaming, Clera.'

'We've got Shade next.' Jula came to join them, squeezing between Nona and Ruli. 'Have you told her yet?'

'Told who what?' Clera fell silent as Arabella walked past with several girls in tow. She always seemed to be laughing. Nona didn't think she would be laughing if she'd had to leave the luxury of life in a noble family for the convent and had assassins trying to kill her.

'About the Poisoner!' Jula said as soon as Arabella had passed.

Clera rolled her eyes. 'I hope nobody tells Arabella.'

Jula turned towards Nona, face earnest. 'Mistress Shade always poisons new girls.'

'What!'

'*Tries* to,' Clera said, as if it were nothing.

'Well I haven't seen her fail yet.' Jula pressed her lips into a thin line, remembering. 'She got you, Clera. And me. And Ruli.'

'I was sick for days.' Ruli mimed throwing up. 'I played up in Blade just to get my head shaved so I wouldn't get vomit in my hair.'

'So don't eat anything she gives you,' said Jula.

'Or let her touch you,' said Ruli.

'Best just let her do it. She'll get you anyway,' Clera said. 'It will be fun to watch at least.'

'Cle—'

'I meant funny to watch Arabella get done.' Clera spoke across Jula's objection.

'That's terrible.' Nona scowled. 'Doesn't the abbess know?'

'I think the abbess encourages her!' Clera gave a crooked grin. 'If being poisoned is the worst thing that happens to you in Mistress Shade's class then count yourself lucky. She's the meanest bit—'

'Clera!' Jula seemed to suffer coarse language as though the words were physical blows.

'Well she is! Nobody gives punishments like her. It's her sharp tongue that's the worst though. Never answer her back, Nona, she can take you apart with a sentence.'

Bray sounded, sonorous and lingering across the cloisters.

'Time to go.' Clera got to her feet in a hurry. She'd never looked properly worried about being late before.

'You could have warned me earlier.' Nona grabbed her shawl. 'About the poisoning.'

Clera shrugged. 'There's nothing you can do about it. Besides, it's not something anyone wants to talk about over lunch.' They joined the elbowing crowd struggling to leave through the main arch. 'She poisoned the soup for Grey Class once. Got all of them, just because none of them passed an exam.'

They got to Shade breathless. The lessons were held in the natural caves that riddled the thickness of the plateau. Mistress Academia had been explaining something about their formation in the previous class … rainwater dissolving paths through the rock, if Nona remembered right … it didn't sound right…

'We're not last!' Clera slapped Nona's arm. 'You never want to be last to this class.'

They came up short at the steps down into the caves, a narrow flight sealed with an iron gate just a few yards in. The steps lay behind Heart Hall and were so close to the plateau's edge that Nona wondered if the caves might not reach the cliffs and open out like hungry mouths.

A tall, slender novice with dead white skin and dark hair stood at the top step, marking off the girls' names on a slate as they arrived. She glanced Nona's way with blue eyes of an unnatural and alarming shade.

'That's Bhenta,' Clera whispered, 'from Holy Class. She's the Poisoner's assistant in the laboratories. Don't mess with her.'

A minute later Bhenta looked up from her slate and took a hefty iron key from a pocket inside her habit. 'All here, then. Novice Hessa, good to see you've graced us with your presence this time. Novice Jula, you appear to have had a close shave since our last lesson.'

'She tries to be snarky like the Poisoner,' Clera whispered. 'But she can't really do it.'

'Novice Clera, get your tongue out of that new girl's ear

and pay attention to the steps.' Bhenta clipped Clera around the head as they passed her.

The steps led steeply down, the limestone in places oozing and thick with slime. In some spots Nona thought that Bhenta, bringing up the rear, would have to duck in order to avoid scraping her head. Within a few steps a faint stink began to wrap them: the sting of lye, sour wine, and other components Nona couldn't name. She wrinkled her nose as the smell grew stronger.

The daylight followed them further than Nona had imagined, and just as it grew so dim that she started to have difficulty seeing the steps another source of illumination took over. The new light turned out to be a fat candle positioned in a niche at a bend in the descent. Its light carried them down to a section of hand-hewn tunnel with a wooden door to one side, before which the girls started to queue.

Bhenta came down, snuffing the candle then squeezing past the line to push into the room beyond. The girls followed her.

This chamber was also hand-hewn, though perhaps from a smaller natural cave as some areas on the soot-stained ceiling looked irregular and didn't show any pick-marks. Light entered by several horizontal shafts in the far wall, each five or six foot long and showing patches of sky. Nona guessed they must open on the cliffs.

Three long tables ran the length of the room with benches to either side, and all manner of jars, pots, glass bottles, and sealed gourds arranged along the middle of each. At the far end a nun stood with her back to the door, writing on a chalkboard. The novices seated themselves at the tables without the usual fuss of who sat by who.

The woman at the board was neither tall nor short, shapely certainly, but Nona couldn't guess at her age other than to say, 'not old'.

Bhenta closed the door, and Mistress Shade, the Poisoner, turned around with a warm smile for the class. 'Ah, Nona dear, do come up here. And you, Arabella. I always like to take a good look at the new girls.'

Nona blinked and stood. The Poisoner had had a pretty good look at her already in the bathhouse. 'Yes, Sister Apple,' she said.

They came to stand before Sister Apple, Nona shooting a sideways glance at the Jotsis girl, apparently serene despite just two nights ago sinking a knife into the spot where Nona had been sleeping. The idea that Arabella could hide her murderous instincts so deep that not a trace showed on the surface unnerved Nona more than the act itself. She knew her own emotions were written across her face the moment she felt them, possibly even before.

'I do believe you're less skinny already, Nona. Another year of convent meals and we might have a decent amount of meat on those bones. And Arabella Jotsis … a pleasure to have you join us. What *is* it like to be part of prophecy?' Sister Apple raised her hand as Arabella opened her mouth. 'Best not to answer that one, dear.' She took an embossed tin, enamelled in black and white, from her habit and opened it with a squeeze that sent the lid springing back. Inside were a dozen translucent yellow balls, each no larger than a thumbnail. 'A sweetmeat to welcome you to Shade Class. We're going to have such a good time.' She smiled that same slow and easy smile she first greeted Nona with on the way to the convent.

'I've stuffed myself.' Nona held her stomach. She had in fact stuffed herself as she did at every meal, but the sweetmeats did look enticing, glowing like the stained glass in Path Tower.

'A pity.' Sister Apple turned to Arabella and held the box out.

'Thank you.' Arabella reached out and took one daintily between thumb and forefinger. Nona noticed that both digits had a waxy sheen to them. 'I'll save it for after class.'

Sister Apple closed the box and tucked it away. 'To your seats then, girls. We've a lot to learn today!'

Nona followed Arabella back to the nearest of the three long tables. The older girl returned to her place first, wincing as she sat, then shifting position with a frown. Nona found her place and lowered herself towards the bench before pausing, held by a sudden suspicion with her backside just an inch or two from the polished wood. She shifted and turned, narrowing her eyes as she made a quick study of the area beneath her. Something glinted. A short pin held upright on a tiny dark base. She flicked it to the floor and sat. Bhenta must have placed the thing while Nona was up at the front of the class.

'Well done, Nona!' Sister Apple clapped her hands. 'Arabella … less well done.'

Nona looked across at Arabella. The girl's face had a peculiarly stiff look to it, just her furious eyes and twitching grimace to indicate she wasn't simply concentrating on Mistress Shade's words. She jerked her body minutely to the left but seemed incapable of more movement.

'You passed the test, Nona.' Sister Apple smiled. 'I won't try to trick you again.' She turned back to the chalkboard, where she tapped her chalk against a leaf-shape then underlined the word beside it. 'Today we will be learning how to brew catweed to potency, a close cousin to segren root from which I made the tincture that was on the pin-trap Nona so cleverly avoided and Arabella did not. Commonly we call the tincture lock-up. The first—'

A tap-tap-tap on the door turned Sister Apple back towards the class. 'Come.'

Sister Kettle poked her head into the classroom, a mischievous grin on her face. 'I've just come from the scriptorium to give Nona her writing supplies.' She pushed fully through the half-open door, a dark slate in one hand and chalk sticks in the other. 'For our lessons together.'

'Go on then.' Sister Apple smiled tolerantly and waved Sister Kettle in.

The younger nun – Nona thought Kettle might be twenty-something to Apple's thirty – tiptoed over in exaggerated fashion and placed the slate and chalks before Nona on the table. She removed a folded wiping cloth from her habit and set that down between them before mouthing 'sorry' at Mistress Shade and tiptoeing out, waving to the novices from the doorway once out of sight from the board.

'As I was saying.' Sister Apple rapped the board. 'Catweed.'

Nona looked down at her new possessions. Her only possessions other than the quill, scroll and ink the abbess gave her … and a briefly-owned knife. She picked the slate up, marvelling at its even corners and uniform thickness. The bigs in Nana Even's seven-day class sat with rough pieces of slate they had dug themselves from Ebson's Hole. While Sister Apple continued to describe the locations in which catweed might be found Nona set the slate back down before her, finding it slightly sticky. Her fingertips held a brownish stain where she'd touched it, and had a faint smell of rot.

'Catweed in its natural state can be eaten without adverse effects,' Sister Apple continued. 'Though you would be advised against consuming it in quantity. That would lead to stomach cramps and numbness in the extremities. Besides, it has a sour and unpleasant taste.'

Sister Apple continued to expound upon the merits of catweed for several minutes before pausing to look at Nona. 'And how are you feeling, novice?'

Nona licked her lips. Her mouth felt strangely dry and cottony.

'You … lied.' She discovered herself weak in every limb. An attempt to rise merely made her slump over the table.

'It was entirely evident that I was trying to poison you, Nona dear. You don't think that someone who would poison you might also stoop to not telling the truth on all occasions?'

'L…iar.' No part of Nona's body would obey her. Where Arabella had gone rigid Nona had turned limp, but neither of them had command of their muscles.

Sister Apple crossed the room to stand beside Nona, setting a hand to her shoulder. 'Do you know what the most insidious poison is, Nona?' Sister Apple pursed her lips. 'That means "worst".'

'N—' The table filled most of Nona's vision now as her head met it. She could see Sister Apple from hips to ribcage, Arabella's arm, Clera behind them both.

'N—? Catweed got your tongue?' Sister Apple retrieved the slate with a cloth-wrapped hand. 'Trust, Nona. Trust is the most insidious of poisons. Trust sidesteps all of your precautions.' Behind the nun Clera rolled her eyes. 'So give your trust sparingly. Or better still, not at all. And, Novice Clera … you will be grinding stinkcorns in the fume cavern for an hour after the lesson finishes.'

13

Shade class passed slowly but with little else to pay attention to Nona learned a lot about the properties and preparation of catweed, the primary ingredient of the preparation known as 'boneless' with which she had been poisoned. She also learned about segren root, from which the 'lock- up' tincture with which Arabella had been poisoned was distilled. The most memorable fact was that catweed had an unpleasant aroma of decay whereas segren root when cut smelt like cat urine.

'Segren root smells like a cat weed. Catweed does not.' Sister Apple tapped the board. 'That should be easy to remember!'

Nona didn't see the demonstrations, though she did get to see Clera pinch the immobilized Arabella, twice.

About ten minutes before the end of the lesson Nona found herself able to lift her head. All about her the novices were boiling small iron pans full of catweed and vinegar over trays of glowing charcoal. The stench was incredible.

By the time Nona could sit up, Sister Apple was moving around the class checking the preparations for colour and consistency.

'You should all be decanting the liquid now. Use a fine sieve, and make sure you've added the alkoid salt before sieving, and the quicksilver after. Next lesson we'll be distilling our liquor to recover the essence with which Nona's slate was coated. It will penetrate the skin, though slowly and less effectively – for optimal results it needs to be consumed while fresh.'

Nona and Arabella brought up the rear when the class climbed the long stair to escape into fresh air at last. Sister Apple supported Nona while Bhenta helped Arabella along.

'You'll be fully recovered within the hour,' Sister Apple said, sending Nona on her way at the top of the stairs with a pat.

Nona didn't feel entirely herself until bedtime. She sat on her bed chatting with Ruli until Clera finally showed up from the bathhouse.

'I had to soak for *hours* to get the stink off me! Look! I'm all wrinkled up!' Clera held her fingers out, the pads of each ridged from too long in the water.

Nona sniffed but didn't like to say she could still smell the stinkcorns. 'How did she know?'

'That I was cheeking her? Eyes in the back of her head!' Clera snorted.

'How did she know, that she would need Sister Kettle to trick me?'

Jula leaned in from the next bed. 'If the sweets or pins had got you both she would have ignored the door and Kettle would have gone away. If Arabella wasn't poisoned when Kettle came in then she would have taken out something for her – a message from her father or something… The Poisoner always wins!'

'I hate that woman,' Clera said.

Morning came and Nona, first out of bed, had to be reminded by a sleepy Clera that there were no classes on seven-day.

'The older novices are allowed to go down into the city on supervised excursions.' Clera sat up, yawning and stretching. Her nightdress was thin and grey with a number of tears but better than nothing, which was all Nona had. 'I'm going down to see my father. With Sister Flint, worse luck. She is *no* fun at all. The abbess gave me special permission even though I'm still in Red.'

Nona said nothing. She knew enough about prisons to say

that she would not want her father in one. However, if being in a prison meant that her father was there to visit one day in seven rather than lost beneath the ice, she would step into Clera's shoes.

Hessa poked her head from beneath her blankets, yawning hugely. 'I had an awful dream.' She sat up, shuddering. 'About a wolf—'

'—in a trap,' Nona said.

'Yes…' Hessa frowned. 'Did I talk in my sleep?'

Nona didn't answer. A dream of a wolf with its leg in an iron trap had woken her in the night. She hadn't remembered it on waking until Hessa spoke.

'We're going to swim in the sinkhole.' Jula tugged her underskirts on and promptly tripped over her bed into an undignified fall, face first, bottom up. She rolled to the side, bucking to get the skirts up. 'Coming, Nona?'

'I have extra lessons with Sister Kettle.' Also, Nona couldn't swim.

'Be careful she doesn't poison you again.' Clera grinned.

Nona met with Sister Kettle after breakfast in the Academia tower. The classroom seemed very large with just two of them there, their chairs side by side at the table where Sister Rule's mysteries were normally on display. The slate and chalks that Sister Apple had taken charge of during Shade were set on the polished wood before them.

'You poisoned me,' Nona said.

'I did.'

'Don't do it again.'

Sister Kettle sucked her lower lip, studying Nona. 'I don't believe I shall. That's a very fierce stare for a little girl.'

'I made both Tacsis brothers bleed, and they didn't even try to poison me.' Nona took out her quill.

'They underestimated you, Nona. I've seen you on the blade-path. I wouldn't underestimate you.' Kettle took a flat case from her habit and opened it to reveal her own quill, the feather black and stiff, perhaps a raven's. 'I told Sister Tallow about your jumping between the tops of the spiral.'

Nona said nothing, but took out her scroll, watching Kettle's dark eyes.

'Sister Tallow said you took the warrior's route. She said most take nothing with them on the path except the fear of that fall. Even when they no longer care about the height of the drop they fear the possibility of failure – just as the fear of death weighs so many down when they fight. The warrior, though, hates the fear: it's an attack like any other and must be fought. She throws herself at it, all or nothing, she dares it and disdains it. Death claims us all in the end, but the warrior chooses the ground on which she meets it, and the manner, she makes death run to catch up.' Kettle smoothed out her own scroll. 'So there!'

'How did Mistress Blade get hurt?' Nona asked.

Sister Kettle dipped her quill and wrote a letter on her scroll. 'This is the letter A. I brought the slate and chalks so you can practise copying it.'

Nona peered at the glistening letter. Hessa had told her the basics. A is for apple, and so on. The wet ink reminded her of blood in the dark. 'A is for assassin,' Nona said. 'They say the emperor's sisters Sherzal and Vel… Vel…'

'Velera.'

'Velera. They say they would rather see Arabella dead than in the emperor's hands.'

'Well, she's neither is she?' Kettle said.

'I know stories about the Noi-Guin.' In Giljohn's cage Hessa had told about Noi-Guin, singular hunters of men, invisible in the night, insinuating themselves past any defence and taking lives with impunity. Markus had always asked for tales of the assassins, the bloodier the better. 'Did Sister Tallow fight one of them?'

Sister Kettle gave Nona a measured stare. 'It would take more than one Noi-Guin to injure Mistress Blade.' She sniffed. 'Now. B is for blade.' Her quill flowed across the parchment leaving a glistening black trail.

'It looks like a P,' Nona said, squinting, trying to remember the shapes Hessa had drawn for her over and over. She drew one on her slate and turned it upside-down. 'There.'

Sister Kettle grinned. 'B is for blade, P is for path. It's a little-known thing but blade and path are two sides of the same coin. The blade-path isn't just a game to occupy the pathless: one really does help the other. Also, what you have there is a Q if it's anything…'

'You're the best at blade-path,' Nona said. 'Does that mean you're quantal too?'

Sister Kettle's grin became a laugh. 'Ancestor, no! But I *am* very good at the Path-drawn mindsets Sister Pan teaches. I can be as *serene* as all hell! And nobody does *quiet* like me! Except Appy of course. I mean Mistress Shade.'

Nona tried to imagine Sister Kettle serene … or even quiet. She failed. 'I thought the Path-trances were clarity, serenity, and patience?'

Kettle shrugged. 'Patience, quiet, another coin with two sides. And you need to know all the sides of a coin before you can earn it and spend it. Sister Pan will teach you that.'

'The novices say that Sister Pan's just an old woman who talks a lot. They say she hasn't got any magic left.' Actually, when she thought about it, Nona found it easier to picture Sister Pan working magic than Sister Kettle's chat and humour replaced by quantal-serenity. Sister Pan at least looked the part: as ancient and haggard as any tree-witch in the stories whispered around the village fireside.

'This is a C. I want you to write A, B, C. Over and over, until your hand remembers them.' Sister Kettle gestured to Nona's slate.

Nona drew the letters out, following the line of each in her mind.

'Good. Do it again.'

Nona did it seven more times before filling the slate.

'Good. And no, I don't know if Sister Pan can touch the Path any more. She was old when the abbess was a novice. But what I can tell you is that she was once one of the great Holy Witches and she followed the Path that runs through all things. High priests came to see her. Emperor Xtal, the third of his name, and his son, the fourth, summoned her to court. And when the Durnish sailed against us more than fifty years ago, so many of them in their sick-wood barges that they almost made a bridge across the Corridor, it was Sister Pan and Sister Rain of Gerran's Crag that met their storm-weavers and swept them from the sea... So don't bury the old girl yet. And don't call her "old girl". Or tell her I told you that story... Let's draw some Ds, shall we?'

The best part of the day passed before Nona escaped the horrors of the alphabet and hurried from the Academia tower too exhausted to go in search of her friends. Overhead a rook fluttered, black against the sky, descending towards the many-windowed spire of the convent rookery. They came and went together normally, a clamour of them raucous and wheeling. A single bird meant a message. Nona wondered what words those dark wings brought and from how far. She also wondered if they'd been as much of a pain to write as her endless letters.

Nona lay relaxing in the dormitory, nursing a cramped hand, when Clera returned. The sun had already started to sink, its red light painted in bars across the ceiling now.

'You're supposed to put the ink on the parchment.' Clera nodded towards Nona's fingers before slinging herself down on her bed.

Nona spread the ink-stained digits of her right hand before her. At Nona's insistence Sister Kettle had let her try with quill and lowest grade paper after hours with chalk and slate. It had been more difficult than Nona expected, the result a scratchy mess of jerky lines and ink pools.

'How was your father?' Nona asked.

Clera rolled onto her back and stared at the ceiling. 'Where is everyone? Did they all drown while swimming?'

Nona shrugged. 'I don't know. I saw Ruli going into Blade Hall. Some of them must be practising blade-path.' Clera looked worn out. Sad too, flipping her penny up high, catching it, flipping it. 'How was—'

'He's fine. He has an appeal hearing in a month. It looks promising.'

'That's good?' Nona wasn't sure what an appeal hearing was.

'Yes.' Clera caught her penny in her palm and closed her hand about it. In the dying light it looked silver. 'Did you ever consider just running away, Nona? Just running and running and losing yourself somewhere?'

'Where?' Nona had considered it, but running to was better than running from.

'Just anywhere. Making a new life.'

'It's hard out there.' Nona gazed towards the windows. 'Running's all right, but when you stop there's the freezing and the starving and the dying. If you had money then—'

'Yes.' Clera sat up suddenly. 'Yes, money makes it better. Money fixes everything.' She stood. 'Let's go find them. Have some fun, make trouble, make a noise. Classes tomorrow. Classes forever. Let's—'

'That's a silver crown!' Nona pointed to it in Clera's fingers.

'I made one become many.' Clera tucked the coin into her pocket. It dropped with a faint chink. 'I had some luck.' She smiled but she looked sad.

'How—' But the door flew open and Ruli raced in shrieking and wrapped in towels, Jula and Ketti hard on her heels.

'Catch her!'

'Get her!'

And Clera leapt into the chase, her grin both wide and wild.

14

Nona's first full week in the convent passed in a blur, exhausting herself in Blade's endless repetition of punches, throws, and holds, straining her brain in Academia against topics like glaciation, erosion, and the formation of rocks, gorging herself at meals, still unable to truly believe they would keep coming three times a day.

In the dormitory Nona shared two more dreams with Hessa, both nightmares. Hessa said they must be echoing down the remnants of the connection through which she had shared her memory. The phenomenon would fade away, she said. Also, Ketti had a fight with Ghena and both were put on laundry for a week. And, to Clera's delight, the abbess's cat urinated on Arabella's habit on three-day night.

In Shade they brewed two more poisons, one to cause blindness, another confusion, learning the nature of the ingredients, the antidotes, where such existed, and the means by which the resulting pastes might be introduced to victims or avoided by novices. Sister Apple proved as unpleasant within her cave as she was sweet while outside it. Ketti spent a day without sight after failing to prevent the Poisoner from duping her with the same trick she had just described on the chalkboard. Ruli spent a day in the Necessary after whispering too loudly with Ghena at the back of the class. Nobody knew how the Poisoner got to her, but she was vomiting by the time she reached the top of the stairs on the way out. And Jula caught the sharp edge of Apple's tongue for a moment's daydreaming – reduced to tears by a critique of her alchemical failings that had the rest of the class laughing despite themselves.

Path proved to be Nona's least favourite class, worse even than the tedium of Spirit where Wheel led them through the endless small ceremonies that seemed to occupy every Holy Sister's day. She soon came to dread Sister Pan's room, alight with colour and harmony. She stared at the patterns until she thought her eyes would bleed but nothing the old woman said to do made the mystic Path open up before her. There was none of the strange and alarming energy that Arabella had spoken of during her first Path class, just a boredom so profound it made her want to scratch her eyes out. The visualizations for serenity made Nona angry; the ones for quiet filled her head with clamouring for something different.

By the time the seven-day came around again Nona was starting to consider the convent her home. Memories of the Caltess seemed distant, those of Giljohn and his cart a dream, and recollections of the village a story told about someone else.

On the walk to Academia Tower Nona paused to make a slow turn on the spot, taking in the buildings that had so quickly grown familiar: Heart Hall and Blade Hall, with the Dome of the Ancestor looming behind them, the dormitories and the refectory, the nuns' cloisters and the wide courtyard before the bathhouse. A lone chicken strutted in the shadow of the scriptorium, pausing to scrape and peck as if looking for any dropped punctuation. Between the laundry and the sanatorium Nona could see a wagon parked outside the winery, loaded with barrels of the latest vintage to be released. The novices in Holy Class were allowed a glass of the convent wine with their evening meal on any seven-day that happened to also be a holy holiday, which most of them seemed to be. Ruli claimed the convent earned far more of its income from shipping barrels of Sweet Mercy around the Corridor than from educating and training novices.

'Of course, if any of them had met the Poisoner they'd all be emptying their wine jugs down the sewer.'

* * *

Clera was waiting in the dormitory when Nona returned from her next lesson with Sister Kettle, hand cramped, white with chalk, and ink-stained about the fingers. Sister Kettle's parting words had been about Clera and Nona had crossed the wind-swept courtyards frowning under the weight of them.

'A word to the wise.' Kettle had set her hand over Nona's as she reached for her slate. 'The hardest lesson I ever learned was that every bad thing you see a friend do to someone else they will some day do to you. Some people in this world are users and some givers. When two such form a bond it often ends poorly. Find more friends, Nona. Clera Ghomal spends enough time thinking about herself without you to help her do it. Don't—'

Nona had pulled free and hurried from the tower, but she could still feel the sister's fingers on the back of her hand, still hear her speaking. She rubbed hand against habit and tried to shake off the foul mood that had risen in her. She had had few friends in her life and the bonds that bound her to them were more sacred to her than the Ancestor was to any nun. Friendship wasn't something you gave up on or let slip: it wasn't something to be done in small measure or cut in half.

She had still been angry when she thrust the dormitory door open.

Most of the novices had yet to return from their various diversions but Jula lay across her own bed, head hanging over the edge as she studied a scroll, and Ghena lay sleeping – the girl always seemed to be rushing about or sleeping, with no real pause between one and the other. Ketti raged past in her smallclothes holding her habit before her, nose wrinkling. 'Someone let that damned cat in here! He's peed on my underskirts! Sister Rule should drown the thing!'

'Malkin's nice,' Jula said, not looking up. 'Just a bit old and confused.'

'Needs drowning!' Shouted back through the door as Ketti vanished in the direction of the laundry.

'The only male in the convent and he spends his time pissing on everything.' Clera from her bed.

'There's the roosters too.' Jula still not looking up.

'Who spend their time crowing and strutting about,' Clera said.

'And the pigs.'

'Who eat and shit,' Clera said. 'I rest my case.'

Nona crossed to her bed.

'Is Sister Kettle getting those letters to stick in your head, Nona?' Clera looked up from the silver crown she'd been walking across her knuckles. Her tone held something distant in it: perhaps her day at the prison had given her bad news this time.

'She's having more luck with it than Sister Pan is with her stupid Path.' Nona flomped down on her bed, stretching her hand out and sighing. 'We need to get her to let us off to practise blade-path next time.'

'We do.' Clera nodded. She studied Nona as if she were something new to her. 'Anyway, hurry up and learn to read. You don't want to take up too many of Kettle's seven-days or the Poisoner will not be a happy little Poisoner.'

'Why?' Nona frowned.

'You don't know? Really? Oh come on—'

The ringing of a bell cut across Clera. A bell Nona hadn't heard before, sharp and very loud. Three rings, a pause, three more. A steel bell.

'Ancestor bleed me!' Clera looked shocked. 'That's Bitel! We have to get out, now!'

Moments later the Red Class girls were crowding out through the dormitories' main door, along with a dozen or so older novices. Outside in the growing gloom nuns and novices were on the move, streaming from all directions, some running, others striding briskly, all headed towards the abbess's house.

Bitel found its tongue again. *Clang*. Rooks broke for the sky from behind Heart Hall. *Clang*. Clera and Nona broke into a run. *Clang*. Somewhere in the distance a woman started to shout.

The entire convent gathered before Abbess Glass's doors. Nona and Clera pushed in among the novices, some still wet and steaming from bathhouse. The senior nuns arranged themselves around the perimeter of the crowd, several carrying lanterns.

'It's a fire?' Jula elbowing through behind them.

'I heard it was a collapse in the Shade caverns…' Ruli, her long hair in a bathhouse towel.

'Ssshh!' Ghena pointed towards the abbess's doors.

Sister Tallow and Sister Apple preceded the abbess, Sister Tallow with her arm in a sling. Abbess Glass followed, crozier in hand, and halted on the steps from where she commanded a view over her gathered flock.

'Sisters.' Abbess Glass smiled for them though it lacked joy. 'Novices. Word has just arrived that High Priest Jacob and the four archons are approaching. They will be with us within the hour. This visit is a great honour for us and for Sweet Mercy. I expect you all to be on your best behaviour.

'The high priest and his retinue will be accommodated in Heart Hall, which will be off limits until further notice. Novices will be expected to stay up to greet High Priest Jacob, after which they will retire to their dormitories. Sister Rule will lead the choir in Aethsan's Hymn to the Ancestor, and Saint Jula's Requiem.

'The high priest will undoubtedly wish to lead a service in the dome, and all sisters will be expected to attend.' Abbess Glass clapped her hands. 'We have an hour! Get the lanterns lit, food and wine prepared, the choir properly attired… Go! Go!'

Nona looked around for a direction in which to go, only to find a broad, brown hand descending upon her shoulder.

'Red Class,' Sister Oak called from her considerable elevation. 'With me to the refectory. We will be carrying out tables and chairs to set before the Dome of the Ancestor for the welcoming ceremony.'

Waving a fleshy arm, Sister Oak led off and the Red Class novices filed after her. Clera should have joined the choir but instead she stuck with the class, perhaps not ready to perform for such a high audience. Nona glanced back as they left. The abbess descended her steps, the golden curl of her crozier stealing the lanterns' brightness. Her lips made a grim line in the gloom beneath.

15

Lights blinking in and out of view among the pillars gave the first visible sign of the high priest's arrival. Nona imagined the churchmen dwarfed among the hugeness of the columns, their small patches of illumination in all that darkness, shadows swinging around them. She wondered how many had come and to what purpose. Raymel Tacsis's brother, Lano, had said his father knew High Priest Jacob. How far did Thuran Tacsis's influence reach? Abbess Glass must know the high priest too – surely that would count for more?

'They're here for you. You know that, right?'

Nona turned to look up at Clera, standing behind her a little to her left in the second row of novices. Each class stood in two lines, the shortest to the fore.

'It was all over town, Nona. You should have told me.' Clera kept her gaze on the approaching lights. To either side of her Ruli and Ketti turned to stare.

'Told you what?' Jula asked, beside Nona.

'Nona half-killed Raymel Tacsis, Thuran Tacsis's son – the ring-fighter. And when Lano Tacsis came up here with a high court judge the other day—'

'He didn't!' Ghena from Nona's right. 'Did he?'

'He did, and Nona nearly cut off two of his fingers. It took a marjal wizard from the Academy to save them. Raymel's still under the care of four other Academy mages.'

'Where did you get a knife?' Ghena hissed.

Nona glanced along the line and saw Arabella staring at her with startling intensity.

'Why did you attack him?' Jula whispered.

Nona made no reply. She looked down into her empty hands and wondered why Clera hadn't asked her questions back in the dormitory. She must have been angry at being misled by Nona's story of Amondo in the forest. Though that story held more truth in it than the first one Nona had told her… Had she learned about Raymel last seven-day or just today? Clera had held her anger so well, kept it cold and close, then used it like a blade. Nona hadn't understood that about her friend – but then she understood so little about people. She expected them all to be like her and found instead that each of them was a mystery, from Clera with her copper penny that became a silver crown, Ruli so easy in her skin, kindness without ambition, to Jula and her faith, Hessa and her magics, even Ghena's anger, so close to her own, never yielded to explanation or prediction.

The churchmen came into view, picked out in the guttering light of the bonfire the nuns had set burning in the fire-pit before the convent. Under Sister Rule's direction the choir gave voice to Aethsan's Hymn, the younger novices first, piercing the night with high, sweet notes, singular and wind-torn, hanging a moment before the sisters underwrote it with more strength, the words flowing together into melody. Sister Mop stood to the fore, dumpy, her face plain and careworn, but her voice a marvel, sending chills along the backs of Nona's arms.

First came a dozen church-guards in polished steel breastplates, the visors of their helms smooth, reflecting the world. Four drummers behind their armoured ranks started up a grim beat that drowned out the voices of nun and novice, the beat at odds with the metre of the hymn. Behind the drummers, eight priests holding aloft the standards of the four archons and of the four states of the empire. Each standard fluttered beneath a short crossbar on the bearer's long pole, a boss of silver and brass gleaming at the very top.

The archons came on horseback, their stallions similar enough to be brothers from the same sire and mare. Two clerics attended each archon, riding smaller ponies. Even these attendants wore silver chains of office and plush robes, trimmed with the fur of ice lynx. A dozen men bore the high priest's sedan chair between them on two poles.

The drummers ceased their beat only when the high priest's bearers set down the sedan chair. The choir had fallen silent and nobody spoke as a lone bearer hurried from his position to open the door to the closed sedan.

A young man, blond and handsome in black velvets, ducked out through the open door, a leather-bound book clutched to his chest. Nona wondered at priests and judges: did they also carry a book to the Necessary with them to tell them what to do?

High Priest Jacob followed after a dignified pause, a small man almost swallowed by the robe of his office, a thing of deep purple folds, embroidered with enough golden thread to weight him down should a gust try to make him take flight. Short grey hair escaped beneath a black headpiece rising in scrolls. He stood thirty yards from Nona, lit by flickers, but even so there was something familiar about the man. Something that made her lip curl.

The high priest looked around, sharp-eyed, ignoring the hand his bearer offered to help him down. His assistant reached into the sedan and brought out a long straight staff, a couple of feet taller than him and made of wood so dark it might be black, the end of it stamped in gold with the interlocked alpha and omega of the Ancestor. The high priest took the staff and cast a disapproving eye over the welcoming committee.

Sister Knife approached with a bow. With eyes lowered, she gestured towards the steps where the abbess waited. The abbess stood flanked not by Sisters Apple and Tallow as so often before but by Sister Wheel and by Sister Rose from the sanatorium, their funnelled headdresses now seeming to indicate some kind of church seniority.

Taking his cue, the high priest approached the abbess. He walked with a pronounced limp, leaning on his staff. Behind him the four archons dismounted and the bearers began to remove luggage from the sedan.

'High Priest Jacob! Welcome to Sweet Mercy.' Abbess Glass nodded towards the choir to begin the requiem.

The high priest raised his hand to forestall them. 'This is not a visit that I am happy to be making. If you would join me, abbess…' He beckoned her to his side.

'I know him…' Nona hadn't meant to say the words but they emerged as a whisper.

'You do *not*!' Ghena hissed to her right. 'That's High Priest Jacob, primate of the faith. Not some wandering preacher a peasant might have seen.'

'Abbess?' The high priest beckoned again.

Abbess Glass pursed her lips, eyeing the two bearers approaching from the sedan, carrying an iron-cornered box between them on rope handles. With a sigh she descended between Wheel and Rose to join the high priest out before the fire-pit.

'The girl too.' High Priest Jacob scanned the Red Class line, the fire glinting in his eyes. The light and shadow made something skull-like of his face. Nona knew him then. The man from Hessa's memories. The man who had beaten Four-Foot to death.

The abbess looked puzzled. 'What g—'

'Do not,' the high priest said.

'Nona!' Abbess Glass waved her over, and without thinking of escape Nona came. She shot a narrow look up at the high priest, meeting his pale eyes and registering the surprise there. For a moment she imagined leaping for his throat. The image pleased her.

'This is the novice?' he asked as she drew near.

The abbess nodded. 'She's a small thing to bring the high priest and all four archons up such a steep and winding path, is she not?'

'This was not well done, Shella.' The high priest frowned. Behind him the bearers opened the box and began to remove something heavy and clanking.

'Is this necessary, Jacob?' Abbess Glass glanced at the box with distaste.

'Do you truly not understand who Thuran Tacsis is?' High

Priest Jacob shook his head. 'I thought you were clever, Shella, devious even. This makes … no sense.' He waved and the bearers stepped forward, heavy iron yokes in their arms, trailing lengths of chain. 'Abbess Glass, Novice Nona, you are both to be placed under church arrest pending trial at sunrise.'

The larger of the two men opened the iron yoke in his hands and stepped forward to place it over the abbess's head. Nona heard gasps and cries from behind her. The other man stepped towards her and she backed away.

'Let him do it, Nona dear.' Abbess Glass smiled, then winced as the weight of her yoke settled on her shoulders. 'The high priest has spoken. The Ancestor will watch over us.'

Nona willed herself to stop. She didn't much care if the Ancestor watched or not, but she knew the abbess stood before her humbled and in chains because she had taken her from the very shadow of the gallows, moments before they tried to set the rope about her neck. Nona didn't understand why the abbess had done that but she understood the debt upon her.

'I would kill him again.' Nona stood straight as the yoke descended upon her. 'I would kill his brother too, and his father if they think this is right.'

'She condemns herself.' The high priest spread his hands. 'Do we even need a trial?'

'She's a child, Jacob.' The abbess stumbled as she stepped towards him, her features strained.

As the weight settled on Nona her legs gave way and she fell to her knees on the rock. One bearer supported her while the other man tried to lock the yoke in place, encompassing her neck and both wrists. It took the use of a spanner to tighten the yoke sufficiently that her hands wouldn't simply slip out.

'Give her up now and there may still be a place in the church for you, Shella. It isn't like you to get sentimental over a child. And why *this* child?'

'My name is Glass. We will have a trial and see what that name is worth.'

The high priest sighed. He removed his hat, smoothed his hair into place and resettled it before the wind could undo his work. 'Take them to the recluse.'

And so with the convent watching on and the welcome meal cooling on the long tables, Abbess Glass and Nona were led off to wait upon their trial. Nona looked towards her classmates as she staggered by, partly supported by one of the church-guards. Some looked away or at their feet, Clera among them. Others stared in horror. Even Arabella Jotsis looked stricken, though Nona couldn't imagine why.

Sister Apple had to lead the high priest's men to the recluse – every convent had one but the location varied from site to site. Sweet Mercy's recluse was a cavern at the end of the tunnel that led past the Shade classroom. Sister Apple took them more than a hundred yards further into the bedrock of the plateau, holding her lantern high. In the depths the darkness moved aside before the nun's intrusions only with reluctance. She navigated past half a dozen junctions where the tunnel forked into smaller or larger ways and eventually the corridor ended in a small cave where the walls had been smoothed by waters that had long since found a swifter course, leaving an almost spherical chamber. Iron bars blocked the corridor and the smaller entry path of the vanished stream. Sister Apple unlocked a gate in the bars and the abbess walked through with as much dignity as she could manage. Nona's guardsmen helped her in. Sister Apple locked the gate.

'I shall pray for you both.' She offered a narrow smile and walked away, leading the four guardsmen. She left nothing but an echo of her lantern light, soon consumed by a night so ancient that it never truly left such places.

'She didn't seem very upset.' Nona's voice surprised her. She hadn't meant to speak but darkness gives the tongue licence – like a mask – or a judge's crown.

'Apple is a Grey Sister,' the abbess said. Nona heard her sit down. 'She wears many guises, and she herself would tell you to trust none of them. Only remember that she is your sister, as true to you as you are to the Ancestor.'

'What will they do with us?' Nona asked. The ground was damp, uneven, and hard and the place held a lingering scent of the sewer, perhaps remembering the last nun or novice sent down here to reflect upon their sins.

'Find us innocent, I hope.'

'And if they don't?'

'Ah, well, then we will be subject to church justice, which sadly rests upon some very old and rather barbaric laws. I will have my tongue split and be scourged before being driven out of the convent. And you will be put to death.'

'Oh.'

'You did ask. And you were on the gallows steps when I found you…'

'I thought you liked to lie.' Nona wriggled her hands in the yoke's grip. It hurt.

'I said lies can be very useful. Even children deserve honesty in the dark, though.'

'How?'

'How?'

'How will I be put to death?'

'Ah.' The abbess sucked in her breath. 'Each convent has its own method. Silent Patience and Chaste Devotion burn, but in different ways; Gerran's Crag opts for crushing with stones. We drown. Not in my time, but they say the bottom of the sinkhole is thick with bones…'

'Why are you telling me this?' Nona might only be ten but she knew that adults were supposed to comfort children, even if all they had to offer was false comfort.

'So that tomorrow you hold your tongue and let me do what needs to be done without your temper digging us deeper.'

Nona bit her lip at that and drew her knees to her chest, resting part of the yoke's weight against the cave wall. She kept silent for what felt like an age, remembering her classmates' faces as they watched her being led away.

Finally, 'Why *are* you helping me?'

Abbess Glass didn't speak for the longest time, and when she did all she said was, 'Perhaps because I really do know who Thuran Tacsis is.'

16

Church-guards brought Nona and the abbess blinking into the light of day and led them past the scriptorium and Blade Hall to Heart Hall. Nuns and novices lined the final fifty yards to the steps and pillars of Heart Hall's grand entrance. The sisters and older novices muttered the Ancestor's first prayer. Nona didn't know the words by heart but had heard enough of it to recognize it when it was spoken.

'*Ancestor watch our journey. Ancestor guide us in the from and in the to. Ancestor help us to carry the weight of our years, and evening—*'

'Don't they say that at funerals?' Nona asked, stumbling as she tried to keep step with the abbess.

'And at births, Nona. And at births.'

Great doors of ironwood gave onto a foyer, more pillars rising to a vaulted ceiling, the floor tiled in black and white. Other doors, bronze and of smaller scale, opened into a domed chamber where the high priest sat upon a dais in a chair whose gilded back rose above him in scrolls. The four archons sat at the base of the dais, two to either side, each clad in their finery and on chairs scarcely less impressive than the high priest's. Nona took them in for the first time, having seen only their grandeur and the symbols of their office on the night of their arrival. A fat and pallid man, gone to grey, his eyes deep-set, his lips wet. A stern old woman, dark as pitch, head shaven, wearing a single golden earring. A tall and narrow man, younger than the rest, dark-haired and with a look of great melancholy. A solid man with an air of restless energy about him, head square upon a thick neck, half his face laced with ridges of old scar as if some clawed hand had tried to tear it off. This last official shot a quick tight smile towards the end of the hall – gone so swiftly it might never have been there.

Half a dozen assistants, some with leather-bound law tomes, attended the archons, the whole assembly before the dais apparently too deep in various muttered conversations to note the prisoners' arrival. Sisters Wheel and Rose waited before an area close by the door cordoned within a short wooden wall that reached to Nona's chest. Church-guards lined the chamber walls, five to each side.

Abbess Glass led the way into the enclosure, Nona following. 'Are you scared, child?' the abbess asked, turning her head and arms with difficulty to look down at Nona.

'I don't know.' Nona knew that she should be scared. She had been scared of the fall when she had stepped out onto the blade-path. Not of the ground below but the helpless drop before it. She had been scared of losing Saida when the cart took them to the prison. Here though, in irons and with the sinkhole waiting, skulls in the black water looking upward for her arrival, she had yet to find room for fear. This came from Raymel Tacsis, his actions, his evil. That man would die by her hand and if the church supported him, it too would be her enemy. The high priest, she had already decided, would pay more than a crown for Giljohn's mule. 'I'm angry, mostly.'

Abbess Glass blinked, shook her head, then smiled. 'Of course you're scared, Nona. I am.' She went to one knee to be on a level with Nona. A few strands of iron-grey hair had escaped her headdress; sweat beaded on her brow. 'Do you know why they call this Heart Hall?'

Nona shook her head.

'It's named for the shipheart that's kept in a cavern far below our feet. The heat for the bathhouse and dormitories comes from there, the pipes reach down, close enough to the shipheart to heat the oil…'

Nona let the abbess calm herself telling her stories and

looked instead at her own wrists, held level with her shoulders by the yoke. The iron clamps had taken the skin, leaving wet red flesh beneath, the fingers above were numb and barely responded when she tried to wriggle them. If they threw her into the water still yoked she would sink and vanish. Even without the yoke she would drown, unless swimming proved to be an easy thing to learn in a hurry. But such a weight of iron … would they cast it aside as easily as her life? Or remove it for later use? That would be her chance.

'…took it from the vessel that brought our forebears from the darkness above the sky. Did you know that, Nona?'

'No.' Nona looked away from her inspection of the damage to her wrists and faced the abbess. 'Will they start soon?'

'In a short while. There's nothing a church court likes more than delay and debate, but I have a feeling that our high priest is anxious to be on his way. He must have a pressing appointment in Verity. Or perhaps he's worried that other parties might show an interest in the proceedings given enough time to notice. I'm not without friends in court.'

As if hearing her across the length of the room and through the ebb and flow of the archons' chatter, the high priest stood, bringing the heel of his staff down sharply upon the dais. 'I, High Priest Jacob, holy of the church, declare this extraordinary meeting of the Ancestor's court in session.' He nodded to an assistant seated to his left, bent over a large and open scroll, quill in hand. The woman began to write.

'Gathered with me in judgement I have the four archons of the faith. Archon Nevis, to bring the gravity of the gerant.' The fat man bowed his head, deep-set eyes glittering in a pale face. His girth aside, he didn't seem a particularly large man to Nona, not a blood-gerant for sure. 'Archon Anasta, to bring the swiftness and precision of the hunska.' The old woman nodded, the day's light gleaming across the bald dark dome of her skull, lone earring set to swinging. 'Archon Philo, to bring the mystery and insight of the marjal.' The tall man made no sign of having heard, save perhaps in a deepening of the sadness on his narrow face. 'Archon Kratton, to bring the direction and balance of the quantal.' The last archon dipped his head, the scars across the left side of his face livid in the morning sun slanting in from narrow windows. He clenched his fists before him. Nona imagined those hands might crush rocks, leaving only powder.

The high priest bowed to each archon in turn then returned his gaze to the prisoners. 'I expect this to be a swift trial. The facts are indisputable, the sentences prescribed by precedent, and it is hard to imagine that there can be any defence. We will listen to Abbess Glass's apology and consider what measure of mercy may be open to us in this case.

'The facts are these. Raymel Tacsis, son of one of the realm's highest families, born of the line of emperors, given his name in the Ancestor's holy cathedral, was mortally wounded by Nona Reeve—' Nona opened her mouth to protest that she wanted nothing of Partnis Reeve, but the abbess shushed her, her look so fierce that Nona bit her tongue. '—said individual then being found guilty of murder and sentenced to hang at the emperor's pleasure in Harriton prison.

'Abbess Glass of Sweet Mercy Convent secured the release of the criminal into her care under false pretences and subsequently brought her to the convent where, with indecent haste, she was inducted as a novice.

'The matter now sits under church law, which on matters of murder and attempted murder is no more forgiving than the emperor's commandments in such regards. Our duty is clear. Firstly, we must sentence Novice Nona to death for her crime against Raymel Tacsis. Secondly, we must impose sentence upon Abbess Glass for gross interference with secular affairs of state – a transgression for which an example must be set before both the church and lay populations. Failure to hand out a severe sentence will cause unrest, both among the populace and within the emperor's own court. The church cannot afford to be seen as thinking itself above the civil law.

'Unless there are any other opinions at this stage…' he glanced at the archons to either side, '…I will call upon Abbess Glass to make her apologies and appeal for clemency.'

All eyes turned towards the abbess, who took a step forward, now resting herself against the prisoners' wooden enclosure.

'Have you asked yourself why I would take a child from the hangman, Jacob?'

The high priest coughed into his hand and cleared his throat. 'You will address me by my title, Abbess Glass. There are no ties of friendship here. Only the law.' Seated, his robes rose about him, setting his head afloat on a sea of purple and gold. 'We understand weakness, abbess: all of us are human. We lack the perfection of the Ancestor. A mother's instinct perhaps overwhelmed you. It is not uncommon in women of a certain age, but you chose poorly when picking this one...' he waved a hand towards Nona, '...to adopt.'

Abbess Glass straightened her back against the yoke's weight and managed a wry smile. 'I have many faults, high priest, too many to try to conceal. But even my enemies have yet to accuse me of owning a soft heart. I believe the word most often used against me is "cunning". So it pains me to see you leap so swiftly to the conclusion that I stand before you yoked by my own stupidity.'

Nona noticed a smile twitch on the scarred lips of Archon Kratton on the far right, and a broader one spread on the wet lips of Archon Nevis on the far left.

'Trials seek the truth, high priest. Something that singularly failed to happen during the conviction of the child beside me. Perhaps you might ask me why I acted as I did before you demand an apology for those actions? Certainly the men who convicted this small girl of killing a famed gerant ring-fighter should have asked that question before sentencing both her and the girl Saida Reeve to death.'

'Saida didn't do anything!' Nona blurted the words, afraid that the abbess might try to lay Raymel's injuries at Saida's feet.

'Hush, Nona,' the abbess said in a low voice. 'You'll drown yourself with that mouth of yours.'

The high priest rose from his chair, staff in hand. 'A lack of humility will do you no favours here, Abbess Glass—'

'Even so, I would like to hear the why.' Archon Kratton spoke with a tremor in his voice as if some powerful vibration were running through him. It struck Nona then that the high priest was less of a king than he might appear, and the archons were not merely part of his show.

Abbess Glass inclined her head towards the archon. 'I heard about Nona's case while in Verity to negotiate the induction of the Jotsis girl. The Argatha prophecy has considerable influence among the populace, and whatever weight we may or may not place behind the words it is certainly true that the belief of the common man has given the prophecy a power of its own. It could, for example, quite easily see any suspected two-blood killed or kidnapped as part of empire politicking.

'I mention the prophecy because it's an example of words gaining power because we let them. Two other words that have gained too much power because we let them are Thuran Tacsis. High Priest Jacob asked me if I really knew who Thuran Tacsis is? Well I know that he is a man whose eldest son has killed at least five young girls in acts of cruelty, on occasion as a result of his temper, and on occasion for his own sadistic pleasure, and has in each case been allowed to walk free without even an attempt at arrest or prosecution. Tacsis money has purchased the common law. Even in the higher courts where others of the Sis and merchant classes might seek justice, Tacsis gold often speaks loudest. Louder indeed than any of those charged with the duty to enforce the statutes set down by our ancestors.

'So, curious as to how a small girl could fell a gerant ring-fighter, I enquired further. I found many whose reports of the event, at least in private, ran quite differently to those of the "witnesses" produced to support the death sentence imposed on Nona and Saida Reeve. It is certainly true that Nona inflicted the injuries on Raymel Tacsis. She did not, however, assault him by surprise and from behind but did so to defend her friend, also a small girl, from his attacks, having first warned him to desist.

'In Nona we have a rare talent, the purest hunska I've seen in years, born with an instinct for battle and to defend the weak. A girl, innocent in youth, in whom the faith's seed will find fertile ground. Sweet Mercy scours the empire for girls such as these … was I to let her be sacrificed to the unhealthy appetites of a murderer too rich to pay for his crimes?

'The Ancestor directs us to follow the tenets of our faith and the church is our armour. I saw the common law fail and I have replaced it with the church law. We here, in this hall, are bound by duty and by faith to show that as sons and daughters of the Ancestor we cannot be bought and sold. Ancestral law is gold to the base metal of common law. We lead where others fall. I saved a child who will serve the Ancestor well, but more than that I struck a blow for the ideals that are written in the Ancestor's own book. If we return Nona to this false justice that blow of mine will not strike against corruption but against the foundations of the church itself.'

Abbess Glass drew a deep breath and allowed her shoulders to slump in concession to the yoke upon them.

The fat archon licked his lips and nodded slowly to himself. Archon Philo, the sorrow-faced marjal, lifted his head from contemplation of his knees. 'A better path would have been to demand a stay of execution while you sought a judge to hear the case.'

'That is perhaps true, archon.' The abbess nodded. 'But the case would have had to have been made very loudly for any judge in Verity to hear it above the clinking of golden coins.' She sighed. 'I acted rashly. I saw that I could take Nona. The trip from *could* to *should* is short and allows little time for reflection. But I do not think that the result was the wrong one. Except that I should have found a way to save both girls.'

'It is, as the high priest says, a dangerous game to play.' Archon Anasta spoke for the first time, her voice deep and thick with age. 'Invoke church law over common law outside our doors and with both hands you are taking the emperor's power as your own.'

'Also true, Archon Anasta. I could never argue politics against the woman who taught it to me in the first place.' The abbess managed a smile, as if she were not yoked and bleeding, but instead discussing the finer points of academia over a school desk. 'However, at no point in removing Nona from Harriton did I invoke one law above another. I made no mention of my office. I simply reminded the guards of my long friendship with Warden James and said that I was taking the girl. None of them attempted to stop me or even ordered me to desist, and so it seemed a perfectly reasonable assumption that they were happy for me to take her. I am more than willing to submit to any test of truth… I hear that there are graduates of the Academy who can deduce whether they are being told a lie, and—'

'The truth is a very nebulous concept.' Archon Philo took on a still more doleful look and returned his gaze to his lap.

'Ha!' The bark of laughter burst from Archon Kratton. 'They didn't even try to stop you?'

'No.'

'Well, it's their incompetence. If they let you take the girl that's tacit permission!' He smacked his fist against his thigh.

'If you've nothing more to say.' High Priest Jacob, realizing that he was still standing, sat heavily in his grand chair. 'If you maintain your refusal to apologize, then we can move on to the sentencing.'

'I move for the charges to be thrown out.' Archon Kratton waved a hand dismissively above his head. 'Who's with me?'

'Kratton!' The high priest struggled back out of his chair. 'You would be advised to give this matter serious con—'

'I have my own mind, Jacob. Old debt and old secrets be damned if they mean selling my soul for Tacsis gold.'

Archon Philo raised his face to the room. 'There seems no case to answer.' He didn't sound happy about it but Nona wondered if he had ever sounded happy about anything.

Archon Anasta fixed Abbess Glass with a stare so hard that Nona could imagine reaching up to find it a physical thing, an invisible bar of iron between them. 'This could have been done better, Glass.'

'I know.'

'Cleaner. Sharper. Clearer. As I always instructed.' The archon narrowed already narrow and bitten lips. 'This … this is muddy, messy, unsure.'

Abbess Glass bowed her head.

'But the child should not suffer your mistake. There is no case to answer here.'

The abbess slumped, a guard stepping forward to prevent her falling.

'Archon Nevis, the decision rests with you.' The high priest walked to stand behind the fat archon's chair. 'You at least I know can be relied upon to understand where the best interests of the church lie.'

Archon Nevis glanced across the line of his fellow archons. He looked nervous, sweat making small ringlets in the grey hair sticking to his forehead. 'I—'

'It's been more years than either of us would care to mention, Nevis,' Abbess Glass said, shaking off the guard and standing straight. Speaking as if there were only the two of them there, Nona and the rest no more than shadows. 'That boy and that girl would not recognize us. We are old. Changed. But I remember. One time, you said. Once. That I could ask anything of you. I doubt you thought it would take me this long to ask it. That one time is now. That anything is this.'

'I remember.' Nevis went still more pale, every vein blue upon the marble of his flesh. 'We were children, Shella. Playing children's games. You can't expect—'

'It was in the focus of the moon, Nevis. The ice lit red about us and began to steam…'

'…and the crakes took to the sky and their song—'

'Very touching.' High Priest Jacob brought his staff down with a crack. 'But Archon Nevis is no longer a moon-eyed boy panting over a tanner's girl. Great Ancestor, woman! Nevis honours the debts of the entire church. The master of the faith's coffers concerns himself with debts of a rather more adult nature. Archon, let's end this farce.'

'I…' Archon Nevis held his finger to his chest, out of the high priest's view. A 'one' for the abbess's eyes. 'The case has no merit. It cannot stand.'

Across the hall, murmurs of approval spread among the guards and attendants. Outside cries of delight went up, though how word reached the women and girls in front of the hall so swiftly Nona had no idea. Archon Kratton was already on his feet, his chair rocking behind him. 'Get the damned yoke off her! She's an abbess of the church!'

Nona found herself standing straight and unsupported, her restraints no burden now, a shout of defiance on her lips.

A guard moved to obey, the heavy key ready in his hand. The loud crack of the high priest's staff against stone cut through raised voices.

'Overruled.'

'What?' Nona stared. Even the archons looked shocked. She looked up at the abbess. 'He can't...'

Of all of them only Abbess Glass seemed unsurprised. 'That's a big step, Jacob. Are you sure you want to—'

'This is a court of law and you will address me by my title!' High Priest Jacob slumped back into his chair of office. 'Your concern is noted, abbess. I'm sure your concern is for me rather than for your own imminent and … uncomfortable … exit from this convent, and from the church as a whole.'

Abbess Glass pursed her lips. 'The office of high priest rests upon four pillars. It's my duty to counsel you against kicking them out from beneath you.'

'Noted.' The high priest turned to his black-clad assistant, scratching at her scroll. 'Make sure you get that down, Greha. *Now* – to the sentencing.'

'I took Nona from the prison because she is The Shield. The Ancestor told me to do it in a vision.' Abbess Glass didn't raise her voice but somehow she gathered all the attention that the high priest held a moment before and focused it upon herself in the quiet of the hall.

'Nonsense! Nonsense...' The high priest tried to wave the idea away. 'This is foolishness, desperation. It would not have been credible if these words were the first out of your mouth on our arrival. To speak them a moment before you're sentenced to have your tongue split … well … it's beneath you. It's beneath an abbess of the Ancestor!'

'Wh—' Nona wanted to ask what a Shield was but the abbess set her large foot over Nona's small one.

'The Shield will have almost as many enemies as the Argatha. It was my duty to protect her until she is able to protect both herself and the Chosen One. She is just a child. Her safety lay in secrecy. Unfortunately, now you have forced a damaging choice: reveal the truth of her identity or let you drown her in ignorance.'

'This is ridiculous, Abbess Glass. Anyone can claim a holy vision to save themselves from justice.'

'Were not my first words to you in this court an invitation to consider *why* I would do such a thing? Rather than giving serious thought to that question you preferred to blame it on a mothering instinct that was singularly absent before my courses ran dry. I ask you once more – knowing what you know of me – do you seriously believe the words that came from your mouth?'

Nona knew herself a stranger to tact but even to her ears the abbess didn't seem to be doing a good job of convincing a proud man to change his mind. She gave him no retreat, no escape, and yet he held all the power. Not even the archons could tell him what to do.

High Priest Jacob cleared his throat, gathered his robes about him as if he might be chilled, and stamped his staff beside his chair. 'I am unconvinced, abbess. The sentence of this court is that—'

'I demand the test.'

'Test? What test?' The high priest glanced to either side as if missing something. Answering his rhetoric, a black-clad assistant leaned in to whisper into his ear. The high priest frowned, the furrows across his forehead growing deeper from one second to the next. Then a smile. 'You want to set this child before the Red Sisters and let them shoot her full of arrows? It's certainly a more interesting form of execution than drowning the girl.' The assistant raised his head from the open book in his arms and leaned in again. 'The child would have to agree to such an ordeal though. Apparently.'

'No.' The pressure on Nona's foot increased as the abbess shook her head. 'That would be ridiculous. The ordeal of the Shield is for any sister that claims the title. It was never intended for a novice. Certainly not one who has worn the habit little more than a week. The test I refer to is the one that became legal precedent after Sister Cane's vision of the Three Arks.' The abbess lifted her foot, freeing Nona's. 'You will have to look in Lorca's book on ecclesiastical proof. I believe Archon Philo's attendant has a copy at the bottom of the pile he has stacked by the archon's chair…'

'Why don't you save us the bother, Abbess Glass, and just tell us?' The high priest clapped one hand over the fist of the other and rested his chin upon it, elbows on his knees.

A smile twitched across the abbess's lips. 'I'm tempted to say that I must affirm my vision to each archon and as a bride of the Ancestor that would be sufficient.' She held up a hand as High Priest Jacob raised his head to object. 'Sadly the ordeal that Sister Cane endured to prove her words was a rather unpleasant one.' A quaver in her voice now.

Archon Anasta spoke into the quiet moment. 'The nun in question held her hand just above the flame of a votive candle until she was believed. The precedent is that either the presiding official is swayed to believe the testimony and allows the witness to withdraw their hand. Or the witness withdraws their hand without permission and by doing so admits the lie. Or, I suppose, the candle burns out, which should be proof enough for anyone of something extraordinary. The whole thing is archaic, barbaric, and rife with superstition, but then again the prophecy to which Abbess Glass refers is archaic and rife with superstition, and the punishment that High Priest Jacob seems determined to impose carries an even greater degree of barbarism and antiquity...' The old woman raised her hands in a gesture of helplessness. 'Who has a candle?'

The archon's request passed via a chain of assistants and guards to the sisters waiting outside and a silence followed as presumably nuns scattered in search of a votive candle.

'How will burning your hand change his mind?' Nona asked. Her wrists had started to hurt and some sensation had returned to her fingers, though the yoke was no less tight. 'He won't care: he likes to hurt things.'

'The high priest will see the depth of my conviction. Every second he delays will shame him before the archons against whom he has set his opinion. He will know that a woman who can stand the flame is capable of anything, and it will sway him.' The abbess spoke with a calm serenity, her eyes fixed on High Priest Jacob in his chair across the chamber.

Nona wondered how Abbess Glass could be so calm. She had burned her fingers in the embers of a fire when she could barely walk and the heat had seared those hot moments of agony into her mind ever since. 'If a woman like that is capable of anything, then she's capable of lying too?'

'Would he care about that? This has never been about truth.' The abbess kept her eyes on High Priest Jacob. 'If he decides to hurt me he will also at the end of it have to set me loose in the world. You think he has the balls for that?'

Nona knew she would be sweating in the abbess's position. Looking for an escape. Ready to fight. But the woman looked so … serene. 'You're doing it, aren't you? That mind game Sister Pan teaches.' Shadowing the Path the novices called it. Not following it like a quantal could, but coming close enough to alter the way their minds worked.

'Serenity.' The abbess made a slow nod.

Nona frowned. Serene or not the abbess would still burn.

A young church guard bustled in, cloak rain-spattered, helm askew. She approached the archons, clutching a votive candle as if it were a holy artefact.

'Remove the prisoner's yoke and bring her before us,' the high priest called. 'Set a table … there. And a rope, to keep her from raising her hand too high above the flame.'

'That hardly seems necessary. I—'

'She's proving herself to me, not to you Archon Kratton, and *I* deem it necessary!' He wiped at his mouth. 'Bring the girl too.'

Beside Nona a guard was working with a heavy key, rotating a screw that allowed the slow separation of the yoke that held Abbess Glass's hands up to either side of her head. The device made a painful sound, sometimes a squeal, sometimes a deeper scraping.

'It would be best if you looked away for this, Nona dear,' the abbess said, easing one hand out from the yoke as the guard moved to release the other. 'Don't interrupt – you won't be helping. I'll need to concentrate.'

Nona watched as the yoke was lifted from around Abbess Glass's neck and, flexing her wrists, she walked out to where the candle had been set upon a table. Nona wondered if the abbess had saved her from the noose as she first said on some point of principle, outraged at the corruption and failure of the empire law? Or because she valued the skills Nona had shown? Or had she truly been led by a vision? Or was that claim made in desperation? None of it made sense. The abbess had said *words are steps along a path: the important thing is to get where you're going.* Nona wondered if the abbess knew where she was going now or if the game had got away from her the day she walked out of Harriton prison holding Nona's hand.

The church-guard who led Nona after the abbess reminded her of the man who had led her to the gallows: tall, greying, probably someone's grandfather. If the abbess failed her trial then he might be the man who pushed Nona from the edge of the sinkhole and sent her sailing down towards the water.

'She's secure?' The high priest descended from his dais to stand over the table till he was almost face to face with Abbess Glass, as if concerned that there might be trickery. Two ropes bound around the abbess's sore wrist led to opposite legs of the table where they had been secured. She could move the hand from side to side, but not raise it.

The votive candle, fat but short, sat close by, its flame flickering as guards moved around the table checking the abbess's restraints.

'Abbess?' The high priest gestured to the flame. 'I wait to be convinced.'

Four archons leaned forward in their chairs and the room held its breath. Nona could hear the rain drumming on the roof above them, splashing from high gutters. Abbess Glass moved her open palm above the flame, a single inch between the tip of its tongue and her skin. The trial hardly looked dramatic. To prove themselves Nona knew the wildmen in Durn hung from trees by ropes attached to iron hooks set beneath the muscle of their chests. But despite the blood and groaning of such theatrics the abbess's trial held its own fascination. Every person in the hall had their own memory of fire's kiss. The one that taught them the lesson you need learn only once. Hot, don't touch.

Abbess Glass kept her gaze upon the high priest, upon the

cold grey of his eyes and the smirk twitching across his lips – amusement? Embarrassment? Her face remained serene and Nona imagined that in her mind the abbess must be following the broad strokes of some path that led to peace, gentle turns finding their way to the quiet places of the world where the wind holds its tongue and the light of the dying sun rests gentle upon the ground.

Long moments passed.

'Ah.' A quick intake of breath. Tension in the abbess's cheeks, a distant pain in her eyes.

'You should give up this foolishness now, Shella.' High Priest Jacob leaned in, his voice falling to a murmur. 'You could burn your whole hand to blackened bones and I'd still know you were lying. This time you're out. You've played your game and lost.'

Abbess Glass clenched her teeth, eyes wide and locked on the high priest's, her breath tight in her throat. 'Glass. I am Glass.' A faint sizzling noise came from beneath her palm. Nona sniffed. It could have been bacon, hot from the pan and heaped in the refectory bowls. Her stomach growled even as she retched.

The abbess's breath, gasped in in tight little bursts, counted out the duration of her ordeal. Nona's shortness made her the sole witness to the flame's damage, first turning a circle of the abbess's palm red, then raising white blisters upon it, then setting them to bubble and blacken.

Tears filled the abbess's eyes and rolled across her cheeks, sweat beaded on her brow, gathered in the folds beneath her chin. The scream that broke from her came so sudden and so loud that Nona jerked backwards and half the guards reached for their swords. The abbess fell to gasping and groaning, deep guttural noises that hurt to hear. She strained to raise her hand, but the ropes held. Her arm shook with effort but moved neither left nor right to escape the heat.

'This is pointless!' The high priest threw up his hands, looking around at the archons. 'Give it up, Shella, you're embarrassing yourself.' If anything it was the high priest who looked embarrassed, almost as red in the face as the abbess.

She was beyond any shame, deep in some place where nothing existed but her and her pain.

'Arrrrrrgggghhh!' A roar of agony this time. Nona could see fats dripping down from the puckered ruin above the candle's flame. It seemed to reach higher now, as if trying to lick her. 'Arrrrrggghhhh!' A cry so awful that Nona would have put her hands to her ears if they were free.

Nona saw again the fluid motion with which the abbess's clever hand had caught her image on her work scroll back in Sister Wheel's class. How would those fingers function now? Could they ever draw again?

'Move your hand!' Nona found it was her saying it. She wasn't alone though – all around the room men and women were muttering it. 'Move your hand!' Archon Philo's assistant lost his composure and shouted at the abbess, his own hands clenched together, white-knuckled.

'This is ridiculous!' The high priest stamped his staff in anger. 'I won't be blackmailed—' Another roar of agony cut him off. Nona could hardly see for tears. Her nose ran and she couldn't wipe it; her throat was raw with shouting for the abbess to stop.

High Priest Jacob's face was set in a rigid, sickly grimace. He turned and walked back to his chair, taking the three steps to the dais in one, his journey punctuated by the abbess's screams. He turned, tucked his robes behind his knees and sat down.

'I will watch the flesh—' Another scream. '—drip from your bones before I let you sell me this—' A scream that had nothing human in it. '—this pathetic lie.'

'I'll take the Shield test!' Nobody heard Nona amongst the shouting and the abbess's almost unbroken howling. She lunged forward, smashing the weight of her yoke into the table. The candle jolted, fell, and rolled away. 'I'll take the Shield test!' Nona yelled it into the stunned silence. For a moment nobody spoke. Then the abbess collapsed and everyone started talking at once.

17

The rain hit Nona, cold and hard, as she stepped through the doors of Heart Hall, the shock of it seeming to wake her to the truth of her situation. Standing in the chamber before the archons in their finery had been so far outside her experience that events took on a dream-like quality, ending in a nightmare. Out there in the freezing rain the grim reality regained its hold.

She could see little but the backs of the guards leading the way, and to either side, almost lost in the downpour, the grey shapes of sisters and novices huddled in their habits, pressed to the walls for shelter. The icy water burned on her wrists where the yoke had taken her skin off. She flexed her hands rapidly, knowing she would need them soon. The rain ran off her fingertips as if they were pipes spraying it from within.

The procession kept a brisk pace. Nona had no problem keeping up. Free now from the yoke's weight she felt as if she were floating, as if with one hard kick she could shrug off the earth's bonds and reach the roof of Blade Hall, a dark shape wavering ahead of them. A few moments later they were through the doors with more men pushing in behind them.

Two guards took Nona off to one side, paying no real care to how they held her, as if she were really just a little girl, not a prisoner accused of murder preparing to take some trial that few full-fledged Red Sisters would try.

The high priest and archons came through the doors and

stood dripping on the sand, finery bedraggled. Nona's mother used to say that the rain didn't care how long you'd spent brushing your hair, it'd fall on you just the same. The villagers had it that there were gods in the rain, just as there were gods in each river and wood. You could pray to them but generally by the time they got close enough to hear you it was too late to stay dry.

Once through the doors the archons didn't get long to find their bearings as more figures pressed in behind. First priests and the attendants from the church party but then the nuns, and on their heels the novices, and nobody moved to stop them.

With hardly a word spoken the entire assembly shuffled along the left side of the hall and up onto the tiered seating at the far end. The last few backsides were settling by the time Abbess Glass came through the main doors, escorted by two church-guards, supported by Sister Rock, a solid and hatchet-faced Red Sister, on one side and by Sister Rose on the other, still adjusting the edges of a mass of linen bandages that bulked the abbess's hand into something almost spherical. Abbess Glass seemed unsteady on her feet, allowing herself to be led. The guards took her to stand before the lowest tier of the seating. When she passed Nona the abbess shot her a quick look, fleeting but long enough for Nona to see those same shrewd dark eyes that had assessed her that first day back at the base of the gallows.

Nona searched the stands. The classes were mixed together, novice sat by nun, but she spotted Clera and Ruli huddled together on the second tier. A glimpse of colour drew Nona's gaze a little way behind the girls: Sister Apple's red hair escaping her headdress, Sister Kettle tight beside her, no less close than Clera sat with Ruli.

The high priest stood in the highest tier, his hat discarded, wet grey hair plastered back across a reddened forehead. 'Sister Wheel … Sister…' He glanced at the black-clad man beside him who muttered something. 'Sister Rose. You are, I understand, the Sister Superiors at Sweet Mercy? Deputized with authority in the abbess's absence. And as a prisoner of church law she is absent from authority. So, it falls to you to administer the ordeal of the Shield to this … novice.'

Sister Rose said something inaudible and hurried over towards Nona, her fatness jolting and jiggling around her. 'Oh my dear…' She dropped heavily to her knees, ignoring the guards, and took Nona's hands in hers.

Suddenly Nona wanted to cry. She felt like a child, as she had been in the mists of her memory, when her mother's arms were a fortress and a haven. She shook herself free of Sister Rose's embrace. Her mother had let them give her to the child-taker: the weakness Sister Rose offered wouldn't help her.

'What do I have to do?' she asked.

Sister Rose's eyes darted past her, to where the practice dummies stood, crowded together on their round bases, each of them a leather man-shape about six foot tall, battered by innumerable punches and kicks. The dummies would rock back when struck, absorbing the force of a blow, then bounce forward as the lead in their base pulled them upright once more. 'Well … with the bigger girls, the new sisters I mean … it's been a few years now … Kettle was the last … she took spear and dagger…' Sister Rose struggled to her feet, shaking her head. 'You there!' She waved to a couple of guards by the main door. 'We need one of the practice-shapes moved against that wall.' She turned back to Nona, looked to the stands, then back at Nona. 'But … but this is madness!'

Madness or not the two church-guards crossed to the dummies and began to haul one to the spot that Sister Rose had indicated, its base leaving a smooth and wide depression in the sand.

'Wait!' The high priest rose from his place on the highest bench. 'The Shield protects the Argatha, a precious gift from the Ancestor, not some lump of leather-bound horsehair. Let us have her defend flesh and blood at least, so there is some echo of the pressure under which such work must be done.' He held his hand out towards Nona and looked around, his smile returning. 'Who will volunteer?' He turned his gaze left, then right. 'Have you no faith in this Shield?'

Sister Kettle made to stand, biting her lip, but the Poisoner caught her arm and dragged her back, her brow furrowed, eyes intense. They fell to furious whispering.

'No one?' The high priest spread both his hands and his grin now.

'I will.' Sister Tallow got to her feet just five places along from the high priest, unwrapping the wet sling from her arm as she did so. She started to move along the bench towards the steps, nuns and archons standing to let her by.

'I think not.' The high priest leaned his staff into Sister Tallow's path as she reached him. 'Mistress Blade, is it not? How would we know, those of us with slow eyes, if it were the child who defended you or if you defended yourself?'

'I would tell you.' Sister Tallow narrowed her eyes into a stare whose discomfort Nona could feel across the hall. The high priest wilted before it.

'Yes, yes…' He rallied as a new thought struck him. 'But the child could hardly defend someone as tall as you, Mistress Blade. She barely reaches past your hip. We must pair her with someone close to her own stature, no? For a fair test.' He didn't wait for an answer. 'We need a novice. If there are no volunteers then that lack of faith speaks for itself – she can hardly be the Shield if no one believes in her. As well as defend, the Shield must represent and carry our belief.' The high priest looked around, his gaze running across the crowded seating. 'A novice! A girl from her own class would be most suitable. Who is ready to put their lives in this criminal's hands?'

Nona wondered how many of those present had seen the ordeal of the Shield undertaken. None of the novices, if Sister Kettle had been the last to take it. Perhaps there were demonstrations, or maybe just stories, and sometimes the story of a thing created more fear than the reality. Either way, none of Red Class were leaping to their feet. Clera had her eyes down, staring at the back of someone's head. Beside her, Ruli was at least looking at Nona but with a wide and hopeless stare. She spotted Ketti and Ghena together, the former pale, her mouth half-open, the latter scowling furiously as if she'd just been insulted. Behind them and to the right two shaved heads. Jula seemed to be crying, Arabella about to open her mouth, perhaps to laugh.

'No one?' High Priest Jacob pressed his lips into a thin smile. 'The matter is settle—'

'I will.' Hessa had been bending down for her crutch. Now she used it to get to her feet.

Nona's eyes misted. The story running wild through the convent was of how she'd failed to save Saida. How she'd let her friend die. She hadn't expected any of them to trust her to protect them. She looked down at her hands, made fists of them, and squeezed until it hurt.

Hessa made her way down from the seating with agonizing slowness, awkward on the steps, all eyes upon her. The high priest leaned forward to the tier below him and tapped Sister Wheel on the shoulder. In the hush as Hessa descended the last steps High Priest Jacob's voice carried further than perhaps he intended.

'—not chosen to be a Red Sister. She's not quantal?'

Sister Wheel muttered something in reply. Nona heard the word 'waste' in the high priest's answer. Maybe he thought quantal blood too precious to spill in such an exercise, but Sister Wheel seemed unconcerned, perhaps willing to pay that price to rid the convent of a peasant. And a crippled one at that.

Hessa stumped across the sand to join Nona and Sister Rose, swinging her withered leg, the foot leaving shallow scuff-marks behind her. She offered Nona an uncertain smile, the blue of her eyes darker than Nona had ever seen it.

'You shouldn't do this,' Nona said.

'I'm your friend,' Hessa said. 'Besides, you'll protect me.'

Nona's eyes widened. 'Friend?'

'Of course, silly. You don't think Clera's your only friend, do you? People can be friends without saying so.'

Nona opened her mouth and found that she had run out of words. She had vowed that she would never let a friend down, that she would do anything, anything at all, to protect them. A vow more sacred to her than the Ancestor, more holy than the church from tallest spire to lowest crypt. The idea that someone might count her as a friend without her knowledge or agreement suddenly complicated things.

Sister Rose set her hands to their shoulders. 'Do you both understand the trial?'

Nona shook her head but Hessa replied, 'I have to stand still and Nona has to defend me from a thrown spear and a throwing star, and … are there four stages in the full trial or three?'

'There are—'

'Sister Rose!' The high priest calling down from the back of the stands. 'Get them ready if you will. And provide Captain Rogan with a spear.' At his words one of the church-guards standing at the main doorway stepped forward, not a gerant but well over six foot and solid in chest and limb. He removed his helm and brushed back short brown hair sprinkled, like his short brown beard, with grey. A pallid scar pulled his mouth into a sneer. His eyes, though, were neither cruel nor kind, only incurious, as if throwing a spear at little girls was just another of the day's duties.

Sister Rose steered the two girls towards a part of the wall covered by a splintered wooden hoarding. Nona felt a tremble in the woman's hand. 'Do your best, Nona.' Her voice wavered. 'Oh dear. And Hessa, don't be scared. Sister Tallow says Nona is very fast … and ... I'm sure the abbess is right… She had a vision, and…' The nun choked on the next word, instead taking them into her arms, pressing them both against her fatness. Nona was surprised to find herself not wanting to be let go of. The ordeal hadn't scared her until the high priest had put a person's life in her hands – and now that person was Hessa. Her friend, Hessa.

'Sister Rose!' The high priest's voice, not well pleased by the delay.

The nun struggled, weeping, to her feet and let Sister Flint lead her off. Flint glanced back once, dark eyes finding Nona's. A curt nod and she looked away, helping Sister Rose to the back of the hall.

Nona turned and stepped closer to Hessa, so close their

noses almost touched. 'Don't move. I won't have time to look at you. I have to know you're where I put you.'

'I'll do my best.' Hessa gave a weak smile, very pale now, glancing towards Captain Rogan, now being presented with a spear from the stores. 'In any case, it takes me ages to get anywhere.'

The captain hefted his weapon, a plain ash shaft nearly two yards long, iron shod, the blade narrow, designed to penetrate armour. 'You have anything heavier? Broad-leaf?'

Sister Tallow narrowed her eyes at the man. 'Nothing heavier. We have blade-headed spears, if your desire is to cut as much flesh as possible, captain.'

The man shrugged and waved away the suggestion with no apparent embarrassment. 'This will serve.'

The high priest stamped staff to floor. 'Let's get this nonsense over with.'

Nona looked towards Abbess Glass and the abbess gave her the same calculating look she'd given that day at the prison, tossing hoare-apples at her. Nona turned, set her hands to Hessa's shoulders, positioned her, then faced the captain, taking five paces forward. Less time to see the spear coming – more time for any slight deflection to grow.

'Sister Wheel, if you will adjudicate.' The high priest opened his palms in a gentle shoving motion, and taking the hint, the nun descended to the sands, moving in that strange gangling way of hers that seemed as if it should belong to something not born of a woman.

Nona spent the wait studying the captain, watching the gleam of his breastplate, the sway of the iron-studded leather tongues of the undershirt as it divided into a skirt to protect his upper legs. The bright point of his spear. The thickness of his arm.

At last Sister Wheel took her place at the middle of the hall and raised her hand. 'Ancestor witness this our trial of faith and swiftness, the Argatha's Shield.' She looked left, right. 'Ready?' She let her arm fall.

Nona lengthened her heartbeats and watched. The captain's arm hooked back, launched forward, sliding through the air, a wordless roar on his lips. Fingers opened at the full extension of his arm, releasing the spear's shaft. Nona wrapped the world about her, watching the bright steel point of the blade pulse slightly up and down as the spear's shaft flexed with the power of the throw.

Captain Rogan aimed his throw at Nona's heart. She began to twist to the side. Swiftness depends on reaction, on the speed with which the mind understands what the eyes show it, and with which it sends its orders to the body. No matter how fast those messages though, there are limits to what muscles can do. Nona knew that a finger can be moved more swiftly than a hand, a hand quicker than an arm, an arm faster than a body. She worked to move her torso from the path of the spear's flight, her thin body suddenly heavier than iron, sullenly resisting her strength as she strove to shove it aside.

While she twisted she raised her arms, readying her hands, one atop the other, backs flat to her chest. Every part of the hall lay frozen, faces, eyes, the shower of sand from the captain's heels hanging in the air. Only Nona moved, Nona and the spear, sliding inexorably towards her heart.

By the time the steel point reached her, in the thick deep silence of her speed, Nona had almost twisted clear of the line that joined its sharpness to her friend's heart. The widest part of the blade touched her fingers as it passed. The tickle wouldn't reach her for a while yet but her muscles had already been primed to push, and with near perfect timing they did, driving her palm against the haft of the spear.

At speed everything refuses motion with an obdurate stubbornness, as if the air itself were thickest mud. Although the weight of the spear proved problematic Nona had two advantages. Firstly, she was applying pressure right at the end she wished to deflect, just behind the spearhead. Secondly, she was sufficiently in advance of her friend that moving the spearhead just an inch at this point would see it miss Hessa entirely.

Nona shoved with all the strength and speed that lay in her limbs. The wooden shaft slid across her palm. A moment's panic washed through her as she realized that if she continued to push after the spear's midpoint had passed across her hands she might be turning the spearhead back towards Hessa. Her mind spoke but it took an age for her arms to cease their advance. The spear's midpoint had passed her hands, and several inches more had travelled across her palm, when the contact ceased – the spear now on its new path, her only chance to influence it passed.

Nona let the world spin up to its given speed around her, her gaze locked on Captain Rogan. If his spear killed Hessa she would give him a new scar for his collection. And more besides. The impact thundered around her, echoing back from walls and ceiling. For a moment there was only the voice of the spear, the shuddering of its shaft about a point now bedded deep. And then … a rising cheer. Nona turned to see Hessa, just as she had left her, eyes crinkled shut but beginning to open, the spear standing proud of the wall, a three-inch gap between its shaft and her upper arm.

'Thank you,' Hessa gasped. She came forward on her crutch and put Nona in an awkward one-armed embrace.

'Proceed!' On the stands the high priest thumped his staff down. 'I assume this gets more taxing as we go?'

'The throwing star!' Sister Wheel's cracked voice silenced the last remnants of conversation. 'Mistress Blade, if you will?'

'Not her. Wheel, you do it.' The high priest waved Sister Tallow back to her seat. 'And put your damn arm into it.'

'Sister Wheel?' Nona snorted under her breath. She turned to Hessa. 'Good. What can she do?'

'Bad!' Hessa shook her head. 'You don't know? She took her orders as a Red Sister. She passed all the trials. Then renounced it to be a Holy. She doesn't think Red Sisters are proper nuns – not close enough to the Ancestor. She—'

'The throwing star!' Sister Wheel had taken the captain's place and now held her hand overhead, a steel throwing star catching the light from the windows. The thing was almost unbroken blade: a small heavy centre, five broad, bright blades, gaps behind and between them where Sister Wheel held it. Quite how she would release it in the throw without slicing her own fingers off Nona didn't know.

'Ancestor witness this our trial of faith and swiftness.' Sister

Wheel narrowed her eyes at Nona, as if she were the target, not Hessa. She shook her long arm, twisting the over-flexible wrist. Her eyes, normally wide as if in permanent and vaguely comical surprise, became something else entirely when slitted: in those moments something baleful and other than human watched the world through them.

Nona brought her arms before her, hands crossed.

Without further warning Wheel shook her arm, cracking it like a whip to set the throwing star flying. The motion looked too casual to have imparted such speed but the star sliced through the air considerably more swiftly than Captain Rogan's spear, revolving around its centre, blades cutting sparkles from the light. It came spinning around the vertical axis, the disc of it parallel to the floor, aimed at Nona's chest. Even if she could deflect the weapon by pressing at the side of it she would need to push the thing off course by a large enough degree to send it over Hessa's head or into the ground before her feet. A huge deflection. To move it the small amount to miss Hessa to the left or right Nona would have to press against the whirling blades… Even as she considered the matter the throwing star devoured a third of the distance between them, and for once in her life Nona found she could burrow no further into the space between her heartbeats.

She started to extend one arm towards the oncoming star. With the other she started to run her nails from the habit's cuff towards her armpit. The tough cloth parted beneath her fingers without resistance. When she was tiny Billem Smithson had tried to hurt her. Nona had held her bloody hands out to her mother. *This was what was inside him.* The boy's skin had sliced where she touched him, four parallel wounds, as if she had invisible blades reaching from her fingers. The same had happened when she struck Raymel Tacsis and again when she had reached to fend off his brother on the abbess's steps. She'd tried to make it happen many times, in long boring hours, on dull days when the rain fell thick with ice … but only in Harriton prison had the sharpness come to her outside a moment of panic or rage. The ropes that had bound her hands behind her had given way beneath her touch.

Now her fingers sliced the sleeve of her habit into long ribbons. Perhaps they were shredding the skin and muscle beneath too – there hadn't been time for any pain to reach her yet or for any blood to fall.

The throwing star approached Nona's outstretched hand just as her other hand reached her armpit and continued, now with just one finger extended, to slice a line across her chest. The star passed within a breath of the veins in her wrist and whirred along just beneath her reaching arm where the ribbons of her sleeve had not yet had time to fall. It swept through them, cutting through whatever opposed it, but tangling other ribbons in the narrow spaces between the blades, winding them up about itself as it flew beneath Nona's elbow.

When her finger reached her breastbone Nona stopped cutting and reversed the thrust of her arm, pushing against the momentum of blood and bone, fingers cupped to scoop up the flap of cloth sliced free before them.

The bundled throwing star travelled the length of her arm, reaching the point where it would start to pass beneath her shoulder. Nona's other hand met it, the cloth of her habit balled into a palm angled down and to the side. The force of the impact rippled up through her arm. Nona had done everything she could. She let the moment go.

The thud of the cloth-wrapped star, the jolt of its impact up her arm, and the sharp pain in her hand, all reached Nona at the same time. The star fell to the sand, its energy spent. Looking down she saw her hand filling with blood and thought for a moment that her whole arm might be sliced open, but a darker spot among the crimson wash revealed the truth – one point of the throwing star had penetrated all the cloth layers to puncture her palm, a small hole but deep and bleeding freely.

The cheering rose around her as she tugged free a trailing strip of her sleeve and bound it tight about her hand.

'Cover yourself, girl!' Sister Wheel stalked towards her, scowling her disapproval, peering at the shredded sleeve and the broad flap torn loose across Nona's chest. 'What have you done?'

'I protected Hessa.' Nona bit down on the harsher words queuing behind her lips.

'You've ruined your habit!' Suspicious eyes ran over exposed flesh and the sharp upper edge of the rip across Nona's chest. 'How…'

Nona waved her sleeve, fixing Sister Wheel with her stare. '*Your* throwing star chewed this up.' *Would you rather it had been my flesh?* Something in the glare the Holy Sister returned suggested she just might.

'I hope the last round of this ordeal is rather more testing!' The high priest broke the line that joined their eyes. Nona blinked and shook her head. She hadn't thought enough time had passed for the old man to limp down all those steps. She looked up at him, his scowl as ugly as Sister Wheel's, and found herself dizzy. The hand she raised to her face seemed to take an age – voices buzzed around her like angry flies.

'—wrong with the girl?' The high priest snorted. 'She's hardly a Shield if the sight of a few drops of blood has her reeling around.'

'I'm all right.' Nona didn't feel it though. She felt weak in every limb, tired beyond endurance. A puppet with one string remaining, and if that would just let her go she would lie face down in the softness of the sand and sleep.

'The last trial is the bow,' Sister Wheel said, mouth pressed into an unreadable line. 'Fetch me a bow!'

'No!' The high priest raised his hand. 'You've had your chance, Wheel. I have just the man for this – and just the bow. Devid?' He raised his voice, looking around. 'Devid!'

A big man vaulted down from the first row of seating, one of the bearers for the high priest's sedan chair, his arms roped with muscle.

'Fetch the eagle-bow from my luggage train. Go! Quick about it!'

The man sped off, sand flying from his heels. Nona stepped away until her back was against the wall. Hessa took her shoulder and tried to turn her. 'What's the matter? You look awful.'

Nona slid until her bottom touched the floor. She bowed her head. 'Long night. Just tired.' The words slurred from her mouth. Had the throwing star been dipped in some kind of venom? 'Just … close my … eyes.'

'You can't sleep—' But Hessa's voice seemed to be coming from a long way off, becoming little more than muffled echoes in the cavern whose darkness swallowed … everything.

A slap brought the world back, the daylight streaming through the narrow windows, the low murmur of conversation, and beneath it the distant thunder of rain on the high roof.

'Get up, girl!' Sister Wheel's other bony hand, knotted in the remnants of Nona's habit, hauled her to her feet.

Behind the nun Devid stood ready, his tunic soaked and sticking to him, sculpting the muscles of his chest and shoulders. The bow before him was nearly as tall as he was, not a single arch like the hunters of the Grey used but a composite of different curvatures and woods. In the hands of a skilled archer such a bow truly could bring down the white eagles that rode the Corridor wind. Though no peasant would ever protect his herd with one – the price of such a weapon would exceed that of any shepherd's flock, and his land to boot.

The high priest stamped his way to the man's side. 'Get this done.'

Half the seats lay empty now, nuns, novices, guards and bearers all crowding to either side of the line between Nona and Hessa against the hall's north wall and the archer before the south wall. Even Abbess Glass had been allowed to approach, her guard close by. Nona glanced at the abbess's right hand, fat with bandages, and at her own, the strip of fabric black with blood, the skin from fingertips to the heel of her palm red and sticky. Abbess Glass met her eyes and gave that same nod, sure and intense.

'Ancestor witness this our trial of faith and swiftness.' Sister Wheel waved the onlookers back.

Devid pulled a long arrow from the quiver over his shoulder, white fletched, perhaps with eagle feathers, the steel head long and narrow, designed to penetrate rather than slice. He nocked it to the bow and looked to the high priest who gave him an impatient wave.

Nona watched, her hands before her chest as before, one atop the other, the back of the left against her sternum, the palm of the right facing Devid and his bow. The man had a raw-boned, brutal face, as if the clay from which he had been formed had been in the Ancestor's hands for no more than a moment, just long enough for bold strokes.

'She's only a child.' The words rumbled out of him so deep and low that Nona had trouble picking them apart. 'Both of them, little girls.' He looked at the high priest again, helpless.

'You'll shoot that arrow hard enough to put it through the damn wall, Devid.' The high priest thudded down his staff, though the sand deadened the impact. 'The Ancestor will decide who is worthy of tomorrow. There will be no sin on your hands. Now do it!'

Devid lifted one huge hand to rub an eye, shook his head, then returned the hand to the bowstring. He drew in a smooth motion, muscles bulging, veins standing proud along his forearm, the bow creaking with the strain. Held. Held. And with a cry of anger or shame, let fly.

The arrow came fast, no matter how hard Nona clung to each passing fragment of the moment. It flexed back and forth like a decked fish, shuddering with the power of the bowstring's push as it flew towards her. Its path from Devid's height to Hessa's heart would take it just over Nona's left shoulder.

She threw herself backward towards the ground and watched, helpless, hands outstretched and rising.

To push against that thin shaft – to do so hard enough to deflect it from Hessa, and to give that push in the tiny span during which the shaft passed her by – would likely just break through it. And that would leave the arrowhead or the shaft behind it still travelling towards Hessa at lethal speed.

Too quickly, allowing no time for thought, the arrow was before her. Hands, already in place, already closing, now clamped upon the arrow. Nona saw her skin exit the tight curl of her fingers, carried away on the first emerging inch of the arrow shaft, the next inch slid out bloody. She wouldn't feel it until long after the arrow had found its final destination.

The emerging, blood-slicked arrow moved more slowly

than it had covered the yards between Nona and the archer, but it was not slow, and lubricated with her blood her grip would not reduce its speed below a lethal level before the arrow left her hands. Nona pulled down, hoping she could be gentle enough to draw the arrowhead down rather than snap off the rear portion.

She watched the arrow's flights escape her hands. In the same instant the steel point, deflected slightly downward, touched her beneath the collarbone. By the time her hands caught up with the end of the arrow the arrowhead was buried three inches deep in her shoulder, slowed by the thickness of her flesh and turned further from its path by the rotation of her body as she fell backward. She grasped the wood again, willing some sharpness into her touch, hoping it would help to grip rather than reduce the shaft to sections.

Still no hint of the pain had reached her. She knew by the length of arrow that had vanished into her that the arrowhead must have emerged high on her back, but she felt nothing. The sharpness in her fingers shaved pieces from the arrow like a carpenter's plane on timber. The rear of it fell into tumbling inch-long sections. They bounced off her, peppering the area around the bloody hole beneath her collarbone as she fell.

She knew her head would hit the sand hard. But the impact never came. She fell and there was no bottom to it, just whiteness, and then no colour at all.

18

Nona spat sand from her mouth, finding more between her teeth and behind her lips than she could get rid of. Something cold and wet covered her face. She tried to push it away. The pain arrived in that instant, all at once, something too huge for her body, trying to explode out from beneath muscle and skin. She screamed, or tried to: it came out more as a whimper. The wet thing moved and through eyes screwed tight in agony she saw the blur of someone leaning over her, cloth in hand.

'Stay still.' Sister Rose set a hand to Nona's chest.

'Hessa?' Nona tried to roll but the white fire in her shoulder stopped her more effectively than the nun.

'Hessa's fine.' A smile. 'The arrow hit the ground a foot before her.' Sister Rose looked to the side. 'We need to move her!' Called to someone else.

Other voices reached into Nona's awareness. She focused on the roof high above her, the sand beneath her heels. She was still in Blade Hall. People were talking to her right. A roll of her head brought them into view.

Abbess Glass stood there, free of the yoke, head high, Sister Apple at her shoulder. The archons and the high priest faced her, all of them on the practice sand now. Looking the other way, she saw a host of nuns and novices, church-guards escorting them from the hall and everyone leaving as slowly as possible so as not to miss anything. Sisters Flint, Kettle and

Mop were approaching, presumably to carry Nona to the sanatorium, though any one of them could lift her.

'…irregular! In this day and age, to be thwarting the due process of the emperor's law with archaic texts and talk of prophecy… You would do well to give the child over to the civil judges, abbess, however thick the hunska runs in her veins. It's very disappointing. This matter could make all kinds of trouble for us – not the least of it in the emperor's own court—'

'What disappoints me, Jacob, is that you appear to have been purchased wholesale, along with your staff and office, for something as worthless as money.' Abbess Glass raised her voice, not shouting but lending it the power to reach the rafters. 'The church of the Ancestor is not for sale. You bring the archons here, racing from the four corners of empire, and then slap them in the face with a veto when their opinion is not the one Thuran Tacsis purchased? I say there should be a vote of no confidence. Here and now!'

The high priest snarled: the same look he wore when he raised his staff to strike a blow across Four-Foot's back. 'It's not your place to call any such—'

'I call for a vote.' Archon Kratton rubbed at his scars, scowling. 'Can't say I'm impressed, high priest. Three days on horseback to reach Verity. From what the bird brought wrapped around its leg I thought to find the walls fallen, or the emperor proved a bastard, the Scithrowl heresy afoot in the streets… Instead a child has humbled a bully. And if we're to believe she's the Argatha's Shield, then you've put a hole in her just because you wouldn't trust the abbess's word.'

'I vote for vacation of office.' Archon Philo, looming over his fellow clerics, lean and languorous, in sharp contrast to Kratton's compact strength and restless energy. 'Anasta?'

The eldest of them rolled the ball of her earring through long fingers then lowered the hand to fold into her other. 'You have no idea how uncomfortable it is to spend five nights on the Bluewine when it's in full spate. A riverboat's no way to travel at the best of times. I get seasick looking at a cup of water. But,' she raised her hand, 'it would not have concerned me had the summons been for a matter of import. It might even have been forgivable as a lone lapse of judgement … if our decision had been respected. But to bring us scurrying to Verity like lapdogs just to underwrite your own sentence on poor Glass here… I vote for vacation of office.' She turned to her left. 'Archon Nevis?'

The fat archon ran both hands over the grey curls of his hair, still thick at the sides, and at the top as bald and shiny as Anasta's head was all over. 'Vacation.'

'Which leaves me,' Kratton said, stepping sharply across to the high priest until they stood face to face, eyes on a level. 'And as the vote would have to be unanimous to remove you, I find myself mattering…'

'Kratton, we should discuss this in private… There are *issues* that—'

'I've never had a particularly good opinion of your term in office, Jacob. The staff does things to a man – most of them bad. Doesn't do to have too many people around you whose position depends on their being agreeable. Even so, I would have voted to keep you … but for one thing. A high priest can be stupid, he can be greedy, he can be wrong: but what he can't be is purchased. I voted to put you in the office and I'll stand by that. I didn't vote to put a Tacsis in the robe and hat though. You'll have to go. I'm sorry. Vacation of office.'

Someone had their hands on Nona, crouched over her, ready to lift, but nobody was going anywhere until this was done. The silence behind her let Nona know that the nuns had given up any pretence of leaving.

'This … this is outrageous!' The high priest backed away from the archons and abbess, limping on the leg the roof-tiles had injured, his staff held defensively before him. 'No high priest has ever—'

'High Priest Albur was removed by his archons forty-three years ago during the last narrowing,' Abbess Glass offered.

'And High Priestess Sartra a century before that. For … indelicate relations,' Archon Anasta added, nodding.

'I won't. This is … a conspiracy.' High Priest Jacob purpled.

He stared in Nona's direction. 'A trick! Guards! Take these archons into custody. Yoke them!'

A pair of church-guards moved to flank the high priest; the rest were at the fore of the hall to usher out the now-unwelcome audience. The first of those guards to move took one step before Sister Tallow's foot found the back of his knee and he collapsed to the floor with a clatter. Another guard reached for her but Tallow caught the woman's wrist and with a twist had her tumbling to the sand. The guard behind reached for his sword.

'My title is Mistress Blade, young man. I have been a Red Sister since before you were born. Do not try me.'

The guard – who didn't look particularly young to Nona – stopped with just an inch of steel gleaming above his scabbard and looked across to the far end of the hall. The two church-guards beside High Priest Jacob had their hands on their sword hilts but showed no enthusiasm for arresting the archons.

Archon Kratton raised his voice before the high priest could master his outrage. 'Captain Rogan. Your loyalty to the high priest is not in question, but this man is no longer the high priest. You will have to put your faith in the judgement of four archons and a convent full of nuns when it comes to the legalities of the matter, but I can assure you that our proceedings have been every bit as correct here as they were in the court in which we served immediately prior to these events. Please tell your men to stand at ease.'

The silent moment that followed seemed as long as any that Nona had clung to in the ordeal.

'At ease, guards.'

'This is treachery! Blasphemy! The emperor will hear of it and set your heads on stakes!' Jacob seemed half-crazed, clutching his staff as if it were his former rank and not some piece of gilded wood. 'The emperor will hear…' A whisper now.

'And you are welcome to tell him, Jacob,' Archon Nevis said, his face near as solemn as Archon Philo's. 'You are free to go. In time I hope you will agree to serve in one of my dioceses. Priest Martew of Gellim passed to the Ancestor last month and his flock would benefit from the wisdom of a church elder—'

'Gellim? Are you mad? It's a wild ice-swamp on the margins!' The former high priest started towards the main door, half-stamping, half-limping. 'I'm going to the palace. Anyone who tries to stop me will hang!'

The archons watched him go.

'We should recover the staff…' Archon Philo said.

'Let him keep it.' Abbess Glass smiled. 'It's just a stick. Besides, he'll need it on the way down. The footing can be treacherous.'

'We find ourselves in need of a new high priest.' Archon Philo flexed his long hands and interlaced his fingers before him.

'Well, we're all here,' Kratton said. 'We could retire to a room and talk in circles for hours, or just get done with it and go home. Damned if I want to spend any longer than I have to on this windswept lump of rock. No offence, Glass.'

'None taken.'

Archon Anasta swept the crowd with a dark gaze. 'We could ask for no better witnesses.'

'I vote Anasta,' Archon Philo said.

'I vote Nevis.' Archon Anasta inclined her head. 'He showed the greatest courage today and will make fewest ripples with the emperor.'

Archon Nevis looked surprised. 'I vote Nevis too.' He hugged his belly, smile spreading.

'I suppose…' Kratton waved a hand as if the matter were trifling. 'Nevis then.'

The three of them turned to look up at Archon Philo. 'Really, Anasta?'

She nodded. 'At my age what I want is a comfortable chair, not too far from the privy, not too close. And chamile tea. Lots of it.'

'Nevis then.'

'That's done then.' Archon Kratton dusted off his hands. 'Congratulations, High Priest Nevis. You can pay for your own staff. Now, if you don't mind I have a church to consecrate, an outbreak of shellpox to deal with, and a prize mare that may already have given birth. Shall we go?'

'You forget, Kratton.' Anasta raised a hand. 'We're short of one archon. I suggest the new high priest pick Abbess Glass.'

Nevis frowned and bowed his head, chins doubling, then tripling. 'That would be irregular, but—'

At the far end of the hall the main door slammed shut behind the former incumbent.

'Thank you.' Abbess Glass took a step towards High Priest Nevis. 'But no, my place is here, I have my sisters to serve, novices to raise to nuns, and besides, politicking has never been my forte.'

The high priest and all three archons spluttered with laughter at that, Nevis and Anasta laughing longest.

'Abbess Glass.' Nevis wiped at his eyes. 'Sometimes I think that if you ever gave up the great game the ice would close on us.' He looked at the sisters to either side of her. 'Get this woman to the sanatorium, and the child – she probably bleeds faster than anyone should too.' He clapped his hands and Nona found herself lifted easily in Sister Kettle's arms. The pain bit once more, hard, making her cry out and she buried her face against Kettle's shoulder as the nun carried her from the hall.

19

Sister Rose had given Nona a bitter drink that looked like ditch water. Sleep had taken her almost immediately. Now she cracked open a bleary eye and tried to focus. She felt much like she imagined the sheets in the laundry must after being trampled in the tubs.

'Abbess?' Nona finally made sense of the blurred shape beside her. Her voice escaped in a cracked whisper that seemed to go unnoticed. She brought up a hand to examine the hole beneath her collarbone, only to discover both it and her other hand were bound in strips of linen, stained across the palms with some kind of orange paste. She rolled with a groan and felt an echo of her earlier pain. Linen sheets limited her movement and she discovered herself naked beneath them, save for the broad strips of gauze wrapped around the injured shoulder, across her chest and beneath the right arm. 'Abbess.' The word came louder this time.

Abbess Glass leaned over from her bed and held a cup of water for Nona to sip from. She looked older, papery wrinkles around her eyes. 'More. Drink it all if you can.'

Nona found she could.

'Now sleep.'

And Nona found she could do that too.

Within the sanatorium Sister Rose's opinion held ultimate authority. It didn't matter who had just been offered an archon's chair or who had just passed the ordeal of the Shield. The small ward boasted five beds, all in a line, opposite a large window overlooking the private herb garden. Abbess Glass lay in the bed furthest from the door, Nona in the one next to her.

That first day Sister Rose allowed no visitors. By evening Nona lay propped up on pillows watching the sun set behind the rooftop across the garden. Abbess Glass sat reading from one of several scrolls piled on the table beside her bed. She had bandages on both wrists and her right hand was still heavily wrapped. Awkward with her left, she cursed like a woodsman the third time the scroll escaped her and rolled itself up, only to remember Nona's presence and break off into a fake cough.

'Your name has been spoken before the emperor in his throne room, Nona, did you know that?' The abbess looked across from her work.

'My name?' Nona blinked. She couldn't imagine even her name entering the palace.

'A high priest has fallen. It's no small matter. The church is one of the pillars upon which the emperor's power rests. He has considerable interest in it being solid from the foundation to the highest point. Thuran Tacsis was summoned to court. He has pledged to put aside his grievance against you, and by extension the convent that shelters you. The matter is closed.'

'And you believe him?' Nona saw Raymel Tacsis's face, the same arrogance had been mirrored on his brother's. They would not forgive or forget.

'Thuran Tacsis is a cold and ruthless man. He would murder a thousand small girls if they stood in the way of his ambition. But he is not a mad dog. Oaths are not lightly given to the emperor. He will move on. Our Lord Tacsis has bigger fish to fry than you, novice, and this matter has already set him back. Don't forget him though, for he will surely not forget you. Some people have a slow anger in them, that builds up a piece at a time so you won't see it coming. Such anger has a momentum to it, so it'll come to the boil sometimes even when the thing provoking it has stopped. Thuran Tacsis is not alone in that – watch for such people, Nona. But yes, I believe him, for now.'

Nona let the tension run from her, giving herself to the pillows' embrace. Outside the rain fell at a steep wind-borne slant.

'Did that old nun really talk about me a hundred years ago?'

'No.' The abbess didn't look up, only tilted her scroll more towards the candle she had just lit.

'But…' Nona hadn't wanted it to be true but the sudden dismissal left her feeling slightly put out. 'But they said Sister Argatha was a famous Holy Witch. She made a prophecy…'

'There's no such thing as prophecy, Nona. Or rather there is but it's madmen that tell them, or people who were once listened to for their wisdom and have found themselves growing old and unwise yet still wanting to be heard. There's no magic in it. Magic doesn't work that way.'

'Sister Argatha was feeble-minded when she said it?' Nona watched the red glow fade above the rooftop. 'I didn't want to be the Shield in any case – I wanted to be the Sword.'

The abbess laid down her scroll with a sigh, straightening it out. It promptly sprang back into a tight coil the moment she lifted her hand. 'You deserve the truth, Nona, and I don't want to stain Sister Argatha's good name in any case, but you must promise to keep what I tell you to yourself. Can you do that?'

'Yes.' Nona was good at keeping secrets.

'No telling that Clera you're so tight with?'

'No, abbess.'

Abbess Glass folded her hands in her lap, then winced and unfolded them. Sister Rose had given her three doses of sorrinbark for the pain but Nona saw that she still suffered, moving with the brittle delicacy of those who carry the worst kinds of hurt.

'Sister Argatha did a great many things, most good, some bad, and twice to my knowledge they were plain stupid. What she did not do is make prophecies. The Argatha prophecy was the work of two archons about thirty-five years ago when Emperor Crucical's grandfather, Edissat, was on the throne. They were troubled times: Edissat was in his dotage, his eldest son in exile, war threatened with the Durnishmen, ice-winds ruined several harvests. The prophecy gave us focus. It reminded us of the salvation the Ancestor promised us. It reminded us that the Ark could be opened, would be opened, and that we owned it, together.'

'What's inside?' Nona asked.

'Nobody knows,' the abbess said. 'But given that the emperor's authority rests on the fact that he controls the Ark, it would be nice if he could open it, no?'

'But someone must know.' Nona frowned.

'Maybe someone does. The trouble is that so many people claim to know and their claims are so varied, that it's hard to know which, if any, are correct. A lot of people believe that it can control the moon.'

'The moon? But—'

'The point is that the prophecy told us that the key lay among us, among our children or the children yet to be. I believed it heart and soul. I was a young woman then, and zealous.' She managed a smile though pain still haunted her eyes. 'In any event, it served its purpose. I didn't learn the truth until I became abbess here and had access to the sectioned histories. It doesn't matter much now – but this is not a tale that should spread. I'm trusting you, Nona. And that's a burden rather than a gift. Do you understand that?'

'I understand.' At least she half-understood. 'But didn't the high priest know? The archons too?'

'Jacob was never a great one for reading. Or listening.' The abbess's smile was fuller this time. 'The archons? I'm sure Anasta knew. Philo too, probably. Kratton? I don't know. He often surprises me. Nevis, perhaps not. Or perhaps like Sister Wheel they know but choose to believe anyway.'

Nona frowned. 'So why *did* you save me?'

'You heard what I told the archons. It was enough for them to find me innocent.'

'But you said you had a vi—'

'I lied, Nona. I do that sometimes even when someone isn't threating to fork my tongue and whip me from the convent.'

Nona remembered what the abbess had said when they were hurrying from the prison. *Words are steps along a path: the important thing is to get where you're going.* And where had the abbess got?

'You didn't like the high priest.'

'No.'

'He was a thorn in your side.'

'More like a knife in my kidney.'

'And you don't like Thuran Tacsis.'

'No.'

'And now Thuran doesn't have the high priest for a friend.'

'He doesn't have the high priest in his pocket, no. For all his faults Nevis will not sell himself so cheaply as Jacob did.'

'Why are you telling me these things?' Nona frowned, trying to see if the abbess was mocking her.

'You asked.'

'But … you shouldn't talk about archons like that… Not to a novice. Not to me. I'm so new.'

'Your shoes may still be shiny, Nona, but your habit has several holes in it.' The abbess regarded her, unsmiling. 'You bled for me. I owe you some answers. Or perhaps I want to see how closely you keep secrets?'

'If the high priest was such a bad one, why didn't the archons vote him out before?' It had seemed a simple enough matter.

'The archons each have their own see to govern and their cathedrals are very far from Verity. You have to move mountains to get two archons in the same place, let alone four. It's an assembly I could never have called.'

'But the high priest didn't even need them to throw you out?'

'He needed them to make it look like something other than a grudge. We have a history, Jacob and I. Just declaring me guilty would make him look weak. A man who spends as long as the high priest does in the emperor's court can't afford to look weak. There are too many sharks in those waters. He thought he had more of a hold on the archons than he did. More sway. If just one of them had agreed with him there would not have been an issue. So Thuran Tacsis floated all four archons to my doorstep on a river of gold – just to get at you, dear.'

'And you knew he would…' Nona started to see the shape of something. The outline of a plan.

'I thought it likely.' The abbess nodded.

'But … but, you burned yourself. Even though you knew it wouldn't help. You knew it wouldn't change the high priest's mind.'

'Yes.'

'Because … you knew it would make me say I would take the ordeal. But I said I would at the start.'

'If I had accepted your offer at that point the archons would never have voted the staff from Jacob's hand. They had to see me suffer – they had to see *him* make me suffer. Getting four archons in one place is a feat, but it is nothing compared to the task of getting them to agree on something of import.'

'So … all this … from that first day … was to bring down the high priest and hurt Thuran Tacsis.'

The abbess just watched her.

'How … how could you know I would pass the ordeal?' Nona shifted her shoulder and winced. Hessa almost hadn't survived, and even a scratch on her would have seen Nona drowned.

'Sister Tallow watched you that first day at Blade. A small girl who could wreak such harm on Raymel Tacsis that it takes four Academy men to hold him on the edge of life … a gerant pit-fighter… I thought that such a child would be fast. Sister Tallow watched you on the sand and told me that she herself was not so swift in her prime.'

Nona lay silent then, the pain of her wound pulsing, her hands and wrists burning with a deep fire. Abbess Glass was neither fast, nor strong, she had no obvious wealth, her office held no great sway, and yet with her truth and with her lies she had turned one wheel against another against another and in due course mountains had moved, the mighty had fallen, and the world sang the song she chose for it. Nona didn't know how she felt about that. She knew that she had tried to lay some portion of her guilt over Saida's death on the abbess's steps and that in truth the guilt was hers and hers alone. She should never have stopped fighting, never allowed them to be taken to face 'justice'. Nona knew that she didn't understand people. Not how they worked in their webs of fragile, flexible friendships and shifting loyalties, not how the games of smiles and hugs, scowls and turned backs were played at court or over a convent breakfast table, and not the workings of their hidden hearts. She knew she didn't understand these things, but with Abbess Glass she understood still less. They had wanted to throw Nona chained into the black and unreflecting waters of the sinkhole, where novices swam and bones crowded in the silt deep below the kicking of their legs. Abbess Glass and that sinkhole perhaps had more in common than their name.

Glass and her church. Nona had no loyalty to either now. And perhaps that was just another of the abbess's wheels turning … but the time to run had passed her by. She had called Clera and Hessa friends and that bond ran deeper than blood: it was the foundation of a world that she *could* understand.

A faith that mattered.

20

Abbess Glass returned to her house and to her duties after that first night. Nona lay abed three more days with Sister Rose in close attendance.

Clera and Ruli came to see her on the first morning, released from Academia for the visit. Ruli shy at first, hiding behind her hair, Clera all smiles and hugs from the moment she burst through the door. They sat on her bed and chatted, about everything except what had happened. Clera told them of a ball her father had taken her to back before his fall from grace.

'...and then Velera came in. She's the younger sister but that never stopped her complaining that her brother sits on the throne while she slums it in her palace on the coast. Anyway, she had Lord Jotsis on her arm, the young one, and the Gersis heir on the other side. And her dress! She looked like she'd been poured into it. My father said she spilled some...'

Hessa came that evening on her own, stumping in on her crutch.

'I see Sister Rose gave you my bed.' She lowered herself carefully to sit on the end.

They spoke of the ordeal. 'I didn't see anything,' Hessa said. 'Just the guards and Sister Wheel getting ready to throw, and in the same moment something hitting the wall beside me. I jumped so hard I nearly fell over. I *did* fall over when you did. I had to wave my arms and tell them I hadn't been hit!'

Jula came the next day with Clera. 'We can only come in twos. Sister Rose says we'll tire you out. Sister Kettle wanted to send you your slate and some lettering but Rosy wouldn't let her.' Clera sat down breathlessly. 'Imagine that, wounded *and* having to do letters!'

Jula came to Nona more cautiously, hugging her as if she might break, her short hair bristly against Nona's cheek. As they parted her lower lip trembled. 'Thank the Ancestor you're all right! I thought—' Her voice broke and Nona was amazed to see that she was crying.

It wasn't until the morning of the third day that Nona told Sister Rose her fear. The hole that the arrow put in her, and the damage to hands and wrists she knew would heal – but her body had let her down, had failed her when she most needed it.

'The abbess thinks I'm fast.' Nona said it between gulps of a sour brew that Sister Rose kept tipping to her lips, though she could hold it by herself. 'But I'm not. I tried to be fast with the arrow – I thought I could – but I just couldn't. I got so tired.'

'Tired?' Sister Rose laughed, her face mounding and crinkling. 'That's the hunska burn. Everyone gets it. Leastways all of you with lightning in your veins. I can't move that quickly but I can lumber on for hours.' Sister Rose took the cup away and squinted into it, checking that Nona had had the nasty gritty bits at the bottom. 'You're using up your resources when you do those things.' She pinched Nona's arm. 'And you're all bones anyhow – what have you got to burn? I'm amazed you managed what you did. Most hunska are ready to fall over after just a few seconds of fighting at speed. Drinking sugar-water after helps. But there's only so much your body can give. Take too much and something will break. With hunska it's normally the heart. Not that you last long one way or the other…'

'We don't?' Nona sat up, her shoulder an ache now rather than a pain.

'Mistress Academia hasn't— Of course not.' The humour left her. 'I forget how little time you've been with us, Nona.' Sister Rose set the cup aside and drew her chair as close to the bed as her legs would allow. 'The four tribes that came to Abeth found it a harsh world, even before the ice. It was mixing their blood that bred a people who could live here. The hunska and the gerant live short lives, one too fast for their hearts in this land, the other too large. Sister Tallow is the oldest hunska I've known, and she isn't as old as she looks. Not by a long margin…The quantal and marjal draw on the power of place, tapping into the magics that lie beneath and above and through all the things of this world. But this is not the land that bred them and its magics are sharp, quick to burn the unwary, or warp them…'

'I—' A knock at the door cut Nona off.

Sister Rose patted her hands. 'Those that burn short burn bright. The shortest lives can cast the longest shadows.'

Nona thought of Saida, cold in the ground, and the shadow she cast. The knocking came again.

'Come.' Sister Rose struggled to her feet.

The door to the foyer opened and Arabella Jotsis stuck her head around, her scalp now covered with short blonde hair making something boyish of her. 'Sister Pan has asked to see Nona and me.'

'Well you can tell Sister Pan that Nona isn't leaving this—'

'It's for the naming.'

'Oh.' Sister Rose looked at Nona, back at Arabella, back at Nona. 'How do you feel, Nona? Could you manage a walk to the Path Tower do you think? I could get some sisters to carry you…'

'No, I can walk.' Nona swung her legs off the bed and got up before Sister Rose could insist she be lifted like a baby. Her shoulder hurt worse than she had thought it would, but she gritted her teeth against it and walked to the door with more care.

Outside the cold made her gasp: an ice-wind had come, blowing off the southern sheet, and three days in the sanatorium's warmth had left her open to it.

'Filthy weather.' Arabella hugged her habit around her but didn't hurry: Nona could see the restraint in her steps and tried to walk more quickly, her shoulder flooding with hot, wet pain at each jolt.

'What's "the naming"?' Nona thought those might be the first three words she had spoken to Arabella. It seemed odd to be walking with her, as if everything were normal, as if Arabella had never tried to stab her in her bed, as if they hadn't been enemies from the first moment. But if that fake prophecy got its teeth into them Arabella Jotsis might be forced to play the role of Chosen One and Nona her reluctant Shield.

'The naming? Do you think Sister Kettle was called Kettle by her mother?' Arabella watched her with a sideways look and an amused smile.

'But … but the older novices, they still have their names! Suleri is in Holy Class and she's still Suleri…' Nona scowled, wondering whether Suleri was the name of a thing like glass or apple, but just one that peasants didn't know.

'Yes, but they all have their holy names. They just have to keep them secret until they take their orders and become nuns. If they get that far. Every novice gets to choose their name in front of Mistress Path when she calls them. She calls most of them during their first year.'

Nona relaxed. She hadn't wanted to give up her name. 'We'll still be Arabella and Nona then.'

'Ara.'

'What?'

'Ara. Everyone calls me Ara. You should too.'

Path Tower loomed above them, dark against the morning, the four open approaches framed in stone.

'I take the east door,' Ara said.

'Why?'

'That's where the Path leads me.' Ara paused, tilting her head to study the smaller girl. 'Try it. Close your eyes and see.' She laughed. 'That's what Sister Pan says.'

Nona closed her eyes. She saw only what she always saw, orange and grey, afterimages pulsing and fading, the last traces shaped into ideas and suggestions – the edges of dreams.

'Do you see it?' Ara, almost at her ear.

'No.'

'Look harder.' A hand touched Nona's shoulder and in that moment what she saw became an edged brilliance and a hot darkness, one cutting through the other like a fracture – though she couldn't say which cut the other – and both driven through her head, hammer-hard, splintering against the back of her skull.

'—ona!'

Nona opened her eyes, slitted against the brightness of a grey sky.

'Nona?' A dark shape looming over her.

'Where?' Nona could feel hands on her arm, lifting her up.

'I'm really sorry!' Ara sounded it too, though she sounded like a really sorry princess. 'I forgot about your shoulder!'

Nona got to her feet, snarling in pain, ready to fight. The girl had pulled her up by her bad arm and her wound felt as though the arrow were back in it and red-hot.

'You didn't—' Nona bit off the words. She couldn't see any mockery in Ara's eyes, no hint of a smile, just concern… Ara hadn't put her hand on the wounded shoulder. She couldn't see the bandaging under Nona's habit: she had just assumed she had because Nona collapsed, and so she had used the other arm to help her up, the wounded arm.

Nona brushed herself off. 'I'll use the door you do.'

Together they covered the remaining distance and went through the east door into the portrait room at the base of Path Tower. The painting directly facing the east door was of a woman's face, half-black, half-white, the black half with a white eye, the white half with a black one. A strip of grey ran between the two halves, but coming nearer Nona saw it was just that the boundary between the halves wasn't a straight line as she had first seen it, but infinitely convoluted, black fingering into white, white into black.

'She's beautiful, isn't she?' Ara came to stand beside Nona. 'It's Sister Cloud. She was a two-blood. Full-blood hunska and full-blood marjal.'

'That sounds … pretty full!' Nona smiled.

'It just means she had the full talents of both tribes.' Ara shrugged. 'Sister Pan says there's one born every generation or so.'

'And this generation has you?' Nona looked at Ara, harder than she had before. How deep did that confidence go? Was she frightened somewhere in there, beneath the face a noble's life had taught her to wear?

'We should go up.'

Ara let Nona set the pace on the steps, following behind. As Nona made her slow turns around the rising spiral she tried to think back to the grievances she had harboured against the girl behind her. Ara's crimes appeared to be confined to being beautiful, being born rich and being the Chosen One. Everything else, Nona realized, was something given to her by Clera, or something assumed. She had assumed that the remainder of half-heard jokes were at her expense, that the laughter that faded as she entered a room had been at her.

'Ready?' Ara asked, her smile nervous.

Nona found that she had come to a halt just below the classroom. She also found in that moment a sudden realization. Arabella Jotsis was very easy to like.

'Ready,' Nona said, and they went up together.

Sister Pan was waiting for them, sitting without formality in a student's chair, and gestured for them to pull up chairs of their own. She looked impossibly old, like the corpses men find in the ice tunnels, blackened skin on bones, folded in on themselves like flowers before an ice-wind. 'It's blowing out there!' When Sister Pan smiled even that had something of a skull about it. 'The Corridor will narrow tonight.'

'And the moon will clear the path,' Ara said, giving the proper reply.

'And the moon will clear the path.' Sister Pan nodded. 'Did you know that the moon is falling?'

Nona glanced at Ara. 'No…'

Again the skull-grin. 'Not to worry. It's been falling all your life, and mine.' Sister Pan raised her hand, leathery but darker than any leather, cupped just a little as if shining moonlight down upon the world. 'It's been falling ever since they put it up there. The light presses against it, the sun's wind too. And as it drifts close it starts to scrape the very edges of our air, touching the highest of Abeth's winds. Then ... then it will be swift.' Sister Pan brought her hand down onto her knee.

'Can we do anything?' Ara asked, staring at the hand on Sister Pan's knee.

'No. At least, nothing good.' The old nun shrugged. 'So ... I called you to this place to hear what you're called.'

'I've chosen,' Ara said. She looked at Nona. 'Shouldn't we ... do this in private?'

Sister Pan turned her head one way, then the other. 'Nobody here but us.'

'But...' Ara frowned. 'But we're not supposed to tell anyone our names. It's a secret until we take our orders...'

'The Chosen One and The Shield don't have secrets from each other.'

Nona kept her mouth closed. She didn't care who knew her name – though she wouldn't tell it. The abbess had wanted to know if she could keep a secret, and she could.

'I'm not the Chosen One,' Ara said. 'I would know if I was. And besides, I can't do anything a marjal can.'

'Doesn't matter one way or the other,' Sister Pan said. 'That prophecy is what's put you in danger – what's keeping you safe for now is this convent, not the walls, not the sisters, red or grey or otherwise. It's that woman in the big house. Glass has a long reach, and a subtle one. Time was when I could have put a big enough hole in this rock we live on to swallow this tower whole. And even then I wasn't half as deadly as that woman. Not half.' She tilted her head as if listening to distant music. 'The prophecy put you in danger because people half-believe it. Make them believe it wholly and it will start to look after you. Both of you.'

'And we need it to look after us ... because the abbess might ... change her mind?' Nona asked.

'Because the wind will always blow and moon will keep on falling.' Sister Pan dusted her palm against her thigh and looked to them, expectant. 'Now, what are you to be called as sisters? Nona?'

Nona hadn't thought about it, not in her days at the convent surrounded by Kettles, Apples, Glasses and Wheels, not on the walk to the tower or the climb up the stairs.

Pan smiled. 'Often sisters choose a name that makes them think of home, of something safe, something they cherish.'

'I…' Nona tried to think of the village, of her house, her mother cutting the reeds, weaving one into the next. She thought of the Rellam Forest – of the savagery and the death – she thought of her mother's face when they brought her child back from the wild, clothed in other people's blood.

'Choose carefully, Nona. Let the Path lead you to a name.'

Nona opened her mouth. 'Cage,' she said. 'Let them call me Cage.'

Sister Pan pursed the wrinkled gristle of her lips. 'Cage.' She turned to Arabella Jotsis who watched them both with a serenity Nona envied. 'And you, dear?'

'Thorn,' Ara said. 'I will be Sister Thorn.'

Grey Class

It is important, when killing a nun, to ensure that you bring an army of sufficient skill. For Sister Thorn of the Sweet Mercy Convent Lano Tacsis brought Pelarthi mercenaries, warriors drawn from the ice-margins east of the Grey, from a tribe considered savage by their savage neighbours. Brawlers, murderers, hard men and hard women who kill for coin. Heretics who set the worship of past warlords, not yet three centuries beneath the ground, above the veneration of the Ancestor on whose shoulders all humanity stands and who makes each man brother to the next.

The throwing star, or cross-knife as the Noi-Guin have it, is typically a weapon of distraction, to put off-balance, to cause minor injury; but in the hands of a Red Sister such projectiles become deadly.

The bandolier above Sister Thorn's blackskin held two dozen stars, pointed for penetration rather than bladed for blood, each set about a central ring weighted with lead. They spat from her fingers as she ran between the pillars, the Pelarthi shocked by the sudden swiftness of her. Eye, throat, forehead. Punching in through soft flesh and hard bone. Eye, throat, a mouth opened to roar for battle swallowing the star's swift rotation amid broken teeth. Forehead, throat. Here a gerant, huge in his armour, pot helm visored, a heavy gorget about his neck. The star arced as it flew, taking him in the wrist just beneath his gauntlet, tearing tendon and artery, leaving his great-sword slipping from numb fingers.

There is, in the act of destruction, a beauty which we try to deny, and a joy which we cannot. Children build to knock down, and though we may grow around it, that need runs in us, deeper than our blood.

Violence is the language of destruction, flesh so often the subject, fragile, easy to break beyond repair, precious: what else would we burn to make the world take note?

Your death has not been waiting for your arrival at the appointed hour: it has, for all the years of your life, been racing towards you with the fierce velocity of time's arrow. It cannot be evaded, it cannot be bargained with, deflected or placated. All that is given to you is the choice: meet it with open eyes and peace in your heart, go gentle to your reward. Or burn bright, take up arms, and fight the bitch.

There is in every delicate thing, no matter how precious, nor how beautiful, a challenge. *Break me.* No bride of the Ancestor can see life as anything but the fragile, wondrous gift that it is. From the alpha to the omega we are all brothers, sisters, children, born of unity, bound for unity. And yet … and yet … those who take the red are trained to listen. *Break me.*

Thorn carried in each limb every hour of her training, every day and year bound into the muscle of her arms, written along the length of her legs, beaten into the hardness of stomach and thigh. She knew five dozen ways to kill, she knew them with a lover's intimacy, and in the execution perhaps lust also played its role – for what is lust but a hunger? And hunger must be fed.

Any weapon begs use. The blade itself incites to violence. And those who mistake the red children of Sweet Mercy for anything other than a weapon are fools of their own breed.

Flicked wrists, arms cracked like whips, and throwing stars take flight, possessed of their own fierce rotation, bound on twisted parabolas. No mother gave her child so much direction, or set them spinning along their course through the world with such care. Governed only by the forces that steer the true stars through dark heavens, Thorn's bright offspring wing their way: deterministic, to known targets, trusted and independent, requiring no more of her attention.

Spears are thrown in surprise, arrows released in confusion. She is among them and gone, a fleeting target in black and tattered red. Spears fly high, hit pillars, find the flesh of allies rather than foe. One Pelarthi, ice-blooded, hawk-eyed, looses at the flickering of her enemy, leading her mark. The arrow glances from Thorn's shoulder as she turns, the blackskin stiffening to resist the missile's speed. The temporary rigidity of her armour hampers Thorn's reply. Her star tears skin at the corner of the archer's eye, rips her ear, and hurtles on into the chest of the man behind.

And at last Thorn's hands are empty, her bandolier slack, two dozen of the Pelarthi in possession of her steel, some lying sprawled, trampled by their kin as they choke on blood; others still standing, hunched about their wound, the fight gone from them, replaced by hurt, the sorrow of steel, tears of blood.

She draws her sword. The blade is long, thin, describing a slight curve, its edge cruel enough to bite through steel. Though it whispers from the scabbard somehow it is loud enough to cut a moment's silence. *This.* This is where the Red Sister's heart beats – on the edge. With her other hand she pulls the knife from her belt.

Pelarthi surround Thorn on three sides, bathing her in the light of their torches, stepping over their dead, their footprints crimson on the limestone. Many and more. A human tide, scores hurrying to flank her, glimpsed between the pillars. The foremost of them are slow now, watching, eyes upon the brightness of her blade, on the cutting edge upon which the fire's light is divided.

Thorn stands savagely still but she walks the Path and with each step she gathers to herself the raw and fundamental power that both divides and joins creation. She is still, but the energies that build within tremble across her, making the air shake and the light dance.

The Pelarthi watch her – the tall and the short, the wiry and the strong, bearers of axe and sword, of spear and bow. Paint-faced women, lips snarled about their teeth, pant for violence, hair wild or in braids, some spattered with the blood of friends. Grim-eyed men, clutching their sharpened iron before them, grind their jaws, muscles twitching beneath chain and leathers, waiting, waiting for the moment.

They expect her to run. They know she will run. And she does. But at them.

There is a joy in destruction and when Thorn raises her head to regard the ruin all about her there is a white smile among the scarlet dripping of her sweat. The blood is not hers, not all of it. The speed of a hunska, the stark efficiency of the sisterhood's blade-lore, and the channelled power of the Path have combined in one young woman to make a slaughter such has never been seen upon the Rock of Faith. She stands panting, both blades crimson from point to hilt, weary enough to fall, but with close on a hundred mercenaries dead about her. In places they are *heaped.*

Thorn straightens, snarling against the pain of broken ribs. She is cut, her cheek opened, a puncture wound high on her thigh. Her speed is diminished: the Path has thrown her and lies now beyond reach, but her foe have known terror and will not approach. The remainder watch her from back amongst the pillars. Jackals stalking a wounded lion, too timid for attack, too hungry to run.

The spear takes her between the shoulders. She should have heard it being thrown, sensed its approach, known it was coming. But it came too swiftly – hunska-fast. Blackskin turns iron hard, moulded about the spear point, driven half an inch into her flesh but arresting the missile, denying it her life. She turns as she falls, sprawling amid the gore.

Someone is leaving the Pelarthi ranks. A woman.

'S-sister?' Thorn's vision is blurred with blood, with sweat, with exhaustion. The woman is not Pelarthi – but she holds a second spear. Thorn blinks and in that moment recognizes one who was once her sister.

It is important, when killing a nun, to ensure that you bring an army of sufficient skill.

The dark-haired woman hoists her spear.

'Don't!' Thorn raises her hand, not asking for mercy but in protest. This is wrong. 'Don't do it, C—'

The spear is thrown.

21

'Welcome to Grey Class.' Sister Flint rose from her desk to take Nona's merit scroll, set with the seals of the five mistresses in acknowledgement of her satisfactory performance in Blade, Spirit, Academia, Shade, and Path. 'You will be sitting by Alata, over here.' The class mistress steered Nona from the door to her own seat. By dint of being considerably over six foot tall, though nowhere much more than one foot wide, Sister Flint managed to make Nona feel smaller at twelve than Sister Oak had when she first arrived in Red Class not having reached her tenth birthday.

Clera, Ara, Hessa, and Ketti grinned at her from their desks, while the remaining eight novices favoured her with the stony looks reserved for any new meat. Clera had been the first of them to move up and let nobody forget the fact. It had been Academia that held Nona back the longest – though she loved both the subject and Sister Rule. Nona had even mastered the much-hated saint's days, ceremonies, and catechism in Spirit under Sister Wheel's unforgiving eye before she passed her Academia finals. It had been the writing more than the reading that defeated her for so long, the business of wrestling her thoughts into a wriggling white scrawl of lines across the test slate.

Sister Flint returned to her desk but didn't take her seat. 'Grey Class meet here on the morning of every first-day for general instruction. I also provide individual tuition in subjects you may be experiencing difficulty with.' The sister paused and glanced out of the window. Grey Class met in a room at the back of Blade Hall that offered views out across to the Glasswater sinkhole and beyond the narrowing point of the plateau to the farmlands north of Verity. Presently the rock lay sun-spattered with just a fleeting shadow here and there where the wind chased a cloud from the sky. 'Today, however, we will finish a quarter-hour early. I shall leave you to introduce yourself to new classmates and gossip with old ones.' Sister Flint closed the heavy book on her desk, letting the leather cover fall with a thump. She said nothing more as she left the room, perhaps eager to catch a moment in the all-too-rare sunshine.

Conversation erupted along with the scraping of chairs as the door closed behind the nun. Clera reached Nona's side first, elbowing her way through the bigger girls. The eldest of the novices were around fourteen and some looked older than their years.

'Thank the Ancestor, Nona! You saved us. Flint was on about girls getting their blood. It was vile. She just wouldn't stop with the detail. I've decided I'm not doing it.'

Ara ducked around a couple of older novices and sat on Nona's desk. 'I've been having mine since the last ice-wind. It's not so bad. The cramps are—'

'Will you just *stop*?' Clera made a face. 'Anyway, I'm safe. Flint said they come later if you're thin.' She eyed Ara's curves.

Ketti, taller and still more slender than Clera raised a brow at the suggestion. 'She said that?'

'If that were true then Flint would never have got hers,' Ara said, raising her eyes to the ceiling. She tolerated Clera to about the same degree that Clera tolerated her, but the claws were never wholly sheathed when the two spoke.

'Perhaps that's why she likes talking about it so much.' Clera waved the topic away. '*Anyway* – little Nona … in Grey Class! It's going to be great. Jula and Ruli will come through soon. I know they will. Ruli's just got to get her stamp from Mistress Blade…'

Nona opened her mouth to say that Jula just needed her

Shade stamp and the test was scheduled for next four-day, but a shadow fell across her and the words stayed where they were. A hand, seeming the size of a dinner plate, reached for her. She grabbed one large, outstretched finger as the rest fastened on her shoulder and heaved her painfully from her chair.

'I'm Darla.' The novice lifted her from the ground, her grip so tight that Nona felt sure the fingers digging into her must have punched through her skin.

'Nona,' she gasped. The girl had looked big when hunched over her desk. In the refectory she stood taller than most of the novices in Holy Class, most of the nuns too. But close up she was enormous.

'You're the Shield, eh?' Darla had a blunt face that looked as if it had been put to hard use scrubbing floors. Her head had been shaved perhaps a week earlier and a pale seam of scar curved from just above her left eyebrow back across forehead and scalp, visible among the coarse brown stubble. She carried Nona, one-armed, pressing her to the wall. 'Don't look so much to me.'

'You saw her in the test!' Ara, loud and angry.

'Put her down!' Ketti reaching towards Darla's arm.

Darla grunted, increasing the pressure on Nona's shoulder until the joint creaked. 'There's more to winning than speed. Don't care what Tallow says.' With her spare hand she poked Nona in the gut, hard enough to make her writhe. 'What you gonna do now, fast girl?'

Another of the older novices pulled Ketti's arm from Darla's and sent Clera staggering back with a bump of her hip.

'This is the first lesson you learn in Grey Class – that it's not all about ratty little hunskas. Least not while I'm in it.' Darla poked again. 'It's not a lesson that gets written in ink either! I'll leave you a few bruises so you can study it again tonight. Your friends all got theirs first day. 'Cept the princess. I let her off.' She drew back her fist.

Nona met the girl's flat brown eyes. The grip on her shoulder was iron. Her feet, dangling above the floor might just touch Darla's stomach if she ignored the pain and thrashed to reach – but she could kick a tree trunk for all the good it would do.

'Nothing to say?' Darla grinned. An ugly thing.

Nona untwisted her mouth and grinned back past the pain. She reached across to grab with her other hand the single finger she had managed to secure a hold on as Darla seized her. And yanked with all her strength.

Darla's scream, the crack of bone, and the thunk of one meaty fist into Nona's face, all joined into a single sound. After that came a fall to the floor, screaming, a torrent of kicks, more screaming. Though dazed and half-blinded with the pain Nona tried to twist to minimize the impacts, folding herself around the heaviest of the kicks. Forged into a tough strip of muscle, gristle and bone by more than two years of training in blade-fist Nona knew how to take punishment. Finally a kick made solid contact and lifted her from the ground, slamming her back against the base of the wall. Even with the breath gone from her lungs she managed to arch out of the way of the next, allowing Darla to kick the wall. The novice howled. She hopped away, scattering desks and screaming curses, clutching at her foot. The other novices leapt clear of Darla's erratic path, leaving her to find herself face to face with Sister Tallow at the doorway.

'Darla. You appear to have broken your finger,' Sister Tallow said without heat.

Darla looked down at her hand, the finger jutting at an alarming angle. She paled, almost to green and straightened, putting her foot down, only to grimace and whimper another curse.

'And some toes.' Sister Tallow frowned. 'Get to the sanatorium. We will speak of this later.'

Darla hobbled out, hissing with every second step. Clera and Ara helped Nona up, and although every part of her wanted to stay there on the floor, coiled about the pain in her ribs and stomach, she let them lift her to her feet. Hessa stood close by, leaning on her crutch looking concerned but also puzzled.

'Nona too – you look to have had the worst of it.' Sister Tallow waved her towards the door.

Nona straightened with a wince, shaking the hands from her. 'I feel fine, mistress.' She spat a crimson mess to the floor and showed Mistress Blade a fierce and bloody grin. 'I've waited two years to have you show me blade-lore. I'm ready now.'

Sister Tallow watched Nona for a long, silent moment, eyes narrow. 'Grey Class to the hall then. Let's see how ready you are, novice.' A curt nod and she left the room.

'What? You need to go to Sister Rose, Nona!' Ara wiped at Nona's mouth with the sleeve of her habit and it came away stained.

'Why didn't you take her down?' Clera asked, not loud, almost lost in the tumult of voices.

Nona cricked her neck and took a pace forward, resisting the urge to clutch her side. 'How would I do that? She's a giant!'

Clera gave her a narrow stare remarkably like Sister Tallow's. Nona shrugged. Taken by surprise and held tight her speed hadn't mattered much. She would have had to cut Darla to win free without injury. She swallowed more blood.

'You should have pounded her.' Clera curled her lip, perhaps imagining herself delivering such a beating.

'Even if I could, it's not worth making an enemy over such a small matter.'

'*Small?*'

'She wanted me to know she's the boss. If you're going to let someone take your measure you should at least get something worth having in return. Mistress Blade taught us that.'

'She did?' Clera looked surprised. All around them the novices were gathering their stuff and starting to head out to the changing room. 'Really?'

Ara came across from Nona's desk with her lesson bag. '*Really*. I think you turn off your ears when Sister Tallow puts down her sword and starts talking theory.'

'I took a few kicks and in exchange I don't have to watch my back or worry about Darla poisoning my food,' Nona said. 'Being feared is clearly very important to her. Why take it away?'

'Why break her finger then?' Clera demanded, deep furrows across her brow.

'She'll remember she beat me so she won't carry a grudge. She'll remember it hurt so she'll convince herself she doesn't need to do it again.'

'And the toes?'

'I got tired of being kicked.' And Nona hobbled through the door.

Hessa stumped along with Nona, keeping pace easily for once. 'Was all that true?'

Nona glanced her way, wincing. 'Yes.'

'Was it all the truth though?'

'Not all of it,' Nona said. There was more, and, as usual, Hessa knew. 'She hurt you. I wanted to break her bones.'

'She knocks every new novice about.' Hessa turned for the exit: she spent Blade class pursuing her other studies.

'Yes, but yours I felt.' Once Hessa had shared with Nona the memory of her last day with Giljohn and somehow her inexperience had led to the forging of a more permanent bond. Perhaps once a month they would share a nightmare. Never a good dream, always something traumatic. And in moments of true panic or pain Hessa's thoughts would reach out and overwhelm Nona's. It happened in the other direction to a lesser degree. When Nona had taken the arrow Hessa had collapsed from more than shock. The pain had echoed in her too. When Darla had knocked Hessa to the floor and set her foot to Hessa's face, Nona had in that same moment shared her skin – the mixture bubbling before her in Shade class forgotten and unseen – had felt the weight of Darla's shoe, the agony in Hessa's hip, the humiliation of many eyes watching as she squirmed. She'd known all of it and been unable to act. 'I'm not going to get beaten twice and not bite back.'

Hessa offered a shy grin. 'Well. She's certainly been bitten.' And with that she took herself off across the hall, the swing of her leg leaving a dashed line alongside each of her single footprints.

* * *

Out on the sands Sister Tallow waited for them, in her hand a naked blade, the long thin sword favoured by the sisterhood, a strip of Ark-steel, carrying a slight curve and an edge that could cut the truth from a lie. Nona jogged after the others, uncomfortable in the blade-habit assigned to her, a heavy tunic of padded leather, bleached to a pale beige. The long sleeves overlapped awkward gauntlets, all designed to minimize the potential for novices gutting each other. She went to stand beside Clera and Ketti.

Sister Tallow always had a stillness about her. Often in blade-fist Nona would start and finish a bout only to find the nun in the same position, watching, as if her flesh was inanimate and she had been carved from it rather than grown. Today though, she paced, glancing up at the windows. Long, swift strides, impatient, spinning to turn and pace again.

Before the novices were gathered and arrayed in their lines the main doors opened and Sister Wheel slipped through, the cone of her headdress scraping the wood. She stayed by the doors, seeming to glare at everyone in the hall.

'Some of you will have seen this before, most will not.' Sister Tallow held her sword up as they hastened into their lines. 'You won't hold one unless you graduate this class – and all your other Grey classes – and come to me again in Mystic Class. But if you do become Martial Sisters it will be through such a weapon that you may need to direct the Ancestor's will. Pray that you are never called upon to use it, but know that there have been few sisters who took the red and kept their blade unsullied.'

'Sullied?' Clera bit back on the question but it escaped even so.

'Blood is always a failure.' Sister Tallow's glance flickered to Nona. 'Often the failure of the sister who holds the sword. Sometimes of those who send her into conflict. Or sometimes the failure lies years back, in the hands of someone who missed an opportunity for peace, who saw a chance to avert a distant violence and did not take it … or who failed to see that chance.' She returned the sword to the scabbard at her hip. 'I spend Red Class, that's two years for most of you, on unarmed combat. One reason I make you dangerous without a weapon – and will continue to reinforce that training – is so that you have an alternative to this.' She slapped her hip. 'You may be called upon to enforce the authority and the will of the church. It would be better if you did so in a manner that allows the transgressor to see the error of their ways rather than the contents of their body. The sword is a final solution.' Sister Tallow looked along their lines as if considering fruit at market and finding none to her standard. 'Knives today – training blades. Equip yourselves. Run, but remember where your blade is and what it will cut if you fall.'

The novices took off running, sand scattering beneath bare feet. Nona brought up the rear, limping to spare tender flesh already turning to bruise. Darla had been a lesson in herself. Take a giant by surprise and you could fell Raymel Tacsis with a blow. Let a giant take you by surprise and your options might dwindle to nothing.

As she turned where the corridor split, changing room to the left, storeroom to the right, Nona caught sight of a figure in the dark corridor that continued to the blade-path chamber. It almost looked like Kettle, but the hard-eyed stare held nothing of the nun's humour.

'She'll shave your head!' Clera raced from the storeroom holding a long knife as Nona approached the door.

By the time Nona had fought her way through the novices bundling from the doorway, all with daggers in hand, the room lay empty. It wasn't clear where the girls had taken their knives from: at the far end of the chamber a bewildering array of weapons lined the shelves, hilts out ready for the taking. Nona passed by the racks. Swords of various lengths and weights, long-hafted axes, climbing picks, hook knives, throwing knives, poniards, killing spikes… She hurried to the furthest corner. Kneeling, she reached up beneath the lowest shelf, stretching. Craw-spiders sometimes lurked in such places but she hadn't time for caution. Her fingers found only space and for a moment she thought it had been discovered at last. One more stretch, cheek hard against the shelf's edge, and she found the hilt. A tug brought it free.

Nona ran back, knife in hand, the one Ara had sunk into her pillow on her first night. Back before they were … almost … friends. The knife had stood between them for two years now, between the Chosen and her Shield, never spoken of, never mentioned, and all the sharper for it. She ran as fast as her injuries allowed, chased down the dark corridor by the ghosts of that distant night, footsteps at her heels.

The others were lined up and ready, Sister Tallow watching the tunnel as Nona ran from it and came to a halt with a wince.

'I repeat this lesson for every novice to join Grey Class. Before you leave you will have heard it a dozen times and still it will not have been enough.' Sister Tallow motioned for Nona to take her place at the rear of the group.

'Yes, Mistress Blade.' Nona joined in the chorus.

'This.' Sister Tallow raised her own knife. 'Is a great leveller. With your bare hands it is hard to disable an opponent – harder still to kill them. Despite all that I have taught you, unarmed you could be defeated by an opponent of considerably less skill if that opponent happens to weigh twice what you weigh, if they happen to be slabbed over with muscle, four times your strength. I am talking here of your average city guardsman. Do not overestimate how much your training will count for in an unequal contest. In such circumstances it may be only your willingness to move swiftly to the most savage of tactics that preserves you. The eyes, the groin, the throat.'

Sister Wheel moved from the doorway, making a slow gangling advance along the far wall, staring at the novices, glancing to the windows and the doors. Sister Tallow continued as if she were not there. 'The sharp edge, however, removes a great deal of an opponent's advantages in strength and size. No muscle, however hard or thick, will stop a sword thrust. A sharp edge applied to the neck will end any contest, and swiftly. A sharp edge applied to an arm or leg will open it to the bone with grievous and crippling injury. Be in no doubt that even a light slash can destroy a limb. Skin, muscle, blood vessels, nerves, all yield to steel with frightening ease.

'Nona – you will find time to visit Sister Rock in the kitchens and accompany her when she next slaughters a pig. The time after that you will make the cut and apply your blade further to the warm carcass to see how easily flesh opens before a honed knife and what lies within.'

Sister Flint appeared from the shadows of the corridor beneath the seating, looking around the hall as if searching for something, though what might be hiding among the rafters Nona couldn't guess. The other novices had noticed Sisters Flint and Wheel, and exchanged glances.

'Pair up. Colour your blades and spar – alpha through delta cuts only.'

Clera and Ara both stepped towards Nona but Sister Tallow saved her from having to choose between them. 'Nona, you'll be with me.'

'Yes, sister.' It was for the best, she had no idea what an alpha cut was, and still less how to pair with Clera without upsetting Ara. Life had been easier in that respect since Clera joined Grey Class six months earlier.

The novices crowded around the stain-stand, each hurriedly wiping their knife against the bundled rags, taking the lamp-black onto the blunt edges and rounded point. Any contact would leave a line or dot on the pale leathers of the blade-habit.

Ara pulled her blade back from the rags, dark as ink, and grinned at Nona, making an exaggerated slow-motion thrust towards her. Nona found she couldn't echo the smile, remembering that the knife in her hand had once been a death threat. Even so, she lifted the knife in response to Ara's thrust. In that instant something exploded from the base of the wall where nothing had been but shadows. A figure, moving with breathtaking swiftness, devouring the scant yards between them before Nona fully turned her head to see. The ground leapt up and Nona found her bruised body pinned to it, her attacker on top of her, securing her by both wrists. She tried to speak but the impact had hammered the breath out of her lungs.

'Nona?' The blurred figure astride her leaned in closer.

Nona managed to pull a breath back in past bruised ribs. She blinked, clearing her sight. 'Kettle?'

'Sister Kettle?' Sister Tallow appeared over Sister Kettle's shoulder, reaching down for her.

Kettle allowed Sister Tallow to bring her to her feet, pulling Nona up with her and keeping tight hold of Nona's knife hand.

'What are you doing, sister?' Sister Tallow asked. Sister Flint loomed over all of them now, with Sister Wheel deploying sharp elbows to find a path through the crowding novices.

Kettle said nothing, only held up Nona's hand with the knife clutched tight.

'An interesting weapon you have there, novice.' Sister Tallow raised a single brow in that manner of hers which Nona had been trying and failing to imitate for two years.

'The assassin!' hissed Sister Wheel. 'This girl is in league with them?'

'Don't be foolish, Wheel.' Sister Tallow waved the idea away. 'Arabella and Nona shared a dorm room for over a year, and will start doing so again tonight.'

'The threads led us here!' Sister Wheel looked up at Tallow, indignant, hands on her hips. 'Not just me. Flint and Kettle too!'

Sister Tallow motioned for Kettle to step back, her eyes on Nona's. 'Where did you get this interesting knife, novice?'

'I...' In the rush and with her mind on Darla, or at least the various hurts the girl had left her with, Nona had been too distracted to notice that the blade in her hand bore little resemblance to those the other novices held, being smaller and razor-edged, the point needle-sharp.

'Show me the hilt.'

Nona opened her hand, revealing a slim hilt wound with a narrow strip of leather and ending in an iron ball.

The novices about them remained dead silent for fear of being noticed and sent away. Sister Wheel noticed them even so. 'Class dismissed! Go and pray. Pray you don't find yourself in this much trouble! Go!'

'Practise your blade-path. Return your practice knives to

stores first,' Sister Tallow overruled. And with reluctance the girls began to retreat to the tunnel. 'Novice Arabella, remain.'

Ara came running back. Sister Tallow motioned for her to stand off to the side.

'That's a throwing knife.' Sister Tallow returned her attention to the weapon. She held out her hand and Nona gave it over. The old nun held it to the light. 'The Noi-Guin take their blades from those they kill. So there is no tell-tale make or style to identify their work.' She returned the knife, her fingers leaving clean steel where they rubbed the lamp-black from its blade. 'But I have seen the twin to this knife before. And its triplet. In the belt of a woman I pulled from the wall of your dormitory on the second night you spent in this convent.'

'A Noi-Guin!' Nona looked at the knife in her hand. She'd had little opportunity to inspect it between retrieving it from her bed and hiding it in the stores the next day. That had been more than two years ago. She wasn't sure why she had hidden it beneath the storage shelf – it had meaning to her, and having it mixed with the other knives and lost had seemed wrong. So she had stabbed it into the shelf support beneath the lowest shelf. That way she obeyed the abbess by returning it, but kept it hers. 'What did a Noi-Guin want here?'

'I opened that discussion with her.' Sister Tallow narrowed her eyes at the memory. 'But a second assassin from her order interrupted us. By the time I'd dealt with the interruption the first of them had fled … and the second, well he was in no condition to answer questions. So I ask you again – where did you get it?'

'It was in the storeroom…'

Sister Tallow raised a brow. 'I inventory the weapon stores on a regular basis. The novices in Holy Class clean and maintain all the blades daily. I've not seen this weapon or its like in two years.'

'It was in the storeroom.' Nona gritted her teeth.

Sister Tallow's narrowed eyes became gimlet. She drew breath for what might have been harsh words, but Sister Kettle spoke first. 'Do you know how it got there, Nona?'

'The abbess told me to put it there.' Nona knew what they wanted but something deep inside her had always kept tight hold on every secret she owned. She found she could no more easily volunteer such truths than she could lie.

'When did she tell you this?' Kettle asked.

'On my second night at the convent.'

'And where did you first get the knife?'

'It was in my bed.' Nona frowned. 'I sat up in the night, and when I looked back at where I had been lying the knife was there, sticking into blankets as if it had been stabbed there.'

'Or thrown there.' Sister Tallow glanced across at Sister Wheel. 'We thought the assassins came for Arabella, but it looks as though they were here for Nona. The Noi-Guin are anything but cheap but perhaps Thuran Tacsis found their prices more reasonable than those of the high court judge whose arrival followed their failure. Ancestor knows what funds Tacsis put behind the visit of our own high priest and archons after that...'

Sister Wheel cast a sour eye over Nona then made a sickly smile for Arabella. 'Our priority should be the Chosen One, the emperor's sister made her interest clear there. A Shield should be able to look after herself or what use is she?'

Sister Tallow made a small sound that might have been all of a long-suffering sigh that escaped her discipline. 'Sherzal is certainly not known for letting slip anything on which she has designs... But these titles are unhelpful. Chosen One? The abbess herself revealed the truth to us, sister.'

Sister Wheel moved behind Arabella and set a bony hand to each shoulder. 'It is called "faith" rather than "reason", sister. The Argatha comes to us out of stories, and even if the stories about those stories differ, they all agree that they came from the mouths of the holy. A nun? A priest? For this purpose, or that purpose.' She lifted a hand as if to wave away smoke. 'The story exists. It was born within the church and many have faith in it. I have faith in it. That is enough.'

Sister Tallow returned her dark gaze to Nona. 'Did the knife in your bed look as if it could have been thrown there?'

Nona screwed her eyes shut, bringing back the image she

had played through her mind so many times before. She'd imagined the knife stabbed there, Arabella Jotsis's hand about the hilt … but the angle… 'The window! It could have been thrown from there – it was open that night.'

'What honest reason would anyone have for keeping a thing like that secret?' Sister Wheel discarded Ara and moved in closer, leaning to be level with Nona, watery eyes studying her face as if a lie might be discovered there.

'She didn't keep it secret,' said Sister Tallow. 'The abbess knew: she told Nona to put the blade in stores… Though that and her silence on the subject are both very strange.'

'The abbess told us Thuran Tacsis pledged to the emperor himself that it was over!' Ara spoke up from the side, perhaps to stop Tallow brooding over Nona's story. She offered everyone a bright smile. 'My father saw him say so, before the whole court. Why should we still be worried about assassins?'

Tallow and Wheel exchanged a glance at that. Sister Tallow answered. 'It pays to be cautious, novice. The Noi-Guin do not like to fail and they are patient. Besides, now Thuran Tacsis has sworn on this matter Nona is a liability to him and his enemies might have an interest in seeing her harmed, thinking to bring the emperor's wrath on the House of Tacsis. And so this blade…'

'How did you all come to be here?' Nona asked, not wanting the conversation to return to her silence on the matter of the knife and to reveal the strong suspicions she'd held regarding Ara's part. 'And...' She turned around to look up at Kettle. 'How did you … you just came from nowhere!'

'I'm a Sister of Discretion.' Kettle offered a tiny grin, just enough to show the whiteness of her teeth. 'You see me when I want you to.'

'Threads brought us here, Nona.' Sister Flint, peering down from her grave heights. 'Mistress Path will teach you about threads soon enough, now you're in Grey Class.'

22

Sister Tallow set Ara to instructing Nona in the basics of knife-work. With the other novices all busy at blade-path the pair of them had Mistress Blade's full attention: never a comfortable thing. They circled, working in a silence cut by the sharpness of drawn breath and punctuated by the distant wails of girls falling from the blade-path.

'No.' Sister Tallow took Nona's wrist and shoulder, moving her arm into the block she had been shown.

After thirty more repetitions of the same block and same cut Nona tried another variation.

'No.' Sister Tallow adjusted Nona's arm again. 'The muscles need to learn it, not the mind. There need to be patterns your body can fall back on when there's no time for thinking. Once those are bedded into you then you start to improvise.'

Nona fell back into the rhythm: circle, cut, block, circle. From the frequency of the distant cries even the novices with most practice were finding the blade-path particularly difficult in their heavy blade-habits. Of the girls who trained on the path in their free time the majority were hunska, half-bloods and primes. Though given that just getting to the end of the blade-path proved a major challenge, speed really wasn't a requirement. Nona guessed that the competitive element just appealed more strongly to those with their eyes on the martial habit; though of late the studious Jula had demonstrated quite a talent for it, completing the whole path, albeit achingly slowly, a feat that of the recent graduates from Red Class only Clera had managed before moving up.

A moment's lapse of concentration and Ara had slashed a black line across the pale leather of Nona's blade-habit.

'Again!' Sister Tallow barked.

Circle, slash, block, circle, slash. Block.

'When you stab you may find the opportunity to mortally injure your opponent, but to sink your blade you must come in closer than to cut with it. When you stab and find flesh your blade may become trapped by the bones of a twisting opponent. Both the necessity of stepping closer and the danger of a trapped blade open you to retaliation. There is almost no stab you can make that is so swiftly fatal that it will prevent the counter-blow.'

Circle. Slash, block. Circle, slash. Block.

'Even the whisper of a well-honed knife can cut through cloth, skin, and the muscle beneath. Knife fights are a war of attrition. Your foe is brought down by the combination of blood loss and the lost mobility due to various wounds, allowing an eventual *coup de grâce*.'

Nona's blade slipped past Ara's block and wrote a black line across her stomach. An immediate flood of guilt washed through her. She had spent two years thinking her friend could have stabbed her in her sleep, or at the least threatened to do so.

'Of course, against untrained opponents combat may often be concluded within moments. A slash to the throat and swift advance to the next target is recommended, though a stab to the heart, the eye, or up under the jaw are possibilities if the opponent's blade is controlled.'

Circle-slash-block. Circle-slash-block.

'Break! You can join the others for ten minutes before next bell.'

Nona straightened, blinking sweat from her eyes. Time had escaped her, but the blisters on her knife hand and the circle of floor kicked free of sand had kept a more accurate measure than her mind.

'Yes, Mistress Blade.' Ara nodded and hurried off towards the changing room.

Nona pushed her wet hair back across her forehead, blinked again, and gave chase.

'It's great you came up.' Ara finished with the last tie and stripped off her blade-habit in one fluid motion. 'I was getting worried we wouldn't range together.'

'We've still got three months for that.' Nona wriggled into her day-habit and brushed her hands through her hair, a short thick shock of it. She wanted to grow it long but it went wild if she let it get past a hand span and brushing wouldn't tame it. When it got long Sister Wheel stopped calling her peasant and called her harlot instead – which made it almost worth it, but not quite.

'I hope more of the others make it up before then too.' Ara picked up her stockings and shoes, ready to go.

'We need Ruli and Jula at least.' Nona nodded. Grey Class went on the ranging every year, the novices sent on a long journey across open country. It was an important part of the year's lessons. Without resources they had to live off the land and pass several convent challenges on the way. On the previous ranging two girls had been injured, one failing to reach the target in the allotted time. The abbess wouldn't throw novices out for failing on the ranging – though her predecessor had – but it was certain that nobody who failed a ranging would ever take the grey or the red. 'It'll be the first time I've got off this rock in … since I arrived here.'

'Come on!' Ara pulled Nona's arm, shaking her out of her contemplation of the fact that she hadn't ever passed back through the pillars outside the convent. 'Race you.'

Nona and Ara scrambled barefoot up the stairs to the platform in the blade-path chamber, Ara bursting through well in the lead and almost knocking a girl over the edge. About half the novices had already abandoned practice in favour of an early bath, but they still had some competition. Ketti sat with her back to them, legs dangling out into space and two older novices stood waiting their turns. Taller of the two, who Ara had nearly pitched into the net below, was Alata. Her dark eyes narrowed in disapproval at Nona's arrival. The girl had ink-black hair so tightly curled it seemed to float about her head, her dark skin had been patterned with darker scars, their raised bumps looking as if they spelled out a message whose meaning lay just beyond comprehension. The other novice was Leeni, a red-haired girl with skin so pale that her veins showed in blue webs across her bare legs and arms.

Out on the path itself Clera, still in her blade-habit, wobbled dangerously as she attempted the first rise of the spiral.

'Watch your back foot!' Ara called out.

Clera twitched, flailed at the air, and fell with a furious shriek, dark hair streaming up to shroud her face. Ara turned to Nona with a guilty look, raising her hands. 'Well, she did have it placed wrongly.'

Nona said nothing, though to be fair, Clera had been poorly positioned.

Alata gestured to the pipe with a broad hand. 'See what you got, new girl.'

'You.' The pale girl pointed at Nona. 'I want to see if the Shield drops faster than the rest of us.'

Nona shrugged. She and Clera were the only acknowledged hunska full-bloods in the lower classes, though Ara might also be, and she was certainly very fast for a prime. Full-bloods always got jealousy and awe in equal measures but Nona's showing at the ordeal had pushed the reaction to greater extremes.

It took a moment to brush the sand from her feet and apply resin. Ara had made her a gift of a small tub of the stickiest blend Nona had seen. The tub itself was silver, embossed and worked, by far the most valuable thing Nona had touched, and yet passed to her as if it were no more than an apple-core.

'Remember, take your time, think!' Ara spoke as Nona set foot on the pipe, arms out for balance. 'You always go too fast.' Ara's first completion was less than a month old and her enthusiasm for giving advice had yet to wane. She had taken a little over four hundred beats compared to Clera's best of two hundred and ninety, and failed to improve on it in her two completions since.

Nona edged out, having to pull to free each foot from the traction that would prove vital in the steeper sections. She still had yet to pass the halfway point. Something never felt quite right, as if the whole shifting shape of the blade-path had been designed just to throw her, Nona Grey, into the net below, as a personal insult. Some elusive part of the puzzle escaped her every time, a sour note in the song, the wrongness of someone else's shoe on her foot.

'You're doing well!' Ara from the platform, already far above Nona's head as she finished the long slow curve of the initial descent and approached the sharp rise of the spiral's first turn.

'The net wants you, little girl.' The pale novice.

'Darla wants you too!' Alata called.

Laughter and hoots rose from below where other novices watched at the doorway.

Nona started the climb, making sure that her back foot held a better position than Clera's had. She rose with slow steps, stuttered corrections here and there as she made the difficult transfer from the inner surface of the spiral to the outer. The structure rocked and swayed on its supporting cables. She drew a slow breath and crossed the vertex of the first loop.

Click. The pendulum swung past its midpoint and the dial advanced another notch, counting out Nona's sloth. The leap to the top of the next spiral tempted her, but the rules of the game said the whole blade-path must be walked. She started her descent, relying on the resin to stop her slipping. Click.

Some yards ahead a heavy section of the blade-path rotated on a joint, reacting to the shifting of Nona's weight on the spiral. Every part of the blade-path levered some other part: the smallest step could set some section in motion, the whole path flexing and reconfiguring.

Nona dropped into the moment, slowing the world to a crawl, the novices' laughter crashing through the registers until it reached the deep rumble of a mud-ox. She reached for support, shifting her own weight to counter the motion beneath her feet. A slow hunt for balance in the space between heartbeats.

Somehow it ended as it so often ended, with Nona understanding that she had passed the point of no return, knowing that no lunge could save her now, and letting gravity take her. She fell without sound, just a silent snarl across her lips. The impact with the net, the bounce, the scramble to the side, all passed without notice: she knew she could walk the blade-path, knew it blood to bone, and yet … and yet…

'Bad luck!' Clera wrapped an arm around Nona. 'You're getting better, though.'

'I'm not.'

'Let's watch Ara fall.' Clera grinned. 'Or just get old watching her finishing it.'

A novice, nearly as tall as Darla but half her width, pulled the lever on the wall, trapping the pendulum at the end of a swing and setting the dial back to zero.

23

'Touching the Path is the second most dangerous thing a person can do.' Sister Pan stalked the classroom with an energy wholly at odds with her ancient frame. 'These games you play with swords and knives, poisons and acids … you think this is danger? You girls don't even know the hurt that a sharp edge can do – a slip of the wrist and you're opened to the world, blood, bone, nerves, guts, all the soft wonder of a body cut through. If you live the pain can last a lifetime, the loss … if you live.' She raised her right arm and gazed at the stump where her hand should be, tilting her head as if perhaps she could still see the missing fingers moving to her will. A moment later the old woman spun on her heel to face Nona. 'I've told these girls a hundred times – it doesn't stick. It's small matter if they haven't the blood for it. But you … you, little Nona, you might yet do it. This ill-advised connection Novice Hessa forged with you is a possible sign. Not a proper thread-bond, but an echo of one.' Sister Pan leaned in and tapped Nona's forehead with a finger as dry and dark as a charcoal stick. 'There might be a touch of quantal locked in there … and all we need to do is find a way to set it free.'

'What's the most dangerous thing?' Nona asked.

'Huh?' Sister Pan blinked as if the path of her own thoughts had slipped away from beneath her feet. She stood dark against the magnificence of the stained-glass windows.

'You said that touching the Path was the second most

dangerous thing a person could do,' Nona said. 'What's the most dangerous?'

'Leaving the Path, of course,' Sister Pan replied, her focus back and razor-sharp. 'And why is that, Novice Hessa?' She pointed at Hessa behind her without turning her gaze from Nona.

'Because when you step from the Path you have to take great care to return to yourself and not to some other place,' Hessa said.

'Some other place,' Sister Pan repeated. 'Some terrible place from which you may never return. A dark place where demons whisper unseen. A hot place where your mind will burn. A place so cold that we who remain will see the hint of its frost in your vacant eyes. A silent place where time does not venture and from which no thing ever leaves… You *must* return to yourself. What else? What else makes it dangerous, Novice Arabella?' She pointed to Ara.

'You must own what you hold,' Ara said.

'Correct.' A nod. 'Every step along the true Path of the Ancestor – a path that runs through all creation – is a gift and a burden. Every step taken is a gift of the raw power of creation, every step increases the potential within you. Sounds good, no?'

Nona nodded. The stories spoke of Holy Witches filling their hands with magics that could blow the strongest door asunder, reduce rock to powder. They said Sister Cloud could throw lightning like a thunderstorm. Sister Owl could scatter men as if they were nine-pins with a wave of her hand.

'Imagine a stream of your favourite drink. Girls like honey-wine don't they? Imagine that.'

Nona had never tasted honey-wine, or wine, or honey, but she nodded again.

'Now imagine it is being poured into your mouth. You like the taste, you swallow and swallow, it's good. But the jug keeps pouring – it's endless – it's too fast – but all you can do is swallow it. Your belly is swelling, your stomach bursting. You can take no more. You break away.

'The Path is like that. You return overflowing with the gift, burning with it, bursting with it. And you must own and shape what you've been given. Fail, and it will tear you apart – never the same way twice. It's not a quick death either. The gift sustains. Even as it destroys you it will keep you there. Even as you burn, whatever pieces of you remain will know suffering sharp enough to make the emperor's torturers weep with jealousy.' Sister Pan frowned as if she'd had more to say, then looked at Nona expectantly.

'I'll stick to swords and poison then,' Nona said.

'Ha!' Sister Pan barked a laugh. 'That's all you'll be good for, young Nona, unless you work on your serenity. Serenity is what will lead you through the fog of this world to the Path. Clarity will let you see it. I've no complaint with your clarity. Your serenity on the other hand…' She waggled her fingers.

Nona ignored the laughter sprinkled across the room. Most of the class knew nothing about her beyond her showing in the ordeal of the Shield. That and the fact she'd broken Darla's finger of course. And pulled a real knife on Arabella Jotsis this morning. And done the same on the first day she arrived. 'I find serenity difficult, Mistress Path.'

Sister Pan patted Nona's shoulder and moved back to the head of the class, a kaleidoscope of colour sliding across her as she went.

Clera winked at Nona. Both of them had scraped through their serenity test long after mastering clarity and then patience. The trances were hard to touch, harder to sink into, and remaining in them despite distraction was the hardest. Sister Pan offered exercises to help attain each state along with explanation of what to expect and why. In class she gave guidance towards shaping one's character and daily being to better fit the requirements. But in the end it was words, words, more words.

'I can show you where it lies,' she had said. 'I can point at it. I can describe it. But I cannot *make* you see it. I cannot put it in your hand. The only person who can see it, take it, and own it, is you.'

The old nun taught them poems, stories, fragments of song, even riddles and jests, all to help them view the world through altered eyes – to somehow see what she saw so easily. On occasion she would open the great iron-bound chest at the front of the class and take from it some pretty object to fascinate the eye with patterns. Pieces of ancient glass rainbowed through with colours, interlocking puzzles of black metal, pictures that deceived – at one glance an old man looking to the right, at the next a young boy staring left, or a hill that with a shift of perception became a pit. Endless variety with one thing held common: all of them led to the same place in different ways, a path to suit each person.

Nona had come closest to serenity when running an old song through her mind. The one children sang in the village. *She's falling down, she's falling down / The moon, the moon / She's falling down, she's falling down / Soon, soon.* When she passed the words over her still tongue again and again until every one of them lost its meaning in a chain of unvoiced sound, when she remembered the shapes of the children dancing black against the focus of the moon, in those moments she reached that calm place where nothing outside could touch her, where every memory was robbed of its sharp edges. It wasn't a state without care or purpose, but one with the serenity to rise beyond the reach of fear or even pain.

Nona found it no use whatsoever on the blade-path though: it just meant she fell serenely and was less bothered by how small a portion of the journey she had completed in a non-vertical manner.

'Let us contemplate serenity, novices.' Sister Pan settled herself on the great chest.

Clera covered her mouth and made an exaggerated yawn for Nona's benefit. Nona pressed her lips together in a thin line and willed herself not to slump. If they had desks in Path she would have been tempted to bang her forehead on hers. Two years and she hadn't come close to touching the Path, let alone walking it. Not only that, she hadn't seen anyone else do it either. Infuriatingly, Sister Pan took Hessa, and later Ara, down the stairs when she judged it time to attempt the Path. The other novices of course abandoned their meditation and ran to the windows, peering through the small, coloured panes, to see where Sister Pan went. But she never emerged. One such time, Ketti returning from the sanatorium after treatment for a wrenched shoulder, reported the portrait hall below to be empty and to have met no one on the spiral stair. The conclusion then was that Sister Pan must take the girls to a secret room in the tower's mid-section. But after endless ascents and descents of that stair Nona had no clue where any hidden door might lie.

With a sigh Nona let go of as much tension as she could without falling boneless to the floor and began her hunt for serenity. *She's falling down, she's falling down / The moon—*

For the first moment she thought the Bitel's voice some figment of imagination, but the ringing continued and the steel bell cut swiftly through the layers of calm Nona had gathered to her. By the second tolling she was on her feet with the rest of the class.

'Ancestor's blood!' Clera was at her side, scattering chairs.

'We will proceed to the abbess's house in an orderly manner!' Sister Pan raised her voice.

Bitel had held its tongue since High Priest Jacob had brought the archons to judgement. Nona took her place in the queue of novices hurrying down the stairs behind Sister Pan.

'Let it be a fire. Let it be a fire.' Ketti, two places behind.

Nona half-wanted her to be right. Some natural disasters were preferable to the sorts that people could wreak upon each other.

The wind had turned overnight and blew from the north in unsteady, cold gusts, stuttering as if even now it might change its mind and let the Corridor wind chase around the girdle of the world. Soon though, if the change held, the winds would howl, ice-laden, blowing in from the endless white, and all of the empire would shiver. Nona wrapped her habit tight and reined in the desire to run, matching her pace instead to Sister Pan's.

Abbess Glass waited on her steps, Sisters Wheel and Rose a step below, and a step below them Sisters Tallow and Rule. Sister Apple came hastening through the growing crowd as Nona's class approached.

Out among the pillars a horseman could be glimpsed from time to time, riding away, a silver and scarlet banner snapping behind him in the wind.

'That's a royal herald,' Ara said, coming up on Nona's right.

'Well yes.' Clera elbowed in on Nona's left. 'It doesn't take a Sis to recognize that.'

Nona stared at the retreating figure. It might not take a Tacsis or a Jotsis to recognize such a standard but it took more than a peasant girl from the Grey. The fluttering of the banner as it vanished for the last time tugged at her memory, the line of it trying to draw her back. 'Is the emperor coming?' The idea sounded silly even before she'd finished saying it.

'The emperor went with the Rexxus army to counter raids by Durnish pirates,' Ara said.

'How do you know that?' Ruli pushed up from behind. She liked to say her family were smugglers, or sometimes fisherfolk, but in truth her father owned several large fishing boats, a good deal more merchantmen, and had people to sail them for him.

Ara shrugged as if everyone knew it.

'A whole army? And the emperor himself? For pirates?' Nona asked.

'When pirates strike shore the hand of the Durnish proctor is always at the helm,' Ruli said. 'It's how they probe for weakness. The emperor is stamping down hard. Showing them strength.'

'Mistress Academia would approve of your analysis, Ruli.' Clera, half-mocking.

'That only leaves the sisters,' Hessa's voice from behind the group.

'Velera then, up from the coast,' Clera said.

'Run from pirates? While her brother marches along the shore?' Ara snorted. 'You don't know sweet Velera! She'll be turning the surf crimson.'

Abbess Glass struck the heel of her crozier against the steps. 'Sisters, novices, we are to have an unexpected visit tomorrow. Sherzal, sister to the emperor, is approaching from the east and has requested a tour of this convent. High Priest

Nevis will be meeting the royal procession at the city gates and accompanying our honoured guest on her visit.'

'Sherzal?' Nona looked around at Ara. 'Wasn't it her soldiers that tried to steal you from your father when he was summoned to court? And now she's come in person to take you?'

'Don't be stupid,' Clera hissed. 'The emperor himself couldn't take Arabella from Sweet Mercy. That's why the Jotsis sent her here.'

The wind swirled cold about them, lifting habits and streaming hair. Abbess Glass bent into it, continuing her address. '…classes are suspended until our visitors' departure. Sisters are encouraged to recruit novices to the necessary tasks of preparation. Girls that Sister Rule requires for choir duty are excused other labour. I'm sure that Sister Chrysanthemum will be happy to find work for any novices at a loose end: there's always some part of the convent that needs scrubbing.

'It goes without saying that we seek to present our best face tomorrow … but I will say it in any event. High Priest Nevis's last visit was somewhat traumatic, so let us do our utmost to replace that memory with happier ones. And Sherzal of course honours us with her presence. Let us strive to deserve it.'

Abbess Glass waved to set the assembly free. Nona's eyes tracked the abbess's hand, still curled around the scar tissue from where the candle had burned her. Any visit that Bitel announced held the potential to prove more deadly than Noi-Guin arriving unheralded in the night.

'Ancestor!' Ruli glanced around. 'Let's run before Sister Mop has us cleaning out the Necessary!'

'Run, peasants!' Clera grinned. 'I shall sing for *my* supper.' And with that she started off towards Sister Rule who stood by the dome, yardstick waving above her head to summon the choir.

Nona tried to smile back, but behind her eyes she saw the scream on Abbess Glass's face as she held her hand above that steady flame. Without warning the ice-wind howled, returning Nona to the present. It spoke again, its voice frost-laden, abrading flesh – as if in place of ice it carried a million tiny throwing stars – and everyone ran for shelter.

24

Nona staggered into the Grey Class dormitory brushing ice from the thick shock of her hair, hair that only minutes before had been steaming as she towelled it dry in the bathhouse. She had thought that Blade class exercised every muscle she owned but three hours of sweeping, scrubbing, and polishing under Sister Mop's beady eye had helped her discover new ones. And they hurt.

'I think I strained my voice.' Clera lay on a bed close to the door, flat on her back staring at the ceiling, outer habit pooled on the floor, long legs stretched. Her silver penny gleamed on an open palm.

'I think I strained everything but my voice.' Nona looked around for an unused bed.

Ara came in behind her, hair caked with ice at the front, still steaming at the back. 'I saw Sister Wheel telling Mop to put you on cleaning the privies…'

'Fortunately Moppy has novices she *really* doesn't like,' Nona said. She knew the best way to earn the nun's ire was to leave a mess in the refectory. The nun approved of anyone who left nothing on their plate, so Nona had become something of a favourite.

'She likes you because you're a peasant,' Clera said. 'Mop likes girls who aren't scared of hard work. *Me* she would have had washing the cliff below the Necessary, while Sister Rule used it.'

Ara pushed on into the room and with a short sprint launched herself over two girls lying on their blankets, belly-flopping onto an unoccupied bed. Nona frowned, still hunting a bed to claim as her own. At the far end of the room Darla hulked, her back to them, hunched over something in her lap.

'Who sleeps there?' Nona pointed at an empty bed opposite Ara's. It was quite neatly made but still perhaps a touch too untidy to be unclaimed.

'Alata.' Clera nodded to the bed behind her.

Nona blinked. Two feet protruded from the heap of blankets but it wasn't the number of feet that drew her eye – just the fact that one was darkest brown, the other milky. At the top end she could see only a fan of red hair, spread across the pillow. They said in Red Class that some older novices kept the same beds but Nona had never seen it before.

The shutters rattled as the ice-wind peppered them with hail. Clera patted the blanket beside her. 'Going to be cold tonight. You can share if you like.' She said it lightly but the words carried a weight even so.

Nona's eyes strayed to the two bare feet again, one rubbing the other now. She felt her cheeks blaze and looked away confused.

'This one's free!' Ara waved, pointing at a bed a few further along from her.

'I ache too much to share.' Nona clutched her side. 'Darla knows how to kick.' She hobbled on down the aisle between the beds, not wanting to see if she'd put any hurt in Clera's eyes.

Nona eased herself into her new bed like an old woman, the bruises from her beating starting to stiffen. She hoped that Darla's injuries hurt more than hers did. The big girl shot her a dirty look but held her tongue. With her right hand and left foot both bandaged she probably had no appetite for further trouble. Either way, Nona lacked the energy to care. She rolled her head towards Ara. 'What are threads?' Sisters Flint, Wheel, and Kettle had been drawn to the assassin's knife, all arriving at Blade Hall within minutes of each other. Quite how that happened had been nagging at Nona all the while she scrubbed and cleaned.

'Threads are complicated,' Ara said, her head on her pillow.

'I'm too tired for complicated,' Nona said.

'They're almost the Path, but not quite. Everything has its own threads and they tangle with each other. A trained quantal can weave one person's threads with another's, or with a thing. Or an untrained one can do it by accident – like Hessa did with you.

'A Mystic Sister must have linked the threads from something left behind by the escaped assassin to some of our nuns. They probably used the twin to the dagger you got, which was why the link was so strong. And they did it so that they might be able to sense if she came back.'

'Sister Pan did that?'

Ara snorted. 'Pan? She's too old. She hasn't touched the Path in years. No, it must have been a proper Mystic. A Holy Witch!'

'So … why didn't they find the knife ages ago?'

'It's complicated.'

'You don't know?'

Ara laughed. 'Not really, no. But I know there are threads to draw you to a thing that is still, and threads that will pull on you when a thing is moving. I guess they chose and tied threads that would pull on the sisters if the assassin was moving close to the convent – and that included her possessions which they assumed she would be carrying. They had one of her other two knives to work with. And then when you moved the first knife … they came!'

'Ouch.' Nona remembered Sister Kettle seemingly unwrapping herself from the shadows at the base of the wall and cannoning into her already beaten body. She frowned. 'The nuns were there before I even touched the knife.'

'They say a really strong bond can give a premonition. Some things bind better than others, but with time the threads always come loose.'

They lay without speaking for a while and the room quietened around them. Eventually another question floated to the surface of Nona's sleepiness. She yawned hugely then asked it. 'Why don't the emperor's sisters have titles? Shouldn't they be Princess Sherzal and Princess Velera?'

'You've listened to too many bards' tales.' Ara yawned her own yawn. 'We haven't had kings and queens, princes and princesses, for hundreds of years. Maybe they still have them somewhere if you follow the Corridor long enough.'

'But they're his sisters and he's the emperor…'

'Crucical doesn't trust either of them further than he could spit them.' Ara snuggled beneath her blanket, only her hair showing. 'Titles would just encourage them. The lack of them reminds everyone where the emperor's favour lies, and where it doesn't. It's like that in high families.'

Nona closed her eyes. Treachery and deceit weren't confined to high families. Blood bonds were neither chosen nor hard to break, whatever the Ancestor might have to say on the subject. She lay still, ignoring her pain, knowing sleep would be hard to find. She thought of her fight with Darla, not that it had been a fight from her side, but Darla at least showed some anger, some brutality. *That* to Nona was a fight. The arts that Mistress Blade taught, while deadly, were without passion. The contests felt to Nona more like dances. Dances that would end in pain and blood if you missed a step, but dances even so, devoid of rage or hatred. Sister Pan told them the serenity trance would help their blade-fist and their blade-path too. It married well to the science of combat that Sister tallow instructed them in. Nona saw the logic of it. But there was a piece missing.

Back in the village the children had always chased Nona for being dark where they were light, for being silent and watchful, outside the circle. They seldom caught her, but sometimes the bigs would come upon her unawares. *Those* were fights. Snarling, desperate, savage, and full of rage.

Control. How many times had Mistress Blade used that word in the class today?

In the Caltess Nona had been caught only once, by Denam, the red-haired gerant who ruled the attic, at least when Regol, swift and dark, wasn't there to keep him in order. She had been in the narrow corridor leading to the exit that looked out over the rear of the stables block. Denam had come up behind her while she gazed at the two stallions being exercised. He had taken her forearms, one in each meaty fist. 'What've we got here?'

Nona had kicked back hard and twisted for all she was worth. The contact hurt her foot more than it seemed to hurt the boy. He stood shy of six foot but his strength was iron: she couldn't slip his grasp any more than she could lift the building. Snarling, she bent to bite his hand, managing to draw blood before he stretched out her arms painfully, putting his fists beyond reach.

'You'll pay for that.' Denam had seemed on the point of saying more but a dull thud interrupted him. The vise-like grip on Nona's arms relaxed and in a moment she'd torn free. She had turned to see Denam clutching his lower back with both hands, and behind him another figure, a touch shorter.

'Go.'

The newcomer hadn't raised his voice but Denam ran for it, still clutching his back, pushing past Nona and out into the yard beyond. Nona kicked him in the back of the knee as he passed, but he hadn't seemed to notice.

'Kidney punch. Be pissing blood for a week.' The man had had the flat eyes and facial scars of one of the ice- tribes, two lines slanting down across each cheek. He had worn a leather jerkin, sealskin trousers, an iron chain loose about his neck, and at his side the flat sword known as a *tular*. Nona had seen one amid the huge variety in the Caltess weapon store: the blade was all straight lines, wider at the end than at the hilt, requiring a scabbard open all along its length. In the village they told worse tales about the ice tribes than they did about the Pelarthi. Nobody knew what they ate up there on the sheet. The consensus being that it was each other. 'You're very small. Smallest Partnis has?'

The man was bald, not overly tall, but solid, and he had spoken slowly and with so deep a voice that each word had been like the rolling out of a heavy stone, both measured and considered. Nona had got the feeling that he might never rush a sentence, whether his firstborn lay dead in his arms or he had woken to find his house ablaze all around him.

She had rubbed her forearms where Denam had gripped her. 'You're a ring-fighter?' She hadn't seen him before, she would have known if she had. His eyes were the faint cloudy blue of an ice-lake, his skin a dark red.

He nodded. 'I fight in the ring – I fight outside it. They call me Tarkax.' He watched her.

Nona had found the man's scrutiny uncomfortable. He had something of the wolf about him, but Nona knew wolves.

'Had trouble before.' The man set his hand to the side of his face, indicating the bruising from where Nona had let Giljohn slap her on the day he sold her. 'Got first blood today though. That's good.' He had looked past her to the yard beyond. 'They going to be teaching you soon enough. Like that.' Outside the horses still cantered around the grooms on their training ropes. 'Partnis's fight-masters will tell you it's a science, this business of fists and knives. They'll tell you, keep a cool head, detached, control.' The man had given a quick shrug of his shoulders and spat. 'He'll tell you the *professional* calculates, watches, plans.'

'Don't they?' Nona had turned back towards him.

'Nature shaped us, little girl. Shaped the animals. Predators. Prey. Millions of years. Fighting, making children, dying. A cycle that hones each to its purpose. And what have we in common, wolf, eagle, man, under-killers, bears, all of us?' His eyebrows had shaped the question.

Nona had waited for him to answer, wondering what exactly under-killers were.

'Rage. We've got hate and anger and red fury, child. Saw it in you too. Got your teeth into that idiot boy. Didn't care that he might snap your arms off.' The man had gone down on one knee, face close to hers. 'Here in the Corridor they teach you to put that anger aside. They got their reasons. Keep a calm head and you'll see more. But on the ice we know better than to let go of the weapons so many hard years have forged for us.' He had jabbed a blunt finger at Nona's chest.

'Keep that fire. Use it. We're wild things us men, and when we remember it we're at our most dangerous.'

Nona hadn't seen the man after that, but his words had struck her like hammers to a bell, and she rang with them, even now in the quiet dark, and she held on to her anger.

'Get up! They're coming!'

Nona opened eyes she felt sure had just that minute closed, and saw only night.

'Quickly!'

She groaned, stiff in every limb, and rolled in time to see a tall figure retreating from the doorway, lantern in hand. All around her novices were spilling from their beds, some grumbling, some anxious.

'Sherzal wasn't supposed to be here until noon!'

'Royals do what they want.' Clera, still a lump in her bed.

'Everyone up! Everyone dressed.' Mally, Grey Class's head-girl, turned up the wick in her night-lantern.

Nona groaned, shrugged off her blanket and started to wriggle into her skirts. Fingers busied themselves with laces and ties, not needing instruction from her sleep-fuddled mind. She hadn't lied about being too sore to share a bed with Clera. Sleep had only stiffened her: she hoped Darla's finger and toes hurt as much as the bruises she gave in exchange.

The novices stumbled out into a freezing pre-dawn, the sun a red promise to the east. The scattered ice melted by the focus moon had frozen into a continuous film, treacherous and hard to see. Clera skated out across the courtyard with a dancer's grace, disdaining the threat of a sudden fall, just as she did on the blade-path.

'Novice Clera! Get in line!' Sister Flint rounded the corner, a thin dark line that the sun could not yet muster the courage to unwrap. 'We're required at the abbess's house. Quickly, quietly, and with decorum.'

The slow, cold passing of an hour found both novices and nuns numb-fingered, shivering in their lines before Abbess Glass's steps, watching the pillars for any sign of the royal party's approach. Hessa saw them first. Nona, following the line of Hessa's finger, had to squint for several moments before she too saw the flicker of motion between the pillars.

The soldiers came into view first: five ranks of five, all in scarlet and silver. The sight of them gave her a sense of unease, something tugging at her memory... The troop wasn't matched in height as the high priest's church-guards had been, but cut from many cloths with varying degrees of generosity. As the soldiers drew closer Nona could see that they all shared two things: none were young and none looked as though crossing them would be a good idea.

Nona had been expecting the emperor's sister to arrive in a sedan chair larger and more grand than the high priest's, but both came mounted, despite the ice-wind. Sherzal cut an impressive figure in the furs of a white bear, astride a huge white horse. High Priest Nevis, on the other hand, looked uncomfortable and ill at ease, huddled in a hooded robe on the back of a grey mare.

Behind the two riders straggled a long train of priests, attendants, and baggage porters, many bent against the wind like ridge-top trees.

The choir started up with the first high notes of Concordiance as the soldiers began to form lines before the steps. Poor Sister Rule had only a moment of song to glory in though before the ice-wind raised its own voice and drowned the novices out, scouring the plateau with shards straight from the northern sheets. Decorum blew away too as Abbess Glass led the charge for the Dome of the Ancestor.

Within minutes the visitors and the whole population of the convent stood packed together in a chaotic and ice-spattered mix, spilling out beyond the foyer's pillared space into the main dome, an unearned privilege for any novices in Red Class who happened to be swept in amid the crush.

Sherzal of course stood in her own space, at the centre of a tight ring of soldiers who had no qualms about knocking young girls or old nuns aside to make room. Nona slipped and twisted ahead of them to enter the echoing space beneath the dome for the first time. Being in Grey Class now she was entitled to stand beneath the dome, though it wouldn't have been untypical of Sister Wheel to delay her introduction by weeks or even months just to keep her in her place. Nona looked up, dwarfed by great walls curving away towards a distant, golden vertex. The enclosed space swallowed the intruders, making them seem few and tiny, enfolding their conversation and complaint in its silence. Nona stood, rooted to the spot, the walls seeming to rotate around her as she gazed at the distant heights. Her habit steamed and fat drops of water fell from the hem.

The underside of the dome lay black and seeded with stars in blood crystal. Here and there the stars took on a paler shade and near the highest point the Hope lay in sparkling white quartz. The skyscape held Nona's gaze a while but the statue at the centre soon captured her attention: a human figure, perhaps twenty feet of gleaming gold. Even if it were gold leaf over stone the wealth it wore could purchase a lifetime's luxury. The figure lacked detail. Was it a man? A woman? This was the Ancestor that Sister Wheel had described as a joining of everyone who had ever lived, an ideal in which the best parts of humanity fused into a joyous whole.

As the voices stilled behind her Nona found that, although she was still staring towards the statue, she was not staring at it, but *past* it. What drew her, and had pulled at her ever so faintly since her first night at the convent, sleeping in a nun's cell, was the foyer at the far side, opposite the one she had entered by. Something there – something beyond the dark marble pillars – demanded her attention, just as it had that first night when Sister Apple led her along the corridor between the convent's sleeping nuns. A fullness. An otherness. A something.

'Hey!' Clera jabbed Nona's ribs then pulled her arm to turn her round. 'You're missing it!'

The soldiers stood in a larger perimeter centred on Sherzal, now joined by High Priest Nevis, the abbess, and a girl of perhaps twelve or thirteen. The emperor's sister had shed her bearskin to reveal a flowing crimson gown edged with silver. The girl, dark-haired and with the flat cheekbones of the ice-tribes, wore a close approximation of the blade-habit, though it too was crimson with silver worked about the collar and had a belt of silver links.

'Who does she think she is?' Clera whispered. 'A Red Sister?'

On Clera's far side Ghena snorted.

'She's whoever Sherzal says she is,' Ara hissed. 'You don't want to cross any Lansis, but Sherzal's the worst of them. Three years ago she had Seema Bresis burned alive as a heretic because the woman made a joke about her hair at the Tacsis's grand ball. They say she owns half the inquisition.'

'...welcome the emperor's sister, honourable Sherzal, to Sweet Mercy...' The high priest droned out his introduction. '...for Abbess Glass to say a few words.' He turned with apparent relief to the abbess.

Abbess Glass made her speech well with ample thanks for the opportunity to show such a high personage around the convent temporarily in her humble charge. She spoke of the famed piety and generosity of the Lancis line and of how the empire had bloomed under Crucical's reign. She spoke until the novices began to shuffle from one foot to the other, and even the nuns' patient smiles grew fixed.

'I would just ask her what she wants,' Nona whispered.

'Which is why you'll be a warrior rather than an abbess,' Ara replied.

'Why won't she shut up?' Clera hugged her belly. 'Breakfast will think I don't love it any more.'

Jula shushed everyone: Abbess Glass was coming to the bit where there was nothing left but for the person to say what they wanted.

'...let us know how we can be of service to you, honourable Sherzal.'

'Thank you, abbess.' Sherzal offered a broad smile, all red painted lips and a bright line that looked too white to be teeth. 'High Priest.' She nodded to Nevis, the mass of dark red curls bouncing slightly about her head. She looked to be in her thirties, perhaps of an age with Sister Apple, almost beautiful but with each feature slightly too exaggerated. An animated face, full of vicious good humour. 'I don't intend to remain long. I'll say a prayer of course. It would be rude not to. After all my great-great-grand-uncle built the place, did he not? Or was it great-great-great? One of the Persuses, anyway.

'You'll take me around, won't you, Nevis?' She slipped a bare white arm through the high priest's. 'I must confess first that I did have an ulterior motive for my visit… Not being blessed by the Ancestor with children I have taken young Zole here under my wing.' Sherzal indicated the girl in the red habit and leaned her head in towards the high priest's. She lowered her voice but by accident of the dome's acoustics or by her own design she remained audible. 'The child was the only survivor from the town of Ytis after the Scithrowl incursion back in '09. I've taken her on as my ward.' She rotated the high priest to face Abbess Glass and continued at more regal volume. 'I've had Zole tutored and trained extensively by a wide range of experts, including Safira, who benefited from eight years of study at this very convent. I think though that the only place where she can truly finish her education to the highest of standards is right here. I'm told that Grey Class would be best suited to her current skills.'

Abbess Glass's smile twitched, just for a fraction of a moment, but Nona saw it. 'I'm so sorry but that is of course quite imposs—'

'Abbess.' High Priest Nevis tilted his head back towards the foyer. 'I'm sure these are matters best discussed in your study, with perhaps a glass of Sweet Mercy's finest vintage to fight the day's chill. It has been a long and … bracing … journey up from Verity.'

Sherzal's smile grew wider than Nona had thought possible, showing more teeth than it seemed likely a person could own. 'We'll leave Zole with her class, shall we? Your nuns can have a chance to assess her talents.'

Abbess Glass frowned and opened her mouth, but the high priest spoke first. 'Of course, an excellent idea.' He bowed slightly and gestured back towards the doors. 'I think we can dare the short trip to the abbess's house now.'

The abbess's mask showed no fractures this time. 'Of

course.' Just a hint of stiffness in her voice. 'Novices, return to your classes. The emperor's sister may stop by to view proceedings before she leaves.'

Sherzal strode towards the main door, with High Priest Nevis – stout and a touch shorter than her – struggling to catch up. Abbess Glass stared after them as the soldiers followed in two files. A moment later she threw up her hands, motioned Sister Tallow towards Zole, and hastened after the emperor's sister.

25

'It seems I will be having the pleasure of your company in Blade Hall this morning after all, Grey Class.' Sister Tallow's hard stare killed the wave of chatter rising in the wake of the visitors departing the dome. 'You still have time for breakfast – at least if you run and manage not to break your legs on the ice. Zole will go with you. Alata, you can watch over her. Go! Don't be late.'

Grey Class's exit began a general rush for the refectory. Clera was first through the doors, skidding to a halt at the head of Grey table. Ara, Zole, and Ketti found their seats a heartbeat later, Nona coming up behind. Within moments the hall around them filled with novices scrambling for chairs, reaching for plates, and trying to push food into mouths faster than words came out of them. Nona sat with Ara on her right and Zole to her left, until Alata pushed their chairs apart and slid herself between Nona and the new girl.

'Safira was expelled from the convent.'

Ara didn't raise her voice or look up from her plate but somehow everyone at the table heard her.

'Who?' Nona asked. The name seemed familiar.

'Safira – the one who trained *her*.' Ara turned to stare past Nona and Alata at Zole, who returned the stare, her face a mask. 'She was expelled from the convent for stabbing another novice when she turned her back on her after defeating her in Blade class.'

'A lie.' Zole's lips gave only the slightest twitch to release the words.

'How do you know stuff like this?' Clera asked.

'Who got stabbed?' Nona asked.

'I know because my father keeps me informed of matters that affect me.' Ara kept her eyes on Zole, her food untouched. 'Sherzal has been hunting all across the empire for possible two-bloods, chasing down any thread her Academics can find. She picked up this one,' she nodded towards Zole, 'after my uncle outwitted her troops and got me safely to the convent. Sherzal will be trying to get her in with us as a spy, perhaps as an assassin too.'

'You think too much of yourself.' Zole bit into her bread and swallowed in two chews. 'Highness Sherzal lost interest in you long ago.'

'Because she has you?' Ara snorted.

Zole didn't reply, just kept on eating. The others, tired from the previous day's labour, from rising early, and from a long wait in the cold, followed her example. While she ate, Nona stole glances at the new girl. She had the flat features of the ice-tribes: broad cheekbones, eyes like black stones. Without any other clues she could as easily be a boy as a girl.

Bray sounded far too soon and Nona limped from the table still chewing, bringing up the rear with Darla, hunched against the wind as the Grey Class novices headed for Blade Hall. Ten yards from the doors, now closed behind the rest of the class, Darla slipped on sheet ice. She fell heavily, unable to break the fall with her injured hand. Nona braced herself and offered her arm for the larger girl to lever herself back up.

'Don't need your help, squirt.' Darla snarled, slipping again as she tried to rise.

Nona stayed where she was. 'When the convent's full of strangers we don't need to fight each other.' She reached for Darla's elbow. 'We'll be sisters one day.'

Darla grunted, but she let Nona take some of her weight as she got up. They came through the doors together, ears stinging from the ice-wind, faces red.

Sister Tallow waited for them on the sands, Zole beside her in scarlet and silver, the rest of the class already vanished into the changing room. Up on the benches Sherzal, the high priest, and Abbess Glass sat surrounded by attendants. Sherzal's soldiers lined the walls, having pushed the stuffed leather combat dummies out into the hall to make room.

Darla and Nona hurried across to the tunnel, heads down to avoid Sister Tallow's disapproval. Nona entered the familiar warmth of the changing room to find Clera just getting up, dressed and ready to return. The heat of the pipes always reminded Nona's body to expect a fight – that and the smell of the place, young bodies and old sweat, something a day's cleaning couldn't erase.

'Fist-habits today.' Clera grinned as she passed them. 'We get to pound on the new girl!'

Nona was second-last out of the changing room, leaving Darla still fumbling with her ties. The broken finger would save her hair – Sister Tallow would rarely shave a novice for lateness if they had a genuine excuse. Nona bit down on her pain and jogged out onto the sand as easily as she could, with every ache and injury from the past two days screaming at her. Grey Class watched her arrival.

'Good.' Sister Tallow didn't seem minded to wait for Darla. 'Novice Clera, a demonstration for the class of the blade-fist kata.'

Clera stepped forward, her smile vanishing as she focused on the complex set of moves required, a long dance of violence demonstrating all the main forms of the art, stressing every muscle and joint a body owns. Zole stood beside Sister Tallow, her face without expression, dark eyes glinting.

Nona glanced across at Ara and found a similar lack of expression on her friend's face. The echoes of unspoken words trembled across her lips, her eyes fixed on some point beyond Tallow and Zole. Perhaps on the tall windows, each offering a deep blue infinity of sky.

Clera moved into the kata, her speed dazzling, snapping out kicks above her head with so swift a tempo that to most of her audience it would be nothing but a blur of motion. She leapt forward, skidding into a crouch with her head almost touching the floor, before jumping up, feet pulled in, leaving almost room for Nona to walk beneath. A series of blocks and punches followed in the prescribed order, intermixed with spins and reversals. Sand sprayed beneath the balls of her feet, a suspicious amount of it in Zole's direction.

A minute later and the performance ended with a jump-kick high enough to break the jaw of a gerant prime. Ninety separate moves woven together and executed at breath-taking speed. Clera returned to the front row, flushed and making an effort to hide how winded the exercise had left her.

Sister Tallow turned to Zole. 'Perhaps you could demonstrate your training for us now?'

Zole inclined her head a fraction. 'I know blade-fist, Noi-tal, the Scithrowl kill-game, and elements of the Torca. Which would you prefer to see, Mistress Blade?'

Sister Tallow frowned. 'The Torca is rarely seen…'

'She's trained with the Noi-Guin,' Clera hissed. 'Must have. They kill anyone else who teaches Noi-tal!'

'If I may?' Sherzal raised her voice from the stands. 'Perhaps a more practical demonstration? Zole could spar with one of your novices. Nevis was telling me that you have a girl who passed the ordeal of the Shield within weeks of entering the convent?'

Abbess Glass glanced down at Sister Tallow, who gave the smallest shake of her head. Nona felt the tension leave her and unclenched her teeth. Tallow knew that Darla could hand out quite a beating.

'A different novice, perhaps?' The abbess turned back with a smile. 'Nona has had a difficult week. Perhaps Novice Arabella?'

Sherzal echoed the abbess's smile. 'I would like to see this Nona of yours against my girl.'

Beside the emperor's sister High Priest Nevis lifted a hand. 'The Shield still has to guard the Argatha, bad week or not. This should be good training for that duty.' He waved proceedings on.

Abbess Glass started to rise from her seat then fell back,

returning the hard line of her mouth to the smile she had momentarily misplaced. 'Of course.'

'Nona.' Sister Tallow beckoned her forward. 'Show our guest how we fight at Sweet Mercy.'

Nona stepped forward, meeting Zole's stare. She felt a heat rise, somewhere deep, just beneath her ribs. The girl's eyes held a challenge – the sort she'd not sensed since she first saw Raymel Tacsis. A killer's confidence. And something inside her burned in answer. Nona had yet to fight within Blade Hall. For two years she had learned and learned, practised until her muscles tore and her bones creaked. Sister Tallow had pitted the novices against each other constantly, and yet to Nona those were not fights. They were contests. Contests between friends, or at least classmates. Even when Darla came against her on the previous morning Nona hadn't, in the marrow of her bones, considered it a fight.

'Mark the corners.' Sister Tallow pointed to the practice dummies and the novices hastened to drag four of them to mark out a square, two girls struggling with each dummy – rough man-shapes of leather stuffed with horsehair, set on wooden posts that bedded in heavy and rounded bases so they would rock rather than fall.

Nona let the others do the work and stayed beside Ara, stretching, trying to squeeze the weary ache from her muscles.

'The princess doesn't want to work up an honest sweat with royalty looking on?' Clera stared in Ara's direction, grunting with effort as she and Ketti heaved a dummy to the nearest corner.

Ara said nothing, just kept staring at the tall windows opposite, the ghost of some rhyme on her lips.

Within a minute the novices stood once more in their lines before Mistress Blade and the four dummies stood at the corners of a square ten yards on a side. At Sister Tallow's nod Nona stepped into the combat area. She rolled her head to one side then the other, stretching her neck, then ran her hands up through the close-cropped thickness of her hair.

Zole entered the square from the other side. She stood a

head taller than Nona. 'I will make you bleed,' she said, her accent clipped. 'Regardless of how swiftly you submit.'

Nona turned side on, one leg forward, crouching in the blade-fist stance, hands raised. 'I'm ready.'

'Fight.' Sister Tallow stepped back.

Zole came forward, unhurried but without hesitation. Nona stood her ground and retreated into the space between moments, freezing the dust motes in place within the shafting sunlight. It took an age for Zole to enter arm's reach, and as she did she snapped a punch at Nona's throat. The girl's fist came so fast that only instinct saved Nona, her arm deflecting the punch into her collarbone. The force of the blow threatened to snap the bone and sent Nona reeling backwards.

Balance lost, Nona let herself fall, narrowly evading a second punch. She kicked as she dropped, aiming for Zole's jaw. The tribe-girl stopped Nona's rising foot on her triceps and came on, lifting into a flying kick aimed at Nona's chest. Nona lacked the balance and time to block. Accepting the impact on her bruised ribs she drove her forearm in hard, just below the girl's knee, using her other arm to break her fall. She hit the ground with a thump, the impact sending up a lazy spray of sand.

Zole continued her advance at exactly the same pace she had maintained from the start, stamping at Nona's hands and head as she rolled away. Nona rolled, contorting to avoid Zole's feet. One heel, aimed at her head, came down on her shoulder, the shock of the blow pulsing into the bone, rippling away through the muscle. Nona hooked an elbow behind the foot and let her rotation drag it along. Rather than fight the motion Zole accelerated into it, then out of it, lifting into a backflip. As Nona's arms came beneath her torso she shoved with all her strength, providing enough momentum to spin back to a standing position in an awkward swirl just as Zole's flip came full cycle. The girl landed on the balls of her feet, crouched and ready.

Most of the audience would have seen a quick flurry of blows, Nona hitting the ground, Zole unbalanced, and both girls gaining their feet with acrobatics – all over in a moment.

Nona and Zole however had both learned a considerable amount in that thin slice of time. They stood for a heartbeat, each watching the other.

Nona attacked, seeking the initiative, a red anger welling up through her, hot enough to burn away both weariness and pain. She came forward, arms raised in defence, in short, high steps that kept a leg ready to block or kick. Zole let her come close, let her punch, punch, and punch again, deflecting each strike with forms Clera had shown in the blade-fist kata. Zole's counter-punch came lightning-fast but Nona caught it in her hand, moving her other hand in to help stress the girl's wrist. Somehow, in moves unknown to Nona, the girl was climbing her, using the trapped fist as an anchor and setting her feet to Nona's knee and hip. The leverage exploited gravity to launch Nona skyward. She had to release Zole's hand to deflect kicks coming up as the girl fell towards the sand.

This time when Nona landed it was all she could do to pull her limbs in to brace for the impact. She rolled to the side to see Zole already coming towards her with the same unhurried pace. Nona reached to slow the world's progress but her grip on time's current was failing, her exhaustion ran bone-deep, and every part of her hurt. Anger flared again. Nona pushed herself up, rising as Zole arrived. She flung herself forward, accepting an agonizing punch to the gut and slipping Zole's blow towards her head, the girl's knuckles sliding across her lips. The move brought them together, Nona's hand on Zole's chest, her fingers tented above the small swell of her breast.

For some fragment of a second they held like that, both looking down at Nona's hand – Nona snarling with the effort it took to hold back the invisible blades that had opened Raymel Tacsis's throat. She could slice through flesh and ribs, cut out the bitch's heart and hold it dripping above her. She could stand panting above the ruin of her foe and howl her victory. The pain in her gut, the blood in her mouth, the rage pulsing through every vein – all these things demanded it.

'What?' Zole's surprise turned to contempt, the moment's

hesitation gone. She drove her forehead into Nona's face and threw her to the ground.

Nona lay where she fell. Zole's kicks and stamps rained around her. She blocked the worst of them, but even the ones that got through had more violence behind them than Darla's. It was a combination of power and accuracy that couldn't help but break things.

'No!'

The voice wasn't Nona's or Zole's. It wasn't Sister Tallow's. It hardly sounded human. It made the stone floor buzz and the sand dance in a golden haze shot through with strange patterns. It made the air brittle. It made Zole stop attacking and Nona stop defending.

Nona let her head flop to the side. One eye wouldn't open but through the slit of the other she saw that a space had cleared around Ara. Something was wrong with her. She looked the same but different, as if she were fashioned from something not of the world, a piece of stained glass cut and coloured to resemble Arabella Jotsis but lit from within, bleeding light in hues that the Ancestor had never intended men to see.

Ara stood staring at Nona on the sand and Zole above her. A trickle of blood ran from her nose, reaching her lip. She shuddered, or the world did, showing her in three poses, each out of line with the others. She stepped forward, or rather one Ara stepped forward, another stayed, a third caught between them, each overlapping, one vibrating through the next.

The Aras, or images of Ara, came together with a snap like the sky breaking and Ara stood there, singular, facing them, eyes blazing as if her head were full of light. She took two more paces towards Zole then with a snarl veered towards the closest practice dummy. Her punch happened too fast to see but it put her fist through the leather and deep into the padding. She ripped it out sideways, shredding the thick leather polished by ten thousand blows, and scattering the horsehair in clumps. Exposed in the gaping wound left behind, the wooden centre-post lay splintered where Ara's fist had found it.

Ara stared at Zole, eyes still burning. 'Let Nona go.' Her voice shuddering with harmonics.

'Or?' To her credit Zole kept any fear from the word – or perhaps she just lacked the imagination for it.

Ara reached into the fight dummy and grasped the heavy post. The noise started as a moan, building rapidly, bursting past Ara's teeth, becoming a yell, and in one moment the dummy became pieces, fragments of leather expanding outward, a cloud of horsehair shaken from its clumps, and in the middle … splinters … thousands of splinters.

A noise like the end of the world shoved Nona, rolling her over and over. She closed her eyes, pulling her limbs in tight, and all around sand and debris began to rain down about her.

'Nona?'

A cold wet something returned Nona to the hall and the sharp angles of her pain. She had been sinking into the endless comfort of deep dark cushions and the transition was not a welcome one.

'What?' She tried to push the wetness away.

'Open your eyes.'

Nona opened them and found herself staring up at Clera, dripping rag in hand. Hessa stood at Clera's shoulder, frowning her concern.

'Are you all right? Anything broken?'

Nona groaned a wordless reply and moved a hand to her ribs.

'Ara's in so much trouble!' Clera sounded awed. Her half-grin echoed conflicting emotions.

'W-what happened?'

'Didn't you see? She went into the serenity trance and walked the Path!' Clera leaned over to brush bits of the practice dummy from Nona's hair. Behind her a wall of backs – novices facing the stands at the end of the hall. 'Ara must have taken three steps at least, maybe more! Did you see what she did?'

Nona struggled to rise, clutching her side. Clera held her down for a moment then decided to help. Ducking under Nona's arm she levered her into a standing position. Hessa tried to help but mostly got in the way.

'Your head?' Nona saw that the left side of Hessa's face lay grazed and bleeding.

'I felt her beating you.' Hessa shrugged, acknowledging the link between them. '…and I fell over.'

Together they edged to the end of the line of Grey Class novices. Nona spotted Zole two places down, her tunic torn, small splinter wounds peppering her face.

Ara stood before the seating stand, Sister Tallow beside her, hand on her shoulder. Sister Wheel had arrived from somewhere and stood at the base of the steps to the seating. The high priest, flanked by Sherzal and Abbess Glass, had come to the front and was staring down at the novice in judgement.

Sherzal wore a broad smile as she leaned out over the rail. 'An impressive display, young Jotsis,' she called down. 'It appears to have broken all manner of convent rules, though.'

Ara stared up at the emperor's sister, making no reply.

The high priest made a curt gesture. 'Novice Arabella, you have used the Path without sanction, without full training, and endangered one of my personal guests. It is my judgement that you be given twenty strokes of the cane, sentence to be carried out immediately.' The high priest nodded to Sister Tallow. 'Mistress Blade to deliver punishment.'

Sister Tallow steered Ara back into the hall, pushing her ahead, and Ara made no protest, still dazed perhaps.

'Maybe…' Sherzal drew the word out, her voice somehow stopping everyone, despite appearing conversational. 'Maybe, as young Arabella is rumoured to be the Argatha, it would be fitting for her Shield to take the beating for her? After all, it was her Shield's failure that prompted the poor girl's indiscretion.'

'Surely that would set entirely the wrong example. And besides, Zole—' Abbess Glass had more to say but the high priest overrode her.

'It would be unusual in the context of our convents, honoured Sherzal, though I quite understand that these practices are common among the highest families. Arabella herself may well have been raised with a whipping girl to receive her punishments for her.'

'I know I was.' Sherzal smiled. 'How my tutors used to beat poor Susi. I never did seem to learn my lesson though.'

'It would perhaps be inappropriate *here*, honoured Sherzal.' High Priest Nevis almost cringed, as if it hurt his mouth to utter any form of contradiction aimed at the emperor's sister. 'Even when the novice is of royal ancestry. Our recruits leave worldly attachments behind them when they join us.'

'I'll do it.' Nona raised her voice and took a step forward.

'What?' The high priest turned from Sherzal, blinking.

'I will do it,' Nona said.

'See,' Sherzal gestured with an open hand. 'The girl is ready to be punished for her mistakes.' Her smile broadened. 'If only all peasants were so obliging.'

'Well…' Nevis frowned. 'If the novice is willing…' He glanced towards Abbess Glass but too quickly to allow her a response.

Sister Wheel advanced from the steps, producing a long cane from the folds of her habit, a black strip of wire-willow, thin enough to cut with each blow.

'I told you.' Zole spoke quietly behind Nona. 'That I would make you bleed.'

26

'Bite on this.'

Sister Tallow offered Nona a leather strap.

'Why?' Nona asked.

'It will give you something to do.'

Nona shook her head, keeping her eyes on Sister Tallow's. The old woman returned her gaze. She had the kind of face that was hard to imagine showing any emotion, a mask of leathery skin, small, tight wrinkles, seams of old scars, cheekbones making sharp angles, her mouth a short and bitter line. Nona always thought of Mistress Blade as old, though no age showed in the way she moved. Sister Rose had said hunskas race through their days: perhaps Mistress Blade and the Poisoner had shared a class once, Sister Apple still sweet, ambling through a long life while Sister Tallow's candle burned at both ends and lighted her way to dusty death.

Nona's thoughts occupied her as Sister Tallow checked the straps securing her wrists above her head. The leather bound her to the lowest of five iron rings set into the wall. Sister Tallow stepped away, leaving Nona facing the stonework, naked. Her habit had been removed to let the lash land; her skirts and smalls taken to save them from the blood. Many of her classmates had gasped as she stripped and they saw for the first time the dark and mottled patchwork of bruising all across her back, ribs, and thighs. Not Zole's work – though that would show soon enough – but Darla's from the day before.

'Ready?' Sister Tallow asked.

'Yes.' Nona hadn't forgotten the Grey: two years of convent living hadn't taken it from her. Sister Wheel called her a peasant still, and if peasants knew anything, it was how to suffer and how to endure.

The wire-willow struck. Left shoulder to right hip, not a crushing blow like the ones High Priest Jacob had struck against Four-Foot, but a cutting one, a shockingly painful line, like acid, burned in and bleeding out into muscle and bone. Nona screamed. She hadn't set her mind to silence – she put no stock in sullen defiance. She screamed out the agony as a wordless curse, a promise of violent retribution, a vow that if Zole or any other came against her outside the rules of the hall she would cut their heart out.

The next lash struck across the first, and Nona roared her defiance, not a girl's shriek but something deep and guttural, a noise she hadn't known herself capable of. Another lash and another. Nona saw all four blows as bright and intersecting lines across the backs of her eyes. A fifth. She roared again, pure threat, animal and free of complication. A hesitation before the sixth, as if she'd given even Mistress Blade pause.

A seventh. Nona's hands tore at the stone, jolting the straps about her wrists and the iron ring above. Eight. The bright lines wove tight into a single writhing cord of light burning crimson and gold across her vision. Nine. Ten. Nona could no longer tell if she were shouting: each new line the wire-willow scored into her flowed into the blazing path before her, becoming a single rope twisted from the whole. It hung before her mind's eye, wrapping about itself, twisting, loops of bright thread seen here and there as when wool is woven into yarn. Eleven. Twelve. Nona's back felt molten: she could feel the blood trickle across her buttocks, down her thighs, feel each drop as if it were burning metal, liquid from the inhuman heat of furnace and forge. But what burned more were the eyes of her enemies upon her: Zole and Sherzal. Nothing else mattered, not novice, or nun, not the high priest, or Mistress Blade striking the blows … just the eyes of her enemies, heavy upon her with the weight of their satisfaction.

More blows, the count lost between them, one so sharp it threw her head back and her eyes open. The wall before her hands lay scored, dark lines against the pale stone, deep and shadow-filled slots in the limestone where the claws of her rage had cut in. Her secret released. Nona's body jolted against the wall, and her fury reached a new incandescence, chasing away all trace of pain. The single path spun from the threads of a dozen and more blows suddenly snapped into a new configuration, a pattern that filled her sight, a single line chasing through hard angles, a corner, a corner, another corner, a surface filled with rectangles, a space filled with blocks, sketched in place with one bright line. A wall.

Another blow hit home and, howling, Nona reached for the Path. She set foot upon it … and was filled. In just one moment the Path poured through her. An awful, wondrous, potential ran in her veins, filled every void, pressed against the insides of her eyes, sang in every bone, bursting, consuming, bleeding from her pores. The fear of destruction didn't scare Nona from the Path – she would have chased so marvellous a doom to the world's end. Rather it was the Path that slipped from beneath her, live and coiling, twisting away even as she tried for her next step. In some complex space with a dozen ups and a hundred swinging downs, Nona lost her balance and stumbled back into the world.

The wire-willow hit her. She heard it crack. The crack ran through her, through her hands flat against the wall, deep amid the pattern of corners, rectangles, and blocks. For one heartbeat a new silence held the hall and in that silence the walls trembled. In the next heartbeat the stone before her began to fracture with a noise like the world ending and everything fell.

'Up.' A strong hand closed around Nona's wrist drawing her up and to the side. Her other arm, still bound to the first, rose too. Pieces of broken limestone fell from her as she came upright. Her feet found the ground and she stumbled against Sister Tallow, hurting her instep on jagged rubble. The surface of the wall had shattered outward to a depth of four or five inches in an area some yards across. The iron ring dangled by the straps still binding Nona's wrists, its pin lodged in a lump of broken stone no bigger than her hand.

Sisters Tallow and Rose wrapped Nona in a sheet. The novices looked on, pale with the dust now sifting down across the hall.

'I'll carry her.' Sister Rose reached for Nona as she had when she lay arrow-struck that second week.

'No.' Nona spat blood onto the sand. Her back hurt as if a thousand scalding hooks were lodged in it, each on strings being pulled in different directions. 'I'll walk.'

She left the hall, head down and eyes on the sand, taking the steps that old women take, with Sister Rose following close behind. She stopped only once, just as she passed Zole in the line of novices. With head still down she turned her face to watch the girl from the one eye not yet swollen closed. She didn't speak, only showed her teeth in a crimson grin, then moved on. Zole had a face on which it seemed nothing could be read but, however deep the girl's faith in herself ran, when Nona smiled she had seen in those dark eyes a moment of doubt.

Nona made it through the main doors and turned from sight. The ice-wind caught her a second later and Sister Rose proved quicker than she looked, snatching her up before she hit the ground.

27

Whatever herbs Sister Rose ground up, whatever unsavoury pieces of unsavoury animals she extracted and refined, none seemed to numb the pain of Nona's lacerations quite so well as distraction. It seemed a shame then that the sanatorium was perhaps the most uniformly dull part of the convent, offering nothing more by way of entertainment than a window onto its small garden.

Nona would have given a lot for some company. The other four beds remained empty and she soon reached the point where pushing someone down the stairs in order to fill one of them seemed quite a reasonable solution.

The first visitor Nona received turned out to be Sister Wheel and even this proved a welcome diversion from the business of lying on her side staring out the window until that side became too numb and Sister Rose rolled her to stare at the wall.

'Don't stay long, Wheel,' Sister Rose said to Sister Wheel's back as the smaller woman elbowed past her bulk. 'And don't upset her.'

Sister Wheel reached the side of Nona's bed then turned to stare at Sister Rose until she coloured, looked away, and finally backed through the doorway, pulling the door shut behind her.

'Couldn't keep me out.' Sister Wheel reached up to tap her headdress. 'Only the abbess herself could – and even she can't overrule both of us. That's why it's me and Rose. Chose us because we never agree on anything.' She pulled a chair close to the bed, the scraping of its feet loud and unpleasant. 'I suppose you feel pretty full of yourself, don't you?' She sat, hands clasped in her lap. 'Because you've got a touch of quantal in you, you think you're a two-blood.'

If Sister Wheel had a better example of a two-blood than someone with quantal and hunska flowing in their veins then Nona would have been interested to hear it. You needed more than a touch of quantal to reach the Path. But she swallowed any reply and kept her lips pressed in a tight line watching the wide and watery hostility of the nun's eyes.

'You're thinking it might be you who's the Argatha. Well, it's not. Nothing good ever came out of the Grey: only broken things. Peasants and lies. The Argatha is sent to save us! Will she be a golden princess of the emperor's own bloodline? Or an urchin taken from under the shadow of the noose? Which do you think? Really?' Flecks of spittle marked the nun's chin.

'The abbess said that prophecy was just made up,' Nona said.

Sister Wheel waved the idea away. 'That's what prophecy is! It's something that's made up and that we have faith is true.'

Nona returned her lips to their line. She wasn't going to argue faith with Mistress Spirit, even if Mistress Spirit was about as sane as a naked stroll in the ice-wind.

'In any event,' Sister Wheel narrowed her eyes, 'it's not you. It's possible that you're the Shield. I'll entertain that unlikely thought now. But don't go getting ideas above your station.' She stood to go, took three paces towards the door, stopped and knitted her bony fists in the material of her habit just above her hips. For a moment she paused, caught on the point of indecision, then looked back over her shoulder. 'By rights you're due two more strokes of the cane. That may not be necessary. Just take my words to heart. The Ancestor has a plan for you, girl.'

As Sister Wheel stalked out, Sister Rose bustled in, her hands full of linen strips. 'I'll change your dressings now, dear.'

Nona sighed and eased herself onto her front as Sister Rose fussed over her, tutting. 'This wasn't right. Not right at all.' The nun peeled off the soiled wrappings with deft fingers. 'It's a cruel enough punishment even when you're guilty…'

Nona didn't want to hear Ara being criticized. 'Why does she hate me?'

'Who?' Sister Rose's innocence didn't so much as approach the foothills of convincing. Nona said nothing more and a moment later the nun broke the silence. 'She doesn't hate you, Nona. Well … she's … that's just Wheel.' She peeled back another linen strip, sticky with blood, and Nona winced. 'She came from the Grey, you know?'

'Who? Sister Wheel?'

'From a tiny village called … I forget, but it sounded like a hard place to survive. We were novices together, you know?'

'Sister Wheel from the Grey?' Nona found that hard to imagine. 'You were in the same classes?' That seemed scarcely easier to believe. 'But she's old!'

Sister Rose laughed at that. 'Wheel's got more than a touch of hunska. The years haven't been kind. And wrinkles don't show on us … well-filled … individuals.'

'She doesn't have the accent.' Nona remained unconvinced.

'You've lost half of yours in two years. Stay here a few more and nobody will know Nona Grey unless you let her out.' Sister Rose began to wash the cuts.

The fresh pain saved Nona from thinking of a reply to that. She gritted her teeth and buried her face in the pillow with a snarl.

Sister Pan came to visit Nona that evening – using her rank to overcome the barriers still keeping the novices at bay. She sat down with one hand in her lap, cradled over the stump of the other. 'Well,' she said.

Nona offered the nun a small smile. Since Nona's first day in Path this was perhaps the only time Pan had looked at her with any particular interest. Nona liked Sister Pan: the old woman had a sharp wit but was never unkind, she entertained and guided, rather than directing or dictating. Even so, she seemed almost blind to those without at least a touch of quantal, as if the novices were interchangeable, save for Hessa and Ara, and she only became truly animated with those two.

'You seem to have reached the Path via a route I didn't teach you,' Sister Pan said.

'Why didn't you teach it?' Nona asked. Perhaps, even with all her years, Pan hadn't known the way.

The nun smiled, ancient in her wrinkles, displaying the worn columns of her remaining teeth. 'Abbess Glass might object if I chained each novice to a wall and beat them bloody on the off-chance they might run from the whip and reach the Path.' She rubbed her chin. 'Also, even on quantals it almost never works. And when it does, it's of limited use. Serenity allows a person to approach the Path in a slow and measured way. To stay on the Path is incredibly difficult. It requires years of training and rare innate skill. Taking more than a few steps on the Path is hard even when a person edges carefully onto it. When rage or pain take you there… Consider the blade-path game that Sister Tallow keeps in her hall. Serenity is a novice edging out from the platform, feet placed with care, arms spread for balance, considering what lies ahead. Rage is a novice bursting from the door at full pelt and racing out over the drop. She may touch the blade-path on her way down, but she's not truly walking it.'

'That was just a touch?' Even as she spoke Nona knew it to be true. She had fallen from the Path as soon as she 'set foot' upon it – not that feet were involved, but the image helped her to make sense of the experience.

'We will examine this matter in class, Nona. There may be exciting times ahead! For now though, practise your serenity. It will help with the pain. That should be motivation enough by itself, even without the Path waiting for you.' Sister Pan stood with an audible creak. 'Seek the Path, but do not touch it!' She glanced around. 'Sister Rose would not forgive you for damaging the sanatorium! Sister Tallow is far from pleased with the damage wrought in Blade Hall. Also, you would likely die. You were very lucky to have been able to shape and push the Path's energies into the wall.' A speculative look. 'We will talk about how you managed that. Later.'

Sister Pan turned to go, shuffling towards the door with the speed of an old lady twenty years her junior.

'Thank you, sister.' Nona spoke the words quietly to Sister Pan's back, but the nun, overturning Clera's insistence that she was deaf, spun around as she said them. 'Thank *you*, novice. When you get to my age you need things like this to keep you alive. Take it from me. I have been too young to know, and I have been too old to care. It's in that oh-so-narrow slice between that memories are made. So enjoy it.' And with that she was gone, the door swinging shut behind her. 'Exciting times. Exciting times.'

Nona lay staring at the door. The animation in Sister Pan's face when she spoke of the Path returned her to that moment of contact, the awful energy that had filled her like a fire under her skin. The memory pushed aside the pain from her wounds, leaving it a mere tickle at the edge of things. There had been an instant of release as she had driven her talons into the wall and emptied the Path's power into the stone. She wanted that feeling again. She hadn't felt anything like it before. Shelter and a fire's warmth after the ice-wind didn't come close, not even food offered to a stomach left empty for too many days. She wanted it again.

Clera, Ruli, and Jula came the next day, bustling in behind Sister Rose, Ruli leaning out to the side to grin at Nona past the nun's rotundity. They descended on her bed, making her wince as the mattress shifted under their weight.

'I'm in Grey Class!' Jula crossed her legs at the far end of the bed. 'The Poisoner finally gave me my Shade stamp!'

'That's great!' Nona would have missed Jula, especially her help in Academia. They grinned at each other. More than for her ability to guide Nona's hand to make perfect letters on the slate in place of her wobbly attempts, Nona liked Jula for the way her bookishness fell away on the sands of Blade Hall. If you didn't keep your wits about you the scribe's daughter would set you on your backside, hard, and all without a drop of hunska in her veins.

'How are you?' Ruli leaned in worried, reaching a tentative hand for Nona's arm. 'You look awful.'

'She's fine!' Clera said. 'She took down the damn wall. Showed that bitch Zole.'

Nona eased herself into a sitting position, manufactured a smile, and let the conversation flow about her. It just took a 'yes' here, a 'why' there to keep it running on and she found comfort in the familiar rhythm of their gossip.

Ara, apparently, would be in to see her later. She wanted to come on her own, feeling very guilty about the whole whipping girl thing. 'And so she should!' Clera cut across Ruli. 'They all do it. The Sis spit on us all the time. Even if they don't mean to. They just think of us as things to be used.'

Zole had remained when Sherzal left, and was taken into Grey Class, where she kept a watchful silence, not rising to taunts or threats. Clera was glad to report that the tribe-girl had fallen off the blade-path within five yards of starting and showed no particular aptitude for Academia. Of particular note and worthy of a mimed impression was her introduction to the Poisoner, one that saw her fleeing the cave just minutes into the class, a hand clutching both main orifices.

Sister Tallow, according to Ruli, had spent the whole of their last lesson aiming a brooding stare at the cratered wall and letting the older novices beat the younger ones black and blue.

'She did promise to teach us to counter that Torca move Zole used on you though,' Clera said. She smiled at that then veered into a new topic. 'And my father's still in the debtors' jail, but they let Mother and my sisters visit him.' No novice ignored the convent's disapproval of discussing family quite so impressively as Clera. She scowled. 'He should have been released by now: the only debts left to clear are ones that everyone knows are fake.'

'Jula's father is working at the palace now!' Ruli chipped in with a bright smile.

Jula, rule-follower to her core just made a quick and agitated shake of her head then looked down.

The chatter bubbled along taking Nona's mind from her discomfort until Bray spoke, the bell's deep voice resonating across the convent, and the three visitors jumped up to go.

'Spirit next! You're better off here!' Clera called over her shoulder.

'Hurry up and get better!' Ruli followed her.

'I'll pray for your recovery.' Jula laid her hand on Nona's then ran to catch the others.

Hours later and the light slanted crimson into the room, the sun's edge burning above the rooftop. Nona thought it would drop away and the day would end before Ara came to see her, but the door opened and there she was.

'I'm sorry!'

'What in the world for? And, that was my line.' Ara hurried across to sit in the chair beside Nona's bed.

'I didn't beat her,' Nona said.

'You can't beat *everyone*! And besides, you were already hurt.' Ara studied Nona with concern, her gaze flitting here and there, looking for evidence of injuries. 'How are you now?'

Nona shrugged, and wished she hadn't. 'Sister Rose will let me go soon.'

'At least you got through the blood-war at the same time as you got beaten. That's not fun either.'

'Blood-war?' Nona frowned. She felt pretty sure that whatever it was it was a blessing compared to twenty strokes of a wire-willow cane.

'When I started to be able to get close to the Path – when my quantal blood started to assert itself – I felt awful. I thought I was dying. Well, not dying, but I felt sick for a week. Sister Pan says it's called the blood-war. But you got pushed through the transition so quickly you missed it!'

'—' Nona shut her mouth. It might be a small blessing but she supposed it *was* a blessing.

'Zole *is* very fast.' Ara looked at her hands, resting in her lap, fingers knotted. 'I should have let Sister Tallow end the fight.'

'Why didn't you?'

'She was taking so long and Zole was hurting you…'

Nona pursed her lips and watched Ara's downturned eyes. Her friend's hair hung about her face, as long and golden as it had been on the day she arrived. 'You were in a serenity trance, Ara. You could have watched her kill me without losing control of yourself. You were getting ready even before the fight started. I saw you.' Doubt struck, cold and hard. 'You didn't think I had a chance, did you?'

Ara looked up sharply. 'It wasn't that at all! It was Sherzal. I wanted her to be afraid of me!'

'Afraid?' The emperor's sister hadn't looked like a woman who knew how to be afraid.

'She would have stolen me from my family – she *did* steal me from my family, only to the convent rather than into her clutches. And now she's trying to reach in here to get at me. So I wanted to show her that the very reason she wants me is the reason she should fear me. I wanted her to know that if she tried to hold me in her palace I'd bring the walls down around her ears… Only *now* she's seen that you're what she wants too – and you haven't got family connections for her to worry about like I have…'

'Is that how you feel? Stolen? You want to be back with your family and your servants? Leave us all behind?' The word 'us' stumbled out at the last moment in place of 'me'.

'I'd like to feel safe to visit them. To see my mother and father. I miss my little sister too. Even Sonella, a little bit … perhaps she's not so much of a cow now.'

Nona smirked. Ara had a hundred stories about her older sister, none of them flattering, some that made you laugh hard enough to wet yourself. 'Well – maybe we both scared her off, or perhaps we both put ourselves on her wanted list. Either way, we're in it together, which is as it should be, the Chosen One and her Shield.'

'You know that stuff's nonsense don't you?' Ara looked serious for a moment. 'Sherzal doesn't want us because the prophecy's real – she wants us because people believe the prophecy.'

Nona nodded. 'Even if I believed in prophecies then Sister Wheel wanting this one to be true so badly would be enough to stop me believing it.'

28

'Who's that?' Nona asked.

A short woman was approaching Path Tower, a black coat flapping about her legs, her dark hair drawn up behind her head in a severe bun, her skin sharing the same reddish hint as Zole's. She carried a sword at each hip.

'Yisht,' Ara said. They had been the first to arrive, coming directly from the sanatorium. Sister Rose had told Nona the night before that she could return to the dormitory the next day and resume all her lessons excepting Blade – which given that Blade was the only class Nona really cared about had been a disappointment.

'Yisht?' Nona frowned. 'That's a real name?'

'As real as Zole,' Darla said, glowering at the approaching woman. Jula and Darla had joined them at the eastern door, waiting for Sister Pan to unlock it.

As Darla said her name Nona spotted Zole, walking in Yisht's shadow.

'She's Zole's bodyguard, if you can believe that,' Ara said. 'Sherzal wanted to station sixteen of her guards to watch over her precious heir. The abbess argued her down to one. She knew they'd be doing more than just watching over Zole.'

Jula nodded. 'I think the high priest has Abbess Glass under orders not to interfere with her, though. Alata came running around the corner and Yisht slammed her into a wall, nearly broke her arm. Said it looked as if she were rushing at Zole … as if Zole can't defend herself!'

'What did the abbess do?'

'That's just it. The abbess didn't do anything. Sister Rose must have told her because she called Yisht a whole bunch of names that I would have sworn she didn't know. And Sister Rose never gets angry!'

'Anyway.' Ara took the lead back. 'Sister Pan won't let her in the tower. She has to stand guard out here.' She shot a dirty look at Zole and her protector as they closed the last few yards. 'I hope the ice-wind picks up again.'

'Yisht is from the ice, like me,' Zole said, coming to stand beside Jula. 'On the ice the wind roars. Here, you hear a whisper and think you know cold.' She shook her head, amused.

Ara carried on as if the girl hadn't spoken. 'Sherzal wanted Safira to lead the sixteen! Safira! An expelled novice who's betrayed the convent and the church, teaching blade-lore outside these walls for money.'

Nona remembered Ara mentioning Zole's teacher on the day the emperor's sister visited. 'She stabbed someone here? Another novice?'

'She stabbed Sister Kettle. She was lucky they didn't drown her. They should have.'

'Kettle?' Nona's mind raced. She'd spent a year having Sister Kettle teach her to read and write, the young nun always full of chatter and gossip, but being stabbed had never come up. Now Nona thought about Kettle's slight limp, and how no one at the convent had come close to her blade-path time and yet she'd never walked it in the two years since Nona arrived. 'You said Safira stabbed a novice…'

'She and Safira were novices together.' Ara leaned in to whisper, her hair falling forward over Nona's shoulder, breath tickling her ear. 'They bedded together in Holy Class, but then Sister Apple joined the convent and … well, you know. Safira was jealous, there were arguments, and Kettle got stabbed while walking away from the last one.'

The door rattled, Sister Pan unlocking it from within. Ara

jerked back as if caught doing something she shouldn't, and Darla pushed on through.

While Sister Pan moved to unlock the next door Nona, Ara, and Jula hurried in behind Darla and up the staircase, sparing no glances for the portraits. Zole was the last up the stairs, behind the rest of Grey Class, following Sister Pan up the steps asking a question in a low voice.

'She's always sucking up to Mistress Path,' Clera said, sitting at Nona's left. 'Probably making notes on everything for when she goes back to Sherzal.'

'And when will that be?' Nona kept to a whisper, convinced Sister Pan's alleged deafness was just the old woman's ruse so she could keep up to date with novice gossip.

Clera shrugged. 'She says she's here to be a nun.'

The first two thirds of the lesson proceeded as usual with meditation and instruction in the vexed business of attaining clarity, serenity, and patience. Clera used to joke that they should all work on patience first because they were surely going to need it to survive the class. But the joke had been old before she was born and now she usually spent the lessons trying to sleep with her eyes open, or badgering Sister Pan to let the class practise blade-path up at the hall while she concentrated on her star pupils.

Nona had never had much greater success with patience than she did with serenity. In fact they seemed almost the same thing to her, though Sister Pan insisted otherwise.

'Patience belongs to the predator. It waits before the strike. Patience is invaluable to Sisters of Discretion. Those that can weave shadows use patience to settle themselves into the darkness with sufficient depth that they can gather it to them.'

'You're saying that if I get this I can do what Sister Kettle did in Blade Hall?' The image of Kettle rising from nowhere returned to Nona. She saw it again and again – Kettle, trailing shadow, leaping up and carrying her to the sand. 'I can be invisible like a Noi-Guin?'

'Noi-Guin aren't invisible, child.' Sister Pan's mouth twisted with displeasure. 'Their shadow-workers are so good because they focus on nothing else. So narrow an education is of limited use. In any event, the answer to your question is no. Only those with at least a touch of marjal have the potential for dark-work and even some of them never manage it. But whether they have the talent or not they will need to attain the patience-trance to make best contact.'

'But what can the quantals do with their Path-walking apart from break stuff?'

Sister Pan raised her voice, drawing the attention of those in the class not already listening in. 'The marjals are conjurers. They touch the world's power in many separate places, far from the Path. Which parts of the secret world they touch, and how deeply, depends on their individual nature and how thick the marjal runs in their veins.

'The Path is different. It divides the living from the unliving. Some marjals touch only the living side of the world, others the unliving, a few touch both. Most marjals work with magics that lie far from the Path. The greatest marjals touch areas that lie close. But none touch or walk the Path itself. Their magics are many and usually minor, though often very helpful.

'But the Path is about power. It is the source of power and the nature of it. Most quantals will only ever gather this power and release it in short, violent bursts. The energy of the Path is dangerous to hold on to. For the rare quantal, however, with sufficient skill, the right training, and years of practice, the energy gathered from the Path may be held and shaped and set to purpose without end. The Path is a line, but it is not straight. It touches and separates all things. The Path gives meaning to identity, to one thing being different and separate from the next. Its power can unravel the world … and create it anew.'

Sister Pan looked around the class. 'Now, if Clera will oblige me by not breaking any of the furniture in her haste to leave, those novices who want to may practise blade-path until the bell.' She set her stump to Nona's shoulder as the chairs clattered and girls started for the stairs in a flutter and flap of habits. 'You, Nona, will be staying.'

As much as Nona would have liked to chase after the others

the stiffness of her scars and the pain when she flexed them were sufficient to keep her seated even without the weight of Sister Pan's attention upon her. Less than a minute later only Nona, Ara, Hessa, and Darla still occupied their seats, along with Zole and Alata's pale, red-haired friend, Leeni.

'Ara and Hessa will accompany me. You too, Nona. Darla, Zole, and Leeni continue your patience work.'

Sister Pan crossed to the great chest and closed the lid before starting off down the spiral staircase. Hessa followed, awkward on her crutch. She glanced back at Nona, *stay close!*

Nona tucked in behind Hessa, Ara at her back, and the three of them tracked Sister Pan down the tight spirals of the staircase.

'Picture the Path, Nona. Don't close your eyes, but see it. Don't touch it but let it lead you.' Sister Pan's voice echoed as if a vast hall held them rather than the narrowness of the steps. 'Follow me. Not the stairs beneath your feet. Just follow me.'

For a moment Nona saw the bright line of the Path across the dark wool of Hessa's habit. The Path drew her – a burning crack, one line and many, straight as a spear and yet also twisting, its convolutions and loops filling the space between Hessa's shoulders, reaching in and through as if she weren't even there…

'Here we are.' Sister Pan's voice returned to its usual surprisingly youthful tone.

Nona blinked. They were neither in the stairwell nor in the vast hall that she had sensed about her. The chamber curved as if it lived between the tower wall and the staircase, occupying a third of the full circle. It had no windows, only a series of small flames burning in alcoves for light. Six black-wood chairs stood in disorder at the middle of the room and every wall, even the floor and ceiling lay crowded with sigils written in silver, bedded into the stone.

'Sit.' Sister Pan waved at the chairs.

Nona sat, staring up at the ceiling, heavy with gleaming silver. The sigils made writing – which had once looked fiendishly complex to her – seem foolishly simple. Each palm-sized symbol was a work of art, a single line folded into a complexity that burned into the back of her eyes and began to fold her mind about it. They almost looked like fragments of the Path frozen into an instant.

'Don't stare, Nona. Generally it's rude. Where sigils are concerned it can be dangerous.' Sister Pan set her fingers to the nearest wall. 'These are the work of a marjal void-scribe, a master of the art, now long dead. They ensure that any accidents you have while attempting to walk the Path are confined to this room. I love this tower, just as Sister Tallow loves her hall, and I'd rather not have a reckless novice knock it down.

'Only the other day … well, before you were born perhaps … Novice Segga touched the Path unexpectedly early upstairs. I'd just shown her the first serenity exercise… Anyway, she screamed so loud it blew the windows out. All my lovely stained glass. We found pieces of it embedded in the Dome of the Ancestor! It was a while before I could hear anything after that…' Sister Pan turned to Ara. 'Novice Arabella, who has already heard me express my disappointment in her over the actions that saw Nona beaten, will begin.' She motioned for Hessa and Nona to join her at the far end of the room, close to the point where the wall's curvature would hide them from sight.

Nona came to stand beside the nun. She had the peculiar smell that old people get, no matter how clean they might be, not musty or sour or stale … just old.

'Now that we know you are of the blood, Nona, you should understand that what we quantal do here in this convent is easier and more effective because of the shipheart. Where it beats, the space between the pieces of the world is narrowed. It is easier to touch the Path here, easier to walk it, easier to shape its energies.'

'Really?' Nona had wanted to use a sharper word, one that might even be new to Clera's foul-mouth, or the sailors who taught Ruli to swear … but she swallowed it. She stared up at Sister Pan. 'Really? Because "easy" isn't a word I'd use for any of those things.' Mistress Blade had beaten her half to death before she could even make glancing contact with the Path.

Sister Pan just smiled a small smile. 'Novice Arabella. Approach the Path in serenity. Take a single step and return, owning what you have been given.'

29

Nona left the hidden room after Hessa and Arabella. The rest of Grey Class was long gone. In the windowless chamber it was easy to miss Bray's call. Sister Pan had held her back, instructing that she set her hands to the sigil-crowded walls and allow any stray trace of Path-energy to leave her body.

She hurried down the spiral stair, still bubbling with exhilaration. Her contact with the Path had been fleeting but glorious. The Path had filled her and in doing so had woken her to the understanding that for all her life she had been hollow. It turned her flesh to gold, her mind to crystal. She wanted more. Even as the power of it terrified her and she felt her body shaking beyond her control, she wanted more.

East door slammed behind her, closed by the wind. Nona paused at the tower base, staring at the greyness of the day in wonder, knowing that behind it all, through it all, ran the Path.

Someone took Nona's wrist from behind in an iron-fingered grip, jolting her from her musings. A hand to her elbow immobilized the limb, and a moment later Nona was bent forward, crying out in pain, her arm raised out straight behind her. Her attacker steered her back against the tower wall.

'You, child, will stay away from Zole.'

'Yisht!' Nona snarled, recognizing the accent of the ice-tribes.

'Tell me that you understand and will obey.'

Nona gritted her teeth against the agony in her shoulder. With her face pressed to the cold stones and her arm locked there seemed no possible means of escape. 'You're going to break my arm?' She snatched a breath. 'How many novices can you break before the abbess throws you out?' Nona hadn't thought about challenging Zole again but she was damned if she would be bullied.

'I could break more than your arm, child.' The pressure increased. 'I could break every joint of every finger.' Yisht spoke without relish but something in her tone left no room for doubt. She would do these things. 'I could tear the eyes from your head—'

Nona lurched away from the wall, shouting against the pain. If she'd left by any other door she might be seen from the other convent buildings.

'A true fighter, I see.' Yisht steered her back against the stonework. 'Too brave for threats. But I have watched you. You care for the cripple. Cross me, in any way, and perhaps she will limp off a cliff one windy night.'

She released Nona with a shove that sent her stumbling forwards as if in demonstration of what might happen to Hessa. A dip in the rock caught Nona's foot and she fell, face first, feeling something tear in her lacerated back. By the time she righted herself Yisht had gone.

'How did it go with the Holy Witches?' Clera wanted to know when Nona entered the dormitory. 'I missed you at Blade, and at the bathhouse, and at dinner! Jula said something must have come up with Sister Pan and she kept you for special lessons, but I said—'

'She said you were dead,' Jula called over from her bed. 'She said, "Nona wouldn't miss a meal unless she was dead".'

'I ate at the sanatorium while Sister Rose changed my dressings and took out some stitches.'

'So…' Clera rolled over and rested her chin in her hands. 'What's the secret? Where does Sister Pan take you witches to play? It's something to do with the tenth step isn't it? I always said it was.'

'Yes. The tenth step. Tap it right and it opens a hidden passage.' Nona climbed into her bed with care.

'Oh you liar!' Clera swung her knees under her. 'Tell!'

'Sister Pan said she'd make an example of—'

'Don't be such a coward. You're Pan's favourite now. She won't hurt you.'

'—of anyone I told,' Nona finished.

'Oh.' Clera slumped, then brightened. 'Tell Jula! She can tell me after.'

Nona snorted and lay down on her side, taking care not to stretch her lacerations. Sister Pan had cautioned her to secrecy but secrecy had been in her nature long before she reached the convent. Sister Apple had told her to strip on that first morning, and she hadn't wanted to, but she'd done it because it was true, she had needed a bath. Giving up secrets though, that left her more exposed than any degree of nakedness. She would rather walk nude through the convent than reveal her true nature. They had seen it at the village. Her own mother had seen it. And she had left there in a cage with curses and clods of earth thrown at her back. The words had been heavier and had hurt the more.

Sleep came hard that night, surrounded by the soft sounds of dreaming. Images of Ara and Hessa working with the Path's energies played across the darkness again and again. Bright and crackling light filling hands to be thrown at the sigil-covered walls, or drawn back into the flesh to imbue an awful shuddering strength.

Visions of the Path finally faded and still Nona couldn't escape into dreaming. Yisht's iron grip held her from sleep, the bruises on Nona's arm anchoring her with a dull ache. She hadn't told the others. It would scare Hessa and gain nothing. All Nona had to do was not pursue any vengeance upon Zole. But, beyond that, it was shame that kept her silent. Shame at how easily the woman had overmastered her, and shame at the fear she had felt. She lay, staring at the darkness. Not until the blaze of the focus moon had come and gone would Nona's mind release her to oblivion.

* * *

The best part of three weeks passed before Nona's back felt fully healed. She returned to Blade classes with a passion, pitting her knife-work against the older and more experienced novices, though keeping clear of Zole. She would of course have to face the girl if Sister Tallow instructed a match, but the nun kept both Ara and Nona away from her.

Nona made sure to get to the blade-path chamber at least three days in every seven now that she never escaped a Path lesson. No matter how slowly she took the course though, and no matter how much resin she applied to her soles, she still managed to get no further than halfway, and usually less than that. The articulated pipes always seemed to end in a different combination of positions at the end of the previous attempt, making the course unpredictable, with sections swinging or rotating in unexpected ways and at unexpected times. Her only consolation was that Zole had yet to cross a third of the way without falling.

One sour note was that Jula no longer practised with them. Clera and Jula had some sudden and one-sided falling out after a seven-day on which both of them were allowed family visits in Verity. Clera wouldn't speak about it but missed no opportunity to apply the sharp edge of her tongue to Jula, who simply looked miserable and confused.

'Why are you such a bitch to everyone, Clera?' Ara asked after one fierce exchange that sent Jula running off in tears.

'Everyone?'

Nona blinked. 'Everyone?' She had been watching Jula turn the corner past the scriptorium at the far end of the courtyard and wondering how after two years of training to accept the fiercest of blows and strike back, mere words got past their defences so easily.

'Everyone.' Ara nodded, eyes narrowed at Clera.

Nona frowned. Perhaps it was true. If you weren't Clera's friend you weren't anything to her.

Clera shrugged and flipped her silver crown, catching the coin to examine the emperor's head on the upward side. 'I don't want anyone to be sad when I die.'

* * *

Ruli joined Grey Class on the day Sister Tallow introduced Nona and at least a third of the newer novices to the throwing star. Nona had held one only once before, and briefly, when it was thrown at her by Sister Wheel and punched a hole in her palm. She still had a white seam of scar there.

Throwing the things proved easier than catching them, but to hit a target with any accuracy proved harder than she had anticipated. Even so Nona did rather well with only Zole and, unexpectedly, Ruli doing better than her out of the girls new to the weapon. And both Clera and Ara were strongly of the opinion that Zole had previous experience. Clera proved to be something of a liability, Sister Tallow expressing doubt at one point as to whether she could even reliably hit the floor with a throwing star.

When Bray finally sounded everyone's arms ached from the throwing action – Sister Tallow insisting that they learn with both left and right hand – and none of the new girls had a finger without at least some minor cuts.

'Novices.' Sister Tallow called the class to her. This was no surprise: Blade was not a class you could run from at the bell. 'It is perhaps timely, given the difficulties presented to this class by Novice Zole's use of combat styles unknown to you, that we are fast approaching the annual Caltess forging. We will be travelling into Verity each day for three days, starting after next seven-day. I expect Grey Class to acquit itself well against the Caltess apprentices. Two among Leeni, Darla, Alata, Sheelar and Croy will be entered into the sword ring; three among those not selected for sword will be entering the unarmed contest.'

The race to the bathhouse after Blade had become a particular point of pride since Zole's arrival, and even burning news like the sudden closeness of the Caltess forging had to wait until the sprint was over. Each novice gathered their day-habit to change into after bathing and collected by the main doors, ready to run. Darla, whose toe was still healing and whose build made her a poor runner in any event, shoved open the doors and the girls streamed out around her.

Nona's size put her at a disadvantage but she'd caught up a few inches on her friends over two years of good eating at the convent. Zole, Ketti, and Clera opened up a lead on the first clear stretch past Heart Hall, with Ara just behind them, but Nona knew she'd close down on them in the tight turns past the laundry and around the long low winery building. Where Zole and the others slowed to make the sharp turn amid the laundry steams Nona ran directly at the opposite wall, leaping up at it to drive off at an angle into the narrow gap between the buildings. By the time the others exited the steam-cloud Nona had the lead.

'How the—' Clera's gasp of outrage lost her a needed breath and several more strides.

Nona and Ketti spun past a bewildered Sister Rock and crashed through the bathhouse doors to victory, with Ara, Zole, and then Clera hard upon their heels.

'How will she choose?' The question bounced around the changing room as habits were stripped with indecent haste. 'How?'

'I don't care how, as long as she chooses me.' Clera kicked off her remaining shoe. 'I don't see how she can't.' And with that she was running into the hot fog of the pool-room.

'Sometimes it's contests. Sometimes she picks her favourites.' Alata stepped out of her underskirts. 'Last year it was favourites.'

More opinions crossed back and forth, but Nona was pursuing Ara and they jumped into the pool's enfolding warmth together. Nona surfaced and let herself hang in the water, boneless, drifting in the white blindness, letting the chatter mix with the sound of splashing and flow around her, detached from any meaning.

'Well!' Clera swam through the steaming water, dark hair fanned out across the surface behind her. 'The Caltess. It'll be like going home for you.' All around them the shapes of novices in the mist, idle and floating in the middle of the pool or in murmured conversation in small groups around the edges.

'What?' Nona came to herself, shaking off the drowsiness. She backed before Clera's advance, swishing her hands before her, feet a yard above the bottom. She had no idea how much time had passed, though her fingers were wrinkly so it must have been a while. The pool's walls reached around her as she arrived in one of the corners furthest from the changing room.

'The Caltess,' Clera repeated. 'Familiar ground for you.'

'I was only there a couple of months.' She had known the forging was coming – nobody passed through Grey Class without experiencing it – but the date was never given far in advance, depending on the fight schedule at the Caltess and any other commitments Partnis Reeve might have.

'My father will bet on me,' Clera said, swimming closer, trapping Nona in the corner, the currents of her approach reaching Nona's legs and belly. 'And win enough to buy his release.'

'I thought the matches were private.' Nona remembered the baying of the crowd beneath the Caltess attic, something living, an animal, greater than its many parts. She wondered what it would be like to fight in the middle of such a thing.

'They are private, silly.' Clera ducked beneath the surface and emerged closer still, squirting water at Nona from pursed lips. 'But that doesn't mean people don't bet on them, or that rich men don't pay to spy on the novices from hidden galleries.

'But the blade-fist is secret…' To be used if required, never to be displayed for mere show – that's what Sister Tallow said.

Clera grinned and reached out to push a steam-damp lock from above Nona's eye. 'They're more interested in us, silly.' She bobbed up out of the water and thrust her chest forward before twisting away with a splash.

Ara took her place, her blonde hair dark with water. 'Are you worried about the Tacsis? You know Raymel doesn't fight any more, yes?'

'I know.' Nona shrugged. Thuran Tacsis had forgotten her. His son was alive. He had more to worry about than a peasant girl who fled to a nunnery. There had been nothing in two long years, not since the Noi-Guin assassins and the high priest's trial. But Abbess Glass still wouldn't let her leave the convent on seven-day, though half the novices went to Verity with a handful of nuns to chaperone them.

In the darkness of the dormitory that night Nona imagined herself once again amid the barrels, crates and coiled ropes of the Caltess attic, surrounded by scores of purchased children, uneasy in their dreams. She wondered about the Tacsis brothers and their father whom she had never seen but who squandered a fortune to see her dead. Even if they still spared her a thought after two long years, a visit to the Caltess would hardly be a sensible time for them to take revenge. Nona would be surrounded by witnesses, not to mention Sister Tallow and several other Red Sisters.

Even so, she couldn't sleep. Something tugged at her. Fingernails drawn across a chalkboard, unheard but still somehow setting that nauseating quiver in the marrow of her bones. Was it just worry?

She slipped from her blanket, and walked on slow feet between the double row of beds. The nightgown sliding across her legs had been a gift from Ara. Nona had nothing that had not been a gift: even her presence at the convent was a gift, her confirmation fee renewed each year by an 'anonymous' donor – though she was sure that was Abbess Glass's doing.

Ignoring the night-lantern glowing beside Mally's bed at the door, Nona slipped out into the communal hall and advanced to the main door. Her fingers found the handle cold. The wind's threats came low and moaning through the door, the draught icy about her feet. Beneath the iron's chill something else tingled at her senses, something darker than the night, colder than the wind, many-angled and strange. She opened the door, just a crack, and set her eye to the gap. The wind whistled in all around, as if mocking her attempts at stealth.

A figure stood so close before the door that the shock stole Nona's breath. For a moment her heart held paralysed within her chest, but the figure's raised hand didn't reach for her, continuing instead to inscribe an invisible pattern upon the moving air between them. The eyes above the black scarf that wrapped the lower face were Yisht's. Shark's eyes, Ruli called them, flat and dead. The woman proved so intent on her work that Nona's small movement of the door didn't draw her attention from it. Nona watched as Yisht finished the pattern, her finger seeming to leave a lingering disturbance in the air, seen as water is seen on glass. She stepped to the right and began again. Was she searching for something?

A white finger, so pale it looked as if the frost had bitten into it, traced a new convolution into empty space. The pattern of it sank into Nona's eye, pressing against her brain, the feeling unpleasant and familiar. Sigils!

Without pausing for thought, Nona hauled the door open. They stood for a moment, Nona in the teeth of the wind, shockingly cold, her nightdress moulded about her and giving no protection, Yisht immobile, hand on the hilt of her sword, a gleaming inch revealed. Without a word Yisht lowered her outstretched arm, turned, and walked away, the night seeming to thicken about her so that in five steps she had gone entirely.

'Shut the damn door!' A shout from the Grey dormitory.

Nona closed it, shivering, and hurried back to bed. She fell asleep quickly, almost against her will, her mind twisting around the shapes Yisht had left hanging in the air.

Cage.

Nona followed a single twisting thread of fire.

Cage.

The word scratched against her concentration. Nona tried to make the voice her own. I'm in a cage – the same cage that's held me my whole life. I was in a cage before Giljohn took me and I've never left it. A cage made of my own bones.

The thread coiled into a spiral of three turns, just like the blade-path. It rose and fell in patterns part-familiar, part-new, flexing as she pursued it.

Cage. Wake up!

I'm not asleep.

The path before her writhed, a serpent in mortal pain, knotting in on itself, and still she followed it, down into the convolutions of the sigil—

CAGE!

Nona opened an eye.

'I was worried.' Ara was leaning over her, so close her hair fell all about Nona's face, tickling her neck. She pulled back.

Nona turned her head. Ara was kneeling on the bed, fully dressed. All the other beds lay empty, the dormitory deserted and full of slanting sunlight.

'W-where is everyone?' The sigil still burned across her vision.

'Breakfast then Blade.' Ara got off the bed. 'You need to get up and dressed right away.' She paused, leaning forward. 'Unless you need to go to Sister Rose? Jula thought we should fetch her. Most of them just thought it was funny when you wouldn't get up, but Jula said you might be ill.'

'She's not gone to—'

'No. I said I'd fetch Sister Rose if I couldn't wake you up. Then Hessa said she thought you were ill too but that it was Sister Pan we should be sending for. She said there was something wrong with you but that it might be a Path-working. She said she would go to Sister Pan after breakfast if you didn't show up.'

'You spoke my name,' Nona said, 'my chosen one.'

Ara bit her lip. 'I thought it might help. I'd tried everything else…' She looked slightly guilty. 'You'll want to dry your face. And your pillow's a bit wet.'

'You threw water on me?'

'Twice. And I pulled your hair. Oh, and you've got nail marks on your arm where I pinched you.'

Nona sat up, wiping her face on her blanket. 'Lucky the name worked! Sounds like in another minute you'd be setting my hair on fire or trying a kiss like that prince in the old story.'

Ara looked quickly down at her feet.

'You didn't!' Nona jumped out of bed, reaching for her skirts.

Ara flashed a grin. 'It would have been the first thing Clera tried.'

Nona frowned, tugging off her nightdress and wriggling into her underskirts. 'Where is Clera? Didn't she have an opinion?'

'She did.' Ara handed Nona her habit. 'Her opinion was that you were fine and if we were late for Blade Sister Tallow would skin us. Or worse, leave us behind when the Caltess forging came.'

'She's not wrong there!' Nona jammed her feet into her shoes and started to run for the door. 'Hurry up! I'm starved!'

Nona devoured her breakfast and ran to her first lesson still chewing over her night-time encounter. Yisht's sigil had sent her to her bed and a slumber so deep she almost didn't wake from it. But what could she tell the nuns? What evidence did she have? The emperor's own sister had sent the woman and she seemed to have licence to do whatever she pleased. Even if Yisht admitted to sigil-work she'd just say it was to warn her of threats to Zole.

The remainder of the week was given over to Blade, much to the disgust of Mistresses Path, Academia and Spirit. Mistress Shade confessed herself relieved to have a break from the thick-wittedness of novices and vowed to spend the time brewing a new toxin that she would be requiring test subjects for on their return.

Sister Tallow drilled Grey Class without mercy, sending them aching to their beds each night. She used Zole and her repertoire of unfamiliar combat styles to wake the novices to the idea that the Caltess fighters would not come at them using forms they knew.

'Nona and Zole.' Sister Tallow waved them together. The meeting had been inevitable.

Zole straightened, wiping sweat-soaked hair from her eyes. Sand coated half her face from where Ara had at last managed to throw her to the ground. It had been Ara's only victory.

'Back for more.' Zole watched her, unsmiling.

Nona offered a fierce grin and shrugged. She had practised the Torca moves Zole favoured and paid close attention as the ice-triber threw the rest of Grey Class around.

They closed, feet making a dozen rapid adjustments before either laid hand upon the other. Nona braced, held her core tight, body low, all counters to the throws Zole liked to use.

Zole's hand gripped her habit just above her breast. Nona reached for the elbow, sinking lower still to resist the throw, but Zole let her grip slide, her other arm fluttering past Nona's defence in a slow and fluid motion that should have been easy to intercept – but wasn't. Both Zole's hands reached Nona's face. Nona clung to the elbow of one but hadn't the strength to stop the larger girl. Zole didn't punch, the lack of speed that had fooled Nona meant there wasn't much power in the blow – rather she achieved some combination of buffeting and slapping that left Nona stumbling past her, disoriented.

'Noi-tal soft-hands!' Sister Tallow called out. 'Just because you have seen your foe fight one way against a previous opponent do not let this make you over-commit to the counter-tactics. Variety is important. A predictable warrior, no matter how talented, will end up dead sooner than a less skilled warrior who can less easily be anticipated.'

Zole remained inscrutable. Nona would have preferred a sneer or a mocking smile: at least then she would have felt noticed.

Sister Tallow saved the final humiliation for six-day afternoon, ahead of the seven-day break and their early morning departure for Verity as the new week began.

'Break.' Sister Tallow snapped the word like a whip, and across Blade Hall pairs of novices stopped their sparring. Nona stood panting, grinning at Clera, who faked a stagger, though the sweat dripping from her fringe wasn't faked. They'd fought each other to a standstill with blinding combinations of punches, blocks and snap-kicks. Nona no longer lacked that much in height against Clera and was perhaps a fraction quicker, but Clera made up for that fraction with low cunning and creativity.

'Zole!' Sister Tallow pointed at Sherzal's ward and Nona groaned, thinking they were to be skewered yet again on the sharp point of the girl's versatility. She'd already been left eating sand on at least four occasions over the past three days. But Zole simply nodded and walked to the main doors, opening one and leaning out. A moment later she was walking back, with Yisht at her heels.

Yisht followed Zole into the novices' midst where she stood surveying them with dead eyes set above raw and prominent cheekbones. She wore her usual black coat, black leather belts beneath it, slung across a tunic that might once have been yellowish, now gone to brown with dirt and age.

Sister Tallow crossed to stand beside the bodyguard. 'Yisht-Raani here is a warrior of some renown whose sword commands a high price. I've asked her to demonstrate her martial skills this afternoon. Unarmed of course – I'd rather there were survivors to take to the Caltess.'

Nona started to raise her hand to volunteer. A fire burned in her and that fire wanted to see Yisht bleed. But something in the woman's shark-dead eyes made her hesitate. She found her hand trembling, and realized that what held her back was fear.

'Who's she going to fight?' asked Darla, face still red from her bout with Jula. She stood a head taller than Yisht and thicker in both body and limb.

'All of you,' Sister Tallow said, as if it were a stupid question.

'Who first?' Darla rarely knew when to stop.

'Together.'

The novices, twelve in all, lined up, ready and eager to attack. Zole positioned herself at the rear of the group and Nona fell back to join her.

'What are you doing?' Clera hissed as Yisht took her position close to the wall and set her blades against the stonework. 'This is going to be fun!'

'Sister Tallow isn't stupid,' Nona hissed back. 'This woman's dangerous. I want to see how she fights. Be careful against her. I mean it!'

'Come.' Yisht beckoned her opponents forward.

Darla, Ara, and Ketti were first to reach her, the others having to crowd in around the sides or wait their turn. Yisht ducked into Darla, evading her blow. The big girl's momentum carried her over Yisht's shoulder and on into the wall. In the meantime Darla's hefty body, flying through the air, provided a shield, beneath which Yisht continued to move, emerging at a surprising angle just in time to catch Ara's wrist in one hand and deflect Ketti's kick with the other.

Once she was caught, Ara's speed meant little: controlled as she was by the desire not to have her wrist broken, she had no option other than to allow Yisht to steer her into the wall. Alata moved in with Leeni, the dark girl landing a heavy punch into Yisht's ribs as she spun with Ara, the pale girl attempting to grapple Yisht's legs and catching one of them. Sister Tallow had not spent long on teamwork as Red Sisters are most likely to be called on to act alone, but she had drilled them on working together against a superior foe. Leeni was following those instructions, making herself vulnerable but isolating a limb. If others did the same the fight should be a short one.

Yisht seemed untroubled by Alata's punch and smacked her elbow into the girl's neck. The ice-triber moved quickly but lacked hunska speed. Somehow though she deflected another kick from Ketti, turning it on her shoulder, and caught Clera's arm as a punch cracked in towards her face.

'She knows.' Nona said it to herself but Zole grunted in affirmation beside her. Yisht seemed to anticipate every attack and end up positioned to defeat it even though the hunska novices were considerably faster than her.

In three short seconds three more girls were on the sand – Jula, Katcha, and Ruli – none of them keen to get up again. Darla and Ara lay stunned at the base of the wall. Leeni had Yisht's foot on her throat and had released the other leg. Ketti, with her legs swept away, landed heavily on her back.

Nona leapt in over Alata's collapse, Zole following behind, Sheelar and Croy closing along the wall from opposite directions, Clera still trying to kick even as Yisht twisted her wrist.

Yisht released Clera – already off-balance and falling – and reached out, catching Sheelar's arm while having her other arm caught by Croy, advancing on the left. With this support Yisht lifted up both legs, a kick to Clera's chest propelling her into Zole's path. Nona, already in the air and under gravity's control, found herself sailing towards Yisht's outstretched foot.

With both arms crossed before her to cushion the blow Nona crashed into Yisht's foot and a moment later everyone seemed to be falling. By the time Nona rose from the sand clutching her ribs Yisht had somehow contrived to smash Sheelar into Croy leaving neither fit to fight on. Clera lay behind Nona now, struggling to heave breath back into her lungs. And Zole … Zole landed, having leapt over Clera. She stood ready to strike as Yisht twisted out from beneath Croy and Sheelar. Zole had her arm crooked, ready to punch the exposed back of the warrior's neck.

Yisht raised a hand acknowledging defeat and Zole stepped back, her blow unstruck. All around them novices lay in the sand, ten in all. Several, Clera included, were in the process of getting up, ready to rejoin the fray, but more than half weren't getting up any time soon, Ara among them.

'The first novices to touch the far wall are selected for the Caltess matches.' Sister Tallow spoke in a conversational tone and for a moment no one fully registered her words.

Clera was the first to start scrambling towards the door. Jula had got to all fours just in front of her and Clera used her to lever herself up, pushing Jula's face into the sand as she did so. She took off, though she hadn't taken the trouble to finish standing up first so it was part-crawl, part-stumble rather than actual running. Zole set off next, quickly overtaking Clera. Alata got up, clutching her throat, and started to run. Croy tripped Leeni as she tried to rise, and staggered to her feet.

Nona watched them. Did she want to go back? Did she want to fight under the Caltess roof, with Partnis Reeve watching on? To put coin in his purse as Verity's wealthy bet on which way the blood would spatter? She thought of Raymel Tacsis. Would he be watching? Would it shame him more if she didn't even rank among the convent's offering? Or did she want to look into his eyes and show him she had no fear?

Jula had got to her knees again, spitting sand. With two of the three places in the Fist rounds gone to Clera and Zole the last would be hers. Nona found herself running. Her mouth shouted a 'sorry' as she shot past Jula, but her legs just pumped harder.

30

The Caltess had a smell all its own. Nona had not remarked it on her arrival with the child-taker but now, among the many stinks of Verity, it was the particular smell of the place that brought Saida's ghost to stand beside her. Sweat, blood, sawdust, sewage, old beer, stale wine – the Caltess could be inhaled and known in a single breath from floor to rafter.

The five competing girls from Grey Class, accompanied by Sisters Tallow, Flint, and Rock, were afforded a corner of the main hall in which to train. Partnis's children had set out chairs and a long table to which the Caltess cooks brought the midday meal and periodic refreshments. This ensured that the nuns and novices would not have to mix with the Caltess's various inhabitants.

The remainder of Grey Class watched from a roped area in the corner opposite the one where ales were sold on fight nights. Sister Kettle kept watch over them. Yisht came too but strode the hall like a predator in search of prey, with no regard to boundaries.

Nona felt on display the whole time, more so than if they had sat at table with the ring-fighters, apprentices, and bonded-children for their meal. She knew that every crack and chink in the ceiling high above her had an eye to it. There would be new kings to rule that particular roost – Regol and Denam would long since have joined the ranks of Partnis's apprentices

– but nothing else would have changed up there among the sacks and dust of the attic.

Several young men from the apprentice hall lounged at the main doors, watching with an amused indolence, though they must surely have seen the same spectacle on several occasions. Even the ring-fighters seemed to find excuses to cross back and forth across the hall more times than seemed reasonable.

Gretcha passed by once, the grizzled gerant fighter who had fought in the second ring that first night when Nona and Saida had watched Raymel at work. She offered the novices a gap-toothed grin.

'She's huge!' Clera whispered beside Nona.

Nona just nodded. The woman's arms were as thick as Nona's whole body, banded by tattoos patterned in red and black like a winding serpent.

Two other gerant fighters paused to watch the novices work through their katas, each a towering mass of muscle, one with what looked to be deliberate facial scars, making something demonic of his smile, though the eyes above lacked malice. The other, balding, his grey hair cut to a stubble, scowled as though he'd happily eat a novice whole, given half a chance. A younger man sauntered by four times, humming to himself behind a sardonic smile.

'That's Aegon,' Alata said after the first pass. 'The Caltess's newest ring-fighter. He sailed from Durn.'

'How do you know?' Croy's eyes lingered on the doorway through which the man had gone. Nona supposed he had been handsome in a lean, dark manner.

'Everyone knows,' Clera said, before a snap of Sister Tallow's fingers set them all back to their tasks.

The appointed hour approached – there were no bells in the Caltess but people began to gather even so. Sister Tallow broke training and allowed the novices to watch the watchers.

'Who's that?' Clera pointed across to where Partnis Reeve stood, wine goblet in hand, amid a collection of ring-fighters and apprentices.

'The owner.' Nona had never quite managed to hate Partnis, though she knew she should.

Partnis Reeve waited, talking with his fight-masters and trainers as he watched his guests from the convent. Nona knew both the fight-masters: lean, grey men in their dark Caltess greens. A woman stood to one side of the group, or perhaps it was a man, hidden in cowl and robe. The nuns' glances strayed towards the figure in quiet moments. On the other side a man Nona thought she recognized. He looked small compared to the fighters clustered around Partnis, though perhaps he missed six foot by only a few inches. He seemed out of place in sealskin trousers and a shirt stitched from the fur of many small animals. The *tular* at his hip and the scars across both cheeks finally hooked the right memory and drew it to the surface. The man had intervened once when the attic's bully, Denam, had caught Nona off-guard. He'd said he was a ring-fighter… Tarkax, that was his name.

At last children began to descend from the attic under the watchful eye of the giant, Maya, who played mother for the Caltess.

'You're up first, Nona.' Sister Tallow nodded towards the ring. 'Don't break anyone.'

Nona climbed up onto the platform and vaulted over the ropes that made the rectangle in which she would fight. The fact they called it a ring still irritated her. A blond boy of no great size clambered in at the opposite corner, looking nervous. Nona looked around, finding that the elevation of little less than two yards offered a profoundly different perspective. She looked down on the nuns, on Zole, Clera, Croy, and Alata; even the tallest of the gerants she could face nearly eye to eye. Gretcha, standing close to the ropes, gave her a grin and banged her barrel-chest with one huge fist.

'Fight!' barked one of Partnis's fight-masters, and the boy came forward, fists raised.

Nona leaned back and kicked him as he closed the last yard. Her heel hammered into his solar plexus and he folded up with an 'ooooff' made by all the air leaving his lungs at once and collapsed onto his side on the boards. Nona glanced around, wondering if she were the victim of some kind of trick. The novices watching seemed just as surprised.

'Next!' the fight-master shouted.

Gretcha stooped and reached in a long, muscular arm to haul the boy out beneath the bottom rope as a hefty red-faced girl clambered in to take his place, her Caltess shift dirty with the attic's dust and cobwebs.

This one absorbed a couple of punches and took a kick to the back of the knee to put down. She tried to rise twice despite Nona's elbow strikes to the back. But not a third time.

The next was a dark-haired girl, younger than Nona. She tried to dodge Nona's first punch and had some speed to her, but not enough. Nona's fist crunched into her nose and the girl staggered back with blood sheeting down her lips and chin, then burst into tears. Gretcha lifted her bodily over the ropes with one hand, frowning, though more in compassion than disgust.

Nona fought six opponents in a row before Sister Tallow called her out of the ring.

On the first day Zole, Clera, and Nona found themselves pitched against a long succession of Caltess trainees. 'Trainees' meant attic-children purchased by Partnis and set to chores by Maya until it became clear what their potential might be. Nona suspected that beyond running laps and watching fights the training the 'trainees' received amounted to little more than feeding up. The fact that many hunska and gerant didn't come into their full speed or show significant size until their teens meant that Partnis didn't want to waste his fight-masters' time on the children he bought by the dozen each year.

Nona saw the fight-masters taking notes, writing down Partnis's muttered comments. It wasn't the novices being forged here: Partnis was getting to see what mettle his purchases had, though why he couldn't use his own apprentices for that Nona had no idea.

Zole fought the trainees with brutal efficiency, seeming intent on putting each onto the boards with the minimum number of blows. Yisht came to the ring for Zole's fights and barked at her in the ice-tongue. Commands, encouragements, threats? Nona never knew.

Nona found herself giving her opponents a chance, letting them swing, punishing them for mistakes rather than for effort. Clera seemed to revel in the chance to hit and not be hit, using her opponents as practice dummies, peppering them with dozens of punches as if seeing how many times she could hit them before they fell. After her first half-dozen, finished by a dull-looking giant of a farm-boy, she jumped out spattered with blood and grinning like a lunatic.

They each faced a second batch of six opponents after lunch. These were older, showing more signs of actual training, or at least more muscle and stamina. Some of the hunskas were half-bloods at least. None presented a challenge.

Come evening the crowd swelled with more fighters and others whose right to be there seemed written only in the richness of the cloth across their backs. Partnis put down his goblet and his chicken leg, moving in for closer observation. If he recognized Nona his eyes let none of it show as they studied the length of her. Nona ignored him, waiting in her corner for the third set of opponents.

The second of Nona's six opponents was the first of the day to hit her. A tall boy with long hair blacker than a raven's wing and a scar that gave him a permanent half-smile. He let her land a couple of punches, clearly relying on what he'd learned by watching her earlier in the day, knowing she wouldn't go for the kill. He disguised his speed and grunted when hit, staggering back. When Nona came in to put him on the ground he struck with the speed of a hunska prime, a straight punch for which his body gave no warning, aimed at her throat. Nona dug deep and managed to take the blow on the side of her face, spinning away, spitting blood. She fetched up against the ropes and found the boy watching her, his scar-smile no longer lopsided.

'Ouch.' She wiped at her mouth, her hand coming away scarlet, and offered a red grin in return.

The remainder of that fight was short, vicious, and one-sided. Nona shouted 'Next!' before the fight-master got a chance to.

Her final opponent made the boards shake as he stepped over the ropes. A dark-haired gerant with muscle heaped along the thick bones of his arms. He was a handsome boy, a couple of years Nona's senior, and popular too, to judge from the cheer among the attic-children – though in truth for the past few hours they'd been cheering anyone who could put up more than a moment's resistance.

'Hello.' The boy grinned down at Nona. 'I'll try not to spoil your face.' Meaty fist smacked into broad palm.

Nona sprinted at him, dropped to her back, and skidded between his legs. She gained her feet long before he had a chance to turn … but he never did. The foot she planted between his thighs, arching up on her shoulders as she slid between his ankles, seemed to have been just as effective as Sister Tallow had promised it would be in her classes. The youth stood without motion, shoulders hunched, silent save for a fierce hissing sound, then with no warning he fell first to his knees, then to the boards, coiled up and clutching his groin.

Day two was given over to blade. In the morning Alata and Croy took to the ring, first with blunted knives and later with wooden swords, facing a small number of the very best trainees. The handsome gerant was among Alata's three opponents. He shot Nona a filthy look as he climbed in, gingerly this time. He lasted no longer with a sword in his hand. Alata parried a blow, ducked beneath a swing, and came up with her sword against his thick neck.

The other bouts were similarly short with no Caltess trainees coming close to victory, though the hunska boy who hit Nona did manage to score a knife-mark against Croy before she 'sliced' his throat.

'Now they'll try us against the apprentices,' Croy said as she climbed down from the morning's final contest. She looked less than enthusiastic.

'You've seen it before?' Nona asked.

'We were here last year with Leeni in the fist battles,' Alata said. 'The Caltess don't train their trainees worth a damn, but they do nothing but train their apprentices. No Path or

Academia for them, just fighting. While we're in Spirit class or grinding poisons they're fighting. We get our fun in the trainee bouts. The Caltess gets its revenge in the apprentice bouts.'

The afternoon proved to be all that Alata promised. The apprentices came to the ring hardened by years of focused training. Alata, with her hunska speed, won two rounds against two gerant apprentices, the first of them the hulking redhead from Nona's attic days, Denam. He now loomed almost eight foot in height and his body looked ready to burst with the pressure of all the muscle heaped around his bones. When Alata spun inside his guard and thrust her wooden blade into his gut he snatched it from her in one huge hand and for a moment Nona thought he would just reach out and crush her head. But the fight-master's shouts reached him and he flung both swords down before leaving the ring cursing.

Croy didn't win a single bout. She had a natural talent for swordplay but just a touch of hunska, and neither was enough to overcome the mismatch between her single year of sword in Blade classes and the apprentices' dedicated training over several years.

It was Regol who first defeated Alata. The tall, sardonic boy Nona had known as king of the attic was now a tall, sardonic young man, the mocking smile and watchful eyes unchanged. He proved both lightning-fast and highly skilled, overcoming Alata's defence in a blinding exchange of parries, thrusts, and feints. Alata lost to all the hunska apprentices and one of the older gerants too.

Both girls returned to the convent that night with the record of their defeats written across them in lines of black bruising. Croy hobbled the last quarter-mile of the Seren Way and Alata looked spent by the time they reached the pillars. As they staggered off together towards the bathhouse Nona wasn't sure either of the novices would make it to the pool.

'Your turn with the apprentices tomorrow,' Alata offered as a parting shot.

On the third and final day of the forging Sister Tallow once again put Nona up first to meet the Caltess Challenge. The crowd had grown greater still. A sword fight can be difficult to see, it can be over quickly, and with wooden blades there is seldom any gore to entertain the masses. Fights without weapons are more of a spectacle: everyone understands them or can at least fool themselves into thinking they can. And blood will often flow.

'Learn something.' Sister Tallow set Nona moving towards the ring.

'Not, "don't break them"?' Nona glanced back.

Sister Tallow gave one of her rare smiles. 'Try.'

Nona vaulted over the ropes into her corner. A moment later Regol climbed unhurriedly into his. The Caltess children began to chant Regol's name, quietly at first, but rising in volume, and on every side the crowd edged closer. Where the trainees had fought in their Caltess shifts, still dusty from the attic, the apprentices fought only in thick white loincloths, the women binding a heavy linen wrap around their chests.

Tarkax, the ice-triber, had moved closer to the ring, dwarfed by the gerant ring-fighters behind him. He watched Nona with mild interest as if waiting to be impressed. Yisht stood by his side, both of them muttering to each other with just a twitching of lips. Nona wondered what they would have to talk about. Perhaps just ice warriors sharing their contempt of Corridor battle skills? But Ara had said Sherzal had attended Thuran Tacsis's ball, and Partnis lay under the Tacsis thumb. If Tarkax was his creature and Yisht was Sherzal's...

Regol raised a hand in salute, turning a full circle before letting his eyes come to rest on Nona. His habitual mocking smile broadened into something more sincere. 'Little Nona. You've grown.'

'You remembered me. I'm touched.' Nona couldn't help but smile back. 'I won't go easy on you though.'

Regol nodded, grave for a moment. He stepped to the centre of the ring, muttering through a fixed smile his voice so low it barely reached her. 'You're remembered. Don't ever think otherwise. Children have short memories, adults long ones.' His eyes flicked to the left and following his gaze Nona saw, out at the back of the crowd, behind Partnis, behind the rich in their furs and jewels, Raymel Tacsis, his nine-foot frame wrapped in a mole-dark cape that couldn't hide the broadness of him. A silver circlet held his golden hair back from his brow, and the face beneath had changed. The veins on the right side of his neck stood black against his flesh, like tendrils of night rising from his cape, and something was amiss with his left eye, though at such a distance Nona couldn't tell what exactly. Perhaps it was just full of blood.

Nona moved to face Regol at the centre. 'He came to see me fight?' Something in that two-tone stare had caught at Nona's guts like a cold hand, waking an old emotion, one she had never had much use for. Fear.

'He came to see you hurt,' Regol said, shaking out his arms and rolling his head.

'You're going to hurt me?' A snarl twisted at Nona's lip, fire rising in her belly to drive out the unease.

'No. I'm going to beat you. Make sure you submit clearly and quickly so I've a good excuse for stopping. Next—'

'Fight!' The fight-master's bark cut through the chanting.

'Next up is Denam. Do not let him get hold of you.'

Regol struck as his lips closed on his last word. A swivelling kick aimed directly at Nona's chest. She slowed the world, stretching each second into an age, but however deep she dug Regol's foot refused to slow. Nona both blocked and deflected but against a grown man neither made much difference, her blocking arm was simply driven against her chest, transmitting the force of the kick. Nona felt her feet lift from the ground, watched the frozen faces of the crowd as she flew, and bent as the ropes caught her in a rough embrace. The rebound took her to the floor where she pushed herself quickly to her feet, fighting for breath, her body a mass of hurt.

Regol didn't press his attack. He stood relaxed, wearing his old smile as the cheers rose around him.

'You're quicker than me…' The words came out in a pained wheeze. The fact hurt Nona more than her lungs did.

'I am.' Regol nodded. 'But you'll likely grow faster, and I'm as good as I'll get.'

Nona adopted the blade stance. Few hunska reached their

full potential before fourteen, but even so it shocked her to find someone so obviously swifter than herself. 'Fight!'

Nona advanced, snapping jump-kicks at Regol, testing his defence with jabs, but hitting only air. His longer reach kept her at bay and combined with his speed left her at a loss for how to proceed. Regol made the decision for her with a lightning-fast leg sweep. Nona leapt above it by the narrowest of margins, throwing herself not just up but forward towards Regol's shoulder as the rotation turned him from her.

It was a trap. Regol had lured her in and his elbow rose to meet her. In mid-air Nona was a slave to events already set in motion. She twisted and raised her arms to block. Regol's elbow knocked her arms aside and hit the side of her head.

Nona found herself on the boards, the roaring of the crowd faint against a ringing in her ears as if Bitel were being hammered in warning. She lifted her head and the world spun around her, the looming shape of her opponent revolving with it.

'…surrender.' A harsh whisper as Regol approached.

Nona lifted her hand, fingers splayed. The blood-roar of the crowd missed a beat then fractured into both cheers and jeers. Nona rolled to her back, panting, fighting nausea, watching Regol's back as he returned to his corner.

Nona didn't see Clera or Zole's fights. She heard the crowd howling, she heard laughter, hooting, gasps, but all that time she lay on a table in what looked to be the apprentice hall, her head ringing, exhaustion running through her though her fight had lasted only moments. Sister Flint gave her sugar in water and told her to rest. Sister Rock leaned over her, a frown on her brutal face, hands surprisingly tender as she pulled Nona's eyes wide and waved a finger before them.

'You'll be all right, child. No more fighting today, though.'

Perhaps an hour later, though it seemed both far longer and far less, Clera came limping to sit on the table. 'We're both done.'

'You look awful.' Nona sat up. She felt much better.

Certainly better than Clera looked, her eye blackening, lip split.

'You should see the other girl.' Clera grinned, teeth red.

'You beat an apprentice?'

'What? No. Are you mad? She pounded me. I meant Zole.'

Nona looked around. She was in the apprentice hall, on the dining table to which she had delivered dozens of meals from the Caltess kitchens during her time there. 'Where is she?'

'Sister Flint's taking her back to the convent.' Clera grinned again. 'On a mule!' She touched her lip, wincing. 'That girl doesn't know when to quit! She did manage to hurt one of them though. Talitha, the tall hunska with the braids, remember?'

Nona didn't but she nodded.

'She had Zole in a lock. No way she could escape. But Zole kicked her in the face anyway.' Clera mimed the impact. 'Brilliant.'

'And then?' Nona asked.

'I think she broke Zole's arm.' Clera shrugged.

Sister Tallow appeared at the doorway, glimpses of the throng behind her, the rumble of them filling the hall. Someone caught her attention before she could turn into the room.

'No. We're returning to the convent.'

Nona couldn't hear the other party above the noise outside.

'That's really not my concern, Reeve.'

'...'

'I don't care what he wants.' Sister Tallow made to turn away but a tall figure closed on her. Partnis Reeve, reaching out for her arm before thinking better of it and withdrawing his hand as she stared at it.

'I don't know what you've heard, sister, but he's not some street-show villain! He's the heir to one of Empire's oldest families, for Ancestor's sake! A refined young man of considerable education...'

'...' Now Sister Tallow's voice fell to a mutter.

And Partnis's rose in response. 'Many young men have ... appetites. Such lapses are unfortunate but—'

Sister Tallow stepped backwards into the room and shut the door in Partnis's face.

'Are you fit to travel, Nona? We're going back.'

Nona slipped from the table. The sound, the smell of the place, both of them filled her head with images – Raymel Tacsis in the ring, seen through an attic slit, bathed in the many-tongued voice of the crowd, Raymel Tacsis on his knees, blood spurting from the lacerations to his neck, Saida on the ground, her arm at broken angles, Raymel Tacsis watching from a crimson eye, black fingers running beneath the skin of his neck. She shook her head to clear the visions. 'I want to fight.'

'Sister Rock says you took quite a blow to the head. There's no shame in leaving now.' Sister Tallow crossed the room to stand above Nona. She took Nona's chin and angled her face, eyes narrowed in inspection.

'I feel better.' It wasn't a lie. She did feel better. Not good, but better.

'Your opponent is ready,' Sister Tallow said. 'There's much you could learn from him, but they would be rough lessons and perhaps you've been taught enough today.'

'I'll fight.'

Sister Tallow chewed her cheek, frowned, then released Nona's chin. 'The world is a dangerous place. We do you no favours if we hide your weakness from you. You can fight.' She turned and walked towards the doorway.

Nona followed.

Not since she felled Raymel Tacsis had Nona been up close with someone as massive as Denam. The apprentice seemed to fill half the ring and she had to crane her neck to look up at his face.

'I'm going to snap you in two, little girl.' Denam curled his lip. He had the arms to do it too, without effort. He'd grown, if anything, less handsome, over the two years, and he hadn't been pleasing to look on in the first place. His face, reddened in anger, sported a nasty collection of pustules, and the beginnings of a sparse ginger beard. More spots had broken out along his arms and his back was thick with them.

'You shouldn't oil your muscles.' Clera from just behind Nona's corner. 'It's bad for your skin!' Nona had to put a hand to her mouth to hide a grin as Denam's face contorted in rage.

Raymel Tacsis had moved closer to the ring, towering above the merchants and lords he now stood among. In all the crowd only one man seemed prepared to stand beside Raymel and an empty area had opened around the pair of them despite the press of people. The other man stood skeletally thin in a robe of sky-blue silk, his head small upon the long column of his neck, eyes pale, dark hair scraped across his head in long thinning locks. He seemed more interested in Raymel than in the fight, constantly glancing at the giant to his left.

For his part, Raymel kept his gaze on Nona. His left eye had no white or iris, just a black pupil surrounded by scarlet. Nona could almost imagine something inhuman watched her through it. The right eye was all Raymel though, blue and full of malice.

'Fight!'

At the fight-master's shout Nona rushed forward. Denam moved like a stone sinking in thickest honey, barely flinching before Nona delivered her kick to his belly. She might as well have kicked a wall. She spun beneath a huge and questing hand to land a series of punches to the nerve centres of the major muscles in his right thigh, following with a vicious kick to the back of his knee. The gerant reacted with such sloth that Nona stayed to drive three more punches into the most vulnerable areas of his left leg, blows that should leave the big muscle of the thigh dead and useless for the best part of an hour. Finally she skipped away from a lumbering swing of his arm.

'Even Regol can hit harder than that.' Nona had expected Denam to collapse but he came on unhindered and she had to dive aside to avoid the wide spread of his arms.

Spinning beneath his guard again, she focused an attack on his right leg, hitting hard enough to hurt her hands, but the thick slabs of muscle seemed impervious. She kicked at his kneecap with all her strength and leapt away from another attempt to seize her.

Nona stood back, catching her breath. Denam weighed at least four times what she did and she lacked the physical strength to hurt him. Punches that would floor another novice he hardly noticed.

'You're not the first hunska I've fought, holy girl.'

Nona pursed her lips and came forward again, weaving around the hands grasping for her. Denam kept his legs tight, wise to the groin strike from her previous fights. Even so, Nona hammered a trio of punches into the fullest-looking part of Denam's loincloth then rolled away. The gerant's roar joined, and temporarily drowned out that of the crowd, his face shaded more deeply crimson than seemed possible without actually bleeding … but he came on undeterred.

Nona kept at it, dancing around Denam's clumsy lunges, peppering the lower part of his body with her best punches and kicks. But it gained her no advantage and she felt the slow but inexorable rise of exhaustion. No hunska can dance between the moments for too long before their body fails, and Nona had already had a trying day.

Even as she ducked and wove Raymel Tacsis occupied the corner of her eye. At each break when she won clear and waited for Denam to catch up she risked glances towards her enemy. He wore an ugly smile now, anticipating the moment when her resources would be so drained as to allow Denam to snag her. The Noi-Guin assassins and corrupting the Ancestor's high priest must have lightened even the Tacsis purse, but how much had it cost to have Denam swear to break her back when he caught her, or put out her eyes with his thick fingers? A sovereign? Nona wouldn't be surprised to learn it was pennies, or perhaps just the cost of a polite request.

Another round of bouncing from the ropes, from one corner to the next. Nona felt herself slowing. Even Denam, crimson and sweat-soaked, seemed to be running out of rage-fuelled energy. Still, in the tight confines of the ring she had little doubt that the gerant would eventually catch her – unless his heart exploded.

The general roar of a hundred voices converged now on a singular cycle of oooohs and aaaaahs, like the watchers of a ball game, as Nona escaped Denam's outstretched fingers by ever narrower margins.

'Enjoy your running!' Raymel's shout reached her through a lull in the crowd's voice. He'd moved closer, only a few yards from the ropes now. 'You won't be doing any more after today.'

The taunt stopped Nona dead, right in Denam's path. Her eyes flickered from Denam to Raymel. The man had killed Saida as surely as if he had throttled her himself. And here he stood in his riches, waiting for his hireling to maim her. Common sense told Nona to slip from the ring, retreat to the convent's safety. But a red anger rose in her, drowning out the voice of reason.

The ginger gerant howled his bloodlust and thrust a hand towards her.

Nona sank into the moment and timed her jump. She landed with legs bent, one foot against the back of Denam's hand, letting his momentum carry them both forward. As he whipped his hand up, trying both to dislodge and catch her, Nona straightened her legs, driving off the broad back of Denam's hand. To the onlooker it would look as if he literally batted her into the air with a fumbled attempt to seize her.

Airborne, Nona sailed across the upper rope, staring at her target. Raymel had time to lift his head and start to move his arms but caught by surprise he had no chance of stopping her. Twisting in the air, Nona brought her feet to the fore and hammered both into Raymel's chest. She caught him around the back of the head to keep her place. Immediately, long before his hands could reach her, something else took hold, as if some unseen and clawed hand had sunk its talons into her mind, cutting through memories, letting emotion bleed out. She felt *them*. She felt whatever it was that now shared Raymel's skull, the passengers that had ridden him back from his long stay trapped on the border between life and death. They lurked under his skin, watched her from his crimson eye.

Nona and Raymel remained in contact for only a split second, but some instinct told her that, although both eyes lighted on her, only the red eye truly *saw* her, and more, it *recognized* her. Something woke inside Nona as her gaze locked with whatever lay hidden inside the ring-fighter's skull. Their communion lasted only an instant, but her speed drew it out into an age. A deep and twisting sensation enveloped her, half-pain, half-sickness.

A dozen different thoughts crowded through the small fragment of time that Nona had left for thinking. She should spring away. She should kill him. She should mark him.

Nona's hands decided for her. 'For Saida.' She plunged her talons into Raymel's throat, drawing them across the thickness of his neck, then sprang away, leaping backwards over his rising hands. She tumbled in the air and landed on both feet, just before the ring, arms spread for balance but looking as if inviting applause.

A shadow fell over her. Glancing up, she saw a hand big enough to engulf and crush her head, and behind it, Denam, crimson and furious, leaning over the ropes to snatch hold of her. For once Nona had no time to move. But, close as Denam was, Sister Tallow reached her first. She caught Denam's wrist in a pincered grip, taking his little finger in her other hand. A moment later he was on his knees in the ring above them, crying for release in a voice hoarse with agony. Sister Rock drew Nona away towards the main doors. To the audience, to Denam, perhaps even to the nuns, the whole exchange would have looked like an accident. Nona swept out of the ring by the gerant, crashing into a member of the crowd, springing away.

Half-pushed, half-carried to the exit, Nona kept her eyes on Raymel Tacsis, the blue-robed man fussing about him. Something was wrong. Blades that could sink six inches into a stone wall seemed to have been turned aside, as if Raymel's flesh held something inimical to their nature. Instead of a devastating wound they appeared to have left just a shallow cut, hardly parting the skin. With the red tide of her anger ebbing Nona realized that she could have been standing there with gory hands before a hundred witnesses to the murder of a lord's son. Even the sisters would have turned against her. If she had managed to escape the hall then the emperor's soldiers would have hunted from the Marn beaches to the Scithrowl borders for her. And yet … *still* some part of her knew disappointment.

Raymel for his part ignored the Academy man before him and stared at Nona in turn, with his scarlet eye and the blue. He kept one hand clasped to his throat, the smallest trickles of blood just starting to seep between his fingers. And as each of them stared at the other that sharp nausea twisted in Nona's gut once more.

31

'What do they even eat?'

'What?' Nona looked back at Clera, next behind her in the queue waiting for Bhenta to open the gate and let them down the stairs to the Poisoner's cave.

'What do they find to eat out there?' Clera asked.

'Who?'

'The ice-tribes. They can't just munch on ice.'

'They hunt.' Nona's father had hunted on the ice.

'What do they hunt?'

'White bear, hoola, lynx. That sort of thing.'

'To eat?'

'My da sold their pelts.'

'And what did the bears eat?'

'They come down into the margins and forage.'

'I'm talking about the deep tribes. Zole said her people roam a thousand miles north.'

'Uh.' Nona frowned. 'Fish, I think. And since when do you speak to Zole?'

'Fish? Isn't it all supposed to be frozen?'

'But there's sea underneath,' Nona said.

'*Miles* underneath! How do—' The clanking of the key in the lock ended the discussion.

Bhenta hauled the gate open and glared at the novices until they started moving. Clera claimed that Bhenta's dead white skin and the alarming, unnatural blue of her eyes were the lingering after-effect of one of Sister Apple's poisons, and her position as assistant was a kind of compensation. But Nona had it from Sister Kettle that such colouration wasn't uncommon if you walked the Corridor for a thousand miles east, and that Bhenta would be taking the headdress next year as a Sister of Discretion.

Sister Apple stood waiting as Grey Class filed in behind Bhenta. Heavy curtains hung over the three shaft-windows tunnelled out to the cliff wall and a shifting gloom filled the place. The three work-benches had been positioned against the walls, chairs stacked on top, lanterns set between, leaving a large empty space. Even the Poisoner's desk had been cleared of its usual vials, jars of pickled organs, and various oddments. Nona stood with the others, uneasy in the flickering shadows. At long last they might perhaps learn something other than poisons. Even so, Nona didn't peel the wax from her fingertips. It never paid to let your guard down in Shade class, and anything you touched could be one of Sister Apple's little traps.

'Light is the interloper.' Sister Apple spoke in the low voice of someone who is certain that they will be listened to. 'Those of you who have heard me give this speech before, attend to your training.' She waved at the group and four or five of the novices backed towards the rear of the chamber where the darkness lay thickest. Nona caught Leeni's smile as the novice ran her hands up across her body from thighs to chest to face and somehow the night seemed to follow, her skin, usually nearly as pale as Bhenta's, growing hard to see, as if the lanterns' shuddering light could find no purchase on her. Beside her Alata's dark brown skin seemed to shout its presence in comparison.

A sick sensation crawled up around Nona's stomach, the same feeling she'd been experiencing since the Caltess forging. In the days since her return it had only got worse. Perhaps Raymel had poisoned her somehow when she had cut him, or had her poisoned earlier in the day. Maybe that's what he had been there to watch – her dying in agony. If so he'd miscalculated the dose. Nona had told no one but Ara and Clera. Ara had wondered if it might not be an enchantment.

The Noi-Guin were said to be able to lay marjal spells that would see the flesh rot from a strong man within a week. Clera had laughed and said that most girls of their age felt the same symptoms every month and to get used to it. Both suggested going to the abbess but Nona wouldn't hear of it. If any of the nuns had realized that Nona's collision with Raymel was other than accidental, or that she had tried to kill him, they didn't appear to have told the abbess. Nona wasn't about to either. Abbess Glass had endured horrors, narrowly escaping an even worse fate the last time Nona enraged the Tacsis family. And now Nona had gone and cut the throat of Thuran Tacsis's firstborn son … again, albeit not as deeply as she wanted to. The fight was hers to finish.

'…light is a temporary kindness.' Nona found that the Poisoner had taken up her theme and was waxing lyrical. She shook herself and tried to pay attention. 'It is made new in the flame of a candle or the sun's hot eye. Before it comes there is darkness. After it leaves there will be darkness. The night is patient, endlessly so. And shadow, shadow is the war, the wound, where the two contest, where the light bleeds.'

The Poisoner paused to tuck a stray coil of red hair back into her headdress. 'Look around you: shadow is never still. Each shadow has two makers, the light and that which blocks the light. Both move. And if we leave this cave of dancing flames and restless novices, still we find no shadow without motion. The sun moves, Abeth moves, clouds come and go. To conceal yourself you must understand this motion. You must learn when to be still and when to move. In Shade I will teach you patience and stealth. We will study them until they become your religion and Sister Wheel marches down my stairs to call you heretics.

'There may be times when your life depends on your ability to stay hidden, or when someone else's life depends on the subtlety with which you insinuate yourself past a defence. If you take the red or the grey this will certainly be the case, but however you serve the Ancestor know that both patience and the talent for passing unnoticed will prove among the most valuable skills you're taught as novices.'

The Poisoner stood dark before them framed by the golden and beaded light where it threaded the smallest of gaps around the curtains' edges. 'For today I want you to find a place to sit. Seek your patience as Mistress Path has taught you, and watch your older sisters as they hunt each other, or watch them as best you can. All hiding is nine parts seeing. So watch. See.'

'Aren't we going to learn shadow-weaving?' Clera stood her ground as the others started to move off.

Nona stopped and turned back. 'Sister Kettle says there was a Grey Sister who could set her own shadow loose and it would go off by itself and do … things…' She trailed off, noting the Poisoner's stillness. Up in the convent she was Sister Apple. In the cave she could be the Poisoner or Sister Apple depending on the moment, but in the dark it was difficult to think of her as anything but the Poisoner, and Nona knew that if she could see the nun's face her eyes would have taken on that hard gleam that always reminded you just how dangerous she was.

'I instruct patience and you answer with impatience?' The Poisoner lifted her hands before her, gathering shadows like cobwebs as they rose. Darkness streamed between her open fingers. 'We don't weave shadow, we weave the light. How can a person cast no shadow? Only if they weave the light so that its path still leads to the spot it would have struck were they not there.' All the while she spoke the darkness thickened in her hands. 'To cut your shadow loose requires little skill, only the right knife. And those, fortunately, are far more rare than foolish novices are common. It is perhaps the most foolhardy and stupid of courses for a shadow-worker to take. A loosed shadow can be a vicious weapon but once free it's apt to cease listening to its owner and is soon lost to the greater darkness.'

The Poisoner closed her hands into fists, squeezing the clotted night within them into an inky darkness that bled between her fingers. She squeezed harder, her lip curling in a snarl, then opened her fists once more. On each palm lay a small black pellet, as if a hole had been punched through her hands.

'Take them.' Mistress Shade glanced from Clera to Nona.

'If you want to work shadows you must swallow the night. No?'

Clera came forward, uncertain, and took the small ball of darkness from the nun's left hand, shadows misting up around her fingers. Nona took the other one, finding it cold and hard.

'Swallow them.'

Nona put hers in her mouth. Immediately a vile bitterness spread across her tongue, crawling up the insides of her cheeks. The nausea already twisting in her gut became razored wire bound tight around her innards. The pain made her want to scream. She wanted nothing more than to spit the pill out, but she clamped her jaws shut and, retching, tried to gather enough saliva to swallow the thing. Her tongue felt as if it were shrivelling in her mouth. With a gurgle of disgust she managed to choke the darkness down. But Clera just spat a great black mess on the floor.

'Ancestor!' Clera spat and spat again. 'That's disgusting.'

'So is spitting on my floor, Clera Ghomal.' The Poisoner wrinkled her nose. 'No matter. The truth is a bitter pill to swallow is it not, Nona?'

'Yes, Mistress Shade,' Nona answered through numb and wrinkled lips.

'And Clera should have had a sufficient dose too.' The Poisoner leaned in towards Clera. 'Have you ever cheated in one of my exams, novice?'

'No.' Nona answered first though she had had no intention of doing so.

'Yes,' Clera said, her eyes widening. 'I swapped crucible jars with Ara last month while she wasn't—' Clera clamped her hands over her mouth. '—looking. And in the antidotes test I—' Clera kept talking behind her hands, her words muffled but audible.

'You would do well to sew your lips together, novices. Truth is an axe. Without judgement it's swung in great circles, wounding everybody,' the Poisoner said. 'Allow me to demonstrate. Nona, what question are you most worried that I'll ask you?'

'I'm afraid you'll ask me what really happened to make my

mother sell me.' Nona struggled with her jaw as her tongue twitched in its eagerness to volunteer the whole story unasked.

A momentary frown crossed the Poisoner's brow. She held her hand up. 'I have a more interesting question: Who have you had a crush on, Nona?'

'Arabella, and you, and Regol—' Nona started running for the doorway, both hands over her mouth, cheeks burning, pursued by Sister Apple's laughter, Clera just a fraction behind.

'She poisoned us!' Clera shouted after Nona as they climbed. 'The bitch poisoned us.'

'She did say she would make something new while we all trained for the forging.' Nona couldn't shut herself up, even as she ran. She glanced back, fearing pursuit, never more vulnerable.

Nona broke from the stairs out into the daylight, the sun's red light fierce after shadow-filled cave. Clera barged past her, turned by the collision and hopping for balance. They ended up facing each other, ten yards apart in the courtyard, which was otherwise empty but for Sister Mop crossing from the laundry.

'Why—'

'Don't! I'll put this in your eye!' Clera's hand emerged from her habit clutching a throwing star – not the five-pointed design to be found in the Blade stores, but a smaller four-pointed make.

'Where did you get that?' Nona couldn't help herself. Besides, Clera wouldn't throw it at her.

Clera's mouth spasmed, her lips writhed. 'Partnis!' She screamed the word.

'Why—'

'What—'

Both girls started questions, but knowing they would have to answer the other they broke off, spun around, and ran in opposite directions, Clera sprinting, Nona hobbled by the agony pulsing through her.

Nona vomited even before she reached the edge of the convent, but it was an hour before the bitterness left her mouth and she could once again tell a lie.

'I am not a monster.' The words tasted sickly sweet on her tongue.

She met Clera hanging by the gate to the Poisoner's caverns, trying to build up the courage to go down. The courtyard lay empty, the rest of the novices at the cloisters or still at their evening meal.

Nona joined her, still in pain but now able to walk without hunching over. 'Where did you get that throwing star? Why have you got it?'

'I told you.' Clera pressed her lips together, scowling furiously. 'Partnis Reeve gave it to me. He wants me to fight for him. My father told him I wouldn't take the red when I'm done here.' She sucked her teeth, wincing at some over-strong flavour. 'Anyway … why *did* your mother sell you then?'

Nona turned towards the gate, which had been left ajar. 'Let's get this over with.' She led off and Clera followed.

Sister Apple sat behind her desk reading from a scroll, the lesson chamber returned to its normal layout.

'Novice Clera, Novice Nona, good of you to return.' She set her pointer stick, a slim length of wire-willow, over the scroll to mark her place. 'I've just been reading about sweet aloe, a plant that's been lost to the ice. Apparently it's very good at mellowing bitterness. I would have liked to try it in my truth toxin – which, as you will have noticed, is not the sort of thing you can slip someone unawares.' She set her hands upon the desk and stood up. 'Perhaps the cathedral archives still hold some seeds…' She crossed the room to stand before them. 'What did you learn, girls?'

'Not to trust you,' Nona said.

The nun laughed. 'I've been trying to teach you that since the first day you came down those stairs, Nona Grey. Will the lesson stick this time?' Her eyes slid to the left. 'And Clera?'

'The truth is a weapon and lies are a necessary shield.'

'Put like a poet,' Sister Apple said. She reached out and laid a hand on each girl's shoulder, ushering them closer together. 'But when I asked what lesson you learned … I wanted to hear "patience".' And with that she banged their heads together.

32

'Is the sea like this?' Nona sat with the others, legs dangling out over the drop to the distant waters. The moonlight revealed the far side of the sinkhole but darkness held the rest. The Glasswater lay many fathoms deeper than the fall from its rocky lips to the rippled surface. Nona found that hard to imagine.

'Ha!' Ruli often spoke her amusement and rarely laughed. 'The sea is huge.'

'I know that. I'm not stupid.' Nona had seen the maps. Sister Rule's charts reached all the way around the Corridor, though those of the most distant lands were centuries old. 'I meant as deep.'

Ruli shook her head and Clera snorted, though Nona knew she had never been to the shore. 'Deeper,' Ruli said. 'My father used to say something he took from a book.' She frowned, trying to remember. '*Whatever befalls it the sea will close upon itself and keep its secrets, erasing with a curtain of waves all that has passed. The deep sea waits. Patient, hungry depths unknown to those who skid over its surface and think they know the whole. There are empty miles, dark places where light has never been, and man's eyes will never know them. What wonders there* … I forget the rest.' She pushed her hair back over her shoulders and leaned forward to stare down past her toes. 'He wants me to come back, when I've finished here. He says there's more in Abeth than the Church of the

Ancestor. But I think I'll stay. If I can't be a Grey Sister then I'll be a Holy.'

'You don't think there's more out there to see?' Hessa asked from her perch on a nearby rock – she didn't ever sit on the edge, perhaps shy of her withered leg, or knowing that if she fell she would drown.

'Oh I do,' Ruli said. 'More than I could ever know. But there's more than I could ever know here too.' She pulled her nightdress tighter around her, the wind warmed by the approaching focus but still too cold for comfort.

'That's how they get you,' Clera said. 'They say you're free to leave and families pay the fees year after year, but how many do leave? There's always something – the faith, the mysteries, pride – this place always seems to manage to hook them.' She put her head back. 'Not me though. As soon as I'm offered the red I'm out of here.'

'You see Yisht watching us?' Ara hissed. 'Don't *look*!' As Ruli started to swivel.

'She's always watching us,' Hessa said. 'Well, watching you and Nona anyway.'

'Isn't she supposed to be watching Zole?' Clera threw a loose stone, arcing down into the water.

'Ghena said she saw her climbing on the dome,' Ruli said. 'She said she told Abbess Glass and she wouldn't listen.'

'Wouldn't listen?' Nona asked.

'It's all the sisters.' Ruli nodded. 'They're all terrified that Sherzal will take Zole back. That's what I've heard. Though why they care I don't know. Maybe the high priest would be angry? Anyway, Zole's getting private lessons from Sister Pan, did you know that? And from the Poisoner!' She crossed her arms. 'And that's why they won't do anything about Yisht. They think if they throw Yisht out then Zole will go too. So Yisht can climb all over the Dome of the Ancestor if she wants.'

'Ghena's always making up stories.' Clera shook her head. 'I hope I'm out of Grey Class before she leaves Red. But she's right about one thing: Yisht is up to something. She *is* always prying.'

'I think she's hunting for something,' Hessa said.

'You think Yisht will tell the abbess about this?' Ruli asked. 'Us being here?' Sneaking out of the dormitories at night wasn't unheard of but it certainly wasn't allowed.

'Well, if she does it'll be your fault,' Clera said. 'You could have shown us in the bathhouse, there's plenty of steam there.'

'I can't do it in the bathhouse. I don't know why. Maybe it's because the air's always moving.'

'The air's moving here too – or didn't you notice the wind?'

'Not down there!' Ruli pointed to the water. 'Well, not so much. I don't know … maybe—'

'Maybe you just can't do it anywhere,' Clera said.

'We'll find out in a moment,' Ara said. 'So there's no need to argue.'

She was right. The focus was approaching, the moon nearly overhead, the sinkhole's shadows slinking away, hugging the near wall. Beneath their feet a second moon, a red rectangle, danced in the water.

The warmth built on Nona's shoulders, and became heat. She narrowed her eyes. Clera and Ara lay back, eyes closed, arms spread, embracing the brilliant light.

Nona watched as the water began to steam, caught between two burning moons. Within a few minutes the whole of the sinkhole had filled with mist, a new surface billowing below her feet and rising swiftly. She was glad not to be in her habit now: the plateau was hotter than the bathhouse and sweat beaded on her arms, trickling across her ribs beneath the thin material of her nightdress.

When the steam reached the lip it rolled out like a hot wet blanket before being stripped away by the wind, swirling and confused in the focus. Ara and Clera sat up.

'Go on then,' Clera said.

'I'm … trying.' Ruli lifted her hands, the mist streaming about them, rising steadily in the void of the sinkhole, shredding around the novices where the wind took it. Ruli's pale brow furrowed and grew more pale, sweat running down the sides of her face.

'I don't see anything,' Clera said.

Nona didn't either, but she could feel something, a tingling in her fingertips, spreading to her palms, an itching across the back of her mind. Her stomach chose the moment to knot itself into a ball of agony, nearly doubling her up and almost pitching her into the sinkhole.

'There!' Ara pointed. Just below them the mist had clotted into a shape … a something.

'It's a person.' Nona gasped it past gritted teeth.

The figure drew closer, a more solid whiteness amid the rising steam. Featureless, perhaps a man, perhaps a woman, it reminded Nona of the Ancestor's statue in the dome.

'I … told … you!' Ruli grinned, the strain evident.

'Do a horse now!' Clera said. 'No! Do Sister Wheel… No! Kettle and Apple. Kissing!'

The figure broke apart and Ruli released a breath.

'That's great, Ruli.' Ara leaned past Nona and put a hand to Ruli's shoulder. 'You're a marjal touch at the least, a half-blood maybe!'

'You'll have no problems with shadow-weaving,' Hessa said from behind them. 'You'll be a Grey Sister for sure if you want to be.'

'I want to see more.' Clera lay back, an arm over her eyes. The focus was approaching its peak, soon the light would be moving on. On the ice margins the thaw would be in full swing, the tribes at the lakes, busy gathering the moon's bounty before the freeze set in again. 'What else can you do?'

'Just that.' Ruli lay back. 'And even that gives me a headache.'

'You should tell the abbess,' Hessa said.

Ruli snorted. 'The abbess only cares about the Path. The whole convent only cares about the Path.' She shrugged. 'The Poisoner will know soon enough if I can work shadow, and she'll help me.' A smile. 'Kettle and Bhenta will too. Us Greys stick together!'

They crept back to the dormitory in the last of the moon's warmth, already shivering as the wind regained its voice and moulded their damp shifts around them.

It took an age for Nona to sleep, coiled around her sickness.

Raymel had poisoned her somehow, and somehow she ne . to fight back.

The next day Nona found herself yawning in Path. She often did, even without the excuse of lost sleep. Serenity proved elusive and the Path always beyond reach. Sister Pan had told her a hundred times that she tried too hard: 'Serenity isn't something that can be seized, taken, snatched up by force of will. It is a gift that you must be open to.'

Even so, however hard Nona tried not to want it, serenity had yet to reach out, take her in its arms and set her gently upon the Path.

Sister Pan summoned the girls' attention from their meditations with a cough. She stood before the great ironbound chest which sat at the front of the room, black against the stained and sunlit glass. 'There is a line that divides and a line that joins, and they are the same line and the line is a path.'

Nona found Sister Pan's pronouncements more and more frustrating, more so now that she knew she had a genuine ability to touch the Path. In Red Class Nona had let the old nun's philosophizing wash over her, just waiting for a chance to escape to blade-path, but now she felt bound to listen, hoping against hope that she might actually say something useful.

'There is a thread that runs through all things, that binds each story to every other, a thread that runs through the veins and the marrow and the memory of every creature.'

Nona sighed. It was all very well Sister Pan making pretty speeches but it would be much more helpful if she would just *tell* them what they needed to know. If you understood something you should be able to explain it: if you didn't understand it then you had no business teaching it. Either way, having the old woman spout poetry at them didn't help at all.

Nona found her head nodding and jerked upright, blinking and trying to keep her eyes wide. Whatever poison the Tacsis had got into her seemed to work erratically, the symptoms coming and going without rhyme or reason.

★ ★ ★

her failures with serenity Nona had on several n away from the convent buildings to try to in the only manner she had ever reached it.

ken to slipping her friends and venturing out wing spur of the plateau. There, she hunched wind, gazing out over the garden lands of Verity and the rridor narrowing away to the east between ice walls. If she looked down she could see the convent vineyards, huddled against the plateau walls, sheltered from the weather.

Pain and anger had driven her to the Path before. Anger had only to be reached for: the fact that Raymel Tacsis still drew breath was enough in itself. She had wanted to kill him at the forging and days later her fingers still itched at night for want of his blood. But she had found her blades unable to do more than scratch him. Had it been the man at his side, working some enchantment? Or the devils sharing his skin, armouring their host against her?

Either way Nona had failed Saida. Within yards of the place where Raymel had hurt her Nona had taken his throat in her hand … and still he lived. She only had to think of her own failings as a friend and the anger was there for the taking. Pain too.

It took time. Time to kindle the rage and let it burn to white heat, time to let her pain rise from the deep and hidden places where she kept it. But she could do it, and on each occasion that she did so the Path would coalesce out of the chaos of her mind's eye. For a moment it would appear, stretching out before her, whipping this way and that, a white serpent in its death throes. And in the next instant she would be hurled at it with frightening speed.

The first time she had touched the Path on one of these excursions she made a glancing contact and the energy of it burst away from her in a boom that had rattled shutters back at the convent and sent birds spiralling towards the ground, killed in mid-flight. The noise had been so loud that nobody knew where it had come from. Sister Rule had suggested some kind of collapse in the many caverns that riddled the plateau.

On the second and subsequent occasions Nona had

managed to drive the Path's energies into the rock, shattering limestone, reducing some of it to powder, but not causing any damage that would be evident from the convent. On a dozen or more attempts though, despite her best efforts to slow her approach, to gain her balance as on the blade-path and make cautious progress, she managed just one step, or perhaps a glancing second step, before the Path threw her.

'Nona?'

'Yes?' Nona looked up, rediscovering the room, the glorious colours of the windows, the novices on all sides in their chairs, and Sister Pan standing before her. 'Yes, Mistress Path?'

'You appeared to be slipping over the line from serenity to slumber.' Titters of laughter around the room.

'Sorry, Mistress Path.'

'I said that you would be accompanying me to the Academy.'

'Me?'

'And Hessa and Arabella. I take the Grey Class quantals every year on the twentieth seven-day. If we have any quantals, that is. It is important that you be exposed to marjal enchantments, and likewise the Academy masters believe their students should know something of Path magics.'

Bray sounded and Sister Pan frowned at the fading bell before waving her hand in uncharacteristic irritation, dismissing the class. Clera's chair almost spun in her wake as she beat the scramble to be first down the stairs.

Nona found Clera already attacking a bowl of stew when she reached the refectory table that evening. Darla had secured a drumstick that looked to have come from a swan rather than a chicken, and seemed determined to gnaw through to the marrow, her cheeks and chin running with grease.

'You're late. Not like you.' Darla managed to get the words around her drumstick. Of all the novices only Darla seemed to have more of an appetite than Nona.

'Sister Wheel caught me for a lecture.' It wasn't true though – she had been trying to walk the Path again, reaching it angry. As usual her attempts to slow down and take control saw her pitched off within moments. A crazing of shattered stone and cracks that ran a yard or more into the bedrock were all she had to show for it.

'I saw Wheel whispering with Yisht behind the pigsties.' Clera didn't look up from her bowl, speaking between spoonfuls. 'I think they're plotting together.'

Nona looked around for Zole but the girl wasn't there. Sherzal often sent her food-parcels to cater to her 'ethnic diet' and Zole could be found eating from them in the cloisters. It looked like dried fish usually, sometimes with disturbing hints of tentacle. At other times it looked like cubes of fat, blackened with age, and the stink made Nona's eyes water. Nobody ever asked to share.

Nona helped herself to stew and a heel of bread, squeezing in between Clera and Ketti. 'Sister Wheel would rather cut her nose off than skip singing the fourth psalm before eating. She's the last nun in the whole faith who would plot against the church.'

'Maybe it's not the church she's conspiring against.' Ara pulled out a chair from the other side of the table and leaned in for the bread. 'Maybe she doesn't consider you a part of the church, Nona. You do manage to destroy every prayer she makes you learn.'

'I get the words right!'

'You make them sound like death threats. Even if everyone didn't know you hate her it would only take them listening to you in Spirit class to be sure.' Ara sat down.

'I don't hate her.' Nona chewed and swallowed. 'I just really, really don't like her.'

'Anyway,' Ara said. 'Forget about Sister Wheel, we get to go to the Academy in four days!'

'I've been.' Nona shoved a big spoonful of stew in her mouth and, finding it too hot, sat breathing rapidly in and out over it while Ara made furious eyes at her, motioning for more information.

'And…'

Nona finally won the battle and started to chew, her tongue a little scalded. 'It's not so great.'

'How did you get to go there? I wanted to visit with my father and they wouldn't let us!' Ara looked up at Hessa, now emerging from a crowd of older novices and stumping towards the table. 'She says she's been!'

'I have too,' said Hessa. 'It's not so great.'

'What!' Ara let her spoon splat into her stew. 'Outrageous. Is there anyone at this convent besides me who hasn't had the tour?'

'All you have to do is get taken by someone who wants to sell you,' Hessa said. 'And Nona hasn't been, she's just remembering my memory.'

Nona blinked and looked up. 'But…' She frowned, knuckling her forehead. Hessa was right – it was the memory they had shared that night she and Hessa had left the dormitory together, all thanks to Hessa's thread-work, something else Nona had yet to have any success in, requiring as it did the ability to move very close to the Path without actually touching it. 'I guess you're right.' She looked across to where Ruli sat staring into the steam rising from her bowl. 'Ruli? What are…' The steam coiled into a pale serpent and a sick agony coiled through Nona. She found herself falling, wordless, pulling plates and bread with her. It took an age to hit the ground.

'Nona! Nona!' Ara on her knees, holding Nona's face between two hands.

'…matter with her?'

'Sister Rose…'

'No!' Nona's hand snapped out to catch Jula's ankle as she made to leave.

'She doesn't need Rose.' Clera – more to contradict Jula than out of reason.

'What are you talking about?' Ara released Nona's head and sat back on her heels. 'You're ill.'

'She's fine. Just slipped.' Clera, standing, waving novices from the other tables back to their seats.

'I'm not ill. I was poisoned,' Nona hissed.

'Well that's even better reason for us to take you to the sanatorium,' Ruli said, squatting down next to Ara, her brow furrowed with concern.

'I'll get thrown out if the nuns find out what I did.' Nona

curled around her pain, which was easing now but still cramping through her. Right now being thrown out didn't seem an unreasonable price to pay to feel better.

'We can't leave you poisoned.' Ara exchanged glances with Ruli. 'It could kill you. And who did it? You really think this is something to do with Raymel Tacsis?'

'I don't have to stay poisoned.' Nona tried to get up and with Clera's help regained her chair. 'We know how to make antidotes.' Two years of the Poisoner's classes ensured that.

'You need to know what poisoned you. We know thirteen different antidotes. We can't make all those, and half of them aren't even safe to take with the others.' Hessa reached for her crutch and struggled out of her chair.

'There's the black cure,' Nona said.

'Which we haven't been taught,' Hessa replied. 'And can kill the patient or leave them blind.'

'Besides, Sister Apple has all the ingredients.' Ruli, back on her side of the table, leaned in, keeping her voice to a loud whisper.

'We don't even know where she keeps them.' Clera went back to eating.

'In a cave,' Nona said.

'Well, duh.' Clera spoke around her mouthful.

'We can search. I've been further in than you have – I saw a few places where she might store them.' Nona rocked to distract herself from the pain, still sharp but easing.

'You've been further?' Ara frowned.

'When she was held for trial,' Hessa said, frowning too, though she'd been frowning all the while.

'Oh.'

'There's the lock,' Jula said.

Clera snorted.

'Well there is,' Jula persisted. 'That gate's always locked. We wouldn't even be able to get to the Shade chamber without Sister Apple or Bhenta to let us in.'

'We?' Clera looked up from her bowl, wiping her mouth with the back of a hand. 'You're going sneaking in the under-caves, Jula? You've never broken a rule in your holy little life.'

'Nona needs us.' Jula looked down.

'She needs me,' Clera said. 'I can open that lock.'

'How?' Ara asked.

Clera pursed her lips and paused, glowering beneath the black shock of her hair. 'I'll steal the key from Bhenta.'

The novices shushed Clera, whose voice had grown quite loud, but nobody seemed to have noticed amid the hubbub of the four classes all eating and talking and clattering.

'I'll open the lock,' Hessa said, voice low. 'I can do it. That doesn't change the fact we don't even know what antidote we need to make.' She stumped off towards the main doors.

The others watched her go, paused for a moment to glance at each other, then nodded. Hessa wasn't given to boasts. If she said she could do it, then she could.

Zole arrived, pushing through the novices standing to leave from the next table. Grey Class shot her sideways glances and the conversation ran short.

'Tonight,' Nona said, then turned her attention to the stew.

Nona stopped at the scriptorium that evening on the way to the dormitory. She knocked and waited. A light rain laced the wind, on the edge of freezing. She huddled in the doorway and had raised her hand to knock again when the heavy door shuddered open.

'Nona!' Sister Kettle smiled down at her, though not from such a height as she used to. 'Get in.'

Nona slipped through the gap and looked around the room as Kettle shut the door behind her. Four large, sloping desks took up most of the space, each with open scrolls secured across them, quills and inks to hand. Sister Scar sat at the only occupied one, a heavy book in a lectern before her, lanterns on stands to either side. She spared Nona the briefest of glances before returning her gaze to her scroll. Clera said the nun had named herself for the scar that divided her cheek, skipped a blind white eye, and ran through her short grey hair. Jula said that Scar had taken the wound on a mission long after she took holy orders and the name related to some other scar or secret.

'What can we do for you, Nona?' Kettle's eyes held their usual mischief. 'You have a book you want transcribed?'

'I wanted to use the library.'

Kettle clapped her hands, delighted, earning a reproving glance from Sister Scar. 'I taught you to read and now you want to tackle a book! This must be what it's like when your baby takes a first step! Come on! Come on!' She hurried towards the door at the rear of the room.

Nona followed Kettle into the convent library, a chamber of similar size to the first but lacking any window, its walls hidden by floor to ceiling with bookshelves. Another door stood open to a long gallery lined with deep box-shelves on which hundreds of scrolls rested.

'So, we have holy texts, spiritual writings, the lives of saints and of revered sisters of our order.' Kettle swung an arm to encompass the whole of the opposite wall. 'Over there we have treatises on fight styles throughout the Corridor and beyond. Here are the histories and genealogies of the Sis. Over there works on the mysteries of the Path – don't expect to find any sense in them.' She pointed out sections on the wall to the right. 'The grey books are up there on the highest shelf. And here…' Kettle spread her fingers over the leather spines of a dozen or so books behind a locked rail, '…we have fiction!'

'Why are they locked in?' Nona asked. She had thought the poisons books might be. But these…

Kettle grinned and lifted her hands from the books with some reluctance. '"Tell me a story" began every seduction ever.'

'The abbess doesn't keep *those* sorts of books!' Nona felt herself colouring.

Kettle shook her head. 'Well, not here at least.' Again the grin. 'But be warned, young Nona: a book is as dangerous as any journey you might take. The person who closes the back cover may not be the same one that opened the front one. Treat books with respect.'

'I can just … read them?' Nona asked.

'Any time you want. Just make sure to put them back when you leave. And don't damage them. They're my babies. My old leathery babies. And I have a very unpleasant poison from Sister Apple for anyone who so much as folds a page.'

'How do I reach the ones on the high shelves?' Nona scanned the highest shelf that ran the circuit of the room just below the ceiling.

'Grow!' Kettle gave her an amused stare. 'You won't want to read any of those books, little Nona. Not until you're taller.' With that she returned to the door. 'I'll be in here with Sister Scar if you want me.'

'Did you find it?' Ara was waiting by the dormitory door when Nona came back. In the hall behind her the other novices were all in bed already, or changing into their nightgowns.

'Yes.' Nona walked past Ara into the room, holding her arms tight across her chest. A fever had sunk its teeth into her and clutching herself seemed to help keep the shivering to a minimum. She fell into her bed, too cold and trembly to want to undress, though her habit stuck to her where she'd been sweating. Clera and Ara watched as she dragged her slate from the habit's inner pocket. With a groan she leaned down to place it beneath the bed so the carefully scratched instructions wouldn't be blurred.

'You got it then,' Clera whispered.

'Yes.' Nona fell back. The recipe had been in a tome by Sister Copper of Gerran's Crag, written more than two hundred years ago. The warnings had been more dire than Hessa's – but she had it. She had the black cure.

33

'Hurry up!' Clera stood with her face pressed to the gap between two bars of the gate across the tunnel mouth. On the other side steps led down to the Shade class chamber. 'Quickly!'

'She's coming as fast as she can,' Ara said.

Hessa stumped towards them, her bad leg swinging with her crutch. With her back to the wall Nona peered at the convent buildings all around them, dark and silent. Somewhere an owl hooted, and in dark corners rats scurried. Ara uncovered the lantern, just a touch, to guide Hessa in.

'Watch the steps.' Nona moved to catch Hessa should she fall.

'Here.' Ara opened the lantern's cowl enough to let its light flood out over the gate.

The sun wouldn't show for an hour: focus had passed, its heat faded from the stones; the stars hid in a coal sack sky. These were the grey hours when mankind lay fast in slumber and the world stood open to the bold.

Should any novice in the Grey Class dormitory rise to use the Necessary they would discover the lantern gone. Apart from that, the danger was discovery by whichever nuns were scheduled to open the bakehouse that morning, or by Sister Tallow or one of her Red Sisters on their nightly patrols.

Hessa came up to the gate. When the lantern's light caught her face it showed the curve of a half-smile, the tranquillity that Sister Pan taught would lead the true-blood to the Path. Hessa set her hand over the lock.

'Don't blast it!' A sudden fear seized Nona, and with it the image of a wrecked gate and Sister Apple standing before it with the morning sun at her shoulders.

'The Path runs through us like our signature, written upon the world.' Hessa appeared to be quoting Sister Pan. 'We are complex and changing, and so is our signature.' Hessa's hand drew Nona's attention. It didn't glow but somehow it seemed brighter and more real than everything around it. 'A lock, though. A lock is a simple thing, no matter how it may be constructed. It is locked or unlocked. Its thread spells one word or the other. And if … I grasp … that thread and pull.'

The click of the lock's surrender made them all flinch.

'I'll go back now,' Hessa said.

'You *all* will.' Nona took the lantern from Ara.

'I will not!' Ara reached to take the lantern back.

Nona held it away from her. 'One can search as easily as three. I don't need you.'

'Nonsense, we can cover more ground if there's three of us. We don't have long!' Ara's brow furrowed into the two vertical lines that developed just above her nose when she was being stubborn.

Nona pulled the gate open just wide enough to admit herself. 'We've got one lantern. We can't split up. Better just one of us gets punished if caught.' She pulled the gate closed behind her as Ara reached for it. 'Help Hessa get back. She could trip in the dark.'

Clera seemed to accept the logic, or realize how much she didn't want to find herself in the Poisoner's black books. Either way, she took Hessa's arm and started to help her back up the steps.

'But you're poisoned!' Ara protested. 'That's the whole point. What if you get worse down there? What if you need us?'

'If I get caught then that's my excuse: I was poisoned. I need this stuff. You two haven't got an excuse.' Without waiting for an answer Nona hurried down the tunnel, feet sure on the familiar stairs.

Once past the door to the Shade class cavern Nona had just a single old memory to follow. Sister Apple had led her and Abbess Glass along this tunnel in iron yokes. To reach the recluse where they spent the night Sister Apple had taken them past half a dozen junctions where tunnels split and wandered into the black secrets of the Rock of Faith.

At the bottom of the steps Nona spent a moment watching the dance of her lantern's flame then turned from it and watched instead the memory of its dance written on the darkness. Of all the paths to clarity that Sister Pan had shown her this one worked best for Nona. Over the course of the next few minutes the trance wrapped her in its cold, tingling embrace, every shadow growing ripe with meaning, every detail in the walls crying out for her attention.

The air held a metallic smell, the scent of deep places. Nona shivered, though the damp air held no particular chill. In her mind's eye she saw herself and her tiny flicker of flame entering a vast labyrinth. Sister Rule had once shown them a cast of the tunnels within an ant mound, so complex, so hugely intricate, that Nona wondered how any ant ever found its way out. Today she was the ant.

She walked slowly, examining the ground. The Poisoner's storage chamber wouldn't be too far from the class chamber, and the path between them would be well trodden. The muddy grit that gathered in the undulations of the rock showed signs of frequent passage. It was at the turnings she would have to pay close attention.

The first choice had to be made where a fissure, barely wide enough for an adult to squeeze through, opened in the tunnel wall. Nona knelt to study the floor. A drop of water hit the back of her neck, ice cold. In the shudder of the lantern's light what she saw surprised her. A few inches into the fissure the rounded edge of a shoe had left its impression where ancient mud gathered in a fold of the rock. The imprint was clear and quite sharp. If it had been there for a long time surely the drip-drip-drip of the tunnels would have blurred its edges... Nona drew a deep breath and, turning sideways, slipped into the fissure.

The crack led downward at a shallow angle, the floor consisting of loose rocks caught where the walls grew closer together. Nona went as swiftly as she dared, expecting to find the way widening and discovering instead that it narrowed. She couldn't picture the Poisoner making her way back and forth with her arms filled with supplies for the novices' cauldrons. And yet someone had come this way.

The walls scraped her on both sides, her breathing the only sound, no scent but that of her smoke and the faint smell of damp stone, aeons old.

Nona pressed on though the way got tighter still. It seemed that the fissure would taper off and narrow to nothing and she became increasingly worried that she might become wedged, unable to turn or retreat, held in the stone's cold embrace until her light failed and thirst drove her mad.

'Whoever it was must have turned back.' The darkness swallowed her voice.

Her fears mocked her, driving her on.

Close to the narrowest point Nona spotted soot on the wall. It was hard to miss, given that her nose was just an inch from it and the back of her head was scraping the opposite wall. The smoke from her own lantern rose along the wall, overriding the earlier blackening.

'They must have turned back here.'

Even so, Nona wriggled on for another yard. No more smoke-blackened walls here. She started to inch back, but paused and sniffed. Her own lantern gave off the acrid tarry smoke of burning rock-oil, but a sweeter scent hung on the air, just the faintest memory of it. Old smoke, but not the cheap stuff novices burned: Nona had smelled such smoke in the entrance hall of the abbess's house, and in Heart Hall when the high priest sat in judgement.

She pressed forward, gripped on both sides now, twisting where the crack in the stone was too narrow for her hips. At one point the rock's jaws gripped her head and she could neither advance nor retreat. Fear proved to be sufficient lubricant and she escaped a moment later. Her courage gave up before the fissure started to widen again but by that point forward had become the only option and, weeping in terror, cursing herself for her stupidity, Nona inched forward.

Finally the walls released her and she stumbled into a wider space. Another tunnel. Above her a shaft opened in the tunnel's ceiling. It looked neither hand-hewn nor natural, having instead a strangely 'melted' character, the walls being smooth and uneven. Debris covered the tunnel floor, rubble from the shaft above, in places fractured, in others smooth, in others bearing pick-marks. Nona could make little sense of it.

The shaft was too high above her to reach, a rockfall blocked the tunnel to the left, and Nona's nerves weren't yet ready to attempt the return, so the passage to the right remained the only option.

She pressed on, scraped and dirty, passing smaller fissures, and once a curtained waterfall where freezing water from the plateau above leaked down. A moment of panic seized her as she imagined the vast weight of the Glasswater somewhere close by. How thin were the walls that held that reservoir in place? What would it take to set those waters flooding along these ancient courses to drown her in the dark?

'Apple never came this way. Not for stores.' The sound of Nona's own voice convinced her and she started to edge back.

That was when she heard it. Just once, and distant. The sound of metal on stone. She held her breath and waited, ears straining. Nothing. She strove for deeper clarity, wrapping her mind in the mantra Sister Pan had taught her. *A single flame in the dark. A single note hanging in an empty place. A single sparkle upon a wind-rippled lake.* Still nothing … no, nothing, except the faintest voice of the pouring water several twists and many yards back along her path. The sound came again. Metal on rock.

Snarling as if to drive away her fear with anger, Nona pressed on. Twenty yards on, the tunnel widened still further but the broad mud floor showed no sign of anyone's passing. The sounds came more frequently now, or Nona heard more than just the loudest of them. A pick on stone. Someone was digging, but the echoing passageway gave no clue to the direction.

Further on and the sounds faded. Nona retraced her steps and found a rocky gullet in the fissure wall, above her head height. The sounds were louder here. She undid the cord that bound her habit and tied one end to the lantern's carrying loop, the other to her ankle. She leapt, catching the edge of the higher tunnel, a thing no wider than a sewage pipe, and hauled herself up, the lantern swaying beneath her.

A minute later and she was inching along the tunnel on her belly. The crashes came so loud now that she cowled the lantern and moved ahead blind.

After what seemed a cold, wet age, in which she banged her head on the rock twice and scraped her knees raw, a whisper of light reached her amid the shouts of pick biting stone. She could see the end of the tunnel, glowing so faintly that only in the blind depths would it be noticed.

Mastering her breathing, Nona crawled to the edge, where some larger, newer tunnel had cut through the old one she was in. Down in the larger passage a lone figure in black was hacking at the wall, already nearly out of sight in the short cut they had made. Debris from the excavation littered the water-smoothed floor behind them. The work must have taken weeks.

Nona watched, fascinated, becoming aware as she did so of a new sensation. Until this point her mind had been filled with the pressing knowledge of the weight of stone above her and how long and narrow the return to the surface – if she could even remember all the twists and turns. But now something larger commanded her attention. Louder than the crash of the pick, heavier than the fathoms of rock. A fullness. An otherness. Something ancient and full of an energy that made her hands tremble and her skin burn.

The digger paused and turned to scoop up a leather bottle set on a rock at the mouth of the cut. She raised a hand, pushing sweat-soaked hair from her brow, and drank.

Yisht! Even as Nona named her in her mind the woman's

eyes swept towards the tunnel mouth. Nona shrank back, pressing herself into the rock, holding her breath. She waited for a moment, long enough for Yisht to return to drinking from her water bottle if she was going to, then started to reverse.

Going backwards through the tunnel, without the space to turn, pulling a smoking lantern whilst trying not to make a sound was not easy. The glow at the tunnel's end grew brighter: Yisht must be approaching! Nona scrambled backwards as fast as she could while still not making a clatter. If Yisht climbed up she might see or smell traces of Nona's lantern. How long then before a knife came flying through the air? And if not a thrown knife then Yisht herself. The woman had practically defeated the whole of Grey Class together. She could easily murder Nona down here and her body would lie undetected long after her bones had crumbled.

Nona's feet eventually found open air and she dangled over the edge before slithering down into the lower tunnel, jolting her chin badly on a protruding piece of rock. Moments later she was hurrying back towards the fissure, her lantern bleeding just enough light through its cowl to stop her knocking herself senseless. She raced on, chased by shadows, slipping and sweating, sure at every moment a hand would close upon her shoulder.

'Did you get them?'

'Yes,' Nona hissed back. 'Shhh!'

Clera rolled from her bed and crossed to Nona's. Ara slumped down in hers, yawning and stretching beneath her blanket. Hessa appeared to be fast asleep.

'Everything go all right?' Clera whispered close enough to Nona's ear to make it tingle.

'Yes, go back to bed.' She counted out the stolen ingredients into her clothes chest. Blackroot wrapped in linen, red garlic powder in a paper wrap, quicksilver in a greased leather pouch, aclite salts, and sulphur. The stores cave had been the next one along, large, easily accessed, the ingredients laid out on shelves in labelled bags, bunches, vials, and pots. If she hadn't been led astray by the mark of Yisht's shoe she would have been in and out in a quarter of the time.

'How are you feeling? I could stay with you?'

'I'm fine. Go to bed.'

'But you got everything? Even the quicksilver?'

'Yes.'

'Good.' Clera squeezed her arm, hesitated, then went back to her bed. 'You stink of mud by the way.'

Nona stripped off her habit and stuffed it beneath her bed. Cleaning it was a problem to be dealt with in daylight. She slipped beneath her blanket, the wool rough against her skinned knees, the darkness full of images of tunnel after tunnel, narrow rocky throats caught in the flicker of a flame, closing ever tighter around her. She turned on her side and coiled herself up, presenting as small a target as she could to the dark. On the nights since the forging it had been the pain she had curled around, the first and growing pangs of whatever poison it was that Raymel had got into her. Nothing swift of course – he would want to know that she suffered long and hard before she died. Sister Apple had told them plenty of horror stories about toxins that would do just that. Venoms that would rot the flesh from bones over the course of weeks, others that would cause first blindness, then peeling skin worse than any burn, and finally madness and death months later. Now she realized that apart from her knees, hands, arms and jaw … nothing hurt. Her head, her guts, and her joints, all of which had been in slow twisting agony, really were fine. She'd said she was fine to get Clera back to her own bed … but it was true … all she felt was that lingering sense of fullness that had invaded her when she spied on Yisht. A sensation she had felt only in one place, and never as strongly – before the black door into the Dome of the Ancestor at the far end of the nuns' cells.

Her last thought before sleep claimed her was to wonder whether Yisht had used the gate and whether she or Sister Apple would notice it had been left unlocked.

On the windswept promontory in the break between Blade class and the evening meal Nona, Ara, and Hessa clustered around a shallow depression, partly sheltered by low walls made by piling up rock Nona had shattered with Path-energy on one of her many secret practices.

The fire had proved a nightmare to light and their few stolen pieces of kindling had burned out before setting fire to the coals stolen from the kitchen store. In the end Nona and Ara sat shivering while Hessa sought the serenity needed to reach the Path herself and eventually set the coals burning with a measured release of Path-energy.

They started to brew the black cure using pots stolen from the kitchens – safer to steal these than try to filch the correct equipment from the Poisoner's stores. Lacking scales, Hessa weighed the ingredients using a measuring rule balanced at its midpoint on an eating knife. Hessa had a collection of pebbles that she had previously weighed in Shade class and claimed that by placing them at the correct distance from the rule's pivot point she could, with some arithmetic, measure any desired weight on the other side. In theory it seemed, at least to Hessa, easy. In the Corridor wind with awkward ingredients that wanted to blow or roll away and couldn't be heaped in one single spot on the wobbling rule … it appeared to Nona to be closer to guesswork than any science taught in Academia.

It took longer than anticipated. Relying on the wind to clear the dangerous fumes meant frequent hurried moves as the direction shifted.

'An ice-wind's coming,' Ara said.

'They might send us on the ranging if it lasts.' Nona tipped another silver drop of liquid metal into the black and stinking black mess simmering in the pan.

'Maybe.' Ara shuddered and hugged herself. The rangings almost always started during an ice-wind. Novices had gone missing on the journey before and been found days later frozen to the ground. Or not at all.

In the end all three of them missed the evening meal and returned to the convent in the dark, their habits reeking of blackroot, the ruined cooking pot abandoned over the cliff, the coals still glowing behind them, hidden in their hollow. Nona held the black cure in a tiny perfume vial that Ara had brought to the convent when she first arrived. When boiled down to a sludge and strained through a cloth, taking care not to let the liquid touch skin, there had been precious little to collect.

'You won't really take it? You know they call it the kill or cure, don't you?' Hessa asked, working to keep up with Nona and Ara. 'Even if I got the proportions right it's a terrible risk. Just tell the abbess what you did. She might be angry but she won't throw you out.'

'I'll think about it. I don't feel so bad today.' The pain, the sickness, all of it had gone overnight, but Nona hadn't the heart to tell the others after the risks they had taken for her. Besides, with an enemy who resorted to poison it never hurt to be prepared in advance. She had little doubt that Sister Apple and others among the Sisters of Discretion carried their own collections of small vials just in case – the black cure among them.

With stomachs rumbling they crept into the dormitory and changed their habits, Nona having to borrow an old one from Ara. The three tainted habits they wrapped in Nona's mud-smeared one from the previous night and took to the laundry. If any nun recognized the smell of blackroot and took a close look at the bundle they would find the entire litany of the girls' crimes written there. Fortunately blackroot was not a common ingredient and Sister Apple seemed never to be on laundry duty.

Nona walked behind Ara to the washroom, her sleeves flapping around her hands, but not as dwarfed by the Chosen One's clothes as she once would have been. It took the best part of an hour to pound the soiled garments clean in the wooden tubs and wring them through the mangle until they were dry enough to hang.

They worked in the dark, elbow-deep in cold water, backs aching despite all of Sister Tallow's training. A light might draw unwanted attention.

'I saw Yisht.' Nona spoke into the dark, her voice barely audible above the splashing.

'I did too, with Zole in Spirit class,' Ara replied. Sister Wheel allowed Yisht into the class, saying that everyone could do with more instruction in holy matters.

'I saw her in the caves.'

'What?' Ara's splashing stopped.

'I took a wrong turn and found her digging.'

'Digging?' Ara asked. 'Why? Where?'

'I think she's cutting a path to something under the dome – there's something hidden there, something powerful.'

'Blood and teeth, Nona! And you waited all day to tell me this … why?'

'Because if I'd said it when Clera was here half the convent would probably know by now.'

'Clera keeps secrets,' Ara said. 'Ones she wants to keep.'

'She…' Nona's denial petered out, the image of that strange throwing star flashed before her. She hadn't ever asked about it again, and Clera hadn't ever asked her about the true story of how she had ended up in Giljohn's cage. It seemed a fair exchange. 'She knows how to keep her own. Other people's she's not so good with.'

Ara snorted. 'So why didn't you tell us when we were out there brewing? That should have been private enough for you!'

'Hessa would have made me tell the abbess.'

'Damn Hessa! *I'm* making you tell the abbess!'

'Tell her that I broke into the undercaves planning to steal expensive convent-owned ingredients because I attacked the man she burned herself to protect me from after I attacked him the first time? For all we know Abbess Glass might have asked Yisht to dig her an access tunnel or given her permission to go prospecting in the caves. She might have opened that gate with a key.'

'She didn't though.'

'No. In fact I saw a new shaft leading up and I'm sure it's under the guest quarters. Yisht must have dug down from her room and set to exploring.'

'Well that's it then,' Ara said. 'She's as guilty as sin.'

'But the abbess would probably let her off. Whatever hold Sherzal has over her, it's a strong one!' Nona heaved a waterlogged habit out into the rinsing tub. 'We need to do something about her ourselves.'

'How? She'd kill us all in a fight!' Ara wrung out her habit on the twisting loom, her face just a handful of glimmers where light from the distant scriptorium filtered from the laundry windows.

'That one I'm still thinking about.' And Nona bent to her rinsing.

They emerged, with sore hands and wrinkled fingers, just in time to meet the rest of the junior novices coming from the cloisters for lights out at the dormitory.

Nona was at the rear of the group by the time they reached the building, slowed by the sickness that had been returning all day. She climbed the steps to the door one at a time. Three things happened together. A fragment of ice sliced past her face, the beginning of a sharp cry rang out, and Ara's foot hammered into Nona's side. The impact was enough to send both girls flying in opposite directions. Before either novice hit the ground a chunk of rotten ice bigger than Nona's head struck the spot in which she'd been standing. The explosion of shards peppered them both.

'Ancestor!' Ara gasped. 'That was close!'

Nona lay on her back lacking the breath to reply, her gaze on the icicle-fringed edge of roof far above. Had there been a shadow there? Just for an instant? Or perhaps tired eyes and strained imagination put it there.

Nona and Ara picked themselves up, got under the door arch, and brushed each other down.

'What a day.' Ara led the way in.

Nona went to her bed, wrapped in thought. Had Yisht just tried to kill her? Did the woman suspect she'd been spied on in the caves? If so, it must be only suspicion or surely she would have taken more direct action…

She flopped down, exhausted and hungry, pushing Yisht from her mind. A whole day gone and not a moment of practice for the Academy visit. Except for Hessa of course, who hardly needed it. Nona could see the Academy school as she'd seen it in Hessa's memories, all grandeur and gravitas set in stone, with the emperor's Academics lined up, waiting to be impressed. And she saw herself before them, one small novice in a habit still damp and smelling faintly of blackroot who could, if she worked herself up into a frothing rage, shatter a few of their expensive flagstones.

34

On six-day the ice-wind blew again in earnest, for the first time since Zole's arrival. In the fire-scorched practice pit where they had brewed the black cure Nona crouched, trying to find the rage she needed to reach the Path. It proved hard to find the heat she required, held there in the wind's frozen teeth. Before her, away across the plateau, the convent huddled under a bleak sky like a beast marked for the slaughterhouse. At last, she abandoned her attempt and raced off towards the Academia Tower, hoping not to be late for the class.

It turned out that she was first, clattering up the stairs into a classroom occupied only by Sister Rule.

'Good morning, novice.' Sister Rule glanced up from behind the desk where she tended to settle her bulk and remain for the duration of any lesson, using her yardstick to point to the headings set out in chalk upon the board to her side.

'Good morning, Mistress Academia.' Nona found her seat at the back of the class.

'Brisk out, is it?'

'Yes, Mistress Academia.' The curved sheet of ice that had formed across the side of Nona's head chose that moment to fall away and shatter on the floor.

Hessa stumped in a moment later, looking surprised not to be the first.

'What's the convent's most valuable treasure?' Nona

surprised herself by asking but Sister Rule always took kindly to questions and asking had become a habit.

'The shipheart.' No hesitation.

'And it's stored below Heart Hall?'

'Yes indeed.' Sister Rule closed the book she had been reading from and narrowed her eyes at Nona. 'Planning on stealing it?' She maintained the stare long enough for Nona to think she might be serious, then laughed.

The rest of Grey Class came in more or less together, Ara looking tired, Clera slumping dramatically over her desk, Jula setting her quill, scroll, and slate out with her usual precision, Darla hulking over her work and managing to spatter ink as she opened the pot. Head-girl Mally at the front. Alata and Leeni side by side, each finding the other's fingers beneath the desk with accurate devotion. Zole took her customary seat at the middle of the room, looking serene, as if she never left the trance.

'Today.' Sister Rule slapped her yardstick down. 'We will discuss the ice.'

The faintest of frowns creased Zole's brow.

'In Red Class we discussed the thickness of the ice, its advance, both historically and contemporaneously. And the cause – the waning of our own dying sun. Today we will address the peoples who make it their home.' She turned her head towards Zole and gave a friendly smile. 'Which is something Novice Zole knows far more about than anyone in the room. So perhaps she would like to tell us something of the ice-tribes?'

'No.' Zole's lips barely moved but the word came out loud and clear.

Sister Rule pressed her own lips into a flat line that managed to convey surprise, amusement, and disapproval all at the same time. 'And why might that be, novice?'

'The ice must be experienced. You have no words in your books that capture it. Journeying the ice is the price for such knowledge.'

'Well…' Sister Rule rapped her yardstick against the desk. 'We have our first observation – the tribes of the deep ice have their own codes of behaviour which can be quite at odds with our own. You would have to travel hundreds of miles east to Scithrowl or west across the sea to Durn to experience significant cultural differences in the Corridor, but a journey of less than thirty miles to the north or south will set you face to face with peoples whose ways are more alien to ours than those of any Durnishman.' She looked around the class. 'I'm sure you've been curious about your new companion and her guardian. Ask me some worthwhile questions and I'll share what…' her eyes flicked towards Zole '…meagre information I have.'

'What do they eat?' Nona's hand shot up but she'd already blurted out the question.

'Good!' Sister Rule banged the desk. 'To the heart of the matter. They eat fish.'

'But how? The ice is miles thick!' Nona had seen the walls of the Corridor and even there just behind the margins the ice lay hundreds of yards deep.

'It is.' Sister Rule reached for the glittering white globe on her desk with its belt of colour almost vanishingly thin, kept clear by the passing heat of the focus moon. 'But there are places above the ocean where the sea lies open, the ice melted by warmer water upwelling from the ocean depths. In some cases the sea is accessible year round. Further north and south, where seasons rule, the ice only clears in high summer. In all cases the open water is limited to patches no more than a mile across but thick with ocean life. The ice-tribes either centre their existence on a permanent spot or range nomadically with the seasons from one temporary oasis to the next. In their travels they explore tunnel systems wherever they are to be found, looking for routes to the bedrock and any of the under-cities abandoned by the Missing.'

Nona's thoughts wandered to the stories her father told about the ice tunnels. The memories of him telling her had escaped, leaving just an impression of being bounced upon his knee, awed by the strangeness of his tales. The stories themselves she knew from her mother's retelling of them when she was still very young.

She watched the class with eyes that saw nothing except dark, glistening tunnels worming their way ever deeper, filled with old night and new possibility. When Bray sounded and shook her from her adventures Nona was startled to find that the whole session had passed and all around her girls were rising from their chairs.

In Blade after lunch they practised with throwing stars. The novices spent the best part of two hours aiming at target boards. Sister Tallow had set up a dozen of the seven-foot boards on which man-shapes had been drawn in sufficient anatomical detail to amuse girls. The first four boards she placed just three yards in front of the throwing line, the next four six yards further back, the last another six yards out.

'If you wish to hit an opponent further away than that you really should have brought a bow with you. Throwing stars are less encumbering and less obvious, ideal for urban situations and use inside buildings. The price paid is that they are less accurate and do less harm.' Sister Tallow paced behind the ranks of novices lined for their turn to throw.

They threw until their arms grew tired and their hands bled from a dozen small nicks. Then they threw some more.

'You think this is difficult?' Sister Tallow continued her pacing, pausing here and there to correct the position or action of a novice. 'You'll be lucky if you ever get a real target standing still and facing you. Aim for the eyes. Anywhere on the head gives you a decent chance of a hit that will take the fight out of someone, but the eye – now that's a guaranteed stop for anyone.'

Next to Nona, Ruli, who had proved annoyingly good with the throwing star since their first lesson, cracked her arm out and with a flip of her wrist put one into the eye of the nearest target, the point bedded in the black pupil.

'Show-off,' Clera said to her right. The target before Clera had three of her stars studding it, one in the forehead, one near the ribs and a third hanging about a foot from the man's neck, having missed completely. 'Do it again.'

Ruli sent another star spinning from her fingers, putting a point into the pupil of her target's other eye.

'That's not even fair! You can't judge where the point will land!' Clera flung her next star and nearly missed the board entirely.

Ruli shrugged. 'If the target were any closer and I had a spear I could practically lean forward and poke it.'

Nona threw her four stars in quick succession. All four thunked home in the head, two into the eyes.

At the end of the line Darla took her last throw and all four of them moved up to retrieve their stars before the next rank had their turn.

'You didn't get the pupils,' Clera said, still raging over Ruli's feat.

'When a sharp piece of metal hits you in the eye you're going to have a really bad day whichever part it strikes.' Nona shrugged.

'Keep telling yourself that.' Ruli grinned. 'One day you'll meet an enemy with *really* tiny eyes and you'll wish you had me with you!'

In the bathhouse after Blade Nona hung in the hot water while the class splashed and chattered around her or sat on the pool's edge recovering in the steams. She put her head back, floating, embraced by heat, nothing but whiteness above her, the steam's slow swirl echoing in her mind. Tomorrow the Academy would show off its students before Sister Pan and some grand audience. Hessa would show them the subtleties of thread-work in return, and Ara the channelled power of the Path gathered over as many as three or even four steps and released in controlled bursts of destruction. And Nona … the peasant girl from the Grey … the would-be murderer spirited from beneath a descending death sentence … what had she got to show them that they wouldn't smirk behind their hands at?

And when she came back she would still be poisoned, still face the dilemma of whether to confess her attack on Raymel or risk the black cure in an attempt to solve her own problems. And on top of all that. Or rather, beneath it, there was Yisht, burrowing into something secret like a worm at the convent's heart.

Nona signed and realized that sometimes even a hot bath couldn't help.

The convent hired a cart to take Sister Pan and the three novices to the Academy. The rest of the class saw them off outside Path Tower. The girls, with the exception of Zole, clustered around, variously slapping shoulders or swapping hugs, dependent on their nature.

'Make us proud!' Darla sent Nona staggering with a semi-affectionate shove.

'Show those Academy brats something new!' Clera mimed an explosion.

'Ancestor watch over you.' Jula smiled and held Nona's hands in a brief clasp.

'Be careful!' Ruli hugged her.

'Don't lose.' Alata with a warning look.

Ara and Nona helped Hessa up into the cart.

'You're lucky,' Clera said, leaning in as Sister Pan took her place beside the driver. 'The church seems to think nuns should walk everywhere. Seriously. Even Sister Cloud didn't get a horse! If Hessa wasn't a hop-along and Pan wasn't a hundred and nine you'd be walking to the Academy.'

The driver twitched his whip over the two horses and the cart lurched into motion. Nona clutched the side and remembered Giljohn's cart. Another journey beginning...

The cart rattled on along the track that led around the back of the piggeries and 'the chicken house' a long hall far too grand for its current purpose. To the track's left the cliff edge lay just yards away over bare rock. Clera claimed a novice's prank had once startled the supply wagon horse and sent it back down to the plains below by the most direct route, along with the supply wagon and the driver. Fortunately on this occasion no such prankster came forward and the cart survived to thread a path through the stone forest. Nona lay back to watch the pillars reaching for the sky as the driver wove his way around them. Even Sister Rule had no idea who had set them there. No book in the library spoke of it. As they broke clear Nona wondered how long the ripples she left behind would last before they faded and Abeth forgot her. Even if she built a thousand stone pillars taller and thicker than the biggest trees, the world would roll on and remember her no better than it did the mysterious founders of the stone forest.

'I know what you're thinking.' Hessa shifted across to join Nona watching the pillars retreat into the distance.

'You do not.'

'I don't think there's enough time left for us to be forgotten. Not if we do extraordinary things. If we burn bright enough we'll be remembered until the moon falls and the Corridor closes.'

'That's not so bad then.'

'It will be if we're still alive to see it!'

Sister Pan eyed them darkly. 'It is never a good idea for two novices to become thread-bound. That experiment of yours was ill-advised, Novice Hessa, even if you didn't know that Novice Nona had the blood.' She rubbed absently at her stump. 'And now you share idle thoughts as well as dreams and pain… The lives of any so closely bound tend to become mirrors of each other, their rhythms coming into time until there are no coincidences, only a sharing in the patterns of crisis and peace.'

Hessa looked down, ashamed. Nona reached out a hand to her shoulder, tentative. 'It doesn't sound so bad. If we stick together it just means we'll share our troubles.'

The cart took the Vinery Stair, a longer descent to the plains but less treacherous than the Seren Way, and despite its name, stairless. Once clear of the plateau they curved back past the convent vineyards nestled in the arms of the cliffs, and took the Rutland Road into Verity.

The grand gates of the city stood open, with as many people seeming to have urgent business inside as had urgent business in the world beyond, leading to a great press of humanity, many employing elbows and whips to forge a path, and all of them shouting.

Nona sat hunched about her knees as the cart inched through.

'I'd forgotten the smell,' Hessa said. She'd been the only member of Grey Class not to come to watch the forging at the Caltess.

Ara wrinkled her nose, watching the crowd with fascination. 'You should come down on a holy-day! There's so much to…' She trailed off, remembering that while she was trapped on the rock by Sherzal's avarice Hessa was trapped by her leg just as effectively. 'Sorry.'

The abbess kept Ara in the convent at her uncle's request, the Jotsis lord still concerned that Sherzal planned to abduct his niece. Practically all of Ara's anger at Zole could be laid at the feet of this fact that loomed over every seven-day. Ara literally ached for Verity. Shopping, she said, was the greatest of pleasures. Nona, having never purchased anything or owned money, had no opinion on the matter, but judging by the street stalls jammed along the high street leading from the gates, it seemed to be one of the more popular contact sports in the city.

Once past the gate the crush eased and within a hundred yards they were moving at walking pace along the broad, cobbled street. To either side grand-looking establishments towered to three and four storeys, restaurants below, guest rooms above. Blacksmiths, wheelwrights, leatherworkers, saddle-makers, tack shops, and all manner of hostelries crowded the side roads. Later the high street gave over to tailors and jewellers, silversmiths and goldsmiths, with luxurious apartments above, occasionally with one of their balconies occupied by some wealthy tenant sipping wine and watching the world go by, literally beneath their attention.

The colours fascinated Nona's eye. In the convent everything was grey or black or the faint yellow-green of limestone. When a Red Sister wore her official habit it was a vivid splash on an otherwise dull palette. In Verity's crowds a Red Sister would scarcely give the eye pause as it swept across the scene.

The driver turned at a main junction and carried on up a gentle gradient into areas given over to private homes. Nona began to get a sense of having already visited the streets they were passing. She turned to see Hessa glancing her way. Hessa looked suddenly very young, her bony body too small for her habit, her face so thin and angular that she might pass as one of the forest nixies that Nana Even used to tell stories about. The sun, still low in the eastern sky, made something ethereal of the wispy curls of her blonde hair, turning it into a kind of halo. It seemed for a moment that Hessa hadn't changed from their journey with Giljohn years ago, not even a little bit.

'My memories.' Hessa leaned forward, steadying herself against the cart's swaying with one hand and touching Nona's arm with the other. 'You're remembering my memories.'

A shadow passed over them and Nona looked up to see a tall brick tower with a great bell hanging above it, open to the elements. She'd seen it before. But with different eyes. By the time they drew near to the Academy Nona could have instructed the driver where to turn left and where to turn right.

They drove around the great hall where Hessa and the others had been tested, past a range of other school buildings, and across a great paved courtyard. A squad of soldiers passed in front of them, twenty men in chain armour, spears across their shoulders, their tunics gold and green, the device across their chests a great tree, black against a red sun rising.

'The emperor's troops,' said Sister Pan. 'And those, novices, are the walls of the emperor's palace.' Sister Pan gestured with her stump to the broad curtain wall stretching in both directions off into the distance. A round keep rose just behind the wall, as sturdy a fortress as Nona could imagine, looking as if it belonged to a different age where giants had built it out of vast blocks of bedrock. Seeming small in the shadow of the wall, but still every bit as large as the Caltess, and far grander, lay another hall. 'And that, poking above the emperor's wall, is the Ark-Keep. And the building we're aimed at is Academy Hall. All these buildings are the Academy, but that hall's the heart of it.'

'Why is it up against the emperor's wall, like that?' Nona asked. It looked strange, as if the emperor and Academy had been arguing over some disputed boundary.

'To be as close to the Ark as possible.' Sister Pan waved

her hand in the air as if trying to collect something from the empty space before her. 'Can you feel it?'

Nona could, though the sensation had crept up on her so slowly that it had passed beneath her notice. The same fullness, the same sense of sleeping power laced the air here as laced the air towards the back of the Dome of the Ancestor. It pulsed with a slow rhythm. 'It's the same … like in the convent.'

Sister Pan gave her a sharp look then glanced to the others. 'Hessa? Arabella? Can you feel it?'

Both shook their heads, looking puzzled.

'Very few can,' Sister Pan said. 'Even among the quantal.' She turned her pale eyes back on Nona. 'It's the same aura that the shipheart has, only stronger, and richer.'

'But…' It was Nona's turn to frown. 'The shipheart is beneath Heart Hall and—'

Sister Pan held her hand up, silencing Nona. 'The shipheart is beneath Heart Hall. Yes. And Academy Hall is positioned as close to the Ark as possible, allowing the Academics to work greater magics here than anywhere else within the empire.

'Without our shipheart Sweet Mercy would be like any other convent. Its presence makes it a hundred times easier to train Mystic Sisters or to let those with a touch of marjal learn shadow-work. The shipheart doesn't just keep us warm. It's the heart of our community. A gift from the Ancestor.' She pointed to the palace walls rising above the Academy's roofs. 'The Ark is the same, but different. Stronger still. In fact you would have to follow the Corridor for many thousands of miles to find an equal to the magics worked here – to one of the other two Arks still said to stand free of the ice.'

'How many are beneath the ice?' Hessa asked.

Sister Pan pursed her lips. 'Who knows for sure? Lost is lost. The old books differ in their opinions. *Palimpest* holds the highest figure and claims one thousand and twenty-four.'

Nona's eyes widened at that. Nations fought for control of the Ark. Emperors murdered their fathers and their sons. A thousand and twenty-four was a vast number.

'Consider, though,' Sister Pan continued. 'Spread evenly across the ice-free face of Abeth that would still put five hundred miles between any one of them and the next. However many there are, they are rare. Rarer even than shiphearts.'

'Shiphearts? I thought there was only one!'

Sister Pan smiled. 'Each ship that bore the tribes to Abeth had a shipheart at the core of its engines. Our forebears did not come here in a single ship. Even if each of the races came in a single ship that would be four shiphearts. I believe Sister Rule has seen texts in Orison that suggest there were a host of ships.'

'A host!' Nona tried to imagine them sailing the blackness between the stars.

'A host.' Sister Pan nodded. 'Though I know of fewer than half a dozen shiphearts in all of the empire, and that number would not double even if you were to scour Durn and Scithrowl too.'

The cart drew to a halt before the wide and many-pillared portico of Academy Hall. The emperor's own soldiers stood to attention on the steps behind the pillars, and behind them great doors of dark bronze, each set with a dozen polished bosses the size of shields.

Sister Pan told the driver to wait and escorted Nona, Ara, and Hessa up the marble steps. At the great doors Sister Pan steered them towards a smaller single door set into the leftmost of the pair. A rap of her hand saw the smaller door swing open and Sister Pan led through into a foyer every piece as grand as that of the Ancestor's dome up on the Rock of Faith.

Nona let her gaze wander up the height of the surrounding columns and winced. The nausea that had plagued her periodically since her return from the Caltess twisted in her gut once more, not so sharp as before, but a warning echo.

'I know what Yisht is after,' Nona hissed the words to Ara as a tall, black-clad Academic led Sister Pan and the novices deeper into the building. 'She's trying to steal the shipheart!'

'But you said she was digging under the dome!' Ara hissed back. 'And the shipheart is under Heart Hall.'

'It's under the dome!' Nona insisted. She'd felt it, but not known what it was. The story about Heart Hall must be a deliberate misdirection in case anyone came hoping to steal it.

'What?' Ara stopped in the corridor. The doors all along it opened onto Academics' offices.

'She's right,' said Hessa, altering course to walk around the pair of them.

'What?' Nona and Ara together.

'How do you know?' Nona demanded. 'You said you couldn't feel it!'

'I don't have to.' Hessa rounded them and carried on after Sister Pan. 'You just follow the hot pipes back to where they came from. And it's not Heart Hall!'

35

The Academic brought them at last to a large chamber cutting up through all four layers of the Hall to a many-windowed dome in the main roof. Galleries surrounded the perimeter at every level and scores of Academics or Academy staff stood watching, some leaning on the stone balustrades, others speaking together in small groups. Some more elderly individuals had had high-backed chairs brought out of their offices and positioned for a good view.

Nona found herself sweating, clutching her belly with one hand. It seemed as if whatever poison Raymel had got into her had merely gone into hiding and for some reason now chose to seep back into her blood.

The chamber itself held no furniture other than a long oak table at the back with a dozen chairs behind it, and eight plain wooden stools against the opposite wall. Four Academics and a priest of the Ancestor sat behind the table in robes of various colours, each a single shade. Sister Pan went to take her place behind the table and the black-robed Academic left the way he had led them.

One of the Academics in particular drew Nona's eye. A sky-blue robe covered his painful thinness, though the ridging of his spine could be seen in the length of his neck, and the small head atop it held a skull's grin. He watched her, eyes pale and without expression. She had seen him before: at the Caltess beside Raymel Tacsis. Perhaps the Academic's magic had saved her enemy's life, or maybe it had been the demons hiding beneath the gerant's skin. Had it been the Academic who poisoned her in the moment she tried to take Raymel's life? Was he here today under Tacsis orders to finish the job? Nona froze, feeling the jaws of a trap around her. She could tell Sister Pan, but what offence would the Academy take? Besides, the nun would just repeat the abbess, reminding her what Thuran Tacsis had pledged to the emperor himself. That the matter was closed. Nona ground her teeth as the nausea rose again.

The oldest of the Academics got to his feet, a white-haired man whose skin looked to have been terribly burned long ago and whose eyes held a milky blindness. 'We welcome the last of our guests – Sister Pan of Sweet Mercy Convent, and three novices of an age with our year three students.' He paused as a polite smattering of applause ran its course through the galleries above. 'My apologies, Mistress Path, but time presses. If you are prepared we will commence immediately.' He gestured to the stools beside the door and Sister Pan motioned for the novices to sit.

Five of the eight stools were occupied. Three Academy students sat in grey tunics, an intense blonde girl closest, then Chara and Willum. Chara looked as severe as Nona remembered her, black hair cropped so close to her skull you could see the darkness of her skin beneath. Willum seemed perhaps a touch less nondescript than he had been, two years leaving his chin more defined and his eyes brighter. Two novices in the brown robes of the Ancestor brotherhood occupied the last two stools: a large sandy-haired boy with red cheeks, and Markus, offering a twitch of a smile. Nona staggered to a free stool without waiting for permission and fell onto it, setting her back to the wall. Hessa settled beside her.

The Academic cleared his throat. 'We will begin with…' He bent to set his ear by the mouth of the angular woman seated to his right. 'With Novice Hessa and Proxim Chara.' He clapped his hands.

Sister Pan got to her feet with a sigh and walked across to a door in the left wall, beckoning Hessa. The Academic seated to the right got up and accompanied Chara through a door in the right-hand wall. Sister Pan had promised to explain what would be expected of each of them before the bouts, and Nona supposed that this was it. Her own chances of doing anything more than collapsing seemed remote.

While both Hessa and Chara were ensconced in the side rooms the black-robed Academic returned to set an iron basket of burning coals midway between the two doors. He retreated and a minute or so later a gong struck.

'Chara's a fire-worker then.' Markus, two places along from Nona. She turned to look at him, managing to echo his nervous smile through her pain. 'Students need an easy source.'

The gong sounded again and both doors opened to reveal the contestants. Chara hurried across to the coal basket and hunched over it, so close that Nona thought her hair must be sizzling. Hessa limped out on her crutch, frowning in concentration as she stared at Chara. Nona had expected Hessa to emerge deep in serenity. Hessa might not be able to manage a step unaided in the common world but on the Path she had more nimble feet than Ara, and both of them far outdid Nona, who was still unable to make more than glancing contact.

'What's she doing?' Nona's pain made the words a gasp.

'Thread-work,' Ara said.

Chara stood and the fire was in her eyes. She shaped her hands and flames flared among the coals, not dying back but coiling and rising until they became a serpent that wrapped around her. Somehow the snake's heat failed to reach Chara, her skin remaining unblistered, her tunic not even singed. But Nona's pain built from bad to worse, ringing through her bones. She hunted the inner pockets of her habit with fingers curled around her distress. After an ecstasy of fumbling she brought out the vial containing the black cure.

'Concede, novice?' Chara asked, her scorn evident. She raised an arm towards Hessa, the serpent coiling along it, raising its head to strike.

Hessa's frown smoothed away as if she had in that moment solved a puzzle. 'There's a thread that binds your fire to the coals.' While she spoke her hand moved, finger and thumb pinched together as if tugging on some invisible string. She stood there, her fingers working, the wisps of her hair lifted on a breeze that wasn't there.

'What?' Chara's turn to frown. Faster than it rose, the serpent spiralled back down her arm, back around her body, back into the fire-basket.

'They're still bound together,' Hessa said.

Chara curled her lips, raised both hands in fists. Once again flames guttered up from the glowing coals, less fiercely than before, reaching for her tentatively.

'And all the parts of the coal are still connected…' There was wonder in Hessa's voice, as if the proximity of the Ark were revealing in astonishing detail something she had only glimpsed before. 'So many…' She leaned on her crutch and raised both hands, cupped, fingers parted, as if sieving strands from the air. The flames above the fire-basket sucked back into the glowing coals, smoke swirled, faster than was natural, and downwards, gathering itself from the heights above. And in the space of moments, despite Chara's snarling resistance, the glow faded, the coals darkened, the fire vanished as if it had never been.

Chara fell to the floor, gasping, as though she had been holding her breath all this time and only now could breathe. Hessa stumped forward to offer a hand up, a genuine smile on her face. 'Thank you for the lessons, proxim.'

Chara shrugged her off and returned scowling to her seat. Hessa returned to sit between Ara and Nona. Behind the table the Academics set to a whispered discussion and in the galleries above onlookers murmured their own observations to each other.

'Sister Pan tells you what to expect,' Hessa said. 'We're matched so that we don't end up hurting each other.'

Nona sat as still as she could, the black cure held so tight in her knotted fist that she feared the flask might break. 'What was Chara doing?' she gasped past gritted teeth, wanting to distract herself.

'A lot of marjals work the elements. Air most commonly. It's easiest with something light. Then fire. Water is rarer. Earth very rare.' Hessa frowned. 'Do you think she didn't remember me? She looked like she didn't know me… Are you all right, Nona? You look terrible.'

Nona waved the questions away. 'How do you know this stuff? Sister Pan never taught us that. Did she?'

Hessa shrugged. 'She covered some of it before you joined Red Class. Most of it I read in the library while you lot were punching and kicking each other.'

The senior Academic took to his feet again. 'The next pairing is Novice Arabella and Proxim Willum.'

As before, Sister Pan went into one room with Ara, and an Academic took Willum into the opposite room. The fire-basket was removed and nothing put in its place. The two contestants emerged at the sound of the gong, Ara golden and glorious, Willum pasty and nervous. His student tunic had been replaced by a long-sleeved robe reaching to his feet and set all about with sigils stitched in gold thread. It looked to weigh as much as he did.

'Like the ones in Path Tower,' Hessa said. 'Sigils of negation, specific to the Path.' She squinted. 'And some more general ones. All negation, though.'

The two stepped closer. Nothing happened. They faced each other, Ara's lips twitching with the echoes of her serenity mantra, Willum ignoring her, staring at his fists, clenched before him.

'Ah.' The gasp escaped as Nona's pain flared. She raised the cure to her lips, her arm responding jerkily to her demands.

'Nona!' Hessa hissed, reaching out to stop her. 'Are you mad?'

'P-poisoned!'

'Ask for help then! We're in the Academy. There are more marjal blood-workers here than in the rest of empire put together!'

'W-what's he doing?' Nona nodded towards Willum to distract Hessa. She wasn't going to put herself in the hands of the Academics. The man sitting behind the table opposite was probably the one who had armoured Raymel against her blades. What other favours might he be prepared to do for the Tacsis?

'He's building a wall,' Hessa said, not looking away. 'An invisible wall. There are faults in … everything … flaws in the stuff of the world, places where the Path has slipped and left a defect. Willum is rotating them and gathering them into a wall. They say it feels like glass if you touch it. It's a rare talent. His wall is static but they say grandmasters can make mobile walls. The Durn-mage was said to have a flaw-sword, an invisible blade that would cut through any steel raised against him!' Hessa put her hand out to cover Nona's, keeping the vial from her mouth. 'Don't!'

'I need to. I—' But as Nona spoke the edge of her agony dulled and her rigid muscles released her to slump forward, retching acid onto the floor.

'He's finished.'

Nona straightened, ignoring the disgusted look from the student to her left. Willum stood waiting. If he'd built any kind of wall she couldn't see it. Minutes passed while Ara settled into her trance, Nona's pain retreating to a dull ache and sharp nausea. She wanted to be back in the tunnels beneath the convent – both to see how close Yisht was to the shipheart, and to seek a repeat of the relief it had given her the last time she had felt so ill.

Finally Ara spoke, her voice deep and resonant. 'You're prepared?'

Willum nodded, wetting his lips.

Nona felt the echoes of Ara's footfalls as she walked the Path. *One. Two. Three. Four.* Ara had never walked so far. Perhaps in the presence of the Ark even Nona could manage a second step. *Five.*

Ara returned, jolting into her body, her hair flying up into a golden cloud about her head. The energies of the Path wrapped her in bright potential, shuddering through her flesh. Nona thought it would be too much for her but Ara swept the power forward and sent it lancing towards Willum in a jagged blaze that looked like lightning might if it were set on fire.

Ara's attack struck Willum's wall a yard from where he stood in a detonation that shook the room. Nona caught a brief impression of white-hot energy flattening out and spilling around a half-dome shape, just a faint echo of it penetrating to strike the student's chest where the gold-worked sigils absorbed it as if they were holes into some other place.

A light round of applause went around the galleries. Willum gave a hesitant bow and retreated to the room he'd come from.

'What? Did he win?' Nona asked.

'No. Ara did. Willum would have been injured if he hadn't been wearing a sigil-robe – and they're worth more than most lords' estates, so not part of the standard Academic's wardrobe. But it was impressive that he could stop so much of such a powerful blast. It's not as if Ara would be able to do another in a hurry.'

The Academics set to their discussions again, the senior man putting questions to Sister Pan in quick succession. Nona leaned forward to look at Markus. He'd grown into his looks over the past two years, or perhaps he'd always been striking and she hadn't noticed. Handsome, but not in the Raymel Tacsis mould, where the arrogance made something ugly of even features and a square jaw.

'What can you do?' she asked him.

'I'm an empath.'

'What does that mean?'

'Well … I can make you laugh.'

'You can't!'

He pulled a face, tongue out to the side, eyes crossed. A laugh burst from her, causing the discussion at the end of the hall to miss a beat.

'That's cheating,' she hissed.

'Isn't that what magic is?' He grinned. 'But I can. I could reach into your head and make you laugh … or cry. Or if we're pitted against each other I could make you surrender.'

'I don't know about the laughing or crying but you couldn't make me surrender.'

'Well. I'd give it a good try.' Markus smiled, without heat.

'It wouldn't work. Giving up is not something I do. You do remember me, don't you?' But as she said it Nona wondered what he might remember of her. She remembered him as a serious, competitive boy, a boy she saw few signs of there in the Academics' hall. Two years at the monastery had changed him, or perhaps it had been his power that changed him. Perhaps you couldn't reach into people's heads without part of them reaching back and shaping you too.

'...Novice Nona and Proxim Luta.' The senior Academic had gained his feet while Nona's thoughts had been elsewhere.

The third student stood from her stool, a tall girl with fair hair that hung across half her face. The visible eye was dark and hostile above a cheekbone that looked sharp enough to draw blood.

Nona followed Sister Pan into the preparation room. Her nausea subsided as she entered. She stood puzzled but relieved, gazing at the paintings hung around the walls while Sister Pan closed the door. Academics in black robes looked down at her on every side, their painted faces uniformly severe.

'Your opponent is a shadow-weaver, Nona.'

'She's going to hide and jump out on me?' Nona frowned. 'Can I hit her?'

'No!' Sister Pan stamped her foot. 'No hitting!' She pushed her chin forward. 'Or kicking, or biting, or head butting, or any other damn thing that Sister Tallow taught you. This is Path.'

'But I can hardly touch the Path. And how's that going to help against shadows? Can I blast her?'

'I don't think you can, Nona, no. But if you suddenly develop the facility – and stranger things have happened this close to the Ark – she will be wearing the sigil-robe and yes, you can blast her. It would be remiss of me not to add that the robe is rated up to ten steps. More than that and you risk putting a hole through an Academy student. Which would be a bad thing.'

'So ... what can I use? Harsh language?' Nona frowned. 'And what can she do to me?'

'Shadow-work is deeper than what Sister Apple has yet shown you. Concealment is the least of such manipulation. A shadow-worker learns to call fear. Others may be able to bleed the darkness into you. Blindness is the easiest harm to inflict but a whole limb may turn traitor if infected with shadow.'

'You're sure I can't just kick her in the face before she starts?'

'You, Nona, will find your serenity, and in its armour be safe from all such attacks.'

'Even the infection thing?'

'Yes.'

'And that's all there is? Serenity beats shadows?'

Sister Pan chewed at the inside of her cheek for a moment. 'A render can use their own shadow to attack. It can tear flesh and there's no physical defence. Clever thread-work can defeat such malice. Or you can just put a hole through the shadow-worker. But rending is a rare skill and in the unlikely event that young Luta possesses such power she will even now be getting told by Academic Untust not to employ it against you, just as I am telling you not to punch the poor girl.'

Nona thought of the audience waiting for her out there. All those stern-faced and serious Academics, their minds filled with the intricacies of marjal enchantment. She felt nervous enough here under the painted stares of the audience on the wall…

'I don't think I can … I'm bad at serenity even back in the convent, with friends. Here … with all those strangers…'

'It's a performance, Nona.' Sister Pan smiled. 'You're a warrior. You might have the Path running in your veins but we both know at heart you're a fighter. And what is a fight if not a performance?' She paused and raised her hand, theatrical. '*Every star, turning in the black depth of heaven, burns for no better reason than that humanity raised its face to look.* Every great deed needs to be witnessed. Go out there and do something great.'

'So…' Nona glanced around at the painted disapproval all across the walls. 'Serene…' She started to run the words of the moon-song through her head.

She's falling down, she's falling down,
The moon, the m—

Sister Pan returned to the door. 'She's going to work fast. So find your serenity faster.'

'You're not helping!'

'The world seldom does, girl.'

36

Nona stepped out into the hall. Luta emerged from the door opposite a moment later, pale behind the pale fall of her hair, her stare intense.

She's falling down, she's falling down,
Soon, soon,

Luta looked around. The hall was well lit by the windows in the dome high above them but shadows lay about the base of the east wall, shallow but there. Darker shadows lay beneath the Academics' table to which Sister Pan was retreating.

The ice will come, the ice will close,
No moon, no moon,

Luta walked to the east wall and where she walked along it the shadows grew thinner, gathering instead about her like a gown of grey mist. Nona ground her teeth as the pain and sickness rose together. She glanced at the blue-robed Academic. Was it him? Toying with her somehow on Raymel's orders?

We'll all fall down, we'll all fall down,
Soon, too soon.

Nona didn't feel serene. She felt like vomiting. She felt like rolling on the floor, writhing to find some relief. She felt like rushing across and felling the girl with a blow to the neck.

Luta passed by the judges' table, muttering her own enchantments. Where once her shadow upon the floor had been slim and comprehensible it had now become a many-angled thing, dark corners moving here, there the legs or back of a chair reaching out like the spindly feelers of some great black insect. The agony flared in Nona's bones but somehow failed to sink its teeth into her.

She's falling down, she's falling down,
Soon, soon.

Nona envisioned serenity as a thick white coat, the fur of the white bear, soft, enfolding, deadening the harshness of the world, taking the sting from any barb. She drew the coat about her shoulders. Her pain became a distant thing that belonged to someone else. An object of curiosity, little more. She didn't allow herself to think about how long it would stay remote.

The shadows around Luta swirled, shapes glimpsed within, ambiguous, allowing every disturbing projection Nona could imagine. Her nightmares lay there, feeding on what she gave them. It was a darkness in which Raymel Tacsis hulked in the background while to the fore a broken Four-Foot fell, tried to rise, and fell again.

Luta raised her arms and the shadows streamed forth, spiralling around Nona, touching her skin with cold, feathery caresses. The fear rose from within her, not from without. The terror she had known on the track through the Rellam Forest, with darkness nipping at her heels and the trees whispering on every side. The fear of drowning in the Glasswater, and of dead girls' bones fathoms deep in the black mud below. The fear of failing. The fear of her truths, of being revealed as a monster; and the end of friendships.

Perhaps without the enfolding serenity to blunt the attack Nona might have run or fallen to the floor, curled foetal around her terror. Perhaps. But Nona didn't think so, not beneath the dome, under the gaze of so many strangers. On a moon-dark night in some lonely quarter … very likely.

The shadows wrapped her close, an irregular tiling of her flesh in shades of grey. She felt it like cold and dirty water, trying to sink beneath her skin, but just like water it ran off.

'Is that all you've got?' Nona spoke past gritted teeth, her pain still huge but distant.

Luta slumped with just her own shadow pooled about her feet. She opened her mouth to speak but in that moment Nona's pain returned to her and in the same instant a spasm took command of Luta's face, a contortion that turned resignation into animal fury. She thrust her arms before her, shoulders forward, fingers spread at uncomfortable angles and her shadow flowed forward as if the sun were sinking behind her, growing from its puddle and fanning out wraith-like, clawed hands reaching.

In the space of a heartbeat Luta went from defeat to blind rage. In the same broken second her shadow surged across the floor. Nona slowed the world but she couldn't stop the shadow climbing her, and where it touched her flesh skin parted as if beneath the edge of a keen knife. Nona had little doubt that once it reached her neck and face the cuts would be deeper: Luta's expression held no room for mercy.

Across the room the Academics at their table had barely even registered Luta's change of mind: in the time it would take them to act it would all be over. Nona started to dive back and to the side but a shadow can move as quickly as the light and she knew evasion would not suffice. In desperation she summoned her blades and hacked at the leading hand as the shadow climbed, knowing she couldn't cut herself. The effect was instant. As invisible blades met shadow they sliced, and every trace of shadow above the slice vanished. And in the same instant Nona's world exploded into bright fragments of agony, so dazzling that she neither saw the floor reach up to take her, nor felt it when it struck.

Nona heard voices, and the voices drew her from the depths that had held her.

'...with her?' A man.

'How did she even fight it off? That was a rending!' A woman, younger than the man.

'Yes.' Sister Pan's voice. 'Yes it was. How could you put such an unstable student up against my novice? There will be repercussions.' She shuffled closer to Nona. 'Many will be strongly of the opinion that this was no random attack. How far into the Academy does Thuran Tacsis's golden hand reach, they will ask?'

Nona realized that she no longer hurt. She couldn't even feel pain where the rending shadow had sliced her legs.

'Look to your own, sister.' The man's voice. They were in a much smaller room than the testing hall. Nona kept her eyes shut, not moving for fear of interrupting their conversation.

'To my own?' Sister Pan raised her voice in outrage.

'Proxim Luta wasn't following some clandestine order. You saw her. She had to be dragged from the hall, raging. Even the damage to her shadow didn't cow her,' the woman said. 'One of those empaths from the monastery put that anger there. You need to be talking to the priest, or to Brother Jax at Saint Croyus.'

'I don't believe for a moment that a servant of the Ancestor, brother or novice, would—'

'But how did she fight it? There are no Path-magics that would do that ... are there? How did she damage Luta's shadow?' The woman returned to her original question. 'And why is she so sick from such minor cuts?'

'She fought it off because she's marjal,' the man said.

'And she's sick because of the blood-war raging in her.' Sister Pan's voice. 'The marjal is fighting the quantal.'

'Blood-war,' the man said. 'Exacerbated by the use of marjal enchantments close at hand... I wonder what set it off, though? It's normally some significant challenge to the system. That Mistress Shade of yours is a marjal prime, no? But would some basic shade-work be enough to spark *this* off?'

'The girl touched Raymel Tacsis two weeks ago,' Sister Pan answered, adding somewhat dryly, 'Didn't your Academy men leave the boy full of demons?'

A pause. 'That *would* do it.'

The woman spoke up. 'Marjal versus quantal is always the hardest of the battles.' She sounded unconvinced. 'But, even so, I've never read of a case so bad. Her metabolism was dangerously out of alignment. She must have been in agony. I don't see how—'

'She's three-blood. She's a full hunska.'

'Ancestor bleed me!'

A moment's silence held the room and kept it.

'Three-blood?' Doubt in the man's voice. 'You realize what—'

'I understand better than you know, Rexxus Degon.' Sister Pan sounded her true age for once.

'You had better get her back to the convent before the emperor hears of it. And tell Nevis. He's the best high priest you've had in a while – not that that's saying much. You've at least a chance with him on your side.'

Nona heard the words but couldn't put them together in her mind, not in a way that would fit. If she were a three-blood… Did that make her the Chosen One? What did it make Ara? She turned her thoughts to something more easily grasped. 'I'm not poisoned?' Nona opened her eyes. The ceiling above her lay the pale blue of a sky she had never seen and stuccoed plaster decorations reached across from all sides like strangely intricate and angular clouds.

'You're not poisoned.' Sister Pan leaned into view. 'And how long have you been eavesdropping?'

Nona sat up. 'But I've always had my blades…'

'Your?' It was the woman speaking, an Academic with long grey hair and a white robe.

'Blades.' They had carried her to a sanatorium not unlike Sister Rose's. She was lying on one of a row of beds in a low-roofed gallery.

'Blades?' The woman furrowed her brow.

With a smooth motion Sister Pan produced from her habit a knife, the serious kind, nine inches of dark steel, honed for gutting. 'Show me.' She held it out.

Nona reached forward, thought of the sick, wet snapping

when Raymel broke Saida's arm, and drew her hand across the knife, close but not touching. Sister Pan grunted at the effort required to hold it steady, and when Nona withdrew her hand three bright lines lay scored across the steel, three corresponding notches in the cutting edge.

'Remarkable!' The older Academic, Rexxus, who had overseen the contests, moved forward to examine the damage.

'I've always been able to do it…'

'We call that a sport,' the woman said. 'An isolated marjal talent. Self-contained and unconsciously generated. It's not that uncommon in children before the blood properly manifests…' She frowned at the knife in Sister Pan's grasp. 'Though flaw-blades are of course almost never seen.'

'Orren of Manners Reach can sustain a mobile flaw-wall…' Rexxus's gaze remained on Nona's hand. 'This though…' He shook his head. 'Get her back, sister. Quickly and quietly.'

37

'They carted you out of there in such a hurry!' Ara sat on the end of Nona's bed. 'We were really worried!'

'I rode a donkey home!' Hessa eased herself into one of the chairs that Sister Rose had brought into the sanatorium. 'It's not as much fun as I'd thought it would be. My backside hurts worse than my leg now!'

Ara shot Hessa a look. 'Mistress Path and I had to walk! And she's at least a thousand.' She looked around the room. 'You should just get your own bed in here. It seems like you spend half your time in the san.'

Nona pursed her lips. It was almost true. She did feel that she was Sister Rose's best customer. Her gaze wandered to the garden. Ice hung from every bush. 'If this gets any worse they'll send us on the ranging. We need to deal with Yisht before then.'

'Or tell the abbess,' said Hessa, exasperated.

'The abbess doesn't want to hear,' Ara said. 'She's got a blind spot for Yisht. I don't know why. And Sister Wheel? Sister Wheel seems to love her. I keep seeing her whispering in Yisht's ear.'

'She would want to hear if the shipheart was about to be stolen!' Hessa exclaimed. 'Without the shipheart we're no different to any other convent. Half the quantals would never touch the Path again, marjal touches wouldn't be able to shadow-weave, it'd take a prime at least. And I doubt the abbess would stay an abbess for long if she lost it.'

'Look, we'll tell the abbess if that's the only way.' Nona really did not want it to come to that. 'But what if I can stop Yisht without having to admit I broke into the undercaves and stole from Sister Apple's stores? If I can do that before the ranging…'

'You need to get better first,' Hessa said. 'What happened to you? Did you take the cure despite everything?'

'No.' Nona patted her habit above the pocket that held the vial. 'Rosy isn't sure what was wrong with me, but it seems to be better now.' Sister Pan had sworn her to secrecy about her marjal blood. The nun had said she would tell the abbess, but no one else for now. The first three-blood in a hundred years would drive the Argathians into a frenzy. The mob would want to carry her to the Ark on their shoulders. They would camp outside the pillars. And what the emperor and his sisters might do to own her … Sister Pan didn't say but the implication was that it might be bloody. The Academic, Rexxus, had agreed to keep the matter confidential but Sister Pan didn't seem to have much faith in his assurances. In addition, with such an audience of Academics to watch the contests it was entirely possible that one or more among their number would unravel the puzzle over what had happened and deduce the truth independently. 'I can leave as soon as she's given me one more check-over.'

The door at the end of the hall opened and Ruli poked her head around. She'd scraped the colourless length of her hair into a tight bun and the change it made to her face made Nona laugh. Ruli stumbled in, pushed by Clera. Both rushed over to her, still damp from the bathhouse.

'What's this madness about going up against Yisht?' Clera flung herself down on the end of the bed.

'She's after the shipheart,' Hessa said. 'Take that and you may as well close Path Tower for good.'

'Excellent! I can't stand all that dreary meditation.' Clera curled her lip in distaste.

'And there'd be no hot water,' Nona said.

'How're we taking Yisht down?' Clera's eyes sparkled with righteous indignation.

'I don't see how it can be done,' Ara said.

'Of course it can be done.' Clera snorted.

'She can beat you all without drawing a sword,' Hessa said. 'The sisters would see you trying in any event and stop you. Then the abbess would take your habits. And even if you could beat her – unseen – what are you going to do with her? Lock her in a store cupboard and hope nobody hears her?'

'Drop her in the Glasswater,' Clera said darkly.

'We're not going to kill her!' Ruli's shock made her paler than ever.

'I have a plan.' Nona sat back. 'For everything but the last part. And no, Clera, I don't want to dump her in the sinkhole.'

'So let's hear it.' Ara slipped off the bed and drew up a chair, as if she needed the distance to properly judge Nona's proposal.

Nona frowned. She had a sense that they were all digging themselves deeper than ever before, a certainty that the things they decided now could not be undone and would steer their fates for many years to come – if indeed any of them had many years, or even a single year, to look forward to. 'If you go to my dormitory bed and reach below you'll find a bag tied to the underside of one of the boards.' Nona glanced at Hessa. 'I didn't just take the ingredients for the black cure when I raided the Poisoner's stores.'

A slow grin spread across Clera's face.

'You'll find a bunch of dried catweed in there, and the—'

'The ingredients for the boneless mix,' Clera crowed. 'We poison her and when she's too weak to move…'

'But everyone will see!' Hessa protested.

'Not if I do it in the tunnels,' Nona said.

'And then?' Hessa asked.

'That… I haven't figured out,' Nona admitted. Part of her wanted to tie Yisht up, drag her to the most remote shaft, and leave her hanging in it.

'Barrels...' Ruli looked up. 'Barrels!'

'What are you talking about?' Ara asked.

'We put her in a barrel,' Ruli said.

'Great. Then we've got a deadly warrior in a barrel.' Ara spread her hands.

'Easy to roll off a cliff though!' Clera said.

'A wine barrel,' Ruli said. 'There are lots of empties at the winery. We put her in, pad it with straw, and set it with the others for the wagon. It's coming tomorrow.'

'And when they open it?' Nona asked.

'Tomorrow's wagon is bound for Marsport. I know because it's the one that goes to my father. He ships some of the wine across the Marn to Durn. They mark the ones for the ship with his name rune. I can put that on Yisht's barrel and they'll ship her to Durn!'

'Brilliant.' Clera clapped her hands. She rubbed her forehead, perhaps remembering how Yisht had knocked her down in Blade. 'Could they push her barrel overboard when they're out at sea?'

'This won't work.' Hessa banged her crutch against her chair. 'A barrel of wine is worth a sovereign at the least. You don't think they might count how many they're supposed to take? There's all manner of notes made on inventory scrolls and—'

'I know,' said Ruli. 'I've been helping Sister Oak with that. She says I'm a natural merchant.'

'But won't Yisht just get out and come back?' Ara asked. 'I mean, fun as it all sounds, won't we be risking getting murdered just to inconvenience her for a few days?'

'You're not seeing it.' Nona shook her head. 'That shaft I saw. It has to lead down from Yisht's quarters. When Yisht doesn't turn up to guard Zole the nuns will go to her room. They'll see the tunnel down. We'll make sure they do. They'll investigate and the abbess will know that the shipheart was the target. By the time Yisht's out of the barrel every sister at Sweet Mercy will have orders to stop her on sight and Sherzal will be in plenty of trouble too!'

Hessa and Nona sat together at the back of Spirit class. Sister Wheel claimed that the further away a novice sat from the chalkboard the more sinful she was apt to be. Nona took pride in setting her spine against the rear wall. Zole sat practically close enough to the board to get chalk dust on her nose. Yisht never sat in lessons, or at least she never sat in Spirit, which was the only class she was admitted to, but stood by the wall as near to Zole as possible.

On this occasion, although her eyes were aimed towards the ice-triber, Nona's focus was actually on the porthole window above her head. Outside, the ice-wind cracked its cheeks, howling loud enough to drown out Sister Wheel's litany. The constant passage of wind-blown sleet created the illusion that the dome was a great ship moving backwards through a sea of ice.

'How does she expect to escape with it?' Hessa hissed.

'What?' Nona glanced back, keeping her voice low.

'The … thing … if Yisht gets it. How does she think she'll get away with it?'

'She got in,' Nona said. 'She knows she can get out. And she probably doesn't know that Sister Pan and I can sense the ship— the thing.'

'She knows about thread-work, though. Sherzal's hardly going to have sent her here without knowing that. There could be a dozen nuns here who would know the moment it had been moved – maybe even a few minutes before! They were on that dagger of yours fast enough.'

'But none of the nuns were even born when the shipheart was put there. How would they be bound to it? And do they even have access to it now? Perhaps it's walled in on all sides. Or threads don't stick to it… I don't know.' Nona's eyes flickered back to the woman, dark against the wall, her attention on Sister Wheel, one hand on the hilt of her tular. It did seem strange that she thought she might just walk unnoticed out of the convent with the shipheart. Or did she really think she could cut her way through Red Sisters as if they were nothing?

'Nona and Hessa – I hesitate to call them novices – will repeat the emperor's prayer seven times before the Ancestor after class.' Sister Wheel lifted her voice so it reached them above the wind's howl. 'Mistress Academia tells me that there was a time when a novice's tongue could be split for idle chatter in Spirit class. So let that stand as an indication that not all progress is good progress.'

Sister Wheel's punishment meant that Clera was left to do the brewing alone, out on the promontory where they had cooked up the black cure the week before. With the ice-wind blowing and no Hessa to light the fire Nona imagined that Clera would have a miserable time of it – if she managed at all.

While Nona and Hessa repeated the emperor's prayer, all fourteen verses of it, time and time again at the base of the Ancestor's golden statue, Ara and Ruli were arranging the barrel and adjusting the records. Ruli was on quill duty while Ara was appointed to 'distraction'. Something her rank and beauty left her uniquely qualified for.

Nona shuffled on her sore knees. Sister Wheel hadn't given them prayer cushions. The nun was a great believer that pain and prayer went together hand in hand.

'Ancestor guide the emperor in his choices and in his actions. May you watch over him at the rising of the sun and at the setting. May you watch over him in the long marches of the night. May you—'

'She's gone.' Hessa shuffled forward. She was allowed to sit rather than kneel, on account of her withered leg – a fact that seemed to give Sister Wheel as much offence as if Hessa had declared for the Hope Church and taken to star-watching.

Nona stopped praying but stayed on her knees, eyes on the distant door. Sister Wheel liked to double back and catch novices in disobedience.

'Is it still there?' Hessa asked.

'Yes.' The shipheart's aura still reached out from the rear of the dome. Not as strongly as it did down in the tunnels though where she had felt the rhythm of it beating through the rock. Yisht must be closer to it down there than they were up top.

'We could look for the way in up here…' Hessa suggested.

'There will be good reasons why Yisht is digging her way to it. If she could just open a door here and climb down some steps she'd already be halfway back to the border with it.'

On their return to the dormitories Nona made a decision.

'You go on, Hessa. I've got something I need to do.'

'You're going to tell the abbess,' Hessa said, no question in her voice.

'How—'

'Thread-bound.' Hessa tapped her forehead.

'I've got to. What if I get one of you hurt, just trying to save myself?'

Hessa gave her a weak smile and made no attempt to talk her out of it. Nona turned and walked away, wondering just how much she might be leaving behind.

It wasn't far to the abbess's steps but it felt as if it were the longest journey of her life. The abbess would have to banish her from the convent at the very least. If Sister Wheel got involved then the punishment might be considerably worse.

The house loomed closer, foreboding, the end to her dreams.

'Where are you going, Nona?' Sister Rock came up behind her.

'To see the abbess.' Nona thought that much should be obvious.

'You'll have a long wait. She's been called to the palace. Sister Apple and Sister Tallow have gone with her. I'll be taking Blade class tomorrow. What did you want her for?'

'I… It's not important.' Gone? How could she be gone? 'When will she be back?'

Sister Rock went up the steps, taking a large key from her pocket. 'A day? Maybe two. Hopefully before Grey Class goes ranging if that's what you're worried about. Something I can help you with?'

'No.' Nona turned to go, not knowing quite how to feel. 'Thank you.' She didn't know who else to tell. The sister superiors were in charge now, Wheel and Rose. Sister Wheel Nona mistrusted almost as much as she mistrusted Yisht. Sister Rose had a good heart but she was timid with it and Nona couldn't imagine her being much help.

Nona walked a wandering path back to the dormitories. Her choices seemed to have dwindled to none. They would have to deal with the thief themselves.

* * *

At the night bell Clera had yet to return. Nona sat on her bed with Ara and Ruli to either side. They had identified a suitable empty barrel and put the export mark on it. Ruli had adjusted the ledgers and Ara had 'borrowed' the cooper's tools necessary for removing and replacing the barrel lid. Quite how to use them was an outstanding issue, but Ruli said she'd seen Sister Scar do it a dozen times and it didn't look that difficult.

'Where is she?' Ruli twisted Nona's blanket in her hands.

'If she doesn't come soon Mally will want to turn the lantern down.' Ara's eyes were on the high windows, all shut and opaque with layered ice.

'Mally'll probably report her too.' Hessa from her bed across the width of the dormitory.

Ruli nodded. The head-girl didn't like Clera.

'You should go and look for her.' Jula on her bed next to Hessa's gave a sad smile, still concerned despite the fact that Clera said something awful to her every day.

Nona was about to agree when the door banged open and Clera staggered in, ice-caked and dripping. 'I think I'm dying.'

Ara reached for her towel. 'Get over here and stop milking it.'

Clera's face was red with cold and she did look to have been in the wars.

'Poo, you stink.' Ara wrinkled her nose.

'Malkin pissed on my spare habit and I didn't have time to change it.' Clera sat down heavily, making the bed bounce. Ara only got the towel under her just in time.

'Malkin peed on your spare habit … and so you … changed into it?' Ara made a face and looked to the others. Nona frowned. The abbess's cat was a liability for certain – but the rest didn't make sense.

'Of course.' Clera rolled her eyes and lowered her voice to a hiss. 'I got out of Spirit and was going to spend the next Ancestor knows how many hours doing unlicensed alchemy. What do you think the first thing I would want to do when I got back was?'

'Change into a clean … oh! I get you.' Ruli smiled. 'So you

had to take off your clean one, and put on the one Malkin had "blessed" so that you'd have a clean one for now.'

Clera nodded. 'I was planning on visiting the bathhouse of course, but it took so damn long!'

It did seem to have taken an age, but in the wind and ice … Nona shrugged. 'So you have it?'

'Of course! I'm Clera!' She took out a small, waxed gourd with its stopper sealed in place. 'Boneless syrup. Guaranteed to make a strong man go weak at the knees almost as fast as I can.'

'You know if this doesn't work she'll kill us?' Ara said, reaching for the gourd.

'Us?' Clera let her take it. 'I thought Nona was doing it.'

'Us. Ara nodded. 'Once Yisht is down it will take four of us to move her. At least.'

'And if it goes wrong the abbess will kill us,' Ruli said.

'Metaphorically,' Ara said.

'And Yisht will kill us,' Nona said.

'Literally.' Ara pressed her lips into a worried line.

38

'We should have tested it!' Clera hissed.

'We did test it. And anyway – you made it – are you saying it's no good?' Ara replied.

Nona edged past them both at the corner of the laundry, checking the courtyard beyond for any nuns. The wind wrapped her habit about her legs, biting through, and her hands were already numb. She hated to think what the ranging would be like.

'It worked on Hessa,' Ruli muttered, and at Nona's signal she sprinted across the yard to crouch by the wall of the scriptorium opposite.

'It did.' Nona replied to the night. Hessa had collapsed bonelessly and they'd left her safe on her side in her bed. Would a full-grown woman go down so swiftly though? Were the ice-tribes a different breed?

Nona waved Clera across and sent Ara on her heels.

A minute later they were all four gathered in the shelter of the entrance to the tunnel that led down to Shade.

'You've got this?' Clera asked.

'I've got it.' Ara grunted. 'Now shut up.' She was on her knees, face level with the lock. Hessa had spent hours trying to teach her the thread trick with locks.

'But Shade has a different lock!' Ara had protested when she had finally worked the lock on the supply cupboard in the dormitory entrance hall.

'You're missing the whole point!' Hessa had thrown up her hands and nearly lost her crutch. 'One lock, another lock, complicated or simple, tumblers or latches … they're all either locked or unlocked. You just need to find the thread for the lock and pull it.

'Like this?'

'That's the thread for the oak that the planks came from.'

'This?'

'You just rotated one of the anchor screws…'

Out in the icy wind and darkness the trick of unthreading a lock was proving no easier than it had in the dorm.

'Hurry up!' Clera stamped in impatience.

'Shut up!' Ara pressed her eye to the keyhole as if the lock's secret might reveal itself to her more easily that way.

Ruli came into sight, rolling the barrel across the open plateau between Academia Tower and the entrance to the undercaves. At one point the wind nearly stole it from her. Nona pictured Ruli chasing the barrel as the ice-wind pitched it over the edge towards the vineyards far below.

'We'll meet Yisht at this rate.' Clera hugged herself while Ara continued to work on the lock.

'She has a tunnel down from her room. I'm sure of it. It's the only thing that makes sense.' Nona gripped the freezing bars of the gate, feeling more vulnerable with each passing second spent out in the open.

Ruli arrived with the barrel, which offered a degree of shelter from the wind. 'She couldn't dig down from there. Someone would have heard her.'

Nona shrugged. 'It's the only way. She must have explored the route I took but not followed it to the end.' Yisht had a room in the guest wing attached to Heart Hall. By Nona's reckoning the tunnel that led on from the Shade cavern would pass below the hall. She had always been thankful that Yisht hadn't been permitted to fill her role as Zole's bodyguard by sleeping with them in Grey dormitory, but it seemed perhaps that it would have been better if she had been allowed.

'You'll have to blast it, Nona!' Clera said.

'Blast it,' Ruli agreed, blowing into her hands.

'I'll blast you if you don't SHUT UP!' Ara didn't sound as serene as perhaps she might.

'I think someone's coming,' Clera said, staring into the dark and open plateau to the east.

click

Ara stood up and pushed the gate open.

'Get the barrel in, quick!'

Moments later they had the gate closed again, with the barrel propped against it.

'That won't stay there,' Nona said, poking at the barrel. 'A strong gust will send it end over end down the stairs after us.'

'Well we can hardly leave someone to hold it. We're going to need all of us to move Yisht.' Ara poked the barrel, frowning as it wobbled. A third of the base overhung the first step.

'We don't need all four of us to take Yisht out though.' Nona patted the bulge where Clera's gourd of boneless, brewed from the catweed, sat under her habit. 'I'll get in position and wait for her. When it's done I'll come back for you to help me drag her.' Without waiting for an answer, she snatched the lantern from Clera and hurried down the stairs.

'Be careful!' Clera called after her. 'If you break that gourd when you're squeezing through then you're going to be down there a while!'

It took perhaps a quarter of an hour for Nona to retrace her route from her first exploration and reach Yisht's excavations. It felt closer to quarter of a lifetime. In the tight sections, through the narrowest part of the fissure and wriggling along the slim connecting tunnel at the end, she expected at each moment to hear a dull crack as the gourd surrendered to the pressure and catweed liquor to begin leaking down her leg. If the victim drank the liquor the effects were said to be almost instant, each muscle relaxing rapidly to the point at which they couldn't so much as lift a finger. The important thing was to make sure the victim didn't swallow their tongue and suffocate. They had laid Hessa out with great care, in line with the Poisoner's lessons, to ensure her safety.

When the liquor was absorbed through the skin the effects

were slower and varied, depending on which part of the body took the dose. Nona's plan was to splatter the gourd's contents in Yisht's face and run for it. The boneless would undo her pretty swiftly. With luck she'd swallow some too and go down even faster.

Nona waited in the mouth of the narrow connecting tunnel, the lantern behind her on its rope. She watched for any glimmer of light, or any hint of sound. Nothing. She waited anyway. In the Blade class after Yisht had single-handedly felled all of Nona's fellow novices, save Zole, Sister Tallow had commented on the display.

'A good fighter lives in the moment, but they see into the future. The better the fighter the further they see. Everyone can develop whatever natural talent the Ancestor gave them for this. Some however, some marjals, have an unnatural talent for it. Seeing five heartbeats into every future goes a long way towards compensating for any amount of hunska speed.' On reflection Nona realized that every move made against her Yisht had seen coming. But had it been experience though, or something more?

She pulled her lantern to her and dropped to the floor of the larger tunnel. The slightest rotation of the lantern's cowl let enough light bleed out to show the dark entrance to Yisht's excavation. Nona could feel the shipheart's power thrumming through the marrow of her bones, singing in her blood, setting every small hair on its end, filling her with possibility. She had but to will it and her feet would leave the floor, she felt sure of it.

Nona advanced, buzzing with energy, but with feet firmly on the stone. Yisht had cut a narrow rising slot into the limestone, tall enough to stand in and swing a pick. The excavation led upward for twenty yards: extraordinary progress that left Nona open-mouthed. In places the walls lay scored with pick-marks, in others they had the peculiar melted quality that Nona had noticed in the vertical shaft she suspected led to Yisht's sleeping quarters.

At the cutting face the air seemed to throb with the shipheart's pulse. Nona's own heart slowed to match the tempo.

She closed her eyes and the Path lay before her, broad as a river, too bright to look upon and too bright to look away from.

She turned and hurried down the passage, her feet slipping on loose stone scattered over bedrock. Hessa had said to ambush the woman as close to the entrance as possible. It seemed obvious now, but Nona hadn't even thought of waiting anywhere save at the cut itself, waiting for Yisht to return to the scene of her crime. She retraced her steps. More climbing, more wriggling, more stealthy advance, and at last she settled herself some yards back from the shaft down which her enemy must come. She turned her lantern low, hooded it, and crouched to wait.

The waiting and the natural darkness put far more fear in Nona than Luta's efforts with enchanted shadow at the Academy had. Yisht scared Nona in a way that Raymel Tacsis never had, not even with demons writhing beneath his skin or peering at her from his bloody eye. Raymel would murder her with glee, with passion: he would enjoy her death. Yisht would cut her down without reflection, with no more concern than the butcher carries for pigs when their throats are cut. Somehow that idea felt worse.

When something slithered and thumped close at hand Nona almost cried out. She pressed herself to the wall, dry-mouthed, the gourd clutched in a trembling hand. A faint glow lit the circle of the shaft in the ceiling, the black length of the rope dangling beneath, twitching as someone climbed down, still out of sight in the shaft.

Nona forced the fingers around the gourd to unclench even as a pair of black boots, the rope trapped between them, slid into view. Black-clad legs. Narrow hips. Without warning, Yisht released the rope and dropped to the floor.

Nona dug as deep into the moment as ever she had, slowing Yisht's descent to a crawl. She flung the gourd out of the darkness of the tunnel, her arm so stiff with nerves that Nona doubted her ability to hit Yisht at all, even if she were standing still, let alone strike her face while she was dropping. Even so, when the gourd left her fingers and passed beyond her control

Nona knew it to be a true throw – the same way that when she loosed a throwing star she might not always hit her target but she always knew whether she would or not.

Yisht raised her hand as she fell. She caught the gourd a foot before her face, her hand moving to reduce the impact as if she knew the gourd to be fragile and dangerous to break. Her off-hand had already dropped her lantern and now produced a throwing knife, releasing it back along the path the gourd had taken. A cold terror gripped Nona even as she twisted aside. It was as if Yisht knew precisely what would happen and had practised exactly this situation a thousand times.

Nona dropped to her left, her mind running furiously through her options and finding precious few that held even a glimmer of hope.

She sees the future. She knows what I'm going to do.

Nona hit the ground and rolled, twisting out of the path of another thrown dagger. She rose, a rock in her left hand and a collection of smaller stones in her right. She threw the stones at the fastest tempo consistent with accuracy, shaking each up into a throwing grip as its turn came. She loosed them, miss, hit, hit, miss, all in flight, their fate known before the first covered half the distance. Another knife angled through the darkness, just the glimmer of its edge to betray its approach. Nona deflected it with the rock.

Nona's first stone passed within a finger's width of the gourd and sailed past to strike Yisht in the chest. The ice-triber already had her hand open, the flask dropping. She'd understood what would happen if a stone broke the gourd while it was in her grasp.

The second stone caught the top of the gourd, shattering it and exploding a modest shower of the liquor within. The third hit Yisht's palm. The fourth would have missed the gourd if it had still been in Yisht's hand but hit the dropping gourd dead centre, completing the job of smashing it and splashing the boneless liquor back across the woman's chest.

The pooled oil from Yisht's dropped lantern flared up, and beads of liquor sparkled on the oily blackness of her jacket.

Nona was far from sure any of it would penetrate to the skin. Of more help would be the rising fumes and the splatters that had reached Yisht's palm as the flask shattered.

'Nona Grey.' Yisht's voice carried no emotion. 'You chose a lonely place to die.' She pulled the tular from its open-sided scabbard. The blade resembled a long narrow rectangle of flat steel, slightly wider at the end than at the hilt, cut at an angle at an the extremity to produce one sharp corner and one more open.

Nona needed to kill time, enough of it to let the boneless drop Yisht, but not enough of it to let Yisht drop her. She could stay in the light and pit her speed against Yisht's sword and her unnatural ability to know exactly what any opponent would do in the next few seconds … or she could run blind into the dark.

She turned and ran. She knew the tunnel well enough for the next fifty yards. She ran with her hands out before her, not at a flat sprint but far faster than she felt comfortable running in total darkness.

The sound of booted feet on stone pursued her into the night. Nona considered diving to the side and letting Yisht pass her … but could the woman's knowledge of the near future tell her what would happen if she slashed left or right? Could her vision of the next few moments be effectively a vision of the next few yards around her in any direction? Nona didn't want to put that to the test.

She had passed the side tunnel. Passed it or almost reached it. Either way, she had no means of finding the opening inches above arm's reach without wasting far more time than she had. Yisht had closed the gap: she sounded so close that a swing of her tular might trim Nona's hair.

Hell. The tunnel might make a sharp turn in the next few yards. Or Nona might sprawl over a rock or break a leg in a fissure. Inevitably, Yisht would find her senseless or injured and kill her without relish or mercy. Nona skidded to a halt, angling to the side. If she had to die she'd do it facing her enemy, blades out.

Yisht came on, swift, not missing a step. Nona ran towards

her, one hand reaching to find the wall, the other before her, flaw-blades cutting the darkness.

Nona tripped on the rougher ground where the floor curved up to become wall. She pitched forward as Yisht came upon her. Something jolted her arm, a metallic squeal and an impact against her blades that echoed through her bones all the way to her shoulder. Nona rolled and came up, arms reaching. Behind her Yisht cursed in the ice-tongue and came to a stumbling halt.

'You poisoned me.'

Nona ran back the way she'd come. Yisht's footsteps followed for a few yards, then came to a halt again. She slurred something.

A moment's silence. The sound of something slumping to the ground.

Nona released a breath and let the tension inside her unwind. She took a step towards Yisht. Another.

What am I doing?

She needed the others. She turned again and started back, slowly, arms searching the space before her.

With a roar Yisht launched herself into a stumbling run, her ruse having failed to bring Nona to her.

Nona just ran, screaming, all control lost in the dark. She hit a wall, bounced off it and fell, her head blazing with pain, wet with blood. Yisht tripped over her before she'd stopped rolling and in a moment the woman's weight had her pinned, elbows holding her forearms to the ground, both hands wrapped about Nona's throat. And there, far below the ground, with the two of them locked together in the blind darkness, Yisht began to throttle her.

Nona couldn't lift her arms to use her blades, couldn't move, couldn't breathe. She raged, blades flexing, body heaving, seeing lights in that dark place that held no light, and the thunder of her heart filled her ears. She fought. She fought hard. And she lost.

'—a—'

It was a small sound to express so much pain but it was

all that could be squeezed from a throat as narrow as a straw. Nothing had changed. Nona was still pinned. She still could see nothing. Still had hands about her throat. Still had her arms pinned. But she could breathe. Everything had changed!

Nona drew and released a few more breaths, each one agony but delicious even so. The hands at her throat just lay there. She struggled and got her arms out from beneath Yisht's pinning elbows. Reaching up, she pulled the woman's unresisting fingers from her throat. 'Got. You.' Small words. Painful. Triumphant.

Nona started to wriggle out from beneath the warrior. For a small woman she seemed to weigh an enormous amount – as if her bones were made of lead. Nona struggled with one limp arm, finding it almost impossible to move. With sudden horror she realized that the boneless solution soaking Yisht's chest had started to work on her. Panic lent her strength. Even so it took several minutes to wriggle out from beneath the warrior and by then Nona felt as weak as a baby and had lost all sense of direction.

'*Think, Nona. Think.*' Hessa's words, penetrating Nona's fog of terror.

Nona drew a deeper breath and stretched out her hands, hunting for Yisht. She took her cue from the orientation of the warrior's body and staggered away, trailing a hand against the wall.

She moved on through the ancient subterranean night, hoping with each passing yard that she would spot Yisht's abandoned lantern. As she covered more and more ground and still failed to see Yisht's light her desperation began to grow again. Surely she hadn't escaped throttling to die lost in the wormholes of the Rock!

Nona called on her clarity mantra, seeking the calm and open mind that Sister Pan had shown her. She advanced more slowly, every sense extended.

Smoke. She sniffed. Sniffed again.

A minute of hunting on her hands and knees and she found the oily residue around Yisht's burned-out lantern. From there it took another minute to recover her own, standing where she had left it, hooded and with the ghost of a flame hovering over a short wick. Picking it up felt like lifting another novice and her limbs trembled with weakness but the comfort of a light in a dark place cannot be overstated.

'Ancestor! You look terrible.' Ruli grabbed Nona's arms and, pulling her forward, wiped her forehead with a handkerchief. 'Oh hells! Your neck!'

'Is she following you?' Clera, eyes wide, peering over the barrel.

'She's down.' Nona whispered the words.

'We'd better hurry.' Ara stepped forward, giving Nona a quick hug. 'Lead the way.'

They found Yisht face down on the tunnel floor, her sword in two pieces against the wall, two deep grooves sliced into the piece of blade still attached to the hilt.

'How in the…' Clera picked it up, holding it towards the lantern in Nona's hand.

Nona pulled the lantern away. 'We have … to move her.' A pained whisper. 'No time.'

Clera knelt at the warrior's side. 'I need to give her the rest first.' She took out another of Ara's old perfume vials and held Yisht's mouth open while she tipped the contents in. Given orally it was the maximum safe dose. Safe-ish. According to the tables the Poisoner had made them memorize it should keep a small adult incapable for several days. The main danger apart from suffocation was dehydration.

While Clera made sure Yisht swallowed the dose Nona made a quick search of the warrior, removing two daggers and five cross-knives for throwing. She didn't want to leave the ice-triber anything that would help her escape or encourage her to return. Reaching into the front of Yisht's tunic, Nona's fingers brushed against something cold. She pulled it out. An amulet, a sigil cast in black metal, small enough that she could just curl her thumb and forefinger about its circumference. Like the sigils Yisht had drawn in the air outside the dormitory it drew the eye, twisting Nona's vision about it. Yisht's fingers twitched and some deep sound escaped her throat, a threat perhaps.

'Is that stuff working?' Nona yanked the sigil and it came free, trailing a broken thong. She slipped it into an inner pocket.

'Give it a few more seconds.' Clera frowned. 'She's tougher than she looks. And she looks pretty damn tough!'

It took forever to drag Yisht all the way back. The scariest part was when her dead, shark-like eyes happened to point Nona's way.

They met their only real problem where the fissure ran between their tunnel and the tunnel from Shade cavern to the recluse. Ara and Clera had had a hard time squeezing through, even with Nona's constant assurance that it widened out any moment. Clera lost her nerve and would have started to scream but for Ara's hefty shove popping her out of the tightest neck and into the wider section.

'How are we getting her through there?' Ruli asked.

'Well we can't get her up there!' Ara pointed at the tunnel in the ceiling.

'Rope?' Nona reached out to tug the rope that Yisht had let down. Ara had already been up to the room above to ensure the excavation would be noticed.

'We'd never heave her up,' Clera said. 'And if we could, how do we get her out unseen?'

'So,' Ruli returned to her theme. 'How do we get her through this crack? She weighs as much as Darla!'

'Cut bits off?' Clera suggested.

'She's not that big,' Ara said. 'And if we scrape her a bit… well, does it matter? We can leave some clues that lead the Poisoner to the digging. After that she won't be coming back, will you, Yisht?'

In the end they dragged her. Clera and Ara at her feet – Clera too scared to take the head end in case Yisht got stuck and blocked the way. Nona and Ruli pushed the ice-triber's shoulders. Though really it was Ruli pushing the shoulders and Nona pushing Ruli's as there was only room for one to fit and Nona had no strength. Inevitably Yisht got stuck.

'Turn her! Turn her shoulders!' Clera, close to hysteria.

'We've turned them,' Ruli called back. 'It's her head.'

'Well cut her ears off! Anything! I don't know. I can't stay down here.'

Nona pushed but Yisht's head had wedged between the two faces of the rock.

'Let me have a go again,' Ruli said.

Nona backed out, seeing that Ruli had a small open earthenware tub in her hand. 'Grease?' The whisper hurt.

'Yes.'

'Why,' Nona whispered. 'Do you. Have grease?'

'I have *lots* of things in my pockets, Nona Grey,' Ruli replied primly and recommenced her wriggling.

In the end the grease worked and Yisht came free with a sudden lurch.

Getting her up the stairs was a nightmare. So was getting her into the barrel, and wedging the padding around her. Getting the lid on was a nightmare too and Ruli managed to crush her thumb with the coopering hammer.

'You're sure she'll be able to breathe in there?' Ara asked as they heaved the barrel onto its side, preparing to roll it to stand with the others in the winery yard.

'No,' said Clera.

'No she won't be able to? Or no you're not sure?'

'No I don't care.'

'She was trying to steal the shipheart, Ara,' Ruli said. 'And you hate her.' Ruli looked as though she were trying to convince herself as much as Ara.

'She's probably going to murder us all if she sees us again, and I doubt we could stop her, so I really don't care if she dies in there.' Clera set the barrel rolling and ducked after it out into the ice-wind. 'Come on!'

39

'She's gone!' Ruli came bustling up to the Grey table, the refectory loud with the usual lunchtime chatter. 'Rattling her way down Vinery Stair as we speak!'

'Thank the Ancestor for that!' Ara glanced towards Zole at the far end of the table. The girl had her head down, attacking her food.

'Thank the Ancestor,' Hessa said, uncharacteristically pious. She reached up to rub her neck. 'I never want to see that woman again.'

Nona nodded, finding her own hand at her neck, touching the bruises there. Hessa had said that the thread-link between them should fade away given time, and Nona had thought it was doing so, but Hessa had suffered through every bit of Nona's choking. It was pure luck that nobody in the dormitory had woken and rushed to fetch Sister Rose: the dose of boneless Hessa had tested helped there, stopping her thrashing and making a noise. But for that, the novices' absence would have been noticed and the whole plan discovered. 'We've just got to make sure the abbess finds out what she was up to now.' Nona scooped more scrambled egg into her mouth, began to say more and thought better of it.

'Let them notice she's gone first,' Ara said. 'They'll check her room. They'll discover the shaft then. When they do it should be easy enough to tell.'

* * *

Nona had been expecting the abbess or at least Sister Pan to come and talk to her about her revelations. She'd been hiding her blades since the day of her arrival. Now, to have them discovered one day and ignored the next and the next left her puzzled. Ara had gone on about how rare a thing any three-blood was, and the Academics had certainly seemed impressed with the discovery. But the abbess had just sat in her house ignoring Nona, doing whatever it was she did in there, and then left for the palace. Was anyone even going to train her to use her marjal talent for anything other than shadow-work?

A cheer went up. 'Time?'

'Two hundred and six,' Ara called down.

Nona blinked. Far below, partly obscured by Nona's toes, Clera was doing her victory dance. A new personal best for completing the blade-path, and a new record for the current Grey Class to boot. She'd beaten Croy's record by four counts.

'Your turn!' Ara pulled the lever to arrest the pendulum and reset the dial.

'Bleed this!' Nona swung her legs up onto the platform and walked with sticky feet to the start of the course. 'I'm going to do it this time.'

She stepped out, cautious, feeling her way. As ever, the whole blade-path felt as if it were somebody else's glove, something that refused to fit her no matter what she did. And if it were a glove then it wasn't just a case of being the wrong size for her, it was the wrong hand too. With too few fingers!

Nona got just past the halfway point. A record for her at least. And fell with a wail of frustration.

Clera, still by the lower stop-lever, followed Nona back up the long flight of wooden stairs offering advice. Nona ignored her.

The ice will come, the ice will close

She called on her serenity mantra. She'd found serenity while in the agony of a marjal-quantal blood-war.

No moon, no moon

She'd found serenity under the critical eyes of a score of Academics.

We'll all fall down, we'll all fall down

She'd found serenity in the face of Luta gathering shadows to strike terror into her heart.

Soon, too soon.

'Shut up!' Nona spun on a step, Clera nearly running into her. 'Shut up, Clera, or I swear I'll push you down these stairs.'

Clera stepped back, hands raised. 'Fine, all right. I was just trying to help.' Hurt in her voice, her expression hard to see in the stairwell's gloom.

Nona turned back and continued to stamp up the steps.

We'll all fall down, we'll all fall down…

When she was up on the platform once more Nona stood with her back against the wall rather than sitting at the edge with the others. She stared at the blade-path, ignoring everything, her mantra trembling unvoiced behind her lips.

'It's your turn.' Clera, braving Nona's threat, stood from the edge and came to wave her hand before Nona's face. 'Are you all right?'

'I'm fine.' Nona stepped forward. She stopped just before the pipe, her feet black with resin. 'I'm serene.' She took her first step. 'I'm so fucking serene that if I miss my footing I'll just walk on the air instead.'

Nona felt as if she were wrapped in a blanket of golden light. She saw the world both with perfect ease and as if she were viewing it from the end of a long tunnel, removed from the currents of its need, distant from its immediacy.

She took a step. Took three more. Another.

And fell. She thought she might waft like a feather, but she plummeted as fast as ever. The only difference was that she didn't mind so much.

Clera fell off before Nona had even reached the lever to time her run. She bounced and flipped over the edge of the net, landing on her feet. 'Too eager. Always happens after I complete.' She paused. 'Anyway, I have to rush, Flinty's taking me to town.' Her smile dropped away. 'Father's back in Rutter – that's the jail they put him in when all this started, the worst one.'

'I thought they were about to clear him?' Nona would never understand the details of the case. It wasn't debt as she understood it – the debts of friendship and duty – Clera's father seemed to be caught in a shifting miasma of paper debts, penalty clauses, interest, dividends, and fines.

'It's all politics.' Clera shook her head, her victory on the blade-path washed away. 'I'm scared he'll die in there. It's not a good place. Rats and disease. And his main creditor has filed for twenty lashes and more fines…'

'I hope he's all right.' Nona reached out to touch Clera's shoulder. 'I'm sorry I shouted at you.'

Clera managed a grin, eyes bright. She stuck her tongue out, turned on a heel, and hurried off to meet with Sister Flint and the other novices allowed into Verity with an escort.

Nona kept at her blade-path practice until lunch, with others coming and going. She had ten tries and got no further than a third of the way. The pipes swung wrong, the sections revolved wrong, the whole thing was just wrong. No matter how slowly she took it, how carefully … the ground just kept reaching up to claim her.

She joined the others at the Grey table, last to lunch, which had never happened before. Clera sat alone at the far end of the table staring at nothing over a bowl of soup. Nona went to join her.

'How did it go?' Nona reached for bread and started to ladle soup from the great glazed bowl between them.

'Family's important, isn't it?' Clera's gaze didn't move from the nothing that had trapped it.

'Well.' Nona thought back to her mother and felt the muscles of her jaw bunching. 'It should be.'

'My mother's not a strong woman,' Clera said. 'You'd think she would be. But she really isn't.'

'Oh.' Nona wasn't sure how long this conversation had been going on without her.

'There was a time when she was my world. When I was a little girl I used to lie in bed crying because I thought she might die and I didn't know how I would exist without her. It sounds stupid, but I did.'

'Have…' Nona put her spoon down unused. 'Has something happened to your father?'

'They're going to let him go,' Clera said. She walked her penny across the back of her knuckles. 'All debts written off.'

'Well... That's brilliant!' Nona said. 'Isn't it?'

'It is.' Clera smiled but only her mouth made the effort. She walked the penny back again.

'That—' Nona saw that it wasn't a penny, not Clera's old copper penny nor the silver crown that replaced it. 'That's gold!'

'Yes.' Clera vanished the sovereign into her habit. 'I took a penny and I bred it into a multitude.'

'Well...' Nona met Clera's gaze. 'That's great news!'

'Yes.' Clera looked away and picked up her spoon. 'I wonder how far Yisht has got to go before she reaches the coast.'

After lunch Nona returned to Blade Hall and the site of her most repeated failure. She joined the others practising and carried on failing.

Later in the afternoon Sister Kettle came to watch them. She stood at the bottom and worked the timing lever for them, watching twenty novices fall in a row before Sessa from Holy Class came and completed a run on her first try.

'A hundred and eighty,' Sister Kettle read from the dial.

Nona tried next and fell off after a count of thirty. She'd barely made it to the spiral before a counter-weight swung and the pipe lifted beneath her. 'Sixty-nine!' she gasped as she dropped from the net to land beside Sister Kettle. 'How did you do it?'

Sister Kettle shrugged and grinned. 'I ran.'

'Not helpful!' Nona scowled. 'And Sister Owl ... twenty-six ... that must be a lie?'

'Or she ran faster...'

Nona trudged up the stairs. Other novices came and went but towards evening the press began to slacken off. An hour later only Ruli and Nona were left. The others, perhaps driven off by the foulness of her temper, had gone to the bathhouse before bed to soak off their efforts on the blade-path.

Nona stood scowling at the twisted pipe. 'It's ridiculous. It's just metal and wires. Why do we spend so long at this stupid game? It doesn't mean anything.'

'Isn't that what games are for? Wasting time?' Ruli shrugged. 'Besides, Sister Kettle says it's more than a game. So does Sister Pan. Perhaps if you think of it as a game that's why you're not winning?'

'You think I should make it life and death?' Nona asked. 'Stop it being a game? I could cut the net down…' That would make it matter. Fall and die. There hadn't been a safety net when she had gone up against Yisht in the tunnels or Raymel in his chambers. 'I should cut the net.'

'Ha! Ha!' Ruli laughed without humour. 'We should go.'

'You should go,' Nona replied.

'Come with me?' Ruli looked worried.

'I'll be fine.' Fast, furious, and without reservation. That was how battle was. That was how the most crucial struggles of Nona's life had been. 'Let me try a few more times on my own.'

Ruli glanced at the door, ducked her head, and started towards it.

'Wait,' Nona said before Ruli left the platform. 'Give me that grease of yours…'

Ruli frowned but reached into her habit and handed over the small earthenware tub. 'Don't do anything stupid.'

Nona waited for Ruli's footsteps on the stairs to fade away. 'Fast.' She stared at the tarry soles of her feet. 'Without reservation.' That was how she had arrived at the Path, swift with anger, and she always tried to slow, and always fell. But perhaps she didn't fit the convent's measure. Perhaps she couldn't bend to fit their mould.

She began to pick the tar and resin from the sole of her left foot. When she came to the blade-path wrapped in serenity she fell serenely. She put more care in, went slower, fell. Sister Kettle had completed the blade-path in sixty-nine counts. She must have run. Sister Owl in twenty-six, the legend said. She must have flown. Nona started to clean her other foot.

Ten minutes later she set the pendulum swinging and stood at the edge of the platform, staring at the pipe an inch before her toes.

'No.' She backed away, backed some more, backed another step and her shoulders met the door. 'No.' She opened the door and retreated down the steps. 'Fast. Without reservation.'

Nona came up the steps at speed, toes curled for grip. She came through the doorway, accelerating into a sprint. She leapt and hit the pipe with both greased insteps. She slid, gravity seizing her, accelerating her with terrifying swiftness. And now, at last, she dived into the moment, letting the pendulum crawl between its ticks.

Nona shot towards the corkscrew turns. There are some things that must be done quickly or not at all. If someone asks you if you love them you cannot hesitate. There are some paths that must be taken at speed.

Nona began to rise with the curve, her feet running before her, and for the first time, although it felt very far from safe … it felt right!

Bray's lingering chime chased Nona from the arch of Blade Hall out across the courtyard. She raced along the dark alley alongside the laundry and came slipping and sliding around the corner just as Suleri was reaching to close the dormitory's main door. The door wouldn't be locked but anyone arriving after Suleri – now the convent's senior novice – closed it, was counted as late to bed, their crime recorded on the records delivered to Abbess Glass each seven-day. Suleri, new to her power, wasn't inclined to leniency.

'Wait!' Nona leapt up the steps and ducked under the novice's arm, skidding so fast along the corridor she almost passed the door to Grey dormitory.

Suleri banged the door shut. 'You're not wearing shoes, Nona!'

Nona didn't deign to reply. It wasn't something she'd failed to notice. She banged through into the Grey dorm hall. 'Guess what!'

'We're going on the ranging tomorrow at first light.' Ara turned from the conversation she'd been having with Mally by the door.

'Uh. We are?' Nona looked around the room. All the novices had ranging-coats either laid out on their beds or wrapped around them.

'Your coat's on your bed. Sister Flint brought them round. There's an oilskin too.'

Nona hurried to her bed, excitement at the prospect of actually getting out of the convent for once driving her own news from her thoughts. Sister Tallow had taught them the basics of making a shelter the previous year, though the lessons now seemed a very long time ago and the details frighteningly vague. 'Do you remember anything about navigation?'

'No,' said Clera, bent over her coat, having some sort of problem with the toggles.

'Where are we even going?' Nona picked up her own coat, a heavy black thing that would hang around her ankles. It looked as fine a garment as she'd ever worn, but where she came from when the ice-wind blew you found shelter and hid. Warm as the range-coat seemed she didn't relish the prospect of open miles with nothing between her and the ice-wind except cloth and padding. 'Do we know our target yet?'

'We're all aiming for the Kring.' Clera tugged and a wooden toggle came away in her hand. 'Piss on it!'

'The what?' The name had something familiar about it – something from Nana Even's tales.

'You should know! I was relying on you to get me there!' Clera pressed the toggle back where it came from as if it might magically re-attach. 'It's up past the Grey. A thing the Missing left behind. A column of black iron taller than a tree and as wide.'

'I've heard of it.' Nona frowned. She remembered the description now but nothing else. She wondered if Yisht's amulet, cold in her pocket, had been cast from the same metal. 'What's it for?'

'The answer to that … is missing.' Clera threw down the toggle and spat. 'Anyway, the ranging isn't about navigation or even surviving the wind. We can ask directions. We can even beg shelter. Who's going to refuse a novice of the Ancestor?' She framed her face with her hands and batted her eyelashes. 'It's about surviving *them*.'

'Who?' Nona asked.

'*Them!*' Clera waved her arms around. 'Everyone else. The

world. Abeth. It's full of hungry people. And hungry people are dangerous people.'

'I think…' Nona trailed off. Zole was walking towards them with purpose.

'Where is Yisht?' Zole regarded them without emotion, her black eyes startlingly similar to the warrior's.

'I've no idea,' said Clera. 'We were discussing it just now. She can't be much of a bodyguard if she can't guard her own body, can she?'

'If you have done something—'

'Yes, yes.' Clera waved her away. 'You'll show us a fancy move from the Torca and then Nona will turn you inside out. Now push off, why don't you?'

Zole gave them both a look that managed to be both calm and threatening at the same time, then turned and went back to her bed.

'I hope we lose her on the ranging.' Nona watched the ice-triber go.

'Most novices band together by the end,' Clera said. 'We can split into our own groups in the first days but we're all headed to the same place so it gets crowded towards the target.'

Nona shrugged, pushed her ranging gear off the bed onto the floor, and started to strip out of her habit. A minute later she was under her blanket, and a minute after that, dreaming.

Sister Flint gathered Grey Class after breakfast the next day. Hessa said her goodbyes as they left the refectory. She gave Nona a one-armed hug and Nona took it woodenly, never having grown accustomed to the business of hugging.

'Be safe out there,' Hessa said.

'It's the ranging – there's no safe about it.' Nona made her mouth into a smile.

'Well, be careful.' Hessa released her. 'If you fall off a cliff and break your arms … I'm going to know all about it.'

'You'll have a chance to work on breaking that while we're away,' Nona said. 'And if you can't do that yet then at least make it so we can share good experiences rather than just bad ones! Don't just send me your nightmares. If I'm lying shivering in a snowbank somewhere, I want you to go for a soak in the bathhouse and for me to be the one that gets warmed up.'

'I'll try.' Hessa grinned. 'I'm going to miss you. I'll be lonely here without you lot.'

'At least you won't have to race Nona for the last potato every night.' Ara hugged Hessa and drew Nona away. Sister Flint was waving them to the exit.

'Follow the Path!' Hessa called after them, leaning on her crutch. 'If you get lost, follow the Path. That's what it's there for!'

The nun took them to the abbess's house where they stood hunched against the ice-wind in their ranging-coats. The novices all had their weather blankets and bundled supplies on their backs. Nona had been issued with a short skinning knife, two wire traps, a tinderbox, and a small iron pot.

'I'm freezing already,' Clera said from inside her hood.

'Who's that?' Ara pointed to a figure coming around the side of the abbess's house.

'It's a man!' Jula sounded shocked.

'Tarkax,' Nona said.

The warrior wore the same black sealskins and fur jacket he had worn at the Caltess and seemed unbothered at being in teeth of the gale. He grinned at the girls, his teeth a white slash in a dark red face. 'Lovely day for it, ladies!' And skirting their huddle, Tarkax went up the stairs to knock on the abbess's door.

Moments later Abbess Glass emerged, swaddled in padded robes, the hand around her crozier hidden in a thick black mitten. Sister Tallow followed her out in a ranging coat.

'Novices!' Abbess Glass had to shout above the wind. 'This will be a great test for you, but one in which I am sure you will all do well. Sister Tallow and Sister Flint will have trained you in the skills required to reach your target: it remains for me to remind you that no matter what conditions you may face on your ranging, no matter what the trials, you are representatives of the church, ambassadors of the faith, and most of all, novices of Sweet Mercy Convent. I expect you to act accordingly. And remember. If anyone lays a hand on you …

you have my permission to cut it off. Be safe. Sister Tallow will be waiting for you at the Kring.'

She made to head back into the warm glow of her entrance hall, then turned, remembering. 'I have with me the renowned warrior and tracker Tarkax, also known as the Ice-Spear. Tarkax will be acting as Novice Zole's bodyguard in Yisht's unexpected absence. He will not be aiding her on the ranging unless in exceptional circumstances.' She turned and went back into her house, shutting the door with a thump that had an air of finality about it.

'The Ice-Spear!' Jula almost squeaked. 'I've read about him!'

'You have not!' Darla, hulking above the scribe's daughter.

'I have too!' Jula looked up at Darla through the tunnel of her hood. 'He's famous! He's in the story-sheets they sell in Verity on seven-day outside the Abon Library. The ice-tribes have songs about him!'

Nona turned and leaned into Ara. 'He works for Partnis Reeve, I'm sure of it.'

'Which makes him a Tacsis man,' said Ara.

On Nona's other side Clera leaned in. 'Don't Thuran Tacsis and Sherzal hate each other?'

'They certainly haven't been friends these past few years. Zole must be horrified.' Ara didn't sound displeased and although Nona couldn't see her face she knew the Chosen One would be smiling. Ara didn't bear grudges, but the emperor's sister and everything associated with her was the exception to that rule.

Clera pulled at Nona's arm. 'If he's Tacsis then you might reconsider how you feel about Zole… The enemy of my enemy may be my friend.' She shrugged. 'Of course the friend of my friend is often a jerk.' She jabbed a black-gloved thumb surreptitiously in Ara's direction.

Sister Tallow came down the steps, raising her hand for the novices to gather around her. Nona came to stand by Tarkax and he looked down at her and grinned. 'My friend from the Caltess.'

'You told me you were a ring-fighter,' Nona said.

Tarkax raised his hands, one to the east, one to the west. 'And what is the Corridor if not a ring?'

'You lied to me.' Nona scowled.

'Pay attention to your nun.' Tarkax slapped her around the back of the head without malice.

'...from where we will journey to the starting station on the margins of the Harran Fens. After that you'll be on your own.' Sister Tallow looked around the group then led off along the Cart Way.

Nona followed, rubbing the back of her head and wondering how Tarkax got a name as silly as the Ice-Spear.

'I don't know how any of us is going to survive this,' Jula said.

The Grey Class novices had been trudging along behind Sister Tallow for several hours and Jula had expressed the same thought in at least eight different ways since they came down off the Rock of Faith.

'Grey Class goes ranging every year, Jula. Croy has been three times! She'd been in the class a week the first time.' Ruli seemed happy to be out and on the move, her cheeks red, her eyes bright.

'But we've had *no* training!' Jula limped on, complaining that her shoes were rubbing.

'We've had some,' Ara said. 'And this *is* training!'

'Stop whining, Jula.' Clera trudged on without looking left or right. 'It's quite unusual for anyone to die on a ranging.'

They came into the open from a small valley and the ice-wind caught them by surprise, howling across an expanse of barren fields. Nona staggered before leaning into the blast. Two novices ahead of her were driven to their knees. Tarkax just bent his head and went strolling along behind Zole as if it were nothing more than a stiff breeze.

Midday saw them huddled in the lee of a cattle barn with the sun dominating the sky above them, huge and crimson, but offering little heat, and what it did give, the wind snatched away the moment it arrived. Nona munched her bread and cheese, staring at nothing, her mind on Raymel Tacsis. Had it been his hand behind the shadow-worker's attack at the Academy? Or had the senior Academic's protest been genuine – had some enemy within the church itself set Markus or his friend to drive the girl mad with rage? She couldn't think it was Markus, but perhaps for him Giljohn's cage was just a memory, a dry fact that could be taken out and studied without emotion.

Thuran Tacsis had sworn in court, sworn before the emperor's throne, that the matter was finished. Her name, Nona Grey, had been spoken in the emperor's hearing: her mother would be… Nona shook the thought away. She'd been covered in blood when she'd left the village, and though the blood had long since been washed away, the stains would never be gone.

'They say there's trouble on the coast.' Darla broke across Nona's thoughts.

'Trouble?' Nona recalled the pirate raids. Without them Sherzal wouldn't have dared come to Verity and risk her brother's displeasure.

'The Durnish have come in force. Regular troops on the pirate barges, just not in uniform. And Crucical's summoned General Cathrad from the Scithrowl border.'

Nona looked up at Darla. 'How do you know this stuff?' It was normally Ara who knew things about the world.

'My father's an officer on Cathrad's staff. He's come ahead of the general to gather intelligence.' Darla nodded. 'He says corsairs have come ashore and sent raiding parties along the northern ice while the emperor and Velera are tied up around Honisport.'

'So … don't go too close to the ice then?'

'Not unless you want to join in the war,' Darla said.

'We're at war?' Nona hadn't realized it was that bad.

'We're always at war.' Darla shrugged. 'As long as the ice is closing we'll always have war – that's what my father says. The only difference is what they call it. Right now they're calling it raids. The church will have to play its part. What did you think has been keeping the abbess so busy? They say she's even been to court!'

'And they're sending us out ranging? In a war?' Nona asked.

Darla shrugged again. 'Technically we'll be fleeing a war.

The Kring is in the opposite direction. That's probably why they picked it this year. Last year we had to get to Hern's Island off the coast. And anyway, the ranging is one of the oldest parts of a nun's training. They say the training fits the times. If it's open war ahead of us then it's not so surprising they send us out in this...'

Marching down the tracks and lanes of the empire's heartland brought back memories of travelling with Giljohn, though the roads he had chosen were more obscure and there had been far less walking involved. Even so, when the ice-wind blew everywhere took on that same bleak look. It wasn't without a certain beauty to it. A thin screed of icy snow covered the fields, hiding the crops. Most would recover – farmers grew the breeds that would – but some would always gamble on a long enough stretch of Corridor wind to sow and harvest something more valuable and vulnerable. The hedgerows stood thick with ice, coating every twig, blunting the thorns, glistening, gleaming, surreal, holding everything behind glass, for observation, not to be touched, put in storage ... for a while. One day it would be forever.

In the woods screw-pine and frost-oak stood hung with icicles, a multitude of them, hanging thickly from every limb, some longer than Nona's arm. At the height of the ice-wind the focus couldn't wholly melt the ice and every night the icicles would grow and multiply, until the wind finally relented or the great weight of the ice tore the tree apart. Men had died passing through forests in the ice-wind. When the focus came every branch of every tree could shed a man's weight and more in yard-long icicles in minutes, turning any wood into a nightmare of plunging ice-spears.

By evening they'd passed the town of Averine and come over a low range of hills to a ridge from where they could see the River Rattle snaking its way towards the Marn. Sister Tallow found them lodging for the night in a hay barn close to the river and the unimaginatively named village of Bridge that sat on both sides of a long stone-built bridge spanning the Rattle.

'You know why they call it the Rattle?' Jula asked as Nona worked herself in amongst the hay.

'No.' Two years ago a hay bed would have felt like luxury. Now it was sharp and itchy and the barn an ice-box. Sweet Mercy might have armed Nona with many of the arts of war but it'd made her soft in other ways. The ranging was an overdue lesson – one that she intended to pay close attention to.

'When the melt-surge comes down – that's just before dawn here – the waters run so fast that all the stones in the riverbed rattle over each other. I read it in Hennan's *Geographical History of the Quantal See.*' Jula wriggled against a hay bale, frowning. 'I'm not going to be able to sleep here…'

'Try,' said Nona. 'You're unlikely to get a better bed tomorrow night.'

The convent had chartered a boat to bear the ranging party to Harran Fens. It looked to Nona like the rowing boats the fishermen used on the White River, only ten times as long. It had a tall mast folded into the length of its hull and a sail wrapped tight; both would be raised for the return journey upstream, but to bear the novices to the fens the Rattle's current was all that was required.

Nona, Ara, and Clera sat together in the prow, braving the weather. The wind's blasts raised flurries of ripples across the river, driving them forward before overwhelming them and beating them flat again.

'I'm going to be something,' Clera said, not looking at either of them.

'You are something,' Nona said.

'I wasn't born to be a high Sis. I'm not a two-blood with prophecies hanging off my shoulders. But I'm going to be something. Whatever it takes.'

'You sound as if you think we're in your way,' Ara said.

Clera looked around as if noticing them for the first time. 'We're a new generation in an old world. It's all ours for the taking.' She returned her gaze to the water. 'It just requires that you pay the price. That's how the world works. Trade and loss. Supply, demand, prices to be paid. At least that's how it works for those of us who aren't born with fortune written in our blood. You do things you don't want to do, for people you don't like, and you keep on doing them, because you know that one day things will change and you'll be the one doing the telling.

'I've got a plan. I can't see how all the pieces fit yet, or even what all the pieces are yet.' She held a gloved hand out as if the components lay there in her palm. 'They're bright and sparkling and complex – but somehow I'll fit them all together, and on that day I'll break the world and make another.'

Ara snorted. 'Are you practising a part for a play, Clera? Or have you been sniffing what's left of the stores Nona stole from the Poisoner?'

Clera put her head down. 'I'm just saying what's on my mind. What's been on my mind for a long time. The ranging's a dangerous thing, whatever they tell you. Not everyone makes it back. So if you've got something to say, the boat's a good place to say it.'

Nona discovered that she didn't have anything to say and they sat in silence.

The boat dropped anchor alongside an icy stretch of beach, the bank behind rising in an earth cliff to overhanging sod and ice-rimed bushes beyond. Jula was the first ordered ashore, jumping from the prow into the shallows. She looked a small and lonely figure, black against the shingle, waiting for the other novices as the boatmen struggled to keep their craft steady in the current.

Ruli was next off, followed by a stream of her classmates. Nona followed Ara. The shingle gave onto earth before reaching the six-foot bank. She scrambled up, muddy-handed. Before her the land stretched out towards a desolate expanse of frozen mire, spotted with bulrushes in brittle stands.

Tarkax came last, clearing the shallows with a leap from the side of the boat. He strode up the beach grinning. 'I'm here to watch over that girl.' A loud declaration, finger pointed squarely at Zole. 'You, you, and you.' He jabbed at the cluster of novices atop the bank. 'I won't lift a finger for. Nuns' orders.

Run into trouble and I'll watch you die. So pretend I'm not here.' He sprang up the bank in two bounds and ambled off to inspect the ground.

Sister Tallow addressed the novices from the boat's prow. 'You'll need to get to the Kring within four days, novices.' Behind her the boatmen busied themselves with the matter of turning their vessel about. 'The countryside will be dangerous. It's possible there will be Durnish raiding parties, but worse than them by far will be our own people. There's not much that's less predictable than a frightened peasant. They'll be on edge, suspicious, ready to strike first and without warning. Our people may also be your salvation: the kindness of strangers is often all that sustains us. If your groups are too large you will be unlikely to find anyone to take you in. If they are too small you will be vulnerable to the ill-intentioned.'

The keel ground against the riverbed and two crewmen with long poles worked to turn the boat as it nosed out into the current. Sister Tallow raised her hand in farewell. 'Ancestor go with you, girls.'

'I hope the Ancestor is bringing sack of food and a warm tent.' Nona managed a grin she didn't feel. Seeing Darla struggling to climb the wet bank, she jumped down to help, only to find herself ankle-deep in freezing slime. 'Bleed on it. I hate mud.'

Darla snorted a laugh and got up the bank by herself with a lunge.

The crewmen leaned on their poles, the boatman turned the rudder, and with a shifting of shingle the boat pulled forward into deeper water. The raised sail filled with the ice-wind and within the space of a minute Nona could cover Sister Tallow, the crew, then the whole boat all with one raised thumb at the end of an outstretched arm.

Suddenly very alone, despite her classmates grumbling on the bank, Nona looked down to see the mud starting to close over the tops of her shoes. 'Damn.'

40

While the dozen novices argued over how many groups they should divide into and which of them would be in which group Nona took herself to the side and watched the river. She knew the direction they had to head in. East, down the Corridor. In the warmth of the convent it had sounded simple enough.

'You'll find your way easy – you grew up in the wild.' Alata had mixed scorn with jealousy.

Nona hadn't bothered to explain that when you lived in the Grey on the sharp edge of starvation you didn't spend your days trekking through the wild, you spent it trying to scrape a living from the mean soil. The village had its hunters who took to the wild in search of game, but for every hunter with their forest-craft there were ten farmers who knew how the winds turned and what to plant where who had never gone more than five miles from the earth-floored hut where their mothers had brought them squalling into the world.

When your path lay between two mile-high walls of ice it sounded hard to get lost. But on the ground with a forest rising about you it was easy to wander a random spider's crawl, lost in the space of a few dozen acres, despite your best efforts to steer a straight course. The Corridor might be a scant fifty miles wide, but walking it, with your view hemmed in by tree and hill, it might as well be ten thousand miles wide. Nona thought of the globe in Sister Rule's classroom: Abeth in white with its narrow girdle of colour, so thin you might miss it at first glance. So many things depended on perspective – on where you stood, and when.

In her class Sister Pan had shown the novices those drawings that the mind could see two ways, or three, or even four. Serenity, clarity, patience were all like that. Nothing changed except the way you looked at the world. One minute you saw it as you had always seen it, but with a mental step to the left, and with the right perspective, everything could flip, everything could find a new interpretation and in a moment the whole world would change.

Nona wondered if the same were true with the wider mysteries of the world. Could Abbess Glass look upon the tangled mess of church and court politics, on the complex web of favour and obligation, and with a small change in the way she saw it, a new emphasis on some seemingly unimportant interaction, suddenly perceive it with new clarity? See it as some simple engine that applying pressure here, pressure there, could drive in the direction of her desires?

Were friendships like that? Could Nona step outside the mystery of her entanglements with Ara and with Clera and see from some new vantage something simple and understandable?

Behind her it sounded as if things were being resolved. She would be with Ara, Clera, and Ruli. Jula with Alata, Leeni, and Zole; with the others in a third group. Argument resurged over the initial routes for each group. Nobody wanted to head through the fens. All three groups wanted to trek upstream to the pine forest they'd passed on the way, hoping to find sheltered paths through. The dispute took an hour to resolve and Nona suspected that in good weather they would have wrangled for days.

'That looks bad!' Darla raised an arm to the west. A dark bank of cloud had been advancing on them for a while but now they saw the white wall trailing beneath it.

'Ice-storm.' Zole scowled. 'We should make for the woods.' She turned to go, ignoring protests that they couldn't all go that way.

'That looks worse!' Nona squinted. There were figures,

perhaps a dozen of them, advancing along the banks further downstream, running ahead of the storm, chesting through bushes.

'Durns?' Ara joined Nona on the highest point of the bank. 'Are those spears?'

'Run!' Jula wasn't given to issuing commands but everyone obeyed this one. Even Tarkax.

Moments later the whole ranging party was sprinting towards the distant treeline. Nona kept her eyes forward, concentrating on the ground ahead. The squall took them all by surprise. One instant they were racing for the trees and the dark spaces between, the next instant the wind rose white about them, a howling swirl laden with sharp fragments of ice. Visibility reduced to arm's length, the wind's roar drowning out shouts and screams. Buffeted and blinded, Nona swiftly lost any sense of direction. When a tree loomed at her she barely avoided running straight into it.

What followed was a nightmare of running and hiding and falling ice. Within a hundred yards the blindness of the storm had been replaced by the blindness of the forest, the pines so tight-packed that Nona could hardly squeeze between them. Dry branches raked her as she forced a passage. The wind's rage and the thrashing of tree-tops allowed only the edges of distant shouts to reach her. Imagination filled every shadowed space with Durnishmen, wild-eyed, knives and axes ready.

When the storm relented Nona found herself cold, exhausted, wet, and alone. She broke from the forest an hour later and tried to orient herself. Eventually she found a trail and followed it.

Nona trudged on, bowed against the wind, feet numb in damp and muddy shoes. Here and there the wheel-ruts lay full of brown water, rotten ice breaking beneath her tread if she put a foot wrong. Her eyes watched the road, her thoughts chased the others. Images rose of her friends skewered on Durnish spears. She shook them from her head. Ruli and Jula would run. Clera and Ara would feed a Durn his own spear. They'd be all right, and the best way to find them again was to head towards their goal. If they had fallen in the forest she could wander aimlessly among the trees for a month and still not stumble upon them.

Nona followed the tracks with most evidence of recent traffic. She knew at this distance it was sufficient to head for the Grey, and that would be hard to miss if she kept generally east and a little north. She checked her directions to the next town with an elderly charcoal burner, located by the thin stream of his smoke slanting through the trees, and later with a farmer bringing a score of ragged goats in off the moor. The farmer offered Nona a place by his hearth, but she mistrusted his eyes, fever-bright above high cheekbones. Neither man had word of her friends.

Nona watched for more raiders – in fact she watched for anyone at all. The charcoal man had wrung his soot-dark hands and warned of Durnish pirates marauding the fringes, killing the old and taking the young to sell in the flesh-markets in Durn. But Nona didn't feel too unsafe. The raiders were at her back. With the ice-wind blowing, all but the most desperate among the peasantry had taken a break from their labours to hide inside their homes, waiting for the weather to break. The Corridor was never as empty as when the ice-wind blew, and whilst the wind might carry a killing edge, at least it delivered a clear view of any stranger approaching bearing killing edges of their own.

As the light failed and a new wildness infected the wind Nona found a drystone wall to shelter behind. It had been built as a windbreak for sheep and several of the beasts huddled there when she arrived. They watched her with goggling eyes, rectangular-pupiled and wholly lacking in comprehension, but they soon reached an accommodation: she would ignore them, they would ignore her, and all of them would crowd together out of the gale.

The wall was an ancient thing, perhaps older than the scraps of woodland close by, built in years when the wind blew too fierce for any tree to raise its head. Nona had considered making her camp in the copse that ran back along the stream, but the sheep preferred to keep clear of the trees and she mistrusted the closeness of them, the slow knowledge of their growing and their endless creaking.

Nona sat there in the gathering darkness, wrapped in coat and blanket with her back to the wall and the moan of the wind across the slopes and the singing of the wind among the trees and the sharp whisper of the wind between the stones. Around her the sheep shuffled their cloven feet to press themselves close.

The sky grew clear. She ate half of her remaining food – hard bread and a boiled egg – then went to sleep hungry.

The wind spoke through her dreams, sometimes pulling her from them, only to release her into the next. And although each dream was different from the one before, some dark, some wild, some full of disconnected joy, a thread ran through them all, marrying one to the next. A single twisting line, dividing and joining, running unbroken like the flowing script from Sister Kettle's quill, spelling out word upon word until the words became a river and the river a story and the story her life.

The dream faded, so completely she could hardly be sure there had ever been a dream, but the thread remained, and the thread was the Path and the Path led her to the moment. Nona opened her eyes. The eastern sky held the very faintest hint of a glow. She had slept through the focus moon, through the shifting and grunting of the sheep, through the wind and the sleet. Somewhere in the night a bright sound had broken across the wind's voice. Metal on metal. Nona moved slowly to her knees and peered through the gap between two stones at the top of the wall. To her left the ridge was a black suggestion against the darkest grey of the sky. To her right the field sloped down towards a thin stream and the straggling copse.

By the treeline a complication of shadow drew her attention. She watched, eyes narrowed. There's nothing so good as a night-dark forest for taking your imagination and giving it form. Nothing. Just black shapes and silence. Even so, one by one the sheep left the wall's shelter and trotted away along the slope, angling towards the ridge.

Nona didn't follow. She had no reason to break cover, no reason to offer motion to any enemy who might be lurking.

The dawn's light spread with agonizing slowness, touching one thing from black to grey, touching the next, making two branches from one threatening limb, making a half-fallen trunk from a silent and watchful monster. As the sun lit the ridge it brought with it the suggestion of green beneath the thin and patchy ice. And still, though it advanced moment upon moment, the light failed to make sense of the dark tangle where the first trees stepped from the field.

Nona drew a breath, sharp and cold across her teeth. That fold was a man's knee, the next an arm, that curve a shield. Perhaps half a dozen of them lay sprawled in death, tangled amid the undergrowth, one hand raised among the thorny coils of the briar.

What to do? Move on in ignorance? Investigate and accept the exchange of risk for knowledge? Nona scanned the ridge, then stared again into the stubborn gloom between the trees. Anyone could be watching … but why?

She called on her clarity. In her mind she began to juggle, directing her hands to the task, guiding each ball through the necessity of its arc. First three balls, the pattern she saw Amondo try to teach the village children, then four, the pattern he employed while delivering his banter to an audience, drawing them in for his show. Then the five with which the juggler dazzled, and the six with which he struggled, sweating and anxious, crowning his performance. By nine the world about her lay bound in crystal, no contrast enhanced, no shadow lightened, no detail magnified, the same but different. She stood and everything around her shouted out its meaning, every part of the puzzle yielded its secrets. She walked in a clarity so fierce it burned her eyes. Nothing had changed, yet everything had, and the world no longer held a place to hide from Nona Grey.

There were five men lying dead, warriors all: raiders, from their garb and the salt stains still bedded in their cloaks. Nona approached on slow feet, the mystery of the forest unfolding before her.

The attacker had killed them with thrown daggers and a thin sword. Precise blows, no frenzy, no mercy. The slaughter had begun among the trees and ended at the margins. Nona came closer, close enough to smell the rankness of the dead men, the blood, the unwashed stink of travel, the sewer stench that gives the honest and undignified truth of sudden death on a sharp edge. Ice-rimed blond hair scattered across blue eyes. Sword and axe lay unattended, some hands open and white, some clenched around a last moment of agony, dark with gore. No breath misted from them.

Nona snagged the loop of a pack with her toe and drew it closer. She took the dried meat and hard biscuit out of its wrap of oiled cloth, and added it to the crumbs of her own supplies. Still ravenous she reached for another pack – and froze. Out of the depths of her clarity a single fact rose to take her by the throat. Somewhere close another human heart was beating. From what evidence this fact had been assembled Nona couldn't say. She knew only that it was true. She stood, watching the silence of the trees and of the shadowed spaces between them.

The raiders had been moving through the edge of the copse where it reached back along the stream. They had been attacked as they moved to leave, aimed at the sheep-wall where Nona had been sleeping. Ten yards past the first splash of the raiders' blood Nona left their trail, written in the patchy ice and half-frozen mud, to strike deeper into the forest. She tore through bramble, broke a path among the sharp and brittle branches of the stunted ardna bushes where they grew thick between the elms. To her own ears she sounded like an army on the move. Every instinct told her to leave, to carry on along her path, reach the target and leave this mystery for others. But why would anyone lie in wait for her in a freezing wood when they could have found her sleeping?

Nona saw blood on the leaves first, then blood against the trunk of one tree, smeared across another. Then the boot. Then the leg. Then, coming around the bole of a great frost-oak, the body, sitting propped against the tree, head down, face hidden within the hood of a convent ranging coat.

She stood, suddenly terrified, her heart unwilling to beat. A moment later what she had taken for her sixth corpse of the morning rolled its head back.

'H-hello … Nona.' Sister Kettle watched her, eyes dark in a pale face, the blood around her mouth a shocking crimson, the smile that was always there, there no longer.

'Kettle!' Nona rushed to crouch beside the fallen nun. 'What—' The white hand clutched around a knife hilt stole her words. The blade jutted from Kettle's side, the coat below glistening with blood. The pommel, an iron ball, was all that showed of the knife: the rest was lost in her grip.

'Little Nona.' Sister Kettle discovered her old smile. 'You found me.' She coughed, sputtering scarlet, her lips very red. 'Oh. I shouldn't do that.' A grimace. 'It hurts.'

Nona found her eyes misting, one hand on Kettle's shoulder, the other in her hair. 'You'll be all right. You'll be all right.'

'You need to run, little Nona.' Kettle's eyes scanned the trees, her head unmoving.

'No.' Nona shook her head. 'You killed them. They're all dead. I checked.'

'Th-that wasn't me.' Kettle licked her lips. 'You don't have any water?'

Nona bent and started to dig out her canteen.

'That … wasn't me.' She smiled. 'N-natural hazard. I wouldn't have stopped them finding you. All part … of the ranging. T-tough break, but these are … tough times, Nona.'

'Who did it then?' Nona glanced around while she held the canteen to Kettle's mouth. The clarity had left her in a moment, taken by shock when Kettle raised her face.

'Noi-Guin. That's why I was set to follow you.'

'Why?' The word sat in front of too many questions and Nona couldn't pick which one to ask.

'Wanted you for herself. Proud, these Noi-Guin. A small girl escaped her two years ago. Wasn't going to let that stand, no matter what promises Thuran Tacsis might have made the emperor.'

'Where is she?' Nona's gaze returned to the knife in Kettle's side. She had held its twin, pulled it from her bed…

'H-hurt.' Kettle showed her teeth, red with blood. 'I got her good. But … she ran.' She winced. 'You have to run too. She could come back. Others with her.'

'I'm not going.' Nona hunted for a reason. 'I'm safer with you.'

'No. They don't know where you're going. They trailed us from the convent or knew we land the novices along the Rattle. But the target's always different. Cover your tracks and head north a way, then make for the Kring. You should be able to catch up with Ara. She's safe, Sister Apple is shadowing her. Takes more than a storm to shake Apple off.'

'Apple! Are we all under guard?' Nona frowned. Even now, with blood dripping from the trees it felt wrong. Like cheating.

'Little Nona…' Kettle grinned as if reading her mind. 'Not all. Just you because of the assassins. And Ara … because of her … father. And the Chosen One.'

'*And* the Chosen One?' Nona frowned.

'Heh.' Kettle spat blood. 'Appy will kill me. But…' She shrugged, winced, and glanced down at the knife, '…she'll have to hurry.'

'What do you mean?'

'Arabella's not the Chosen One. You're not either.' Kettle put her hand on the one Nona had on her shoulder. It felt like ice. 'You're both … shields, if you like. It's Zole. She's a straight-up certified four-blood.' And a tear rolled down Kettle's cheek. 'Stepped out of legend. She's come to save us, Nona. I know it.'

'Zole?' Nona blinked, wondering if Kettle had grown delirious.

'That's what convinced the abbess of Sherzal's good faith,' Kettle said. 'She put Zole into the church's care.'

'With Yisht to guard her…'

'Yisht has a great reputation for her skills.'

'And now Zole only has Tarkax…'

'The Ice-Spear's reputation is greater still.' Kettle drew a sharp breath. 'And nobody knows Zole is the Chosen One. If anyone is out hunting it's Ara they'll be after.'

Kettle fell quiet for a long moment, long enough for the questions to start crowding in on Nona: how could she help? Could she drag Kettle if she made a travois from branches … the raiders had rope…

'You have to go.' Kettle broke the silence. 'Run. Find Ara.'

'I'm not leaving.' Nona sat back on her haunches, arms folded.

'It's not a request.' Another breath hitched past gritted teeth. 'In the absence of the abbess or senior sister I … represent the convent's authority.'

'I'm still not going.'

'It's a direct order.' Kettle furrowed her brow. 'In the name of the Ancestor.'

Nona shrugged. 'I've never been that convinced by this Ancestor business. I prefer the Hope Church myself. Or perhaps the tunnel gods.'

'Nona!' Kettle tried to sit up and fell back with a gasp. 'This is serious. You *have* to go. The Noi-Guin will call others.'

Nona shrugged again. 'I'll kill them if they come.' She paused, thinking over Kettle's words. 'How would your wounded assassin call for help?'

'They're shadow-workers. She could reach out to another, if they had the bond.'

'How far?'

'It depends. A mile? Ten? Most shadow-workers could send a simple call for help a fair distance.'

'So call her.'

'Who?'

Nona levelled a narrow stare at Kettle. 'Sister Apple.'

'But Arabella—'

'The Noi-Guin want me, not her. And they'll track me from here if I run. So we need someone here to stop that happening. And if Ara needs protecting – well, I'm the Shield aren't I? I passed the ordeal. You didn't.'

'But—'

'Call her!' Nona shouted it.

'I don't want her to see me die!' Kettle shouted it back.

Nona sat back, stunned. 'You … you're not going to die.'

The words came rough from a dry throat. 'It's just a small knife.'

'It had venom on it, Nona. It's eating at me. I can feel it in my bones.'

'Wait!' Nona fumbled in her habit, her fingers clumsy with grief. 'I've got the black cure!' She brought the vial out.

'Little Nona.' Kettle's old smile returned. 'Where in the world—'

'I made it.' Nona twisted the cap. 'You've got to drink it!'

Kettle gave a weak grin. 'I'd rather drink ditchwater. You should throw that away. It's dangerous stuff even when not made by novices.'

'But—'

'I'm a Sister of Discretion, Nona. I've already taken the black cure. I took it when I first saw her. It's why I'm still alive. But it's not enough.'

'Sister Apple would know. She could do something. She's the Poisoner! She could—'

'They still call her that?' The ghost of a smile now, a weak thing.

'Call her!'

'No.'

'Call her, or I swear by the Ancestor I'll track and kill this Noi-Guin. And then I'll find the Tetragode and start killing the rest of them until there are none left.'

'Nona!'

Nona shrugged. 'I'm going. I saw her blood trail. It went west towards the river.' She got up.

'I believe you're serious.' Kettle looked surprised, though Nona could see no reason for it.

'I swear that I will do what I say.' Nona sprang away, starting back along the path that she had broken through the undergrowth.

'Nona!'

Nona turned. All around Kettle the shadows gathered, a dark mist bleeding through the wind.

'Can you reach her?'

Kettle sat with her head back against the bark, her face

white as death, a tear running from the corner of her eye. 'I can always reach her. A thousand miles wouldn't matter.' She raised an arm, unsteady, and beneath it a shadow blacker than the night stretched out, reaching for infinity, as if the sun had fallen behind her. 'It's done. She knows I need her. She knows the direction.'

'You swear it?'

'I swear it.'

'By the Ancestor?'

'By the Ancestor.' The faintest echo of that grin. 'And by the Hope, and the Missing Gods who echo in the tunnels, and by the gods too small for names who dance in buttercups and fall with the rain. Now go. For the love of all that's holy, go. You wear me out, Nona. And I've got to concentrate on being alive. It would break her heart to get here and find me dead.' She drew a shallow breath. 'They're both in that direction. If you take it until you find some sort of trail there's a good chance you'll find Ara and the others on it. Try to travel with Ara and Zole. Tarkax may be able to protect you if the Noi-Guin track you from here.' Another shallow breath, snatched in over her pain. 'Go! Now!'

Nona came forward. She set her canteen in Kettle's lap and kissed her icy forehead. Then she ran.

41

Clera found Nona before Nona found Ara. She came hurrying along a forest track in the late afternoon, chased by a dark squall.

'Nona! Hold up!'

Nona turned on the path, relieved, feeling the sweat on her forehead start to freeze as she faced the wind.

'You were racing!' Clera came puffing to a halt. 'My excuse was trying to catch up to you. What's yours?'

'The same.' Nona grinned. 'Are the others safe? I've been imagining awful things.'

'Don't know. You're the first I've seen.' Clera bent over, hands on her thighs, catching her breath. 'I got very lost for a while back there so I'm pretty sure everyone's ahead of us… Ancestor bleed me! Where in the hells did you get that?' She straightened, staring at the naked blade in Nona's hand, a shortsword of Durnish blue-steel, as long as a man's arm from elbow to fingertips.

'I took it off a raider.' Nona frowned. 'Do you think the others are safe?'

Clera puffed through her lips. 'Don't know. We need to find Ara though, and the rest of them… Raider? One of the ones that chased us?' She glanced back along the track and scanned the trees more slowly. 'They're going to want that sword back…'

'No,' Nona said. 'They're not. Come on.' She set off at a jog.

'Wait up!' Clera hurried to catch up. 'Are they after you?'

'Someone might be. And we need to find the others.'

'Someone?' Suspicion crossed Clera's face. She looked nervous. 'You're not making a lot of sense...'

'Save your breath for running.' Nona led off as the wind started to build.

The edge of the squall caught them before they'd covered fifty yards, whipping the screw-pines into a frenzy, howling between the trunks, seizing icicles as long as Nona's blade and shying them across the track.

'You ... you killed the person who had that sword ... didn't you?' Clera ducked beneath a broken length of icicle, hunska-swift.

'They're not alive any more.'

The wind took whatever answer Clera had to that and for the next ten minutes they ran in a maelstrom of ice, wind, and flying branches, dodging what they could, relying on the thickness of their coats and hoods to take the brunt of any impacts they failed to avoid.

An hour later they were crunching their way through frozen puddles on a lane between beleaguered potato fields. The hedgerows bore scattered stands of hoare-apple, the dark red fruit glistening with frost.

'Where is she? Typical Ara. She's going to have me running all the way to the Kring.' Clera pulled level again.

'You're very keen to find Ara,' Nona said, eyeing her friend. 'I didn't think you liked her.'

'Well I do.' Clera snatched a breath. 'And you should throw that sword away. It's weighing you down, and you're hardly going to use it. We haven't moved past knife-work yet!'

'I should throw this sword away?' Nona slowed.

'It must weigh a ton.'

Nona came to a halt. She held the sword up between them. 'I should throw it away?' She met Clera's dark gaze. 'I don't need it?'

Clera looked away, her eyes on the track ahead. '...Nona...'

Nona let the sword fall. It fell point first and stuck in the ground between them. 'Come on then.' And she ran on.

* * *

'Hey! Novices!' The cry came from behind them.

Nona and Clera stumbled to a halt and turned. A moment later Nona had Ara in her arms. The Jotsis heir, eyes bright, face reddened by the wind, returned the hug grinning. 'Who are you and where have you hidden Nona?' Ara squeezed her and stood back. 'Since when are you a hugger?'

'I'm your Shield. You have to hold your Shield tight.' Nona glanced around at Ara's cold camp. Just the windbreak and a log to sit on. 'We have to find Zole next.'

'What the hell for?' Clera looked suddenly fierce.

'Zole?' Ara's smile fell away. 'She's Tarkax's responsibility. We need to find Jula and Ruli!'

'Zole,' Nona confirmed. 'Because Sister Apple isn't looking after you any more and we need Tarkax in case anyone makes a move on you. Also, the countryside is thick with Durnish raiders. I saw another party two miles back. That's the third I've seen.'

'Sister Apple wasn't looking after me in the first place!' Ara glanced around as if the Poisoner might be standing behind a tree. 'Was she?'

'More raiders? I didn't see any!' Clera turned to look back along the road.

'We need to get moving!' Nona started back towards the track.

'Nona!' both of them shouting.

Nona stopped and turned back towards them. 'Sister Apple was shadowing you. She's a senior Sister of Discretion – you would hardly expect to see her. And yes, Clera, *more* raiders. They didn't see us in the squall, or did and weren't interested. They may be next time.' She set off again. 'Let's go,' offered over her shoulder.

Ara wanted to know how Nona knew about Sister Apple's presence or absence given the impossibility of spotting a Grey Sister who didn't want to be seen. So while they hastened along the road Nona told them the whole story, except for the part about Zole being a four-blood-prophecy-fulfilling legend. She wasn't entirely happy with that part herself. Not that she wanted to be Sister Wheel's darling or anything … it just didn't make sense. By giving Zole into the church's care Sherzal had made Abbess Glass trust her intentions. It was a precious gift: it removed any suspicion that the emperor's sister wanted to steal Ara or Nona to control the Argatha or the prophecy. She had just given Abbess Glass the Argatha and put into her hands control of the prophecy, fake though it might be.

And yet … Nona knew that Sherzal's intentions were *not* to be trusted. She *had* tried to abduct Ara. And she had put Yisht into the convent to steal the shipheart… Had Zole just been the price she was prepared to pay for the chance to steal it?

When Nona had finally laid the whole thing out for them Ara seemed satisfied.

'So … if you spent the morning hunting the forest and helping Sister Kettle … that explains why you had to run so hard to catch up with me.' Ara jogged on, gathering her breath. 'But you said Clera was racing to catch up with you … so why was she so far behind too? Sister Tallow said to take things slow and steady – so since I got clear of the chaos at the river I've been doing just that.'

Both of them turned to look at Clera, running beside them, red-faced, holding her side. Under their stares she stumbled to a halt. 'I need a rest. I can't run all the way to the Kring. There's the best part of sixty miles left!'

'Why were you so far behind Ara?' Nona asked.

'Got lost, I said already. All right?' Clera scowled, exasperated. 'I'm a city girl. You may have been brought up by wolves, and Arabella here might have had estates to hunt on, but I know streets and markets and houses, and if I see three trees together I know I've gone the wrong way.'

Shelter that second night came in the form of a pigsty among a collection of hovels that made Nona's village look prosperous. Their initial welcome was the two points of a pitchfork and a hasty assembling of fierce-eyed peasants armed with hatchet and hoe. Through Ara's smooth diplomacy the opening offer of brutal murder was negotiated down to room in the unoccupied sty on fresh straw and the threat of violence if they tried 'anything funny'. Clera, fishing in her habit in the privacy of their new accommodation, came out with a handful of silver from which she dug out a copper and went on to purchase a slab-like loaf of black bread and a wrap of rancid butter.

'Where did you get all that money?' Nona asked, chewing on her portion of the loaf.

'I told you, my father's fortunes have changed.' Clera's jaw bulged as she ground away at the bread. It seemed as if more grit had been used than flour. She played her gold sovereign across her knuckles. 'The church teaches faith – but what you learn is that it's money that moves mountains. The church preaches the Ancestor's creed, but it's gold that talks. Everything we do, all this business of emperors and temples, all the war, alliances, murders, hospitals … all of it floats on money. The currents that move these things, make them dance, are all financial. Politics, religion, love, faith, even hate, are just the things people say. *This—*' she held the coin before her eye between finger and thumb. 'This is what they mean.'

'That's a shallow view of the world, Clera.' Ara watched from the corner, hunched in her ice-rimed coat.

'Says the girl whose whole life was built on gold.'

'There are things that can't be bought or sold,' Nona said.

Clera shook her head. 'Some would say everything has its price, and that it's often surprisingly cheap. Others that if a thing cannot be bought, it has no value.'

'What about friendship?' Nona asked.

'Ah.' Clera lay back, settling herself to sleep. 'There you have to be careful.'

Ara had managed to establish that several novices had passed through the village hours before them, but how many novices or hours proved difficult to pin down. Nona doubted that there were any behind them, though. Not unless the Durns had them.

The novices took turns watching through the night. Nona spent her hours staring at the darkness, wondering if Sister

Kettle still lived and what horrors Sister Apple might have wrought upon her attackers if not. She wondered too at the raiders she'd seen, lying at broken angles where the Noi-Guin had left them. They'd been young men, pale with short, fair beards and eyes the blue of cornflowers. She wondered what had driven them across the sea. They looked too well-fed, too well-equipped, to have come so far in order to terrorize peasants in their shacks. Does a man with a good iron sword cross an ocean to steal a half-starved goat?

She watched the darkness and painted the raiders across it, breathing life back into their pale limbs. Would they come this far inland, or retreat now, fearing to be cut off when the emperor's new armies arrived?

No raiders came in the night. Or if they did they moved on, hoping for richer pickings than promised by the cluster of hovels. The three girls got up as the sky paled and set off towards the valley, a shallow one that stretched east and north towards the distant hills where the sun would soon rise.

'She said it was the only way through. The only easy way anyhow – and if we want to catch the others we want the quickest path.' Clera had taken the lead. The old woman who extorted a copper from her for last night's bread had also furnished her with directions to Aemon's Cut, a gorge that she claimed to be the only safe passage through the colourfully named Devil's Spine.

Nona could tell from the terrain that some river of ice had pressed forward here as it once had across the Grey, but more recently, perhaps only a century or two earlier, retreating to leave the bedrock scraped bare of soil, fierce ridges standing where veins of harder stone ran. The Spine was one such vein of obdurate granite left standing where the slow, implacable currents of the ice carved softer rock away. It stood perhaps a thousand yards proud of its surroundings but near vertical, and honed to a razor-edge running north and south for a dozen miles and more.

The novices had heard of the Devil's Spine. Ara had even seen it before as a small child – a curiosity on a trip to visit some or other far-flung fruit of her family tree. But not until they drew close, harried by the ice-wind, did they properly appreciate the wisdom in seeking an easy passage from one side to the other.

'We'll go to Aemon's Cut and press on. We'll catch the rest or we won't. We can meet them at the Kring if not,' Clera said. 'Apart from not having Ruli, this is the group we were going to be in anyway.'

Crossing the rock wastes took longer than anticipated. Fissures ran across the stone, miles long, yards wide in places. In other areas the stone lay pockmarked with sink-holes, some filled with dark water, some empty with sharp edges, some wide enough to drown in, some small enough to trap a foot and break an unwary ankle.

By late afternoon they had spotted the Cut. By early evening they had reached the approach. The three novices wound their way through a maze of rocky gullies that snaked in confusion across the fractured rock up towards the Cut still almost half a mile off. The wind, that had plagued them since leaving the Rock of Faith, slackened as if daunted by the Devil's Spine, growing fitful.

'It's changing,' Ara said.

'We might find we have a Corridor wind tomorrow to blow us the rest of the way to the Kring,' Clera said.

Nona hoped so. Her father had hunted up on the ice most of his life whereas she had spent most of hers hiding behind whatever walls she could find when the ice-winds blew. Three days bearing up under its breath had only deepened the respect she felt for him. It added a new dimension to her concerns over Yisht. Would a woman raised in such a place truly let her ambitions be thwarted by children or forget the indignity they'd heaped upon her?

A break in the clouds scattered sunlight across the ridged rock. Nona stopped in her tracks. Just as there's a power in many clear voices, ringing in harmonies, it lives too in the shadows of clouds, and in the light moving across landscapes, watched in still moments.

'It *is* changing,' Clera started up again. 'We'll be home and safe in the warm before we know it. I'm going to buy everything in the Pillared Market.' Her chatter had a nervousness to it. She seemed distracted, glancing around.

'We should—' Nona bit off the words, eyes upon the pebble that had just bounced past her. She made a slow turn, poised to spring. Ahead of her Ara and Clera came to a halt. Tarkax stood in the mouth of a small cave some way back along the gully. They had passed just ten yards beneath without seeing him. He beckoned to them, an urgent gesture, one finger to his lips. Behind him in the shadows they could see a smaller figure in a range-coat.

'Come on!' Nona started off towards the warrior.

'No!' Clera called after her. 'We need to push on – you can't trust him.'

Nona looked back. Clera hadn't moved. Ara stumbled to a halt halfway between them.

'That's why we're here!' Nona said. 'We came to find Tarkax. Sister Kettle told me to. So Ara has a guard over her now Sister Apple's gone. Trusting him is the whole point.'

'Well I don't.' Clera raised her arm towards Aemon's Cut. 'That's where we need to go. That's the path to our target. Sister Tallow is waiting there. She'll have half the convent's Red Sisters with her now they know how serious it is with the Durnish.'

'I told Kettle we'd find Tarkax,' Nona said, frowning.

'Well we've found him. Now let's go,' Clera said. 'Remember who he is. I saw him at the Caltess, talking to Yisht. If we hadn't put her in a barrel it would be her standing in that cave. It would be her that Sister Kettle told you to find to look after Ara. Did you trust Yisht?'

Nona didn't answer that, just glanced back towards Tarkax, now crouched further back in the shadow of the cave's entrance.

'Let's go!' Clera started back along the gully towards the Cut.

'No! Clera!' Nona had promised Kettle. She had sworn to a dying woman. To her friend. 'Come on.' She waved Ara after her and hurried up across the steep slope towards the warrior of the ice-tribes.

'Nona...' Ara followed, but slower, faltering. 'What about Clera?'

'She'll follow us,' Nona said, unsure of whether she wanted it to be true.

Nona reached the cave first. Tarkax remained crouched, his eyes not straying to her but keeping to the ridges and gullies. Nona moved past him, seeing in surprise that the gloom held four novices. Her eyes had yet to adjust but one of them was so large she could only be Darla. Ignoring them for the moment, Nona turned to see Ara coming past Tarkax, and running up behind her, a wrathful Clera looking ready to punch someone.

'Nona!' Jula and Ruli closed on her from both sides.

'Glad the Durnish didn't chop you up, squirt.' Darla pulled her hood back. She had a black eye and a bloody nose. Nona wondered how the other person looked.

Zole glanced her way but said nothing, remaining close to Tarkax.

'Why are you here?' Nona asked it of the cave in general.

'There are soldiers waiting by the Cut.' Tarkax didn't turn his head. 'Perhaps a dozen. They're in ambush positions so it's hard to tell.'

'Raiders!' Ara said. 'This far inland?'

'Soldiers,' Tarkax corrected. 'Not Durn men.'

'What's the problem with soldiers?' Clera remained at the mouth of the cave, out past Tarkax. 'The emperor's general probably dispatched them to hold the pass in case the Durnish came this way in force.'

'Get in out of sight, girl.' Tarkax waved Clera behind him. 'And they're not the emperor's men. No uniforms. I killed two in the gullies. One died slower than the other. Said he was a Tacsis man.'

'Thuran Tacsis...' Ruli held Nona's arm. 'But he said he'd leave Nona alone. He swore it to the emperor!'

'He didn't swear he wouldn't come after Ara though,' Clera said.

Tarkax edged back from the entrance. 'Some men will swear anything to anyone to get what they want. I wouldn't place much faith in Tacsis words.' He drew his tular, the flat blade hissing from its scabbard sounding just like Yisht's had back in the tunnels. 'They're coming. They must have sent more scouts out and spotted you.'

'We can't stay here!' Ara started towards the entrance. 'We need to run.'

Tarkax lowered his blade into her path. 'We'd be caught and killed in the open. Here they can only come at us from one direction.'

'There's twelve of them!' Darla from the rear of the cave.

Tarkax rolled his head and shrugged. 'On the right ground twelve I can take.'

'You, in the cave!'

It had taken the best part of an hour before the shout came. Perhaps the Tacsis men had spread out to encircle and catch the prey they expected to run. Nona had seen few hours pass more slowly – as if she clung to every heartbeat of it with hunska battle-speed. Tarkax had returned his sword to its scabbard and told them Sister Tallow would bring the Red Sisters out looking for them in two days. He also said that they would all be dead or on their way again before sunset, so whatever Sister Tallow might do was of no relevance.

'Nona?' Ara leaned forward, her face in shadow. 'Are you all right? There's … something odd about your eyes.'

'We've more to worry about than my eyes.' Nona looked away towards the brightness beyond the rocky entrance.

The shout came again. 'You, in the cave!'

'Only my voice.' Tarkax held a finger to his lips and backed towards the bunched novices, coming to stand between Zole and Ara. 'They mustn't know who or how many stand with me.' He cupped his hands and called out. 'You, outside!'

'We want the girl! Send her out and we'll go.'

'I met two of your number in the gully to the east,' Tarkax shouted back. 'They have joined the Ancestor. I am Tarkax, the Ice-Spear. If you want the girl you must come and take her.' He glanced over his shoulder. 'They'll waste an hour finding their dead if we're lucky.'

'Why would they do that?' Ara asked.

'There's a lot to learn from dead men,' Tarkax said. 'Were they shot with an arrow, taken from behind, garrotted, killed in the same place or apart, by one person or more, were the attackers bleeding when they left?' He shrugged. 'A cautious man would want to know. These soldiers – they know my name. Now they wish to learn if the man calling it to them is really Tarkax. Perhaps they will wait until they can bring more troops. The longer they spend out in the open growing cold, the better it is for us.'

'You couldn't really kill twelve, could you?' Ara asked.

The warrior puffed out his chest. 'I am Tarkax...' He winced and started to turn.

'Ow!' Ara's face creased with sudden pain and she too started to turn.

Nona was already spinning around when she felt the sharp jab in the side of her neck. As she turned Nona saw Clera tangled with Zole, both of them twisting, punching, blocking with a speed that only a hunska full-blood could hope to follow. They fell together, Clera beneath the ice-tribe girl.

'Get Zole off her!' Ara dived in snatching at a wrist and missing.

Tarkax stood unmoving for what seemed an age at fight speed, long enough for Ara to finally catch Zole's arm and hang on despite a kick to the stomach. Nona just watched, flooded with a cold certainty and hot despair. Jula, Ruli, and Darla also stood statue-still, but trapped in the moment as any without hunska blood would be.

Clera tore free, bleeding from the mouth, a hank of her dark hair in Zole's fist as Ara wrestled the girl from the ice away, gaining momentary advantage from the fact that the whole of her attention was aimed at Clera. For his part Tarkax threw himself back and to the left, towards the cave wall. And Nona watched. Her neck stung where the venom-coated pin had been jabbed in.

Ara held Zole atop her, her arms looped beneath Zole's

armpits, her hands clamped behind Zole's head and both legs wrapped around the ice-triber, but Zole still somehow managed to reach down and grip beneath Ara's ribcage, causing her to cry out in excruciating pain. It was all the chance Zole needed to twist out of the hold. She rolled across the floor towards Clera.

Nona didn't act. She couldn't act. She had to see this played out. She had to believe it. She stood and she watched through slitted eyes.

Tarkax landed beside his backpack and tore it open.

Zole rose from her roll, hurling herself bodily at Clera. Clera's foot, aimed at her face, caught her collarbone and brought her down with a snapping sound, the whole of Clera's thigh muscle absorbing the girl's momentum.

Tarkax, fumbling, brought out a leather wrap from among his supplies and began to unroll it. It held close on a dozen small leather tubes, sealed with wax and sewn to the wrap. A throwing star blurred across Nona's vision and took the leather strip, tubes and all, from Tarkax's grip. Clera's throwing star.

Ara got up, stiffly. Zole rolled to her side and jerked into a sitting position, eyes blazing. Tarkax drew his tular in a stuttering motion.

'You?' Ara stared at Clera, horrified. She took an awkward step towards her. 'Why?' She had to jerk her whole body around to take the next step.

Zole tried to stand but fell to her side. Tarkax staggered forward and tumbled, the sword flying from his hand, his head hitting the rocks hard.

'Money,' said Clera, rising smoothly to her feet. 'Lots of money. Enough gold to raise my family to the Sis, and more besides.' She turned to look at Nona, still standing where she had stood since the first sharp prick of betrayal. 'It's Ara he wants, Nona. Thuran Tacsis swore to the emperor not to harm you. He'll take her, get his concessions from the Jotsis and sell her back. All through third parties. She won't lose anything but a month or two and some family prospects. And that scarcely matters if she's to be a Red Sister.' Clera stepped closer. 'So you see, it's hardly anything.' Closer still. Close enough to whisper. 'I'll miss you, Nona.' She pulled her head back and stared. 'What in hell is wrong with your eyes? They're black … every bit—'

Nona's fist connected with the side of Clera's head, the sort of solid blow that puts an end to conversations and to fights. She was at Tarkax's pack almost before Clera hit the ground, but she felt as though she were running through a bad dream. Clera would abandon her for as little as money? Trust, Sister Apple had said, was the most insidious of poisons. It hurt Nona to know how well she had learned that lesson.

'Tie her up, quick!' She threw the rope from the warrior's pack at Darla. 'Quick! Gag her too.'

A moment later she had the leather wrap, crouching so as not to be seen from outside the cave. Clera's throwing star, the four-pointed one from Partnis Reeve, was stuck in it. The contents of four tubes dripped from the leather, unstoppered by the impact.

She brought it back across the cave and threw herself down beside Tarkax. 'Which one? Which one?' She waved it before his face but his eyes were unfocused, blood leaking from beneath his cheek and forehead where he had struck a rock. He had been reaching for the antidote, she knew that, but which tube was it in? She couldn't risk using the wrong one. She might dose him with a whole new poison.

Rising, Nona went to Ara and held her face in both hands, putting herself in her eye line. 'You've been poisoned, Ara. Clera jabbed you with a needle. It was coated with lock-up. Tincture of segren root. You had it before, first day with the Poisoner. You'll be fine.' She glanced across to Ruli, standing helpless, watching as Darla and Jula bound the unconscious Clera. 'Help me lie her down.'

Together they lay Ara on the ground, the unnatural stiffness of her limbs unpleasant to touch.

'Your eyes, Nona.' Ruli looked up from her examination of Ara, one hand still twined in the gold of her hair. 'What's wrong with them?'

'I…' Nona reached up to touch them. 'I don't know. I can see. They don't hurt.'

'But, they're black … like someone poured ink into them.' Ruli looked frightened, but there was plenty more to be frightened about than odd eyes.

'I took the black cure… the one I made with Hessa and Ara.'

Ruli's fear turned to horror. 'Why? Why would you do that?'

Nona pointed towards the brightness of the slopes. 'Those soldiers haven't just come for Ara. I don't care what promises Thuran Tacsis made or where he made them. Raymel Tacsis wants his revenge and someone out there knows that if they don't go back with me they may as well not go back at all. Maybe all of them know that. And if they come I'm going to go down fighting, not poisoned and helpless, ready to be bound and carried off to some torture chamber.' It was almost true. She had put the vial to her lips when she heard that the soldiers were advancing on the cave, worried that they might carry venoms to take her alive – but what had made her tip it into her mouth? That had been the memory of Clera coming back off the plateau having brewed the catweed liquor. She had blamed the stink on poor Malkin because, despite the plant's name, Sister Apple's silly rhyme held truth, catweed didn't smell like a cat weed, but segren root did.

'I took it because I didn't trust my friend.' That was the truth, and like many truths it was hard and it hurt.

When Nona raided Sister Apple's stores she had stolen catweed and segren root along with anything else that looked useful. After Clera's alchemy out on the plateau some of both were missing, the segren root cut to disguise the loss … but Nona had spotted it anyway, because the smell had made her suspicious and, hating herself, she had checked up on Clera. Nona had come on the ranging knowing that Clera was carrying lock-up … she just hadn't quite known why.

'Zole's talking…' Jula was crouched beside the girl that Sherzal had set among them. The four-blood come to claim her place in history.

'Tarkax got the biggest dose, then Ara, then me. Zole got jabbed in the fight but Clera must have been running out of needles, or used one twice.'

'Kill. Her.' Zole watched Nona kneel beside her, her black eyes dull.

'I'm not killing her,' Nona said. Whatever Clera had done she was Nona's friend. It wasn't a bond made for breaking. 'She's well tied.'

'Kill.'

'No!' Nona snapped the word. 'Tell me what Sherzal wants. We're probably going to die here, so you may as well. The Tacsis aren't going to want to leave witnesses. Tell me and I'll do my best to draw things out so you've got a chance to face this on your feet.'

'Argatha.' Zole forced the word past a locked jaw.

'I know she doesn't want that…' Nona frowned. 'She did. Once. But something changed. She gave you to the abbess.'

'Argatha. Not. Four-blood.'

'Yes it is. That's what the prophecy says. Four bloods speaking with one voice, and the Ark will listen.'

'Four. Hearts.'

'Oh gods.' Nona looked around. Only Darla and Jula were on their feet, both looking blank.

'Yisht!' Ruli said.

'Yisht.' Nona nodded. 'Sherzal's after four shiphearts, not one four-blood. And Yisht's not going to have given up on getting the one from the convent.'

Nona bent back down to Zole. 'What can the Ark do?'

Zole shook her head, just a faint vibration of movement.

'You don't know?'

'No.'

'I know,' Jula said, her voice faint.

'You?' Nona got to her feet.

'Well.' Jula spread her hands. 'I know what the books in the convent library say about it. Some of them anyway. I helped Hessa research it. It's what she's been doing for two years while we train to fight.'

'And?' Nona wasn't sure why she cared. There were soldiers

out in the gully with swords in hand and murder on their minds. 'What do the books say?'

'They say a lot of things. Miracles, cures, wisdom, all those things…'

'So they tell us nothing?' Nona had harboured suspicions about whether anything of worth might be found in a book.

'Hessa said there's a common thread,' Jula said. 'That's how she found the right books. She's very good with thread-work. Better than—'

'Tell me!' Nona barked. In her mind's eye the soldiers were already advancing, spread across the slopes, the sun's red light bleeding across their blades.

'Most accounts agree that the Ark can take us to the Hope just like the four tribes were brought here in their ships. And…'

'And?' Nona remembered Sherzal's smile when Ara tried to cow her with the power of the Path. She hadn't looked like a woman who would go to all these lengths to run away to a distant sun. Even one that burned so white amid heavens scattered with the red embers of dying stars.

'And … it controls the moon. It can turn it, change the focus…'

'Ancestor!' Ruli covered her mouth with a hand.

'Shit!' Darla let her jaw drop.

'Gods!' Nona shook her head. A person who could steer the moon wouldn't want to flee Abeth … they would *own* Abeth!

'Send out Nona Reeve!' The shout came from outside. 'The rest of you can go free.'

'I thought Clera said they wanted Ara…' Ruli looked confused.

'They lied to her. Raymel is behind this, not Thuran.' Nona wondered what would have happened if the Tacsis agent had told Clera the truth, would her price have gone up because of their friendship, or down because Nona had nobody to avenge her? She wondered how long Clera had been slipping into the Tacsis pocket. What information had she first sold to turn that copper penny into a silver crown…

'Send out Nona Reeve!'

On the floor Clera opened her eyes and started to struggle in her bonds, grunting around the strip of cloth that Darla had gagged her with. How long had she been feigning unconsciousness? Just one more deception? And why this sudden panic? Nona met her gaze and realized she felt anger, but no hate. Her friend would never have sold her. The Tacsis had used Clera, tricked her, played on her resentment of Ara's wealth.

'Just the girl!' Shouted from the slope.

Nona spun around. 'I'll go to them, but we're going to have to fight either way.'

'Fight?' Darla snorted and kicked Clera into stillness. 'With what? We're going fists against swords?'

Nona pressed Clera's throwing star into Ruli's palm. 'That's one dead right there.' She retrieved Tarkax's forgotten tular from the shadows, surprised by the weight of it, and put it into Darla's hands. 'Get his jacket and trews on. You're not that much bigger. Keep your hood. If they're scared of you it gives you an edge.' She bent and pulled the long knife and hatchet from Tarkax's belt. Close up he smelled of woodsmoke and a spice she didn't recognize. 'Jula, take these.' She pushed them at her.

'W-what are you going to use?' Jula asked, the weapons trembling in her grip. She was a natural warrior despite her affection for books, but also terrified, and why not? The Tacsis soldiers would make as short work of the novices as Partnis Reeve's apprentices had. They were adults against children, and well-trained. Darla might be a man's match in strength but she held an unfamiliar sword and it shook in a white-knuckled grip. Also, there were twelve out there and in the cave Nona was the only hunska standing.

'Let me tell you a story,' she said.

'What?' Darla seemed unimpressed, angry at her own fear.

'A story.' Nona motioned for them to sit. 'We have time. If they weren't going to check Tarkax's kills then they would have rushed us by now.'

'What story?' Ruli asked, turning the throwing star over and over in her hand, her gaze on Clera.

'A true story.' Nona looked across to where Ara lay watching, trapped in her poisoned body. 'I lied before, about why my village gave me to the child-taker … why my mother let them… I lied and lied again. Now it's time to tell the truth.' She had their attention now. Even Darla who she had told no lies would have heard the story from others. Perhaps even Zole knew it.

'A juggler once came to my village. He was my first friend.' And Nona let the words run from her tongue. It had been the truth that she told the second time, of how Amondo had left and her mother blamed Nona for it, and Nona had believed her mother even though the reasons were beyond her understanding. It had been the truth when she said that she had followed the juggler, taking directions from Mother Sible out in the far-fields. It had all been the truth up until the first trees of the Rellam Forest rose around the road.

Everywhere has its ghosts, Amondo had said, but in most places those ghosts are at least hidden in the corners, or tucked away at right angles to the world, waiting their moment. In the Rellam Forest you could see the ghosts, patterned on the gloom beneath the canopy, the distortion of their faces frozen into the bark of ancient trunks. And you could hear them too, screaming into the silence, not quite breaking it but making it tremble.

I followed, not caring about ghost or faerie, because when a true fear takes hold of you it drives out the others, the ones people try to give you, try to put into the heart of you with stories and dark looks. A true fear grows in the bones of you.

I followed because I thought that if I turned back then I would keep turning back, turning away from every other fear, from every new thing, and that I would never leave that place to which my father had brought me. I would live, toil, grow old, and die, all within sight of my mother's hut, and the ice would remain forever a line glimpsed in the distance, and I wouldn't matter to the world nor would it matter to me.

That was a bigger fear than the shadows between the trees.

I let the path lead me, not stopping for it's when you stop

that things catch up with you. And not quickening my pace, for in a haunted forest any increase in the speed with which you walk is a slippery slope to blind panic and the mad dash that sees you lost in the deep wood with a broken ankle.

I walked until it grew too dark to see the trail and then I sat with my back to an oak and watched the dark. Rain came, thick with sleet, pattering down among the leaves, gathering and dripping, sliding to forest floor with the soft wet sounds imagination can fashion into nightmare.

When the focus came it woke me, first patterning the world in glowing red, and black shadow, the undergrowth writhing beneath the sharp relief of branches. As the ground began to steam I thought I heard a shout, far off, and I took to the trail, running hard, knowing it would be Amondo.

I met him on the path, rushing towards me out of the fog as fast as I was running towards him. He nearly flattened me but I'm quick and I slipped aside at the last second. It happened so swiftly that he didn't even see me. I shouted after him, but he was lost in the pink blanket of the fog.

I thought he was gone, but the sound of his feet pounding the track stopped in one sudden moment.

'Nona?'

'It's me! I followed you.'

'Dear Ancestor! Hide! Hide in the trees!'

I heard the sounds of his pursuit, more pounding feet, more shouts and cries.

'Bleed me!' And Amondo came running back, the hot mist swirling as it released him. He grabbed my arm and dragged me off the track, out into the forest. The thorns tore my skirt and cut my legs.

'Shhhh.' Amondo pulled me behind a tree, one hand over my mouth.

The band chasing him thundered by, clinking metal, rasping breaths, heavy boots.

A minute later Amondo drew his hand away and unclenched the other from around my arm.

'Why were they chasing you?'

'I owe them something.'

'Why did you leave?'

'I wore out my welcome on the first day, Nona. The real question is why would anyone stay?'

The focus was passing and already the fog lay in streamers being trailed through the tree trunks by the wind. The moon's light, no longer fierce, showed Amondo's face, worried and watchful.

'I want to know—'

'People always want to know things … until they hear them, and then it's too late. Knowledge is a rug of a certain size, and the world is larger. It's not what remains uncovered at the edges that should worry you, rather what is swept beneath.'

'I don't understand.' He didn't look like the juggler who had thrown and caught for a heel of bread. He looked older and sadder and wiser.

'There's a line, Nona, a burning line that runs through the world. It runs through dreams and beneath roots and across the sky … and it leads to you.'

'Me?' I asked. It didn't seem likely. 'Why?'

He managed a smile. 'We're back to knowledge again. The important thing is that those men who were chasing me – one of them can follow that line. He calls it a thread. A clever man with clever fingers… He can tie three knots in an eyelash, that one. And he'll keep on following that thread. He didn't want to go into the village to get you … so he sent me…'

'You were there to get me out?' I felt a numbness prickling across my cheekbones and a hollowness in my stomach. 'But you said we were fr—'

'And a fine job you've done of it, Amondo.' A deep voice rolled out from the direction of the track. Figures moved from shadow to moonlight to shadow. Tall men in uniform, swords at their hips, the soft metal whisper of mailshirts. 'Just when I was starting to doubt you!' A laugh. 'Nobody took her. Not even an itinerant juggler. She ran away by herself. Brilliant.'

The soldiers closed on us from all sides. Two seized Amondo's arms, another took me by the scruff of my neck.

The leader, the one Amondo said could follow my thread, moved out into the moonlight. He wasn't old, not much older than Amondo, but he didn't look like us, not like a real person. He didn't look hungry. His beard came rolling down to the bottom of his neck and there wasn't a spot of dirt in it. His cloak was scarlet even in the moonlight and the silver bands across his shoulders shone bloody with it.

'We still have to hurt you, of course,' he said. 'For the running.' He motioned to the two soldiers and they began to twist Amondo's arms. He cried out immediately.

'And then of course we have to kill you,' the man added when Amondo paused his scream to gasp in a breath. 'To keep this secret.'

That's when I did it. I reached around to where the man had hold of my neck and I cut him, skin, muscle, tendons, arteries – Sister Tallow is right, men are just like pigs inside – and his blood shot out so fast that it drenched my shoulders even though I was already moving as fast as I knew how to.

I knew I had to reach the man with the beard, the man with the clever fingers, without giving him the chance to show any of his cleverness. I slashed him across the stomach before he even noticed I was loose. I cut him and the bright rings of his mail made bright little sounds as they broke open. He noticed then and folded up, hugging his belly. I cut that beard of his with another slash and left him torrenting blood from an open throat.

Then it was all running and slicing and screaming. I climbed up one man who tried to chase me round a tree with his knife. I dug my blades into his back and hauled myself up him. A foot on his belt – thrust my blades into his neck – heaved up. I jumped from his shoulders onto the last of them. She still had a hand on Amondo's arm, her other one on her sword hilt, half-drawn.

And when it was done and they were sprawled among the bushes and the trees were splashed with gore and cut here and there where the soldiers had swung their swords I stood in the middle of it all wearing their blood and screaming. And I was screaming for *more*. And Amondo ran … although he was my friend and I had saved him … he ran.

* * *

'And that's how they found me the next morning, and that's my secret, and that's why my mother let them give me away. I'm a monster.'

Nona started to walk towards the cave mouth and the day that was dying on the slopes just beyond. 'That's my secret and my shame. I'm Nona Grey, war is in my veins, and the screams of my enemies are music to me.'

'Wait!' Darla shouted. 'That's nonsense. Where did you get your knives from … how did you know how to use them? How did you kill six warriors?'

Nona turned and slashed a hand across the wall. A shower of fragments scattered out across the cave floor and where she had struck four gouges remained in the stone, deep and dark.

'But … they had swords.' Darla waved hers for good measure.

'Never try to swing one in a forest,' Nona said. 'And never underestimate a wild animal, however small it might be.'

Darla had no reply. She set her fingers to the cuts Nona had left in the rock, and stared in wonder.

'Scarlet and silver?' Ruli spoke from the back of the cave where she had crouched, listening to Nona's story.

'What?' With the truth out Nona ached to leave, before they properly understood what she had told them.

'The man was in scarlet and silver? Were the others in uniform?'

'I…' Nona tried to see it. She saw blood mostly, and wounds. 'Perhaps.' Yes.

'Those are Sherzal's colours,' Ruli said. 'The headman at your village would have known that. He would have known that they couldn't keep you – not with the emperor's own sister after you. Your mother would have understood too. The child-taker was your best chance. Hiding in plain sight. A girl with a price on her head, sold for nothing, there in a cage ready for sale… It was all they could do to keep you safe.'

'No.' Nona waved the idea away, as if her blades could slice it into a lie. 'It wasn't like that. They would have told me…'

'Really?' Ruli stood up, staring at Nona with concern. It was more than she could take. 'Not telling you was more likely to stop you coming back…'

'I'm going out there.' Nona started back towards the cave mouth. 'Once it starts you—'

'Nona, there are *twelve* of them!' Jula stepped after her, though stopping short, as if she saw something new in Nona's place. Some wild beast perhaps, with eyes like holes into the night and hands thick with old blood.

'You might have…' Ruli frowned, staring at Nona's hands, 'invisible daggers… But they have swords, as long as you are tall! And we're not in a dark, misty forest! Don't go!'

'I have the Path, Ruli.' Nona offered a faint smile.

'You have the Path at the convent,' Ruli said. 'But let's be honest … you're not very good with it there. Ara is much better. And Hessa – she knows more about threads than Sister Pan does already! But isn't that the whole point of Sherzal wanting the shipheart? This far from it even a Holy Witch finds it hard to touch the Path. And your serenity … well … it's rubbish.' Ruli looked down. 'Sorry.'

'I've given up on serenity.' Nona smiled. 'It wasn't me. But I do have a new record on blade-path…'

'Blade-path?' Darla asked. 'What the hell has blade-path got to do with anything?'

'New record?' Ruli asked. 'You completed it? Well…' She looked around the cave, Tarkax lying in a pool of his own blood, Ara and Zole paralysed, Clera bound and staring dazed over her gag. '…congratulations?'

'I used the grease,' Nona said.

'What?'

'The grease you gave me. I'd been doing it all wrong. I kept going slower and slower and falling off sooner and sooner. It felt wrong. It didn't fit. So I did what I do to reach the Path. I ran at it. I cleaned the resin from my feet and greased my soles. Blade-path's all downhill, except the bits that aren't and by the time you reach them you're going fast enough to carry through.'

'But the corkscrew?' Ruli looked up at her, blinking.

'If you're going fast enough you can slide around the inside.' Nona grinned. 'It's wonderful. Everything fits together. All the choices, all the balancing, they happen at fight-speed, they make sense. I did it in thirty counts!'

'*THIRTY* counts?' Ruli gasped. 'That's impossible.'

'It's not as fast as Sister Owl,' Nona said. 'But I was pleased with it.'

'I still don't care,' Darla said. 'How is that silly game going to help against what's out there?' She waved her sword towards the slope.

'But it's not just a game,' Nona said. 'We do it for a reason.'

'Balance and timing,' Jula said.

'The hunska do it for that. But the quantal do it because it trains the mind for the Path. I had a … I suddenly saw everything in a new way.' Nona turned back towards the daylight.

'An epiphany,' Jula breathed.

'An epiphany.' Sister Kettle had taught Nona the word but she hadn't found it on her lips when she wanted it. An epiphany. Seeing the world anew with new understanding. Like when Sister Pan's trick pictures suddenly made sense and you saw the bump as a hole, the young woman as an old lady. The same thing had happened with Clera. Nona had taken a step back and in an instant seen her treachery whole and clear. The new picture didn't erase the old – the bump was still a hole, but now it was a bump as well; the old lady was still a young one, but now she was old too. Clera was still her friend, and now an enemy also.

Nona saw too that the truth had been hers for the taking. Sister Apple's bitter pill… All that had stopped her asking Clera about the throwing star and unravelling the whole tale was her own desire not to speak of Amondo and the forest where she had stood, clothed in blood, revealed to the world as a monster, hungry for the kill. One truth for another and they wouldn't be standing in this cave. But that itself, like most truths, had proved too bitter for the mouth to speak.

Epiphany? She saw herself. A child of nine, the dried blood of six royal soldiers still in her hair. She saw the child-taker,

Giljohn, with one hand on Four-Foot's reins, the cart and cage behind him, rattling up the lane. She saw Grey Stephen bent in conversation. Her mother weeping. She had stared at the memory so long, so many times… Could it be possible? To see it another way?

'So you think you can walk the Path now?' Ruli asked. 'Even here?'

'I think so,' Nona said. 'I just need to get angry enough.' Rage could throw her at the Path back in the convent, close to the shipheart. Rage would throw her at it now – enough of it would. And this time she wouldn't try to slow herself, wouldn't try to stutter to a halt and gain her balance. She would take the speed and aim it down the Path and take all the power it would give her. And own it. All she needed was the rage. She reached for it … but where a fire had once blazed only an ember remained. Had her mother truly saved her?

'Stay here,' Darla said, looking down. 'You don't have to go out there. Or … we could scatter and run.'

'No,' Nona said. If they ran Darla would be the first caught.

'We can wait,' Jula said. 'The poison will wear off and Tarkax can fight and…'

'And Sister Tallow will come with the others,' Ruli finished.

'Go.' Zole managed to put some heat into the word. She understood. If you wanted to win against the odds you had to carry the fight to the enemy. You had to take them unprepared.

'I have to—' But something dark and vast reached up to grab her and before Nona's mouth closed on the last word she was gone.

Nona had been yanked from her body so swiftly she hardly had time to feel it begin to fall. She saw nothing, not even darkness, felt nothing save the pull and a sense of rushing. Then in one moment she slammed back into herself. She saw a paved yard, Heart Hall on her right, the Ancestor's dome rising above the dormitory block to her left… Nona had been poured into someone's skull, but not into her own. She leaned onto her crutch and took another limping step. Hessa!

Hessa's thoughts rose around Nona, a tide that threatened to drown her. Nona shouted that she had to go, screamed to be released back to the cave, but Hessa just took another step as if she'd heard nothing.

Hessa had known it would be Yisht. Even so, finding the gate to the under-tunnels unlocked put a cold terror in her. She had shared every excruciating moment that Nona endured when Yisht had held her hands tight about her neck. It might have been Nona's throat that was closed, but Hessa's lungs had burned too, striving for a breath that wouldn't come.

'Why would you think you could come back?' Hessa whispered. It made no sense. Did the woman want to die?

'What are we doing here?' Ghena hugged herself against the ice-wind, weaker now than it was, at the end of its reign, but still able to carry a sting.

'You need to go to the abbess. Tell her Yisht has broken into the under-tunnels again.' Hessa had been put in Red dormitory while Grey Class ranged.

'The abbess? You're mad! She'll kill me. It's the middle of the night.' Ghena's habitual temper hadn't been improved by Hessa waking her with a pinch and cajoling her to come out into the night despite her protests.

'Tell her Yisht is back. If you don't she really will kill you! This is serious, Ghena. Deadly serious.'

'Ancestor's tits!' Ghena spat on the ground and took off running in the direction of the abbess's house. 'You better be right about this, Hop-along!'

Hessa turned back to the gate and sighed. She had taken threads from everything of Yisht's that Nona had brought her. Blood, hair, clothes, a boot-knife. And each bright and coiling thread she had pulled taut across her mind, feeling the woman's impotent rage as she jolted westward in her barrel. What had scared her wasn't the depth of that rage, but how cold it ran.

Hessa pushed the gate and it swung open, the tunnel beyond yawning darkly and swallowing the light from her lantern. She sighed again and began her long and painful descent of the stairs.

None of them had imagined for a moment that Yisht would dare return after her efforts had been discovered. Quite how she had evaded the Grey Sisters watching over the convent's approaches Hessa couldn't say, but now the woman would find herself up against Red Sisters. She must be insane to think she could reach the shipheart, let alone escape with it.

The threads had started to tremble as Hessa sought sleep that night. A vibration so slight that she hadn't been able to unravel it from her own nerves. Nona had seen something terrible two mornings before. Death and dead men. Sister Kettle was involved somehow but Nona had become so hardened to fear that whatever had happened wasn't enough to make the full link between them. Even so, it had left Hessa shaken and unable to sleep that night.

This night, despite the trembling of threads, exhaustion had taken Hessa to her dreams. And the threads had jerked her from a nightmare, yanking so hard that the pain filled her sight with sparks for several moments.

At the door to the Shade chamber Hessa stopped and leaned on her crutch. 'What's she doing here? Why this passage?' Hessa knew that Yisht's efforts had been discovered. There had been nuns in and out of the guest chambers all through the evening of the day that Grey Class left to go ranging. They had to have discovered the shaft and set guards while measures were taken to protect the shipheart and to challenge Sherzal about the matter.

'What good am I going to do?' Hessa shook her head and went on down the tunnel, ill at ease on the uneven surface. 'If falling over is the worst that happens to me…' She spoke to give herself courage. Before her the threads that led to Yisht snaked away into darkness.

Ten yards on the threads veered into a fissure in the wall, so low that Hessa would have to abandon her crutch and crawl. 'How did she…' But of course, even though the fissure was so tight that it daunted Nona, the novices had proved to Yisht she would fit through it.

Hessa went to all fours on the muddy floor. Or to all threes – her withered leg would do nothing but drag. She turned around, shuffling backwards into the fissure on her behind. She pushed the lantern ahead of her, praying it wouldn't fall, praying she wouldn't get stuck, praying that Yisht had already been apprehended and wasn't already wriggling her way back through the very same gaps.

The distance to the larger tunnel was perhaps twenty yards, but squeezing through it took a lifetime and left Hessa flat on her back when she finally emerged, gasping and trembling. At the tightest spot Hessa had seen that the rock had been scooped away, leaving strange smooth gouges, widening the passage.

'A rock-worker then.' The rarest of the elemental marjal talents. Yisht's unique qualifications were becoming apparent.

Hessa angled her lantern up. The shaft in the tunnel roof led to a boarded-over entrance. She looked down the tunnel. At any moment a knife could come winging out of that darkness and hammer into her, and Hessa's story would be over, drawn into the great story of the Ancestor, a raindrop in an ocean. She should just wait for the nuns.

The threads running invisible through Hessa's fingers said Yisht was not so close … but had she come alone, or did the black tunnel hold some accomplice, waiting, silent and ready to cut throats?

With a sigh Hessa began to shuffle along the tunnel floor, inch by inch, foot by foot. The seat of her habit would be worn through. 'If I survive this Sister Mop will kill me.'

She carried on, knowing that in the shadows about her lay the spot where Yisht had all but choked the life from Nona.

Some minutes later she sat looking up at the entrance to the crawl-tunnel that joined her passage to the one where Yisht had been digging when Nona had found her. A knotted rope dangled from the hole, presumably set when the nuns came down to investigate. Without it Hessa would have had no chance of getting up there. Even with it she had to touch the Path in order to put enough strength in her arms to haul herself up. She lay in the connecting crawl-way, panting. She preferred not to touch the Path: its energies disquieted her and filled her with dreams of power that fitted awkwardly at best into her ordered mind. Thread-work suited her far better, had greater subtlety to it. She enjoyed working so close to the Path but not allowing its force to dominate and overmaster her. In its way thread-work was every bit as powerful as Path-walking, closer to the wonders Abbess Glass achieved without violence or threat. Path-walking was closer to the blunt and brutal methods of the Tacsis – not that they were unique among the Sis for that.

A gentle pull on Yisht's thread revealed her to be close now, but focused on some task. Hessa could almost see her, high in the rising cut she had made over long weeks of digging. She was digging once more, but pausing every now and then to touch the stone, changing it into something less resistant that fell easily beneath the swings of her pick.

Hessa had never gathered such strong and detailed impressions from a thread before. She stared at her hand where the threads twined. Curious. Then she felt it. The pulse of the shipheart, thrumming through the thread, thrumming through everything, even the stone itself. Eager, she wriggled on through the narrow passage, seeing the space around her fill with detail as the shipheart built upon the power within her. She saw the threads of other people's passing. Nona's, Yisht's, three nuns who she might identify if she were to pick out their threads and examine them. By the time she reached the opening into the wider passage beyond, strewn with rubble, Hessa was starting to see threads in the rocks themselves, their lineage running back across the aeons into ancient seas or the fires of the earth. She even saw the threads of the waters that had once run here, carving out these tunnels, threads that led on to rivers and oceans, up into the sky, down to percolate through dark soil and run in secret rivers.

Hessa shook her head, banishing the visions, focusing on her own task. She understood Yisht's accelerating progress now. The rock-worker had used her marjal powers to aid her excavation, but as she grew closer to the shipheart its aura enhanced her talents and she was able to tunnel ever more swiftly.

Hessa saw then why no thread-warnings could be set

around the shipheart or the tunnels about it as had been done with the Noi-Guin knife that Nona hid. The beat of the shipheart rippled out like waves, unhindered by thickness of stone, and would wash away any such workings. Only true threads survived and no entanglement would last for long under such conditions.

Another rope dangled from the tunnel's far end, anchored on an iron spike driven into a crack in the wall. One of the nuns who came down to investigate lacked the athleticism required to make the journey without help. No Red Sister then.

'Nona! Nona!'

Nona shook her head, spluttering, icy water dripping from her face. 'Where…?'

'They're gathering again outside.' Jula leaned into view, water-canteen in hand. Above her the roof of the cave lay rippled in red and shadow as the sun sank behind the ridges. 'You fell … you've been lying there for ages, muttering … we thought the segren root had got you … or the black cure … or both.'

Nona rolled her head to look towards the entrance. Darla was there, hooded and filling out Tarkax's sealskins pretty well, tular in hand.

'She's been letting them see her so they don't think we're escaping out the back tunnel,' Ruli said.

Nona tried to get up at that, shaking the last strands of Hessa's thoughts from her mind.

'There's no back tunnel!' Jula said, glowering at Ruli. 'We've looked.'

'Let's get you up.' Ruli hooked an arm under Nona.

'Wait!' Nona shouted it loud enough to draw Darla's attention from the slopes. 'I was with Hessa – I mean, seeing what she's seeing. Yisht is back at the convent again. She's trying to steal the shipheart. Hessa's going to try to stop her.'

'Yisht? What are you talking about?' Darla came stomping across, stepping over first Tarkax then Ara. 'How do you know this?'

'How can Hessa stop her?' Ruli demanded.

'She'll get killed!' Jula looked shocked.

Nona sat up. 'She thinks she can do it. She's not scared any more. That's why I'm not there. We only join when something really bad is happening to one of us.'

'Hell, she should be watching us then!' Darla snorted. 'We've got twelve kinds of bad right outside.'

Nona frowned. 'There are no coincidences among the thread-bound,' she repeated Sister Pan's words. The nun had told them that the rhythm of their lives would start to match – and here they were both face to face with death.

'Hessa thinks she can beat Yisht?' Ruli asked, doubtful.

'Yes, but she can't do it.' Nona shook her head. 'It's the shipheart, it does that, it gives you power, makes you think you're indestructible … it's like the Path. But Yisht will kill her!'

Darla returned to peer out at the slopes, knowing that to those out there in the day's last light she would be invisible within the cave's gloom.

'Why is this happening?' Ruli helped Nona up. 'I mean, why now, why is Yisht going for the shipheart just as we're trapped and about to die?'

'We're not going to die.' Nona shrugged off her range-coat. 'They are.' She flexed her fists and felt the flaw-blades form. 'And what better chance would Yisht get? Half the Red Sisters are out with Tallow to escort us back. The best of the Grey Sisters are absent too. And if news of Sister Kettle has reached the convent then the abbess may have sent more sisters to help … it's the ideal time to strike.'

'The soldiers who went looking for Tarkax's kills are back. The full twelve are on the slope again. They're getting ready to make their move.' Darla kept her voice low but it shook with nerves.

Nona started to advance. 'Let me—' But Hessa's terror reached out and seized her. Nona fought the thread-bond, knowing she would only be able to watch Hessa's fight, knowing her friends needed her in theirs. But the bond's strength proved too great. Her body fell, helpless, with her enemies gathering to strike. And once more Nona became bound within Hessa's mind. A silent witness.

Hessa let herself down the rope, good leg questing for the floor, the lantern dangling from her elbow on its strap, smoky and hot. She made it and collapsed to the smooth wet stone, the muscles in her arms burning.

Lifting her lantern, she cried out in horror. Just an arm's length from her face and unseen during her descent Sister Flint sat with her back to the wall beneath the connecting passage. Her long neck lay at an odd angle to her shoulders, the bones making an unsightly bulge beneath dark skin where the angle grew most acute. Her eyes stared at nothing, reflecting the lantern's flame, and a thin red line of drool ran from the corner of her mouth.

Go back. Nona spoke into the clamour of Hessa's thoughts and went unheard.

Hessa looked towards the entrance to Yisht's shaft, glowing with the distant light of the assassin's lantern. The sound of pick-blows and crashing rock echoed back and out into the main tunnel. She returned her gaze to Sister Flint. She had been a Red Sister, as fine a warrior as Sweet Mercy could produce. And Yisht had killed her.

Go back! Nona shouted it but struggled to be heard against the beat of the shipheart's pulse.

Hessa raised her hands. She could see the threads that she had drawn from Yisht hanging in her fingers, golden, silver, scarlet, and black. Pull on this golden thread and a stream of memories would come rushing to flood her with the woman's bloodstained history. Pull it far enough and she would see the ice, see Yisht even before her memory began, swaddled in furs and innocence. Pull on that scarlet one and she could change the woman's mind, pull hard enough and any opinion she might hold would be overturned, however firm it might be set. Pull this silver thread, the one that anchored her to her soul, and the woman would come undone. Hessa knew she could do it. She held Yisht's life in her hands, and the shipheart gave her all the power and clarity she needed.

Hessa edged to the shaft, scraping herself across the rubble, cutting her hands, tearing her habit. Dark splatters amongst the broken rock caught the light of Hessa's lantern and returned it. She rolled and touched a finger to one glistening patch. 'Blood!' Yisht hadn't escaped unharmed from her encounter with Sister Flint then…

A tremendous crash echoed down the shaft and moments later rock dust billowed out, obliterating Hessa's vision, making her cough.

Silence. Then, as the dust began to settle, the sound of loose rock being pulled away. Hessa shuffled the last foot and peered around to see up along the steep slope of the narrow slot that Yisht had carved. The whole passage glowed. Light, from some source far brighter than any lantern, caught the last of the dust and turned it into gold. At first Hessa thought Yisht must have broken through to the surface, but as the dust continued to settle she saw the woman's blurred black outline, and on every side the light shafted around her as if a miniature sun were before her, level with her waist. And if it were a sun then it was the Hope rather than Abeth's red star, a young sun full of white and gold.

And the heat. Even at this distance it made Hessa sweat.

'She'll never get out with it…' Hessa squinted against the brightness.

The light changed, shadows ran and swung, the quality of the shipheart's pulse altered. Yisht turned to the side, her fingers red around the shipheart's glowing sphere, her bones dark within the rosy haze of her flesh.

Leave! Nona shouted it at Hessa and for a moment she thought that she might have been noticed.

Hessa watched, just one eye at the very edge of the cut, her resolve blown away like focus mist in an ice-wind. Yisht would never get out with the shipheart. She started to pull away. Yisht held the shipheart before her and thrust it towards the wall. The air whined as if a thousand mosquitoes had gathered to feast … and the rock flowed away as though it were liquid mud. Yisht stepped forward into the void.

'No!' Hessa understood now. Yisht might be a marjal half-blood, or even a prime, but her rock-work was only sufficient to aid her in digging, weakening the stone ready for the pick's swing, or allowing a slow and silent start to the shaft she had sunk beneath her guest quarters. Perhaps it also gave her intuition as to where the tunnels and fissures ran... But as she had come closer to the shipheart her skills had been magnified, allowing the last yards of the cut to be hewn away in just a few hours. And now – actually holding the shipheart – the rocks moved to her will. Hessa had no idea what such a gift must be costing Yisht. There was a reason that the shipheart lay buried rather than in the hands of a nun ... but whatever it cost her it also afforded a marjal rock-worker their escape. She could tunnel out, closing the shaft behind her and emerging at some pre-arranged location, no doubt to be met by Sherzal's troops.

Hessa reached her arm around the edge of the cut and pulled on all Yisht's threads at once. The warrior came flying backwards out of the hole she had created. The opposite wall arrested her motion with a crunch that made Hessa wince. For a moment she felt guilty – she hadn't meant to injure the woman – then ridiculous, knowing exactly what Yisht would do to her given a chance. In the moment after that Yisht's thoughts and memories flooded her, drawn out when Hessa pulled on the golden thread of her being.

Images washed over Nona, trapped at the back of Hessa's mind. One image, burning with importance, caught her attention and Nona seized it as it passed: the amulet she'd taken from Yisht, the sigil black against a tide of moments, recollections, sensations. And with the amulet's image came understanding. A sigil of negation, fashioned with vanishingly rare talent by a master of the art a century before. Yisht's key to the defences on the abbess's house. Her secondary mission, to claim the secrets there, now abandoned... Pressed to any enchantment the amulet would erase the magic or at the very least disrupt it.

Yisht unfolded herself slowly, the light from the shipheart breaking around her as she straightened to expose it.

Kill her! Nona shouted. *Quick!* This close to the shipheart, and with threads drawn from Yisht's own blood … she could snap the silver tie that bound Yisht's spirit, and the woman's warm flesh would topple to the ground, empty.

Hessa worked quickly, the deft fingers of her mind sorting and plucking the threads that connected her to Yisht.

'Put it down.' Hessa only mouthed the words but Yisht found herself lowering the shipheart to the ground, not against her will but because her will had changed.

End her! Nona knew killers. Yisht was a killer. Hessa was not. The killer always has the edge. *Don't give her a moment!*

Yisht raised a hand and above Hessa a thickness of rock fractured away from the ceiling.

There was no time to react, no pain, no memory of the impact, just the knowledge that the world had turned upon its side, that the lantern oil was flaring somewhere around her legs, and that she now saw Yisht through a single eye full of blood. Nothing hurt, and that worried Hessa most of all.

Yisht approached down the cut, a slim knife in her hand, her gait uncertain as if her collision with the wall had broken something inside.

'The personal touch.' Hessa thought the words but her lips scarcely moved and her breath sputtered out wetly.

Nona threw every ounce of her will against the bond that tied her to Hessa, but all that happened was that the world started shaking, as if Yisht had decided against the knife and raised all her earth-magics to crush her foe.

'Nona!' A slap that made her cheek blaze. 'Nona!' Screamed at her face, full of desperation.

Nona didn't open her eyes – they were already open – but she started seeing through them again. Darla was shaking her. 'Wake up! They're coming! All of them!'

'Buy me a minute!' She gasped the words out and Darla dropped her in shock.

'What?'

'One minute.' Nona sat. 'I need to help Hessa.' Her shadow

lay before her, thrown by the descending sun, stretching out to the rear of the cave where it joined the general gloom. Nona made a fist and extended one finger from it, sheathed in a single flaw-blade.

'Wait, we're sending her out,' Darla shouted from the cave entrance. She ducked back. 'If they're going to kill us anyway why are they so keen we send you out?'

'So I don't get killed in any fighting. Once swords start swinging anything can happen.' Nona started to cut at her shadow, slicing it away from below her feet. 'Arrrgh! Gods damn it, that hurts!' She'd known her blades cut shadow – that lesson had been taught to her at the Academy. She hadn't known that cutting her own shadow would hurt as much as cutting her own flesh.

'What?' Ruli stared in horror at the ragged edge of Nona's shadow and the strange twisting of the light about the gap. 'How will that stop them?'

'Not them. *Her!*' Nona slashed again, a long tearing motion, screaming out the agony of it.

Behind her, Darla scooped up Ara's stiff body and carried her towards the cave mouth. 'We had to subdue her with poison!' she called out.

'What are you doing?' Jula joined Ruli, dagger trembling in her grip. Whether she was talking to Nona or to Darla was hard to say.

'I'm breaking rules.' Nona threw herself onto her severed shadow before it could escape into the greater dark, and then hurled herself back at Hessa, terrified that she would be too late, terrified that she would throw herself along the threads of the bond forged in such sorrow and so long ago only to find a nothingness, just the vacant space that her friend had once occupied in the world.

The point of Yisht's knife waited just a finger's width from Hessa's eye. Yisht herself sat on the rocks just before her. In her other hand Sherzal's assassin held the shipheart, a blue-white ball of wonder, its surface a multi-layered thing across which floated the ghosts of forms both familiar and unknown.

She kept it pressed to a rip in her tunic, the flesh beneath torn and bloody.

'...I am not given to cruelty, child.'

Nona realized that Yisht was speaking.

'But you reached into my mind, and a violation like that cannot go unanswered.'

Hessa could smell meat burning and knew it was her – but still no pain reached her. The knife at her eye terrified her, but she had drawn her head back as far as she could, and still the point advanced.

Nona found herself lost, an impotent observer, her plans ridiculous. Somewhere she had hands, and those hands were full of shadow, but her ambition to draw that unleashed shadow through to Hessa lay so far beyond her talent she had no idea where to start.

Help me, Hessa!

And where Nona's orders and demands had gone unheard and unheeded, her cry for help caught her friend's attention – even beneath the heel of Yisht's revenge.

'How?'

Help me draw it through! She tried to show Hessa what she needed.

'Easy!' Hessa felt herself drifting away, beyond pain, beyond struggle. She heard the Ancestor's song, many-voiced and more beautiful than anything she had ever imagined possible. Even so – her friend had asked for help...

With the shipheart so close it seemed simplicity itself to take the dark threads from Nona's clumsy fists, beating ineffectually at the walls between them, and to pull those threads through the bond they shared. *We're Giljohn's children.* The thought rolled across the smoothness of her mind as the Ancestor's song grew louder. *Sisters of the cage.*

Stay! Nona tried to hold onto Hessa. She could feel her leaving but had no sense of where she might be going or how to follow.

The point of Yisht's blade traced a hot line down the side of Hessa's face, and in that moment of hurt the shadows suddenly swirled, rising from the ground so fast and thick and black that the broken stones rattled with their passage. Nona's shadow broke from Hessa's and threw itself at Yisht like an extension of her will, rending, tearing, screaming its hatred in registers above hearing.

From the fading, blood-soaked view that Hessa's eye provided Nona saw Yisht fall back, open wounds torn across her, shredding her jacket. She twisted, and staggered away, thrusting the shipheart at Nona's shadow to ward it off. Nona saw her shadow grow huge and monstrous, as if it were the shadow of her true self, barbed with hatred, swollen with rage. Yisht stumbled back, retreating up the shaft she had spent so many hours and so much sweat cutting into the bedrock. The shaft that led nowhere and offered no escape.

'…coming…'

'Wake! Up!'

'I'm awake.' She opened her eyes.

'Nona—' Jula, reaching out, her face without hope and full of goodbyes. Outside the tramp of many feet approaching. An arrow glanced from the wall and rattled on into the cave.

Nona shook her head, rising smoothly into a crouch. The rage she had needed now filled her from toe to head, her body vibrating with it. 'I was born for killing – the gods made me to ruin.' She batted aside an arrow and snatched another from the air before it reached Jula's neck. She tucked it into her belt.

Nona launched herself into motion, driving up and forward, aimed at the bright entrance where tall figures crowded like the shadows of teeth in the cave's open mouth. Ara lay at their feet, a helpless offering. Arrows, shot blindly into the gloom, ricocheted from the walls, clattering around her on the stone floor. Behind her she heard Darla's shout as the novice found her courage and defiance. Something sped past Nona's ear while she closed the distance to the enemy, overtaking her, spinning and scattering the sun's last rays. Clera's throwing star, released from Ruli's considerably more skilled fingers, found the face of the foremost soldier.

As Nona's feet drove her forward across the uneven floor

of the cave she let her anger, every piece of hurt and rage and despair, throw her mind towards the Path. Nona had no trouble gathering what she needed. She had felt Hessa leave, felt her sweet and clever soul join something larger and more distant, as streams find the ocean. Hessa had gone, her last mile not limped or shuffled, not even walked upon her own two feet, but run. Hessa had not feared dying. But Nona feared living without her.

As she hit the Path Nona made no attempt to slow herself or find the balance she had always sought: instead she used her speed as she had on the blade-path, letting rage propel her where serenity had held her back, riding the twisting impossibility of the Path, shooting through the convolutions and relying on instinct to keep her on course, whatever came.

At the same time that Nona's mind ran the Path her feet drove her towards the soldiers crowding through the cave mouth. She angled herself towards the wall, leapt at it, and kicked off, gaining height. Her speed and the unexpected nature of the attack, coming at the day-blind men from the darkness of the cave, took her over the points of their swords. Her target, quicker than the rest, managed to raise his blade but she twisted about it, her movements in the physical world somehow complementing and complemented by her simultaneous running of the Path.

Nona flew, arms extended, and hit the man in the face with both fists. Her flaw-blades, six inches long and spiking from her knuckles, gave her the purchase to leapfrog him, bringing her feet to his shoulders and springing away, her blades slicing clear as she jumped. A sword hissed towards her while she sailed over the last of the soldiers. She managed to swing her arms wide before her as it cut across her path. There was a moment's contact, a bright metallic sound, and she came to ground tumbling across the rocky slope with sections of neatly-divided longsword clattering down around her.

Nona fell from the Path at the same moment as she hit the ground. The impact against rough stone could have broken bones, at the least torn flesh and left her too injured to put up much of a fight. Instead, wrapped in the Path's power, Nona left a channel of shattered stone in her wake and rolled to her feet, crouched in the fighting stance. She didn't know how many steps she had remained on the Path for but there were many of them, the energies building inside her with each one. Past the tenth or twelfth step Nona had noticed that energy was bleeding off her, and that each new step built her reserves a little more slowly than the one before, but still, the build-up was inexorable and exhilarating. Such a magnificent feeling, in fact, that had she not fallen then she would never have voluntarily left the Path.

Crouched there, with the soldiers still turning to follow the line of her attack, Nona knew that the impact with the ground had saved her life. Even now she struggled to own what the Path had given her. The raw energy of it smoked from her skin. All about her the rock trembled, and the broken fragments, shattered loose by her passage, now started to rise, each making slow revolutions as it lifted from the ground.

Nona opened her mouth and the scream that came from it was larger than her body, a hammer that smote the rock, cut down the soldiers like wheat before the scythe, and rattled away down every gully, even reaching out to smite the distant walls of the Spine and come echoing back. The scream tore her lungs and throat, spattering bright crimson blood across the rocks before her. Nona felt herself separate into broken pieces, each an image of herself, resonances in time as the power she struggled to contain vibrated through the stuff of reality.

Ara had been broken into three pieces by the Path energies she used on the day Zole came to the convent. She had struggled to pull herself together. Nona stood in nine parts, some captured in the moments as she had tumbled across the rock, others held around her, some just rising into the crouch, others lifting from it.

At the same time as Nona's borrowed power threatened to scatter her across the slope something stabbed at her chest. A cold, sucking something, lanced into her, a hungry void syphoning off some of what she had taken.

Nona knew that in a heartbeat each piece of her would fly apart, torn one from the next by the Path's energy. She needed to pull herself back into one unified whole, to find a common thread that would bind them together. All she could think of, all that was in her mind as she watched the soldier she had jumped from, still in the act of falling, his head a ruin, was that she ached to kill the rest of them.

It was enough.

With a snap like some deep bone clicking into place Nona stood whole, the Path's energies owned, bound into her flesh, armouring her, strengthening her. All around her the rocks, once suspended, began to fall.

Nona tore at her breast where the coldness somehow knifed through her new-found strength. Her habit shredded and Yisht's amulet fell from the torn inner pocket. Nona batted it away before the iron sigil of negation could drink any more of her power.

She slowed the turning of the world, dug deeper into the moment that she had ever been. The falling stones seemed to crawl towards the ground, and when she launched herself at the tall axeman who stood closest to her she hurtled through the air fast as any spear was ever thrown. Her cry of rage had set him falling, but she didn't give him time to hit the ground.

Nona moved among the mailed bodies of her foe spinning and swinging, opening disastrous wounds wherever her hands passed. Shields and chainmail offered no resistance to her blades. With the Path-power bound into her, muscle and bone, a well-placed kick could shatter a grown man's hip through his armour. Her blood sang with the violence. Ducking beneath the swing of a sword, she clawed through a woman's knee and threw herself onto the largest of their number, a seven-foot warrior, thick with muscle. Nona sprang up the height of him. The punch she delivered to his throat held such force that her arm passed through his neck, scattering the small bones of his spine in a crimson splatter.

The red work of killing carried on. At some point in the midst of it Nona took the arrow from her belt and stuck it into the eye of the man who had fired it at her. Nona had hidden her secret so long, worked so hard to be … normal, but the truth lay all around her in crimson arcs of gore written out across the rocks. She had come to Sweet Mercy bearing the title 'murderer' and come to that deed from a cage where her first act of slaughter had placed her. Even before that the children of the village had seen her for what she was, a fox among hens. *Billem Smithson tried to hurt me* – she had said – *this was inside him.* She must have been all of three or four years old.

She twisted away from the lazy descent of two swords and a thrust spear, diving between a forest of legs, slicing into the meat of a thigh, opening muscle and arteries, scoring the bone. The novices, the nuns, the abbess herself, would all know her now for the monster she was, a rabid animal unfit for the company of decent people, holy or otherwise.

An axe scythed towards her, the wielder white-faced and desperate, more likely to wound a friend than to connect with Nona, and yet by luck he caught her on the turn with almost no time to act.

Her blades divided the hilt into tumbling sections that she dived through. The axehead flew free and bedded itself in the chest of the woman whose knee Nona had ruined, who was still in the act of collapsing.

The men who had been at the fore of the rush into the cave now returned to a scene of carnage. Apart from the four emerging into the light only one soldier stood uninjured. The four paused – an ill-advised hesitation that allowed Nona to leap at the face of their companion and bear him screaming to the rocks amid the wreckage of his comrades.

When Nona lifted her head, gore dripping from her hair, the four survivors took a step back. Darla's tular came down in an inexpert but devastating swing, nearly beheading the leftmost of the men and embedding the blade deep in his sternum. Jula appeared with her arm around the shoulders of the next, screaming and stabbing furiously at his neck. Ruli felled another of them by smashing a rock, two-handed, into the back of his knee.

The last man started to run, angling away across the slopes.

Nona plucked a blood-slick spear from its fallen owner and threw it. The Path-energy was burning out of her limbs and the spear felt heavy. Even so it flew true and took him between the shoulder blades, carrying him to the ground.

Nona stood, panting, blood dripping from her hands, blood in her hair, the taste of it in her mouth, blood running down her legs, blood cloaking her habit as if she were already a Red Sister. She looked up, her gaze travelling slowly across the twitching of the injured and the stillness of the dead, dreading to see the condemnation in her friends' faces.

The three of them stood over the bodies of the soldiers they had brought down. Jula with her mousey hair wild and sticking up at all angles, her face, neck and shoulders spattered with gore, Tarkax's knife glistening in her hand. Ruli raised her face, the rock in her hands dark with gore. She had shattered the soldier's head when he fell and the splash of it decorated her in scarlet. Darla freed the tular with a wet wrench and held it above her head. All three of them stood for a moment, panting. Then as one they roared out their victory and, raising her hands, Nona howled it out with them. She stood, her heart pounding, eyes full of tears, her chest full of that strange mixture of sorrow and exultation that she could never explain, a feeling that words could neither shape nor own.

It took her a moment to remember Hessa. Her death didn't feel real yet. Nona stood there, casting no shadow, and found she could feel nothing for her friend. Some emotions are like that, too big to be seen from within, like the ice patterns, written across empty miles, which make sense only from a great height. She slumped, staggering as weariness caught up with her. She would find that distance in time, and there would be sorrow enough to make the dead weep, and she feared it.

Nona went across to Ara who lay by the edge of the slope, rope around her wrists where one of the soldiers had started to bind her. They hadn't trusted the poison to keep her immobile but it was still doing a good job. Nona met Ara's eyes as she sliced away her bonds.

'They're all dead, Ara.' Nona looked down at herself, still red with slaughter. She couldn't bring herself to speak of Hessa yet. She wanted to set off for the convent, to run all the way, to kill Yisht with her own hands.

'Some are just wounded.' Ruli came across, empty-handed now. Nona became aware of groaning behind her as Ruli spoke.

'We should do something about that.' Darla raised her bloody tular and eyed it speculatively.

'They're no threat,' Jula said, the sleeve of her habit red and dripping. 'We need to get the others moving. Then we can go.'

The slope stank of death, an ugly smell. 'Let them be.' Nona shook her head. 'Help me with Ara.' She made to stand. As she moved, the gleam of sunlight on metal further down the gully caught her eye.

The last edge of the sunset still caught the Devil's Spine, and its light beaded on the smooth curve of a steel shoulder-plate as it came into view. The man walking towards them was armoured from head to toe, lobstered in interlocking steel, his helm a cylinder faced by perforated doors. Nona was amazed anyone could walk in such a weight of metal.

'Get Ara back into the cave!' she shouted.

At least five of the soldiers still had breath in them, though perhaps none would last the night. She crouched by a woman, a scar-faced veteran, her breathing shallow, the point of an axehead bedded in her ribs where it had driven the links of her chainmail into the wound, and shook her roughly. 'Who is that?'

'Can't … you tell?' The woman grimaced. 'Wait … until he gets … closer.'

'It's Raymel Tacsis?' Nona understood. Only a gerant could carry such armour.

She advanced down the slope, skidding on loose stone, into the gully where a small stream gurgled. When Raymel drew closer, Nona once again got that shock of realization as her eyes understood the scale of him. The sword he drew from over his shoulder must have been six foot in length and heavier than her.

'It always pays to bide your time with witches.' Raymel Tacsis set the point of his sword upon the ground. 'Perhaps I should have brought more soldiers. I would have preferred you captured so we could spend a while together. But my father keeps a tight rein on his troops and he felt that you're not worth breaking a promise to the emperor over. Not this year anyway. I disagreed.' His voice was as deep and rich as Nona remembered, but beneath it, just at the edge of hearing, it seemed that she heard other tones, other voices whispering the words, voices that were older, crueller, and more hungry.

Nona backed off, matching Raymel's advance.

'I thought you were a fighter, little girl?' Three more strides. 'You seemed keen enough at the Caltess. Both times.'

Nona continued to back away.

'Not so brave now you've spent your magic?' The trailing tip of Raymel's sword rattled through the loose stones by the stream, scoring the bedrock with a discordant noise.

Nona blinked. The ghostly echo of the Path hung in the darkness behind her eyes, but it lay beyond her reach, like a spent passion. She might be able to reach for it by the next morning, but not any time soon. And her flaw-blades – she had seen that they barely scratched the man, warded as he was by the devils that shared his skin. She kept backing away.

Raymel stopped advancing.

'Trying to lead me away from your nest, mother-bird?' He turned his head to stare at the cave and the bodies sprawled beneath it. Darla vanished into the cave mouth, Ara in her arms. A moment later and she would have been out of sight. 'All this—' he raised a gauntleted hand to the steel plates over his neck where she had cut him years ago, 'was over another nestling. I had to find out her name after I got better. Saida. A dirty little peasant just like you. That's not something a Tacsis heir dies over!' He beckoned Nona closer. 'Are you still angry about her? I bet you are. You should come and show me.'

Nona snatched up a rounded stone from the stream and kept backing away.

'No?' Raymel paused. 'I'm glad she died. My regret is only

that I didn't get to do it, and in my own time. But Father just had her hanged, and quickly. Not one for scandals, my father.' He sheathed his sword and held his arms wide as if daring her to attack. 'Do you remember how she screamed?'

At the back of her mind, where Nona had expected anger to flare, an image of Saida rose instead. Her broad face with its mixture of timid and friendly. If she had been here she would be treating the wounded. The soldiers that Nona had torn open. Saida had wanted to mend, not to break. Nona took another step back.

Raymel shrugged, his armour squealing in protest. 'It looks as if some of your friends won't be able to run away as fast as you can.' He started to march towards the cave, striding at a pace most men would have to jog to keep up with.

Nona threw the stone. It bounced off Raymel's helm. He didn't turn.

'Ruli! Jula!' Nona screamed. 'Darla! He's coming. He's coming for you.'

Fear ran through her, cold water through the marrow of her bones. For the first time in an age she felt the chill of the ice-wind, ragged now as it lost its strength but still icy now that she had no range-coat. 'He's coming!' She didn't know what to do. She wanted them to run, but if they left Ara, Zole, and Tarkax then Raymel would make the gullies ring with their screams.

Darla appeared at the cave mouth, Tarkax's tular in her hand, still sticky with blood. Her jaw dropped as she took in the size of Raymel, striding across the corpses.

Nona cast her exhaustion aside and broke into a sprint. She caught Raymel five yards before the cave and threw herself upon him. Leaping and reaching as high as she could she drove her flaw-blades into the small of his back. One set punctured the steel plate armour, the other skittered across, leaving bright lines scored into the metal. Dragging herself higher, Nona reached up, slashing with all her strength to lodge her second set of blades just below his shoulder blades.

Raymel bellowed and began to turn. If the blades were

hurting him, though, it was nothing more than scratches. There was no blood gushing or even leaking from the slots she had driven through his plate mail. She climbed higher as he turned, cutting and hauling her way up, an ice-climber sinking her axes.

A great hand reached back for her, large enough to wrap about Nona's head and crush it like a nut. Releasing her grip, she grabbed a thumb and finger, each so thick in its gauntlet that she couldn't close her own fingers about them.

Hunska speed enabled her to climb his wrist and reach the iron summit of his elbow before the grasping hand could close on the air where she had been. Locking one leg about his elbow, Nona slashed at Raymel's visor, putting every ounce of her strength into two blows, a rising, left-to-right slash and, as she fell away, a descending right-to-left slash.

The obdurate steel resisted her blades until they met the first of the many perforations through which the warrior saw the world. Then, tearing in, the flaw-blades managed to cut from one hole to the next several times before jolting out to score the surface once again.

Nona turned in the air and landed on her feet, stumbling immediately and sprawling backwards across an injured soldier clutching his stomach wound. From her place on the ground she saw that the criss-crossing of her blades had cut out a number of diamond-shaped sections of the visor and she could now see one glaring eye, the cheekbone below, and part of Raymel's nose. But his flesh had resisted her blades better than the steel, showing just red scratch-marks where his face should have been cut into shreds.

Raymel Tacsis's great sword dropped like a thunderbolt, dividing the man that Nona had tripped over. She rolled clear as the blade hammered into the rock. Her speed was leaving her now, spent in too many acts of extravagant swiftness. Raymel straightened, scything his sword across the slope. Nona tried to dig into the moment but the gaps had grown slim and the spaces between heartbeats, once so cavernous, now squeezed her out. She leapt the cutting edge with just an inch to spare.

Where Nona was tiring Raymel seemed possessed of boundless stamina, howling a chilling mix of glee and hatred as he pursued her. Nona grabbed a discarded sword and, running beneath another swing, hacked at Raymel's leg. It was like hewing a stone pillar. The sword jolted from her hands, and the shock transmitted along the blade sent white agonies lancing up her wrists.

The gleaming arc of Raymel's next swing held Nona's attention, and a kick caught her a glancing blow, coming from the side while she watched the sword. The impact spun her and she fell among the bodies, clutching the hot wet pain in her side: broken ribs at the least.

'You're going to wish you hadn't done that,' she snarled at him. 'But not for very long.' She tried to leap up at him, furious, but for once her body betrayed her, too broken and filled with too much hurt to obey.

Raymel towered above her, lifting his foot to stamp down on her legs.

Nona raised her arm in futile defence and as she did, something small and spinning tore through the empty space above her. It vanished through the gap she had made in Raymel's visor and thunked into his eye.

With mad screams Darla, Ruli, and Jula came tearing down the slope, whirling stolen swords above their heads. Raymel, howling, dropped his own blade, and raised a huge hand to his face. The three novices thrust and hacked at every part of him from his ankles to his chest. Nona crawled clear of the melee, sliding down the gore-slick slope, holding her ribs.

Raymel weathered the sword-storm. He spun around amid the clatter and clang, swinging his left arm. Darla took the main force, his forearm slamming into her belly and lifting her off the ground. She landed yards away with a horrifying thump. Ruli and Jula, both knocked from their feet, tumbled down towards Nona.

Iron-shod fingertips closed on the point of the throwing star and pulled it from the ruin of Raymel's eye. He flipped the weapon away. Behind the intact section of visor the scarlet eye, devil-owned, stared at the sprawl of novices, the hatred so intense that it seemed a physical thing, pressing on them, both burning and icy at the same time.

Nona seized a spear and rolled to her back. She would die facing her enemy, weapon in hand, not crawling away. Close by, Ruli lay dazed, her head bloody. Jula rolled over beside Ruli, her wrist at a sick-making angle, and took her knife in her off-hand, eyes blazing. And Raymel stood over them, all in shadow now with the setting of the sun, his huge sword recovered and poised to end three of them in a single slash.

From the darker shadow of the cave mouth a small figure broke, tottering and awkward on stiff legs. Arabella Jotsis, her golden hair in disarray, staggered weaponless down the slope towards them. Nona wanted to scream at her to run, but it was too late. Too late for anything. At least Ara might die with them, in a bloody moment, and escape Raymel's cruelties.

Some warrior instinct – perhaps just sharp hearing – made Raymel glance back, but seeing a stumbling child he quickly returned his attention to the victims before him.

Ara tripped and fell most of the last few yards, jerking her arms overhead only at the last moment. And in that moment Nona recognized the power of the Path shuddering there in Ara's empty palms. Ara clapped both to the giant's backplate and the energies she had gathered, finding her serenity in the worst possible situation, pulsed into Raymel Tacsis. The raw stuff of creation detonated against Raymel as it had once detonated in the fight-dummy that had suffered Ara's wrath in place of Zole. A light lit within Raymel's armour and with a violent and deafening crack things blew apart.

Nona shook the echoes from her head and looked up to find that although Ara had been blown off her feet, Raymel had not. He stood in the fractured remains of his plate armour, five hundred pounds of bleeding muscle stacked three yards tall. The livid purple mark that reached up the side of his neck continued down across the broadness of his chest, swirling out into patterns that remembered the complexity and form of sigils. On his side and below his shoulder great patches of scarlet scar tissue, as if from old burns, seemed to hold leering faces in their ridges and hollows. Flying pieces of his armour had torn the odd furrow through his flesh, but by and large he stood unharmed. The force of the detonation had blown his helm clear and he stared at her with one eye ruined and dripping, the other a scarlet window into the mind of a devil. Below them hung an echo of the smile he'd worn when he broke Saida.

In that moment the warrior in Nona roared again, finding a last touch of speed, a last gasp of strength. She threw the spear she'd being clinging to. It hit hard enough to bury a couple of inches of the blade between Raymel's ribs, enough to keep it there, standing proud. Rising with the throw, Nona tumbled between Raymel's legs, plucking a discarded knife from the ground between them and slashing at the back of his knee where the armour plate hung on one rivet, exposing flesh. She cut deep, slicing tendon and muscle. Unbalanced, Raymel fell with a roar. Ruli and Jula scrambled clear with no time to spare as he fell, crashing between them.

The head of Nona's spear erupted from Raymel's back as the butt of the haft hit the ground when he fell, arms out to take the impact. Nona scrambled up Raymel's pale and naked back as the huge man surged to hands and knees with a muted roar. She plunged the knife between his shoulders. Again and again. The devils beneath his skin screamed and surged, strange and alien forms moving beneath his flesh. Nona sliced at them, like serpents beneath a rug. The blood that spurted from those wounds came scalding and stinking, staining her hands, filling her with a black agony beyond comprehension – but her rage proved larger than any hurt and still the steel in her fist rose and fell. Nona rode her enemy, her howls a counterpoint to his bellows.

And still, despite the ruin of his back, Raymel turned and rolled, reaching for Nona, the spear through his belly snapping against the ground. She scrabbled away on her back but one huge hand closed around her leg below the knee.

'No!' Nona drove her dagger through his wrist, fear warring with her anger now. 'Die!'

'I can't die.' He kept his grip, spitting blood, and drew her towards him. 'They won't let me!' His red eye met her black ones and she knew in that moment that no wound would stop him. 'I can't die.'

In the last heartbeat remaining to her Nona spotted Yisht's amulet gleaming blackly between two rocks almost within reach. She lunged for it, arms out before her. But for the blood she would never have made it. Raymel's gore-slick hand slipped down her leg from knee to ankle, and with the tips of her fingers she snagged the iron sigil.

'I can't die.' Raymel loomed above her on all fours. Nona sat up and pressed the black sigil to his forehead with her thumb. 'Yes you can.' Her other hand pulled the knife from his wrist and drove it up beneath his chin, hilt-deep.

Raymel roared. Nona saw the blade, gleaming behind his teeth. The sigil of negation seared into his forehead, corroding, falling apart, a red mist rising around it, and with a chorus of screams the devils fled his flesh. The grip on her ankle slackened and Nona rolled clear, twisting her knee as she yanked her leg free. Behind her, Raymel Tacsis collapsed, twitching to the ground, arms sprawled, the rocks about him drenched with crimson.

Epilogue

It is important, when killing a nun, to ensure that you bring an army of sufficient bravery. For when Sister Cage of the Sweet Mercy Convent steps onto the battlefield courage is often found to be in short supply.

She came from the undercaves, and the Rock of Faith shuddered to its base as if deep in the blindness of its roots the Rock itself had given birth to her.

She rose amid the convent buildings, behind the great Dome of the Ancestor. The youngest of the novices were still within their dormitory, a single ancient nun seated at the door. They watched at their windows, open-mouthed. Years ago, before some of these girls were brought wet and screaming into the world, a different set of novices had watched Sister Cage first arrive at Sweet Mercy.

There is little of that child to be seen in Sister Cage. She stands shadowless in the torch-ringed courtyard and in one moment the novices know that the stories are true. She glances their way, each eye utterly black, as if that missing shadow had been poured into both until it filled her skull.

A distant scream rings out, past the Dome of the Ancestor, deep among the pillars. Sister Cage turns her head. She is deadly pale, strange in her beauty, her hair jet and jagged, cut close. Her habit is faded, stained, trailing ragged tails of cloth, but it is still red, and as she runs she looks like death descending from some high place.

The Pelarthi stood between the pillars, a loose halo around the place where Sister Thorn lay in her blood. Clera Ghomal stood above the fallen nun, that once and long ago she had in this place called friend. It seemed that the world revolved about them, the pillars spinning about the axis that stood between Thorn and Clera as all the stars in heaven revolve around a single point of darkness.

Clera Ghomal opened her mouth to speak, and said nothing, for the years rob us of the words for such moments, making each truth too bitter for the tongue, too heavy to be spoken. She stood among strangers before the body of a sister.

Sister Cage drew her sword as she ran towards the first of the Pelarthi. Sister Tallow had pressed the weapon's hilt back into her hand less than an hour before. A long blade, thin, carrying a slight curve, its edge cruel enough to cut silence and make it scream.

She didn't seek the Path, uttered no battle-cry, made no challenge. She spun through a group of six and the clash of her sword upon the metal collar of the last of their number announced her arrival.

Sister Cage stopped, head down, sword trailing at her side, a crimson line stretching out across the rock from its point.

Before her dozens of mercenaries turned their heads to see what threat faced them, and behind her six bodies collapsed to the stone, some not yet realizing they were dead, for death had come among them so swiftly.

Out in the convent compound Bitel rang out. Where Sister Thorn offered protection Sister Cage offered only war, utter and without quarter. The years when they had called her the Shield were long past. Sweet Mercy would open her doors. Everyone who drew breath within its walls would issue forth, from youngest novice to ancient nun.

Sister Cage lifted her face to her enemies, night-eyed, a narrow beauty among the scars, half a smile that promised her to be more than a little in love with death, and invited them to dance.

Bows creaked among the Pelarthi ranks, spears were lifted, knuckles whitened on the hilts of sword and axe. A hawk-eyed archer, her cheek torn and bloody where Thorn's throwing star had sliced past, took aim at the new nun's face.

They knew her by many names, the Pelarthi did, but 'Cage' held as much fear as any other. Cage. She would not release you: you would not escape. The tales said she made her first kill in the same year she learned to walk. They said she tore a boy apart with her bare hands and took his heart to show her mother.

Sister Cage found the torn-faced archer among the crowded strength of the Pelarthi and a knowing passed between them, between the archer's cold grey eyes and the Sister's black orbs. The arrow fell with a clatter. The archer turned without a word and began to push her way back, past the warriors of her clan. To her left another turned, a man thick with muscle, the names of his forefathers inked in runes along his arms. Two of those he pushed aside turned and ran with him.

A trickle became a flood. The Pelarthi left the scores of their dead, still scattered or heaped where Sister Thorn had killed them. They ran, pursued by a terror they couldn't name, something larger than the sister who stood behind them, but perhaps as small as the disappointment in her eyes when they turned to flee.

Clera waited beside Ara as Nona strode towards them through the pillars. In the heavens above the first crimson stars dared open their eyes.

'Is she dead?'

'How are you here?' Clera ignored the question. 'You weren't supposed to be here! How did you know? … and even then, how did you get here?'

'Is she dead?' Nona rushed forward, pushing Clera back, away from Ara, who was still coiled about the spear. She knelt, reaching out to touch the spread gold of her hair. 'Ara?'

'You should never have let me go.' The words sputtered

from Clera as if she were hurt, as if it were her wrapped around a spear. 'You had me bound. Guilty. You should have let them drown me.'

'I wouldn't do that to a friend.' Nona set her fingers to Ara's neck, seeking a pulse. The smallest of groans, the smallest tremble of a hand.

A short laugh burst from Clera, sounding as much like pain as mirth. 'They all think you're the big bad. The church's hammer. Cage the Shadowless. And you're still a child, Nona! You run into everything heart-first, expecting … what? You didn't understand how people work when the abbess brought you here, a dirty-footed peasant. You didn't understand when she sent you away. And you don't understand now. People lie, Nona, they steal, they cheat, they're unfaithful. People hurt you, they let you down. They sell you out.'

'It doesn't mean I have to be like that.' Nona stared up at Clera who flinched, guilty before those black eyes. 'We have a whole church built on ancestors.' She waved an arm at the dome. 'Family. Dead family.' She took Ara's hand in hers. 'You *choose* your friends. If you're going to worship dead people you didn't choose, then perhaps the bonds of friendship shouldn't be so easily broken. No?'

Clera shook her head. 'You're a fool, Nona Grey. Are you going to kill me now, or let someone else do it?'

'Ara could live. If we get her to Sister Rose. Now!' Nona glanced back towards the convent. They were coming. The old sisters and the young girls. Sister Thorn had vowed to protect them. Sister Cage to fight alongside them.

Clera waved her hand at the distant nuns, exasperated. 'Let them take her. I don't care. I didn't come for Ara. She was just in the way.'

Nona released Ara's hand with a squeeze and stood. 'I've missed you, Clera. It's been too many years.'

Clera glanced out across the plateau. 'We were children, Nona. Children make and break friendships all the time. It's not important. This, what we're doing now, this is important. It's about sides in the great game that's being played. And you're on the wrong one. The losing one. You should change sides.'

Nona shook her head. 'I'm not playing. And I've always been on your side, Clera. You've just not properly understood it.'

Clera looked down at Ara. 'I wanted her to run.'

'I know.'

'She should have run. There were too many of them for her. Why did she have to be so stupid?'

Nona shrugged. 'Where is Lano Tacsis?'

'You know the Tacsis.' Clera nodded towards the plateau stretching out beyond the pillars. 'They like to let you spend your power against people they consider expendable, then arrive to finish the job if anything's left to finish.'

'They do.'

'He's out there with his soldiers and eight Noi-Guin. His teachers from the Tetragode. Others too.'

Nona looked down at her sword. 'My power's not spent.'

'You think you can kill me without reaching for the Path, little Nona?' Clera drew her sword, a twin to Nona's, taken from the body of a Red Sister.

Nona turned away, her back to Clera, looking out across the plateau.

'I think I won't need to kill you,' Nona said. 'I think you'll fight them with me. Sister.'

Acknowledgements

Many thanks to Jane Johnson for editing this and my previous six books. Not only has Jane helped to shape the work but she has also helped to inspire it and acquired the trilogy for Voyager. That's a lot of help!

Thanks also to the other good folk at Voyager who have worked hard to put this book in your hands, including Emma Coode, Natasha Bardon, Katie Sadler, Jaime Frost and the HarperFiction sales team.

Agnes Meszaros has also been very supportive during the creation of this trilogy, both as beta-reader-in-chief and as supplier of chocolate!

Thanks too for early reads from Mia Caringal, Tom Brown, Nimue Brown, Nadine Kharabian, and Helen Mazarakis. Finally, let's have another round of applause for my agent, Ian Drury, and the team at Sheil Land for all their sterling work.

Turn over for chapter one of the second novel in the Book of the Ancestor series:

GREY SISTER

Coming soon

1

There are many poisons that will induce madness but none perhaps quite so effective as love. Sister Apple carried a hundred antidotes but she had drunk that particular draught of her own free will, knowing there was no cure.

Thorn and briar tore at her, the ice-wind howled, even the land opposed her with its steepness, with the long miles, the ground iron-hard. The Poisoner pressed on, worn, feeling each of her thirty years, her range-coat shredded in places, the tatters dancing to please the wind.

When the deer-track broke from cover to cross a broad and rutted track Apple followed without hesitation, eyes on the ranks of trees resuming their march on the far side.

'Stop!' A harsh cry close at hand.

Apple ignored it. Kettle had summoned her. She knew the direction, the distance, and the pain. Kettle had called her. Kettle would never call her from her watch, not even if her life were in danger. But she *had* called.

'Stop!' More voices raised, the dialect sharp-angled and hard to attach meaning to.

The treeline stood ten yards away across a ditch. Once she reached the shadows beneath the branches she would be safe. An arrow zipped past her. Apple glanced along the road.

Five Durnishmen spanned the width, their quilted armour salt-stained and mud-spattered, the iron plates sewn on shoulders and forearms, brown with rust. Apple could reach the trees before the men caught her – but not before the next arrow or spear did.

Cursing, she reached both hands into her coat pockets. Some of the obscenities she uttered had probably never been spoken by a nun before. Even the Durnishmen seemed surprised.

'Don't kill me. I'm worth more to you alive.' Apple tried not to sound as if she were lecturing a class. She drew her hands out, a wax capsule of boneless in one, a wrap of grey mustard in the other, and a small white pill between finger and thumb. She popped the pill into her mouth, hoping it was bitterwill. She had all the antidotes ordered inside the many inner pockets of her habit, but reaching in to recover one would be asking to get shot, so she chanced to memory, feel, and luck, fishing in the outer pocket of her range-coat.

'You . . . are nun?' The tallest of them took a pace forward, spear levelled. He was older than the other four. Weathered.

'Yes. A Holy Sister.' She swallowed the pill, grimacing. It tasted like bitterwill. The four younger raiders, all with the same dark and shaggy hair, tightened their grip on their weapons, muttering to pagan gods. Perhaps one nun in a hundred was anything other than a Holy Sister but with the stories told in Durn they couldn't be blamed for thinking every woman in a habit was a Red Sister, or a Holy Witch just itching to blast them to smoking ruin. 'A nun. From the convent.'

'Convent.' The leader rolled the word around his mouth. 'Convent.' He spat it past frost-cracked lips.

Apple nodded. She bit back on her desire to say, 'With the big golden statue.' The men had to walk into the trap themselves. If they sensed her leading them she would be dead in moments.

The leader glanced back at his men, gabbling out words that so nearly made sense. Durnish was like empire tongue put through a mincer and sprinkled with spice. She had the feeling that if they would just speak a little more slowly and change the emphasis it would all become comprehensible. Apple caught the two words that might keep her alive though.

'Convent' and 'gold'. She broke the capsule of boneless in her fist and rubbed her fingers over her palm to spread the syrupy contents before wiping the hand over the back of her other and her wrist.

'You. Take us to convent.' The man advanced another two paces, gesturing with his spear for her to move.

'I won't!' Apple tried to sound scared rather than impatient. She thought of Kettle in danger, injured maybe, and fear entered her voice. 'I can't. It's forbidden.' She had to get them close. She couldn't do much if they prodded her ahead of them at the point of a spear. She let her gaze flit between the faces of the men, offering a wavering defiance. A defiance that they might enjoy breaking.

The leader motioned and two of his men advanced to grab Apple's arms. A third kept his bow ready, half-drawn, arrow pointing her way, daring her to run. The last leaned on his spear, grinning vacantly.

Apple feigned panic, raising her hands to intercept those that reached for her, but offering too little resistance to invite blows. One of the pair seemed to need no excuse and slapped her anyway, a hard, calloused hand across the face. She spat blood and cried out for mercy. Both men were smeared with the clear boneless syrup now, sticky on their fingers.

The slapper twisted one arm behind her while the other made to open her coat, perhaps forgetting that the Ancestor's brides take a vow of poverty. Knowing he would find her array of poisons and cures rather than any gold or silver Apple wailed piteously, raising her clenched fist to remind them she had something more obviously hidden.

Slapper grunted incomprehensible syllables to Robber and the man abandoned the coat-ties to prise Apple's hand open. In taking hold of it he got a second dose of boneless wiped across the palm of his hand. With the bitterwill to counter the poison Apple felt only a numbness where the syrup coated her, the strength in her arms untouched.

Apple began crying out, keeping her fist clenched against Robber's weakening efforts. Slapper tried to twist her into submission and it hurt like fire but she managed enough resistance to stop him breaking the arm behind her. At the same time Apple threw herself left then right, her progress always towards the leader and the archer though she never once glanced their way. The Durns' hobnails slid on the mud. The remaining subordinates laughed uproariously at their comrades' efforts, making no move to help. The leader, snorting in disgust, motioned the archer forward then jammed his spear-butt into the mud and followed to intercept the group as they made a weaving approach.

Neither Slapper nor Robber yet seemed to understand that they had been poisoned, presumably believing instead that Apple was an abnormally strong woman, perhaps drawing some animal strength from the depths of her terror. Apple wrenched her fist to her face as the officer reached them. She blew through her closed hand, a short sharp puff, and a cloud of powder from the crushed wrap bloomed around the man's head. The edge of the cloud caught the archer just behind him.

True terror loaned Apple the strength to throw herself backwards, falling from the Durns' clutches to the rutted mud. She had seen what grey mustard could do and nothing in her array of antidotes would reduce the pain and disfigurement of it to an acceptable level.

The officer's screams shattered the air, the breath for his second cry sucking mustard spores into his lungs. The archer fell back, scratching at his eyes. Slapper and Robber staggered away, tripping and stumbling. Which left Apple empty-handed, on the ground, with one able-bodied foe just yards away, spear in hand.

Another person's distress exerts a certain fascination; the man stood in slack-jawed horror watching the officer claw his face to ruin. Apple glanced at the shadows between the trees. So close: a quick scramble could see her safe in their embrace. The need to be speeding towards Kettle drew at her even more strongly than the desire to escape. But Sisters of Discretion swear more than just vows of piety and poverty. Suppressing an impatient snarl, Apple drew her knife. She rose slowly from the mud amid the officer's bubbling screams, the archer's curses, and the struggles of the other two Durnishmen trying and failing to get to their feet. Her head-dress had come loose and red hair spilled around her shoulders. The last of her coat-ties gave and her range-coat opened about her like the dark wings of a raptor. She held her knife ready to throw, a pouch of ground deadruff in the other hand in case she got the chance to take the spearman alive.

The raider saw her at the last moment, dragging his gaze from the frothing officer, now fallen into the ditch. As he lowered his spear Apple's hand rose in an underarm throw and an instant later the hilt of her knife jutted beneath his chin. He sat down, clutching his throat in confusion.

The archer stumbled close by, blinded with tears and blood. Apple took up a dropped spear and ran it through the man's chest. Next she went to offer mercy to the officer, now a twisting thing of mud and grass in the icy ditch water. She left him in a crimson bath and considered the two fallen Durns, Slapper and Robber. One had his face towards her and tracked the bloody tip of her spear with his eyes. Apple frowned, her gaze wandering to the treeline again, eager to be off. She had no stomach for killing helpless foes. In truth she had no stomach for killing. She had always been a better teacher than a doer.

Apple crouched. 'Sisters of Discretion are supposed to pass unseen and be impossible to take unawares.' She took two purple pills from her habit, brilliant groundwort. She had cured and prepared the roots herself, pressed the pills and sealed them in wax. 'It's all very embarrassing. I won't tell if you don't.' She peeled the pills quickly and popped one into the mouth of each man then rolled them so they wouldn't choke. 'If nobody finds and kills you before you can move again – and believe me you deserve to be found and killed, then my advice is to run all the way back to your boat.'

She wiped her hand on Slapper's cloak. The groundwort would make them sick for a week. A month if they swallowed too much. She considered leaving her dagger in the spearman's neck, but went to retrieve it, pulling the blade free with a shudder of revulsion. In the next moment she was moving, running for the trees, red blade in hand.

Apple had always been a teacher first, lacking the iron for the darkest shades of grey-work. Kettle though, she would never fail to do what was required, without relish or complaint. A perfect weapon. When duty called her she had the capacity to put her sweet nature in a box, ready for collection when the mission was complete. The thought of what it would take to get her to call for help made Apple shudder. Kettle would never willingly make Apple abandon the abbess's orders. Arabella Jotsis stood alone in the wild now, unwatched.

Apple pressed on, using all her resolve to pace herself rather than to sprint. Miles lay ahead. She dodged around trees, following a deer track for a while then leaving it to pursue a stream, rotten with ice.

Kettle had been watching Nona. Had something happened to the child? She was fearless, fierce, and quicker than thinking, but there were more dangerous things out in the Corridor than Nona Grey. Perhaps it was Nona that needed help. . . Apple shook the thought away: the pain had been Kettle's, and the fear.

A swirling fog came in, lifted somewhere by the moon's focus and carried perhaps for days in the ice-wind. The forest clutched at her, sought to trip her at every step, tried to lure her from her path with easier tracks. In the blind whiteness Apple found her way, following the faint echo of Kettle's cry through the shadow.

Many miles became few miles and, as the fog cleared, became a singular remaining mile. The land had opened up into heath where the soil stood too thin and too sour for crops. Farmsteads lay scattered, raising sheep and goats, few houses stood close enough to see one from the next. Apple picked up speed, running now as she crossed rough ground, divided here and there by grassed-over lanes and collapsed walls of dry stone. Ahead the land dipped. In the broad valley a stream threaded its path between stands of trees before losing itself in a thicker extent of woodland. Kettle waited among those woods, Apple could feel it; her nearness tugged at the scar her shadow-cry had left.

Apple slowed as she approached the first trees. She had been careless before: her haste had delivered her into the hands of men she could have stepped around unnoticed if she had kept her focus. She moved between two elms and the shadows flowed around her, raised with both hands. Shade-work had always come easy to her. Darkness pooled in her palms. When the shadows answered her will it felt as if she had remembered some name that had long escaped her, or recognized the solution to a puzzle, a sort of mental relief, joy almost. Other shadow-magic had been worked within the woods. The empty spaces shivered with the echoes of it. Kettle's cry lay there, sharp and deep, but other traces too, the sour workings of Noi-Guin. Apple had tasted their like before, back at Sweet Mercy on the night Thuran Tacsis had sent two of them to kill Nona. Quite how they had failed in that task was beyond her.

Apple wrapped herself in darkness and sought the patience of the Grey Sister. Mistress Path had taught her the mantras twenty years ago and Apple had made them part of her own foundation, woven through her core. Today though, with Kettle's distress throbbing through the shadow, patience came hard.

The undergrowth scratched and tore and rustled with each step Apple took. She felt as raw as any novice, her woodcraft rusty with disuse, certain that her advance would be heard by any foe within a thousand yards. Bait the trap. A tactic as old as killing. Leave a comrade, a friend, a lover wounded, then wait and watch. A Noi-Guin could be resting among the branches of any tree, crossbow ready, bolt envenomed.

Kettle wouldn't have called me if that were true. Apple advanced, leaving patience behind her but bringing the shadows.

All that drew her eyes to Kettle was the bond between them. The nun lay at the base of a great frost-oak, the length of her body fitting around the rise and fall of roots. Leaves and mud covered her range-coat, her headdress gone, the spread of raven hair showing the paleness of her face only in thin slices. She lay sprawled like a dead thing, a part of the forest floor, a work of camouflage of which any Grey Sister would be proud.

'Kettle!' Apple came to her side, the fear of an assassin's bow crushed beneath the certainty that Kettle lay dead and that no purpose remained to her in the world. She took Kettle's muddy fingers in her own, shocked by the coldness of them. 'Kettle . . . it's me.' She choked on the words, overwhelmed, while her other hand, still calm, sought the nun's pulse with practised ease. Nothing. No . . . not nothing, a whisper.

Apple reached to pull Kettle to her, to lift her from the cold ground, but saw the hilt of the knife, jutting from her side just above the hip. She touched a finger to the pommel, an iron ball. Leather binding wound the grip. She recognized the dagger. Kettle had shown one like it to her after it was confiscated from Nona. Noi-Guin for certain then. The one that got away. Apple eased her lover onto her lap and sat for a moment, hugging her, eyes squeezed tight against the tears. Seconds later she drew a deep shuddering breath and strove for calm.

Think.

Apple set Kettle back upon the ground and stripped her own range-coat to lie her on. With Kettle arranged on the coat she examined her for other injuries, checking the colour of her skin, lifting an eyelid, listening to her breath, watching the speed with which circulation returned to her extremities when pinched. She took a thin leather tube from the collection within her habit and broke the seal. Already the cold was making her shiver. She tipped the liquid into Kettle's mouth, sat back, and watched. The knife was the only wound. It must have been coated with blade-venom but there were no strong indications to narrow down the type.

For the longest minute in Apple's life nothing happened. All about her the trees groaned against the wind, their leaves seething. Then Kettle twitched, spluttered and started to choke. Apple seized her head. 'Easy! Just breathe.'

'W-where?' Any further question became lost in coughing and choking. One hand clutched at the range-coat just above the knife. 'Hurts.'

'I told you to breathe, idiot.'

'A-Appy?' Kettle rolled her head to see, eyes squinting as if the light were too bright. Her skin was bone-white, lips almost blue. 'Sister.' The faintest smile.

'I've given you adrene, it won't last long. Tell me what you've taken. Quick!'

'Nona. She made me call.' Kettle slurred the words, staring past Apple at the leaves, black against a white sky. 'Gone now.'

Apple shook her. 'What did you take? It's important!'

'B—' Kettle blinked, trying to focus. 'Black cure.' Her breath came shallow and fast. 'And . . . kalewort.'

'Kalewort?'

'I. . . was cold. Thought it . . . might be nightweed on—'

'Who puts nightweed in blade-venom?' Apple shook her head. 'Where's the assassin?'

'Gone.' Kettle's eyes closed and her head flopped back.

Apple bit her lip. The black cure should have had more effect whatever the Noi-Guin had used. She tasted blood and frowned. Her mind lay blank. Nothing in her great store of lore suggested a cause or cure.

Despair closed about Apple. Her lips moved, reciting venoms, none of which fitted the symptoms. Tendrils of shadow caught around Kettle, moving across her in wisps. Apple stared, her brow furrowed, mind racing. On the white inch of wrist exposed before Kettle's range-coat swallowed her arm, a line of shadow followed the path of the largest vein.

'No?' Apple motioned the shadows around her forward and like a dark sea they washed over Kettle. As they drew back traces of shadow remained, held by her veins as a lodestone will hold powdered iron, revealing the invisible lines of its influence. 'Yes!'

She grabbed Kettle's face in both hands. 'Wake up! Kettle, wake up!' Kettle lay, as boneless as the Durns in the road. Apple slapped her. 'Wake up! It was dark-venom.'

'I'm dead then.' Kettle rolled her eyes open. 'I'm so sorry.'

A glistening tear pooled in the corner of her eye. She lifted a hand, as if it were the heaviest thing in the world, to Apple's cheek. 'You're bleeding.'

Apple took the fingers and kissed them. 'You are my blood.'

The darkness began to thicken around them, shadows streaming towards Apple, clotting about her.

'What are . . . you doing?' The smoothness of Kettle's brow furrowed and her hand dropped back to her side.

'Saving you,' Apple said. The effort of drawing so much shadow so fast tightened her voice. She felt a coldness in her bones, an ache behind her eyes.

'H-how?' Kettle sought her eyes. 'There's no way.'

'There is a way.' Apple saw Kettle only because the darkness ran so deep in her. Night enfolded them both now, a fist of darkness within the depths of a forest grown lighter as its shadows were stolen. 'I have to push you into shadow.'

'No.' Kettle managed to shake her head. 'The Ancestor—'

'I have to. It's the only way.' Apple gathered the darkness around her hands until even to her night-born sight they were holes cut in the shape of her body, without depth or contrast. The Noi-Guin pushed the best of their killers into the shadow, as far as their minds could bear it. It broke some of them. Others were lost in the dark places behind the world. But the price Kettle feared to pay was her soul. The Church taught that those who walked too far into the shadow would never join the Ancestor in unity.

'Don't.' Kettle lacked the strength to raise her hand again. 'Sister Wheel . . . says the Ancestor—'

'Fuck Wheel, and fuck the Ancestor.' Apple set one hand to Kettle's chest, kneeling above her, ready to push. She took the hilt of the knife in her other hand. 'You're mine and I won't lose you.' She bent her head and tears fell. 'Let me do it.' Her mouth twitched and the words came out broken. 'Please.'

'Poisoner.' Kettle found the strength to raise a hand, running white fingers into the flame of Apple's hair. She held her a moment. 'Poison me.'

And with a cry Apple pressed down with one black palm,

all her strength behind it, and with the other drew the assassin's knife from the wound, pulling with the steel and blood an inky venom born of the darkness that dwells between stars.